Comments about author

"This is certainly a thriller that builds t̲ ̲g̲l̲o̲b̲a̲l̲ ̲d̲i̲m̲e̲n̲s̲i̲o̲n̲s̲ and I liked the way Mr. Easterling tackled the plot by having his journalist–Lassiter–slowly piece together the clues. The final revelation is also believable and consistent with the pervading paranoia in Washington. I was also impressed with Mr. Easterling's knowledge of research and development."
Shawn Coyne, as Senior Editor, Doubleday / Random House

"Strong writing, strong characters, solidly researched, exciting novel. Great love scenes, powerful imagery. I think this is the best written book I've read for you. A very strong novel, and a good writer who, frankly, I think has more and quite possibly better books in him."
David Stein, Simon & Shuster

"The writing is good and atmospheric. Todd Easterling is an author with talent."
Joseph Pittman, as Senior Editor, Dutton Signet, a division of Penguin USA

"Todd Easterling certainly tells an intensely emotional story that features many sympathetic characters and he sets it convincingly in two vividly depicted, distinct locales. It has great cinematic potential."
Maggie Crawford, Senior Editor, Bantam-Doubleday-Dell, Random House Publishing Group, New York, NY

For current digital and print domestic and international rights and translation opportunities, please use the contact form at www.ToddEasterling.com.

The First Witness
ISBN-10: 0988988011
ISBN-13: 978-0-9889880-1-9
Library of Congress Control Number: 2013935683

Virgin Iconic Entertainment

Manufactured in the United States of America

For my grandparents Juanita and Harold Fletcher (US Air Force B-29 Captain / WWII POW)

"There is nothing to writing. All you do is sit down at a typewriter and bleed." This is one of the most famous quotes by Earnest Hemingway. When I first set out to write a novel, I never would have believed this statement. I thought, what could be easier than sitting down at a computer and dreaming up a story. Now, many years later (and three daughters later!), I'm sure if I pulled out that first manuscript I'd be terrified. Writing isn't easy. Yes, it's not rocket science, and no one writing novels is saving lives, as a doctor or other professional. But I'd like to think that a work of fiction can stimulate minds, make people think and act, and perhaps lead to changes in the reader, when they discover a writer they like and a moving or exciting story.

For me, three writers motivated me to write that first manuscript. First, as a kid I was fascinated with Michael Crichton's movies, especially *West World*. Later, when I discovered his novels, I was impressed with his amazing ability to dream up "big ideas," such as the cloning of dinosaurs in *Jurassic Park*, or the harvesting of organs in *Coma*. Or the biotech thriller *The Andromeda Strain*. Crichton taught me to try (emphasis on try) and come up with big, world-changing stories. It is truly sad for book and movie lovers to have lost Michael Crichton before his time. He was the master of the big story.

Two other writers motivated me, both very different than Crichton. When I discovered Fitzgerald's *The Great Gatsby*, I was blown away at his command of language and style. I had never seen words as art, before Fitzgerald. Fitzgerald "wrote art." It reminds me of a quote from Anton Chekhov, "Don't tell me the moon is shining; show me the glint of light on broken glass." Words can be art. And getting there isn't easy.

Lastly, I was motivated by Nicholas Evans and *The Horse Whisperer*. That book taught me about the power of including a romantic relationship in a story, even if it serves as a backdrop in an adventure or thriller novel. With a degree in psychology, I guess it is just in me to include some relationship dynamics and romance.

So, while writing this novel, Crichton kept whispering in my ear, "make it a big story." Fitzgerald kept telling me to at least try for atmospheric writing and artful word use (I tried here and there, at least). Nicholas Evans reminded me to create strong relationships within the story, not "just" make it a suspense-thriller.

Earlier, as a kid in high school and student in college, a few teachers encouraged my writing. So here's a thank you to the teacher in a writing class and the stories and scripts they liked, including an episode of *The Cosby Show* I still have, with those encouraging words. And a thank you to the professor, Dr. Leckart, who took the extra time to write thoughtful comments on all those psychology research papers in the four or five classes I had with him. I even named a character after him in this book. It only takes a little encouragement from those we admire, to make a difference and light the flame in a child. So thank you to all the teachers out there who work for little, yet impact students so much.

I hope you enjoy this book. I enjoyed writing it (blood and all), and blending in actual technologies used by the United States, and I found the tie-in with today's headlines about Iran's nuclear development program interesting—and a bit alarming too. With this novel out, you will soon see the next one, which over ten years ago several major publishers in New York told my agent was "a bit ahead of its time," due to the genetics and cloning topic. Although I had obtained technical input from two prominent genetics experts, including Dr. Ian Wilmut (first to clone; Dolly the sheep fame), and Dr. Raul Cano (extracted ancient DNA from tree amber, which Jurassic Park was based on), New York said "come back later." It's definitely later. After another few editing passes, that book will be available soon. And another suspense thriller will follow that.

So for you writers out there, or whatever you do for a living or artistic pursuit, never give up, even if you do it part time, or take breaks. Thinking about a project and getting the vision of how to create it is half the work. You're almost there! And sometimes timing is everything. For example, *Argo* winning best picture has made a lot of people take notice of this novel, due to the Iran connection. The book I almost have ready is getting attention because the book and movie *My Sister's Keeper* did well. And the novel I have in draft form has gotten interest due to *Jurassic Park 4* coming out in 2014, and huge advances in genetics, biotechnology and cloning over the past ten years. Sooner or later, doors open, and the timing is right for whatever project or goal you have.

I encourage those interested to reach out to me at www.ToddEasterling.com, send me an email and tell me what you thought—the good, the bad, and the last elusive typo we missed. As I turn my attention to finishing the next novel, I promise you I will work hard to bring you a big story, and I'll keep listening to Crichton, Fitzgerald and Evans, and those teachers I mentioned—hoping something sinks in eventually.

I also encourage anyone with a dream to follow their heart, put the hours in (translation: years), and see what happens. Don't do it for the money. Do it because you want to create something special, and unique. And remember that motivation can happen at any moment, to spark your pursuit of *your* dream. In fact, if it weren't for a store cashier at a convenience store taking my check for a drug prescription when I had pneumonia years ago, I might not have even thought to try writing novels. The girl looked at my check and said, "Todd Garland Easterling?" I nodded, wondering why she was reading my goofy name from my check. She then said, "That sounds like an author's name."

For some reason, her unexpected split-second comment made an impact on me. I started writing my first manuscript within days. I don't recommend the pneumonia part, but I do recommend following your dreams, whatever they are. I sometimes wonder what that store clerk is doing these days—who may have changed my life and interests forever. Who was whispering in her ear, as she looked at my check? And what if I hadn't gotten that serious bout with pneumonia? Would I be writing novels and be so excited about reading books?

Since then, I've learned that big things can happen even from little moments. A comment from a store clerk. A scribbled message from a teacher. A pat on the back from a grandfather, saying "Go for it. Don't live your life with any regrets." Listen to the cues and follow your dreams. And ignore the occasional naysayer and pessimist. Build that business. Write that book. Climb that mountain. You only go around once.

Thank you for buying this novel. All of you have busy lives, and I appreciate the fact that you let me borrow a few hours from your work or your loved ones.

Sincerely,
Todd Easterling

CHAPTER ONE

Tom Lassiter always knew he'd become famous someday, though he didn't know how or when. He just knew—that someday something big was going to happen to him, or rather, as his grandfather used to tell him, someday *he* was going to make something big happen. And Tom knew full well that indeed he would need to take the bull by the horns and earn his way through life, create his own destiny. Make something big happen.

You see, he hadn't been born to famous or wealthy parents. And his road to becoming an acclaimed reporter at *The Washington Post* was not the Ivy League, privileged route many of his colleagues had enjoyed. He worked his way through college—journalism B.A. and law school—first as a waiter at the tourist-trafficked Anthony's Fish Grotto on North Harbor Drive on the embarcadero, downtown San Diego, and later as a general manager of an upscale Italian restaurant in the gas lamp district nearby. A student loan also helped and it saw him well into his thirties, a real self-made man. I guess I should tell you that prior to law school his intention was to become a doctor. It sounded nice and prestigious, as did lawyer, but he couldn't stand the sight of blood. So lawyer it was. After law school, things didn't work out as well as he expected. No experience equaled no serious job offers. Just not enough ambulances to chase and too many lawyers. Like everyone had warned him.

Somehow he managed to land a job at Jacob, Lansing, and Evans, you know the firm, right across from the courthouse in that thirty story high-rise with the television and radio antennas on top and packs of pit bulls swarming inside with pinstripe suits and iPhones holstered to their sides or squarely shaping their pant pockets. He shuffled papers there for five excruciatingly long years (in dog years that's thirty-five I think), mostly doing probate stuff, real estate contracts, and divorces. He hated it. Then one day while reading the *Union Tribune* on his break and absorbing some San Diego rays he noticed a want ad. The paper was looking for a lawyer to write a column and cover the local legal scene. He thought, perfect, a ticket out of contract hell. He applied and, much to his amazement, landed the position (sixty-eight thousand a year, two weeks' vacation, almost free dental and medical, his own office, and no lawyers around).

Tom Lassiter was a reporter. Well, almost. He stayed there for four years, learning the ropes of the newspaper business, gradually improving his non-legaleze writing skills, and even sold some advertising at one point. Tom also learned how to format a front page and write a decent lead-in. Given his lack of experience, he knew he was lucky they hadn't stuck him on a bicycle and made him toss papers at front doors.

Tom soon found himself climbing the ranks of the newspaper business. And after a few years writing the column and covering what little legal news there was in San Diego, he asked for more assignments, different sections of the paper. One of his first tasks outside the scope of the legal world was writing obituaries. Sounds worse than it is, really. There are no interviews, no one to sue you for misquotes or defamation, and no end to new material. People just keep dying and you just keep writing. Real steady work.

More assignments came his way. Tom had found his niche. He was the lawyer (with barely an ounce of 'lawyering' experience) who could also write. Yet he had positioned himself as an expert in his field, and he knew full well that newspapers and television stations loved experts. Who knows, he could end up being the next Dr. Phil or Dr. Oz, perhaps focusing on legal issues and news. Tom was on his way.

The marriage wasn't as strange as it might appear. Even Tom would tell you that reporters are actually a lot like lawyers—both want to make a big financial pop someday and get out of the daily grind. And where a lawyer dreams of the million dollar personal injury settlement or being a partner in a major firm, and in the interim does contracts, bankruptcies, divorces, and wills, reporters dream of uncovering

10

something earth-shattering or writing the great American novel. Then promptly kissing their editor goodbye and never hearing the word "deadline" again. They often work for low wages for years on end, cover tons of interesting but not exactly earth-shattering local stories (and a few that are, or have the potential, to be "big"), and serve time until they eventually are forced with a major career decision—the typical reporter's fork in the road. One direction leads them toward ever more prestigious reporting assignments on the national or international scene, and perhaps television or major metropolitan newspapers. The other direction leads them out of reporting and up the org chart and into cushy offices and management jobs where they review circulation statistics and advertising revenues and debate the ever-increasing threat of the internet, especially Twitter, on the newspaper business. Not every reporter yearns to stay on the high pressure, deadline-driven writing treadmill where big stories are few and far between. There are only so many Watergate's, Iran-Contra's, missed 9-11 terrorist warnings and 'Iraq or Iran having or not having weapons of mass destruction' stories around, and everyone clamors for the next *big one*, which, by the way, is exactly what Tom yearned for. And he knew San Diego was probably not the place to discover the big one, at least on the national or international scene. Never would he guess, not in a million years, that his life would soon change and he'd find himself in the middle of what can only be called an international incident.

  The big one.

  It all started when *The Washington Post* was looking for a reporter for the City Room. Tom saw it as not only a chance to move into the major leagues, but also an opportunity to move back to the D.C. area to be near family. With two little girls, he knew it would be best to have them near his parents. And since Helen, his wife, had died a few days after a car accident up in the San Diego mountains several winters back, Tom hadn't cared for the suburbs of San Diego much. There was nothing holding him there but memories probably better off forgotten. Helen, too, had tired of the curve-filled commute to the city and long trips to the grocery store and Target. They often spoke of buying something in one of the coastal neighborhoods, closer to work, but a real estate recession had put that dream on hold. And by the time homes started selling again, she had passed away and all of Tom's life and plans got lost or placed on hold. Eventually, though, he waved goodbye to San Diego County in the cracked rearview mirror of the biggest U-Haul van he could rent, and made the move back to D.C. on his thirty-third birthday, March 1, 2012.

D.C. traffic was terrible. Nevertheless, Tom arrived at seven twenty-five at the Pentagon's fortified main entrance, just north of Army-Navy Drive. Since starting at *The Washington Post*, he had never been late to an interview, though on this morning he did cut it too close. He contemplated whether he should go ahead and turn into the entrance and try to park in the visitor lot which looked pretty full on this morning, or head down the street and park at a strip mall, then walk in. He decided to park off-site, and get some exercise. He left his Jeep in front of Macy's and walked for ten minutes back to the gate. The guard (you know the type, crew cut, thick neck, mirrored sunglasses) tilted his head downward as Tom approached over the top rim of his sunglasses. Tom offered a forced smile in the frigid morning air and said, "Good morning. I have an appointment scheduled with General Kramer. I think he's in ring E, off corridor three. Could you please point me in the right direction? I'm in a bit of a hurry."

Big mistake.

"Sir, the Pentagon covers twenty-nine acres. You're looking at the largest office building in the world. No one gets anywhere in a hurry," he said hastily, his breath leaving tiny clouds visible in the air.

"Sorry. I didn't mean to—"

"Uh-huh. No problem, sir. May I see your driver's license please?"

"Sure." Tom removed his wallet from a rear pocket, pulled the license out, and handed it to him. The guard stared at it for a few seconds, wrote something down on a clipboard, then called Kramer's office. A minute later Tom received a set of ludicrous directions to

Corridor 3, which was one of ten spoke-like corridors connecting five pentagonal concentric rings, according to the map the guard handed him. The guard turned, pressed a button on the wall behind him, and the orange and white striped wood arm lifted out of the way. "Okay, sir. You can go in. Please walk on the right side of the road and watch for cars entering or existing. You'll run into a sidewalk and visitor entrance over there," he said pointing.

"Okay. Thank you."

"When you leave, make sure you sign out at this station. Good day, sir."

Tom nodded then walked away from the gate toward the Pentagon, several of its windows shimmering pale silver in the distance. As he walked, he noticed several cameras in the parking lot following him and heard the subtle zipping sound of their robotic motorized pan and tilts. There seemed to be more cameras than he could recall on his last visit to the Pentagon. He remembered that since tensions with Iran had heated up, all the government buildings in town where under constant surveillance. D.C. security hadn't been this tight in over ten years, not since after 9-11, and there was an air of anxiety hanging over the city which was palpable, especially since Iran's heightened threats to Israel, and Israel's assertion that it would take out Iran's nuclear program if progress wasn't made on shutting down their nuclear program. To wait longer, Israel's Benjamin Netanyahu claimed, could risk their ability to contain the development of nuclear weapons. Iran's rhetoric had grown more and more vehement over the years, and in May of 2011 its leadership had called for the complete elimination of Israel, and retaliation toward any country standing by its side. Even for Tom, who had lived to find and cover such internationally significant stories for years, there was an uncomfortable feeling in his gut that something was about to happen in the Middle East and that it would have reverberations right here in D.C. and the heartland of America. Right here at the Pentagon. And at *The Washington Post*.

Tom walked up to the visitor entrance and entered the building, navigated a security check, and began meandering through what seemed to be a cruel joke of endless corridors. The Pentagon has seventeen miles of them, he remembered reading somewhere. All of the corridors looked the same. In fact, everything looked the same, even the important-looking people who walked stone-faced and emotionless through the halls, apparently on their way to somewhere important. Their heels clicked noisily upon the shiny, too-smooth tile floor, seemingly in unison. Mice in a maze.

His legs were tingling when he finally arrived at General Kramer's office. He opened the door and walked in. The reception area was as gray and uninspiring as the rest of the sprawling building, unusual for a general's office, he thought. Most have posh decor and surround themselves with an army of personnel you can hardly get through. Tom's first thought was that the general must be one of those one-man-show types. He had met a few at the Pentagon before, and over at the Capitol. He'd even seen a few over at *The Washington Post*. These types were usually loners, not trusting anyone else, and not wanting anyone's eyes watching their work. Most of the people Tom had met at the Pentagon were professional, polite, and very business-like, just like at the *Post*. But every organization he had visited in D.C., including government and civil organizations and companies, had a few eccentrics running around.

Tom headed toward the only person he could see and said, "Good morning. I'm here to meet with General Kramer."

"Good morning, sir," the lady replied. "Mr. Lassiter?"

"Yes."

She looked down at a piece of paper on her desk. "He's expecting you." She lifted her eyes briefly and did a double take on Tom. "Say, has anyone ever told you that you look like—"

"Harrison Ford?" Tom interrupted. He'd heard the question a thousand times, especially after gashing his chin playing baseball in college.

"Yeah, you really do, even a small scar on your chin." She flashed a smile and continued, "Please have a seat and he'll be right with you."

"Thanks." Tom paced back and forth a few times and studied her as she grabbed a nail file and bottle of Ferrari-red polish from a drawer. A couple minutes later he heard a phone beep, then watched as she picked up the receiver and said, "Yes sir," and turned toward him and, without even looking up, said, "General Kramer is ready to see you, sir. Right through this door." She pointed toward the door to the right of her desk, then resumed sanding her nails, wrinkling her forehead and peering downward like a Boy Scout trying to make fire out of two twigs. She must be on her coffee break, Tom thought, as there was steam rising from a mug sitting next to the nail polish.

Tom opened the general's door and walked in. The general was sitting behind a large ship-gray metal desk with faux wood grain adorning the top. His high-back chair was turned away from the doorway, toward a large window. All Tom could see was the very top of his bald head which reflected the fluorescent light tubes above almost as much as the too-shiny tile floors which had delivered him to this point inside the Pentagon. He cleared his throat, as a forewarning, then said, "Good morning, General Kramer. Pleasure to meet you."

"Yeah, a regular party, Mr. Lassiter," he replied, not even turning around. "Let me be upfront and tell you that the only reason I'm even talking to you is because our Press Office insisted. I don't usually give interviews."

Tom realized that Kramer's eyes were watching him by means of the reflection in the window. "Well, thank you for the warm welcome. I assure you I don't bite, sir."

Kramer brought his high-back chair about-face, rotating toward his desk with Tom dead ahead, as a machine gunner rotating his crosshairs and gun barrels, and stopping precisely on his target. Some light from a side window filtered down on his face and accentuated its details, the nooks and crannies holding many years, many wars. The light also made the myriad of medals on his chest sparkle. Tom moved closer and finally got a good look at him. The wrinkles and craters grew more pronounced and Tom noticed he had a reddish nose, which seemed slightly wider at the tip than at the base. Tom moved his eyes quickly over the medals and downward. Kramer's hard belly was creating a slight tug of war with the buttons and eyelets of his shirt and it hung over a black belt, which could barely be seen at the hips. Tom sensed that he was being studied. Kramer's gaze was piercing. Tom almost began to speak, but hesitated, waiting for Kramer to get settled. The general leaned further back in his chair, then reached over and grabbed a cigar from a box and some matches. He unwrapped the cigar, struck a match, and cupped his hands seemingly in one motion. A cloud of smoke billowed to the ceiling and he just kept staring at Tom, right through the smoke, a ghost of a man.

"I don't care if you do bite," he finally replied as the cloud dissipated and made its way into an air conditioning duct above. He exhaled loudly, then continued, "I'd just as soon be doing anything than sit here and talk with *The Washington Post*, Mr. Lassiter. But here we are."

The fumes were already starting to make Tom sick. "May I sit down?"

"Sure, why not."

"Thank you."

"Hang on a minute, Lassiter," he said, then picked up his phone and hit the intercom button. "Gladys. Are you out there? Can you pull my schedule out and see if you can squeeze in a free hour sometime before lunch?" There was a brief pause. "Yes, I'll wait." He turned back toward the window. There was silence, except for the sound of his breathing, and puffing.

Tom's eyes moved around the office. He noticed a sign on the back of the door he had entered through, No Smoking. To the right there were several steel file cabinets. And to the left of the general's desk was a metal bookcase. Several shiny silver and gold bowling trophies, and two plastic models (one of a space shuttle, and one of a military-gray 747 jumbo jet) were resting upon one of its shelves, next to two framed pictures of young soldiers standing proudly in front of American flags. Probably Kramer's sons, Tom thought. When preparing for the meeting with General Kramer, he had read a story about how the general had lost both his sons in two separate events in the Middle East. His oldest son died in a crash of one of the helicopters President Carter had sent in to try and rescue the American hostages during the 1979 Iranian hostage crisis. Many years later, the younger son died in a similar tragic manner. He had survived just three days in Afghanistan before being killed by an Improvised Explosive Device, or IED, long before the military reinforced the Humvees with steel plating and ballistic-resistant windows. In certain years of the Iraq war and Afghanistan war, one in four soldiers were killed in Humvees, according to statistics compiled by staff members of the House and Senate Armed Services Committee. Kramer's younger son had just missed the deployment of the new improved models, which Kramer had fought hard for with congressional support.

On another shelf Tom noticed a picture of an attractive older woman with two kids sitting on her lap and another pair sitting on the floor, at her feet. A dusty plastic plant was on the top shelf. And, hanging above the bookcase, on the wall, there was a yellowed plaque, apparently commemorating the Strategic Defense Initiative of the old Cold War days.

Tom finished surveying the office, then turned back to Kramer. He was still facing the window and holding the phone, waiting for his secretary to come back on.

A few seconds later Kramer cleared his throat and said, "Good. I'll advise where I want to meet later. Thanks, Gladys." He hung up then turned to Tom. "All right, Lassiter. I apologize for the delay."

"No problem, sir," Tom answered, half surprised at Kramer's attempt to be gracious.

"So where do you want to start?"

"Well, with the basics first, if you don't mind. Your full name is William Charles Kramer?" Tom asked as he pulled a notepad and pen out of his jacket pocket. "And your rank is general, three star?"

"Yes, that's correct. Now get to the point of your visit. I'm a busy man."

Tom thought, I guess the gracious part is over, then said, "Sir, two days ago *The Washington Post* received an anonymous phone call from an individual who said he worked for British Space Systems Corporation. The caller sounded extremely upset. He said that *The Washington Post* should look into something called the 'High Ground' program—what he referred to as some sort of top secret illegal nuclear weapons activity. He claimed that you are in charge of the program. He seemed very worried, as if his life, or other lives, were at stake. Do you know anything about such a program?"

Kramer tilted his chair forward. With his left hand he tapped out the cigar in the ashtray atop his desk, simultaneously rubbing his forehead slowly with his right. "Son, you interrupt my day to tell me about an anonymous phone call?"

"Well, sir. I—"

"Even if I do know about some damn, so-called confidential weapons program, do you think I would talk about it, especially with *The Washington Post*?"

"General, I assure you I'll keep your name off the story. No one will know where I got the information," Tom said, knowing Kramer probably wouldn't fall for it.

"Lassiter, that call was a prank. We get them all the time. I'm sure the *Post* does too. Now, you're wasting my time. I'm not involved in any 'High Ground' program. Excuse me if I cut our little date short. I have to get some work done here." He paused and opened a desk drawer, then pulled out a bottle of aspirin. "There's no High Ground program."

"Well, I brought a tape of the message the caller left. I'd like to play it for you. I think you'll agree that he sounds very credible and very concerned. It will just take a couple minutes of your time. May I—"

"Oh, certainly," Kramer interrupted. "I have nothing else to do."

"Is there a micro-cassette player I can use?" Tom had wanted to bring one with him, but when he scheduled the meeting Gladys had told him that the Pentagon prohibits anyone from bringing in electronic devices of any type, tapeless or tape-based.

Kramer contemplated his answer. Tom assumed that he wanted to say no, but more than this, the General probably wanted to see if he could recognize the voice on the tape.

Kramer finally said, "Hang on a second, I'll see if Gladys can find us one." He picked up his phone and entered her extension, but she didn't answer. No doubt she was over at the coffee room, or chatting with Donna in Logistics, or doing who knows what in the bathroom with things in that suitcase she called a purse. She often vacated her desk when she knew he would be tied up in a meeting and probably wouldn't need her for a while. He shook his head. "Damn it, where's she run off to now. Sit tight, Lassiter, I'll go get one myself." He stood and walked to the door, then swatted the knob just as he exited, leaving it cracked open a couple of inches.

Tom's chest pounded as he realized he was sitting alone in the Pentagon office of one of the highest-ranking military officials in the country. The stories he could probably tell, he said to himself as he gazed about the room, thinking about the allegations from the caller. God, what if the caller was telling the truth? What if they are developing, or maybe even planning to deploy some type of new nuclear weapon?

Tom's mind swirled with thoughts of uncovering a story that could be of international relevance. A lives-on-the-line type of story. Maybe this was the *big one*.

A couple minutes passed. Tom was surprised he had been left alone for this long. Once again his eyes wandered around the room, and eventually came to rest on Kramer's desk just a few feet away. The in-basket was stacked as high as his own back at the newspaper, and there were notes scattered all over the place. And on one corner there was a stack of file folders. He noticed that several of them were bright orange, which he presumed probably meant that they contained more sensitive information than the plain vanilla ones. And there they were, just three feet or so from his curious, twitching reporter fingers. Just begging for him to casually reach over and have a quick look. Shoot, he wouldn't even have to get out of his chair. He thought, *who would ever know if I managed a peek?*

But, Tom then wondered, what if the files were planted there for him to take? How does a General, of all people, leave a reporter alone in his office, with files on his desk?

To his eyes, this stack of unassuming files was a blinking neon sign screaming *come on, no one will know, take a look. This is the big one you've been dreaming of. This is why you moved to Washington*

D.C. This is why you became a reporter. Make your family proud. Make The Washington Post proud. Make your country proud. Who knows, you might save a life. You might avert another war. This is the big one.

And lord knows he could use a fix. Just a taste of success. It had been three months since one of his stories had made the front page. He had experienced this feeling, this yearning to uncover something significant, a couple of times in the past. And on each occasion he told himself that only a Washington D.C. reporter or a drug addict (we're talking the full-blown heroin sort) could possibly understand such a gut-wrenching craving. The pressure to publish critical, internationally relevant stories was that strong, that compelling, especially in the extremely competitive media environment that had recently evolved, where eyeballs that had once stayed glued to newspapers were now torn between countless cable channels, internet sites, and social media. He had often asked himself what Woodward and Bernstein would do at a moment such as this—when the candy is dangling right before you, your mouth literally begins to salivate, and you think that taking a bite will surely prove some sort of illegal activity, or perhaps save someone's life. An activity that will probably make you rich and famous in one swell swoop. Hadn't every reporter worthy of the job crossed the line on an investigation to get a story out? Didn't the end sometimes justify the means?

Tom glanced over his shoulder at the door. He couldn't hear even the slightest sound. Even the slight hum of the air conditioning had turned off. And judging by the clicking noise Kramer's shoes had made as he walked out, surely he could hear him as he returned. Just a quick peek, that's all he would need. Just a taste of candy and his sweet tooth would be content. It would probably only take a few seconds at the most, he told himself. Again his eyes moved to the stack of files. He took a deep breath, licked his lips, and reached forward and carefully slid one of the orange ones out from the stack, making sure not to disturb the pile too much. He sensed his heart speeding up as he opened the file. But then the rush of adrenaline dissipated as he realized the only thing inside was a list of personnel and, apparently, their salaries next to their names (good god, people actually made less than he did). He closed the file and stuck it back into the pile in exactly the same spot. There were still two more orange files, and they seemed to call out to him, Just a taste, Tom. Again, he twisted his neck sideways and gave a look to the door. Still no change, everything completely quiet. He moved forward and tugged out the next orange file. Bingo. The cover was stamped *Top Secret*. He placed it on his lap and quickly peeled it open. "My god," he whispered as he located several papers labeled *High Ground* at the top. "The bastard is lying." Once more, he turned and glanced at the door, then looked back down. He scanned through what was clearly a memo, but much of the text had been marked out with a black pen. His mind was racing so fast he barely took in every fourth word, but midway through the second paragraph several words jumped off the page at him, *"High Ground Program: Satellite-Based Nuclear Weapon/Mid East."* And just then, as he continued reading, he heard heels clicking in the hallway. He closed the file and started to lean forward to place it back in the stack, but stopped as he detected the voice of Kramer's secretary. She was apparently talking to someone near her desk.

Tom swiftly folded the file and shoved it under his jacket, tucked a portion into his pants, then under the elastic band of his underwear to keep it from falling. Expecting someone to walk in any second, he just stayed still. But no one entered. He settled back in the chair somewhat, his breathing much faster than normal, and contemplated whether he should take the file out and place it back in the stack. Yet here he was, sitting here with Top Secret documents— which were now a folded and creased mess with his damp fingerprints tattooed all over the them—that would clearly corroborate the anonymous caller's allegations.

Seconds ticked by like hours as he contemplated what to do. What if they really are planning to launch some sort of space-based nuclear weapon—and over the Middle East? With tensions already high on Iran, such news would be unparalleled for the newspaper, and any reporter's career. It would make Watergate look like child's play. There was no doubt in his mind that if the U.S. launched a space weapon it would be a disaster in foreign policy, at best. And probably much

21

worse, at this critical time. Of course, stealing a file from the Pentagon wouldn't exactly win him any citizen of the year awards either, but something inside told him he should take the file. *For the greater good,* he told himself. *For the greater good.* Maybe he could stop whatever it was they were planning to do, before some crazy weapon was hovering in the sky over Iran.

He wiped the beads of sweat on his forehead on the right sleeve of his jacket, scratched the scar on his cheek a couple times as he always did when nervous, then tilted his neck left and right, stretching and trying to calm himself. He then leaned back in the chair, crossed his legs, and attempted to at least look relaxed. But then, just as his pulse was turning down a notch and the veins in his temples were retreating, he noticed a small black box above. It was mounted to the ceiling, off to one corner of the room. He could just barely make out a glass lens protruding from it. It was obviously a security camera. "Way to go, Tom," he whispered under his breath, then contemplated whether he should just walk out. But he decided to take a chance that either the camera wasn't in use, or the tape or DVR it might be recording to would not be seen for hours, days, or perhaps never. The thing looked as old as everything else in the office. Maybe, he thought, it's broken, or perhaps it's one of those fake ones used to make people think they are being watched? How could they watch seventeen miles of corridors and thousands of offices?

Just as he began to calm down the office door swung open and Kramer ambled in, charming as ever. What startled Tom most was that his mind was so filled with thoughts he hadn't even heard the general's heels clicking as he approached.

"I had to walk half a mile to get this for you. Where the hell's that secretary when I need her? Here you go," he grumbled, handing Tom a micro-cassette player. "I wouldn't want to be accused of not being cooperative, now would I? You'd plaster it all over the *Post.* You can plug it in right over there. They said the battery is dead." He lit another cigar, sat down, and tilted back in his chair. Then he watched Tom plug the player into an outlet on the floor, insert the micro-cassette, and hit the play button.

"Hello, this message is for Tom Lassiter. I can't talk long. Mr. Lassiter, I work at British Space Systems, a division of an American holding company. We're a Department of Defense and NASA subcontractor. I've learned of a highly classified nuclear weapons program that I'm sure you'll be interested in, as I know you've covered NASA in the past. I believe it's called High Ground and I just learned the scope of what is planned. I'm scared to death about it. I guess you could say it's sort of an orphan of the Star Wars program of the eighties, but it is far more serious. A general at the Pentagon is in charge of the project, a General Kramer. I know this sounds crazy, but what they are planning to do is unconscionable. As you probably know, it's illegal to place any weapons in space, let alone nuclear. Several treaties ban such activity, including the Limited Test Ban Treaty of 1963 and the Outer Space Treaty signed later. You have to do something about this, and bring it to the attention of the public and other nations. I'm afraid I can't—"

The speaker abruptly stopped and Tom hit the stop button. "As you can see, General, the caller was interrupted by a voice in the background which is unintelligible on the recording. Then, the line either went dead, or he simply hung up." Tom paused to take a breath. "Do you have any comment about what was said?" he continued, then readied his pen.

The general tilted his chair forward, reached across the desk, and grabbed the mini-cassette player. He tightened his lips around the cigar and inhaled deeply as he pressed the eject button and pulled the cassette out. He handed it to Tom without any sign of emotion, totally cool. "That was entertaining, Lassiter. Now then, I think we're done. Thanks for stopping by."

Tom tried again. He needed to get a quote, any quite, "Can I just have a few comments, sir?"

Kramer paused, telling himself that it was absolutely crazy giving an interview this close to the culmination of the project. Right when everything was about to finally come together, he was having to sit here and dance around the truth and be interviewed by the *Post*, just to appease a military press officer whose sole purpose was pushing paper and smiling for the local and national news journalists once a week. In his gut he wanted to answer, *You bet there's a High Ground program, Lassiter, and because of it, Iran's nuclear weapons sites are going to be turned into the barren desert they were meant to be in just a few days from now.* But he tried to stay calm and replied, "Like I said, we get crazy messages all the time, with all sorts of allegations. There are a lot of whackos out there. I suggest you write about something more exciting, like the weather or something." He stood. "Have a great day, Lassiter."

Tom always hated being blown off, more than anything. But today he was more than ready to get the hell out of the Pentagon. He tucked the notepad, pen, and the breathtaking scribbled quote from Kramer away then walked to the doorway. He knew he wasn't going to get any information out of Kramer, except of course the file which he, well, let's just say borrowed. He felt it digging into his side as he made his way to the exit. He was anxious to see what else was in it, anxious to pull it from his underwear, and even more anxious to get away, far away, from the Pentagon and that damn camera. "General, I apologize for taking your time," he said over his shoulder, walking as carefully as he could. "I had to at least follow up on the lead. You understand."

"No son, frankly I don't understand."

Tom heard footsteps behind him as he neared the door. He stopped, turned around, and offered his hand, which Kramer shook for a split second. "Good bye, General."

"Bye, Lassiter." He slammed the door just as Tom was out of the way.

Tom felt a blast of air following him as he made his way.

In the reception area Tom noticed that the secretary had returned—full cup of black coffee—and was now painting her nails with the intensity one might usually reserve for brain surgery or lunar landings. She hadn't even flinched, hadn't missed a stroke, when the door slammed. She was apparently used to it, nothing unusual.

Tom left the reception area and walked down yet another sterile corridor as quickly as he could without looking too unusual. He dodged between people left and right as chatter bounced off the walls, and eyes darted about. It felt like everyone was staring at him. As he neared a central hall where three corridors intersected, he could feel the file digging into his skin, is hip, with greater intensity. He tried to tuck a corner into a better position, but it just got worse.

With his office door locked, Kramer reached for the phone on his desk, then stopped abruptly and pulled an iPhone from his pants pocket. After flipping through his contacts list, he clicked on first name *Virginia* and last name *Langley*. Virginia Langley was his not-so-discreet code for a number located at CIA headquarters in Langley, Virginia. It rang only once. The call was expected. "John Broderick here," the voice came on.

"Hearing your new cover name still throws me off," Kramer said.

"It throws me off too. I guess I'll get used to it eventually. And no, you can't call me Virginia like you did yesterday when you called."

Kramer attempted to laugh but was not in the mood for levity. "Well, Lassiter just left my office."

"How did it go?"

"He's digging into things, just as we feared. He had an audio tape from someone at British Space Systems talking about the program. He asked if I would listen to it. I almost declined, but thought I better show some degree of cooperation. Anyway, I went to get a mini-cassette player and—"

"Did you recognize who it was?" Broderick interrupted.

"No. But Lassiter didn't seem terribly interested in digging any further, though he may have been bluffing."

"I'm sure he was, General." There was silence for a couple seconds then he continued, "You didn't leave him alone, did you, when you went to get the tape player? Tell me you didn't leave him."

"Yeah, I left him alone. Only for a few minutes though and I—"

"I assume your desk drawers and files were secure?"

"Of course," Kramer said, then paused as he turned from the window to the files piled on his desk. Under his breath he said, "Good god."

"What's wrong?"

25

"Hang on, Broderick."

Kramer set the phone down and picked up the stack of files. It wasn't unusual for him to have various files on his desk, but he rarely left the high security ones out. He shook his head left and right as he flipped through them, recalling that he had asked Gladys to put them away yesterday. But here they were, in exactly the same place he had left them. He moved through the plain vanilla ones and finally reached the first orange-colored file. He flipped it open—the personnel list he had gone over with HR yesterday afternoon was still there. He then briefly opened the second orange folder, which included a stack of memos on the 747 Airborne Laser program, which had been in development for years, canceled due to budget concerns, then turned back on as tensions in the Middle East escalated with Iran and its threats toward Israel. General Kramer was heavily involved in the program. The Airborne Laser utilized three lasers including a Tracking Illuminator (TILL) to track enemy missiles, a Beacon Illuminator (BILL) to compensate for atmospheric distortion, and a one megawatt High Energy Chemical Oxygen-Iodine Laser (COIL)—whose lens was mounted in a movable turret on the 747's nose which resembled a large eyeball capable of being aimed in any direction. Each Airborne Laser aircraft cost a billion and a half dollars, and it was estimated that the United States would need ten to twenty of the 747's, costing $100 million a year to operate. During tests, which included over 500 flight hours and 100 sorties, the high energy laser had successfully destroyed missiles. If Lassiter had seen that file, Kramer thought, it wasn't a major deal. The Airborne Laser was public knowledge going back to the Clinton administration, and was a well-funded effort to obtain the capability to shoot down enemy missiles in flight. Yes, it wasn't public information that the testing of the aircraft and laser had resumed, but it wouldn't be the end of the world if that word got out.

As he looked deeper in the stack of files, he suddenly felt his blood pressure increase, his temples beginning to throb. He knew he had one more orange file out yesterday. And he knew it was missing. "That son of a bitch." He picked up his iPhone. "I think he stole one of the damn satellite files."

26

Broderick exhaled loudly. "'You think?'"

"Well, it's not here. I know I had three orange security files out yesterday. Gladys usually locks them up at the end of the day and—"

"We better stop him before he gets out of the building," Broderick said urgently. "I'm notifying security. I'll call you back." Broderick slammed the phone down and dialed the main MP station for Pentagon building security.

Two rings then, "Security, Sergeant Williams here."

"This is Broderick over at CIA—authenticator charlie-niner-niner-delta."

A few seconds went by and the guard said, "Yes sir. How can I help you?"

"I was just informed by General Kramer that a reporter might have stolen a file from his office. His name is Tom Lassiter and he's with *The Washington Post*. I want you to stop him. Try not to create a scene, just detain him. You might be able to get him before he makes it out of the building, but you better notify all of the guards at the gates. Tell them to stop all vehicles with males not in uniform."

"Yes sir."

"You have to move fast. Call Kramer and get a description. Got it?"

"Yes sir."

"Oh, one other thing. You have video of his office, right?"

"We should. On DVR, sir."

"Good. Don't worry about it now, but locate the footage of Lassiter and put it on a memory stick. I'll pick it up."

Tom rounded yet another corner in the labyrinth from hell. His feet were aching as he approached one of the main intersections, people zigzagging every which way like ants converging on a picnic crumb. Ahead, he could see two MP's approaching the intersection from the other side, with black armbands about their left arms with the letters MP imprinted. These two were as big as trees and their square chins were raised more than the other workers, and their necks were craned purposely forward. They looked in Tom's direction, then one of them pointed.

Tom figured that his only options were to surrender and take it like a man, or try to get the hell out of Dodge and live to fight another day. He decided on the latter. He walked quickly back down the hall and, as he made a turn, looked over his shoulder and saw the men ushering people out of the way so they could cross the intersection. He continued straight ahead, disappearing down a gray, less crowded corridor with a red stripe on the right side. He picked up speed, made another right, then a left, and realized he was completely lost. He didn't know which way was out, and which way was toward the courtyard. A few seconds later he heard heels clicking behind him, very rapidly, and getting closer. The thought crossed his mind that there was a good chance he would be in jail in less than an hour, wearing striped pajamas and calling a lawyer.

He reached another intersection. Or is it the same one? He turned left and walked against another wave of people. The back of his shirt collar and underarms felt drenched, and he was out of breath, more from anxiety than exertion. Twenty feet ahead, two red doors swung open and a couple of maintenance workers emerged pushing a large cart of some sort. Above their heads was a sign: 'Storage Room/Restricted.' He shifted gears and reached for a door before it could close.

He turned to one of the men and said, "Is Larry in there?" Why he pulled that name out of his head at the spur of the moment, he had no idea.

They looked at him all confused like, shaking their heads, and he walked in. The doors swung shut. Inside, there were dozens of brooms hanging on one wall, a cork bulletin board on another, and a time clock mounted at the back of the room. Several trashcans were overflowing with paper towels, and in the center of the room there were shelves with cleaning supplies and folded towels.

Tom managed to catch his breath, pacing slowly in a circle, running his hands through his hair and trying to think of what to do. Surely those MP's, and a hundred of their buddies, were scouring all of the halls for him at this point. He decided to just stay put, for a while anyway. He made his way over to a dark corner and, as he started to lean against the wall, felt something jab at his upper back. He turned and realized it was a fire alarm switch, one of those pull-down handles. The thought immediately entered his mind that this, a blaring alarm, might create just enough of a commotion for him to get lost in a bustling, confused crowd and make his way outside.

At this point, what do I have to lose? He shook his head in disbelief at his predicament and tried to calm himself with forced humor, a tactic he often used but had little effect at the moment.

The handle pulled down with hardly any resistance whatsoever. An alarm began to blare and he was shocked at how loud it was. Although he was only expecting the sound of an alarm, just as he began to move to a door, water sprayed from sprinklers hanging from the ceiling. He quickly became soaked. He cracked the door open and peered out to the hallway. Water was raining down everywhere, and people were frantically covering their heads with briefcases and folders, not knowing where to go. A lady slipped and fell to the floor by a drinking fountain.

Tom exited the storage room. He didn't see the MP's, but he knew they couldn't be more than a corridor or two away, probably soaked and even more pissed off, he thought. His memory briefly flashed back to third grade when he did a school prank, students streaming everywhere, school out for the day. In his mind he saw twenty-four thousand Pentagon employees flowing out of the corridors for a little recess.

CHAPTER TWO

Tom saw an exit sign with an arrow pointed to the left. He ran down a wide aisle, following a line of Pentagon workers, some wet, some dry. The sprinklers were now off but water was beginning to pool in some places on the smooth white tile, apparently flowing from someplace else, perhaps another floor, he thought. Ahead he saw double metal doors and another sign, *Emergency Exit Only, Alarm Will Sound*. He figured what the hell, the fire alarm is already blaring. One more alarm won't be noticed. He ran through the door on the right as if it wasn't there, pushing it open with both hands and bending the hinges slightly as it pivoted and slammed against a concrete wall outside. Blinding sun instantly met his eyes. He breathed a sigh of relief. At least he had found his way out of the maze.

Swarms of people were walking around. Some looked anxious, probably worried that something ominous had happened. Yet most of the crowd were calm and seemed happy to see something besides gray walls and flickering fluorescent lights. They angled their heads back and worshipped the bright thing hovering in the sky toward the east, peeking through the clouds. Tom saw several women in uniform taking deep breaths and smiling. Two of them slipped off their low-heel navy-colored shoes and walked timidly away from the building, like puppies stepping onto grass for the first time.

Tom ran toward another group making their way toward a parking lot. Several people stared at him. The thought crossed his mind that he was the only one dripping wet. Apparently the sprinklers hadn't gone off everywhere in the huge building. He ignored all the glares and began walking along like nothing was unusual. His shoes left small puddles behind as he made his way, and he could hear a squishing sound with each step, and feel water move between his toes.

He stopped and looked around. Hundreds, maybe thousands of employees were pouring out from every section of the Pentagon he could see. He heard the loudest of the alarms stop and, as if on cue, everyone immediately started to file back in, apparently standard procedure. Chins dropped and smiles vanished.

In the distance he heard sirens getting louder and closer, probably fire engines, at least he hoped anyway. He went against the tide of people and made his way through a parking lot. He saw a guard station ahead, but he knew he couldn't just casually walk out of the complex unquestioned. He figured that the MP's who had chased him had surely already notified the guards at all of the gates to be on the lookout for him. He glanced to his right, beyond an adjacent parking lot, and saw a chain link fence at its perimeter. It seemed too high to climb, and there was a thorny crown of barbed wire curled along the top. He felt like a prisoner.

As he made his way toward the Pentagon's eastern perimeter, out of breath, he paused next to a Ford van with tinted windows and yellow stripes along its side, one of those mini-RV conversions. He wiped his forehead on a sleeve and looked around. The crowd was dissipating. He knew that in a few more minutes he would be one of the few people in this section of the parking lot, and would clearly stand out to any MP's canvassing the area. Suddenly the van looked like the best option to get out of sight, and at least buy some time. He tried to open the driver's-side handle. It was locked, and the van's sliding door behind it was locked. So he walked around and tried the other doors. Everything locked.

Nearby, he noticed a Chevy Suburban a couple of rows away and ran over to it. All of the doors were locked, but one of the rear windows was down several inches. He stuck his right arm in, while pulling the glass pane down with his left hand, and managed to reach the lock. He pinched it and pulled upward then opened the door and climbed in. As he slammed the door shut, a feeling of relief swept over him.

Tom crawled to the back area of the suburban behind the third row seats and rolled out a vinyl cargo cover, making a little tent. He rested his head on a bag of dog food sandwiched next to a Costco-size bottle of laundry detergent and a set of golf clubs. He'll stay here for god knows how long, and hitch a ride out of the place. To where, he had no idea. His mind raced between panicked thoughts of being in very serious trouble, and fleeting attempts to calm himself with the idea that he may have uncovered some covert and possibly illegal program at the Pentagon which, when revealed to the world, might instantly transform him from his current state as a file-stealing criminal to a respected whistleblower whose means justified the end—stopping a greater illegal activity.

Eventually he heard a door open, and then smelled a cigarette. Someone climbed in. He was shocked, as it had only been an hour or so. He assumed he would be there, lying in the dark of his makeshift tent, until five o'clock at least. *Maybe they're going to lunch?*

The engine started and the transmission engaged with a *thunk*. The Suburban backed out of the parking stall and paused. Another *thunk* and it was moving forward and Tom heard music, radio stations being quickly flipped through and finally landing on a talk-radio program. The vehicle zigzagged through the parking lot, then slowed down at one of the gates. He could hear two voices saying something but couldn't make it out. The Suburban then exited the Pentagon, made a sharp right turn and its old V8 sprang to life with a hesitant roar.

A few minutes later the Suburban came to rest about a mile away from the Pentagon, the stoplight near Macy's. Tom peaked his head up just enough to see out. He wished he could open a rear door and run to his Jeep. But he knew that would attract attention again.

Soon he felt the vehicle make a sharp right turn, then he sensed a few bumps. And finally the Suburban came to a stop. The engine shut off and he heard a door open and slam shut. He unhooked the cargo cover and raised his head just slightly over the back seat and the biggest damn bag of dog food he had ever seen. No one was around. The Suburban was parked in front of a laundromat and deli, a small strip mall he had driven by a million times. He opened a door and slid out over the bumper, then closed it as quietly as he could and walked to the street, looking for a taxi. The first three to pass him all had passengers already, but eventually he flagged one down and hopped in.

A few minutes later the taxi arrived at his Jeep. He practically threw a twenty at the driver, said thanks, and walked briskly toward the Jeep. He jumped in and drove like a fireman going to his first blaze. His eyes were intense, body rigid, and he was sitting straight up. His arms extended straight forward and his hands squeezed at the wheel, knuckles white. He couldn't decide what to do next. He knew that if, by some stroke of luck, they hadn't captured him on video back at Kramer's office, he would be home free. *If there's no proof of him taking the file, what can they do to me?*

He decided to just act normal, and head to the *Post*. He desperately wanted to see what else was in the file, but knew it would be safer to wait until he was in the privacy of his own office, or somewhere secure.

He made it just three miles before his curiosity forced him to look for a place to pull over. "Damn, I have to see what I have," he said under his breath. He lifted his foot from the accelerator pedal. The Jeep slowed and he pulled off the road and onto the gravel shoulder. He put it in park before it completely stopped, then hurriedly unfastened his belt and unbuttoned his pants. He pulled out the file.

Breathing hard, Tom opened the folder and removed the first piece of paper, the memo he had started to read in Kramer's office. He set it aside and looked at the next page, wanting to see what else was in the file. 'Kennedy Space Center' was written at the top, and there was a column of numbers down the left side of the page. In the middle was a map with a bright red rectangle labeled 'D.O.D. Staging Building.' A long blue line ran horizontally across the center of the page. It appeared to represent a runway, as there were smaller lines that connected to it, perhaps aircraft taxiways.

At the end of the blue line, on the right side of the page, there was a small square labeled 'Launch Pad 39B.' Someone had penciled-in a line from the D.O.D. Staging Building to the launch pad, and scribbled four or five circles around just that area of the map. Tom paused, raised his head, and struggled to look through each window of the Jeep, checking in every direction. The windows were foggy due to his rapid breathing. No one seemed to be around, so he pulled out another page from the folder. It appeared to be a reduced copy of a larger blueprint. In the middle of the page there was a schematic drawing. It showed a cut-away view of the space shuttle Atlantis, according to the title at the top. Tom knew that Atlantis' last flight, July 8th, 2012, was the official end of the shuttle program, but he'd been told that another reporter at *The Washington Post* had worked on a lead which had come from an anonymous source, purportedly at the Pentagon, who claimed that Atlantis would be kept in near flight-ready status if it were ever needed, though it would go on display at Kennedy Space Center's Visitor Complex.

The drawing depicted two large objects in the shuttle's cargo bay. They appeared to represent some type of satellites, but they each looked different. The shape of one of them was similar to the pictures Tom had seen of typical communications satellites. But the other satellite was more rounded, and it had eight cylindrical objects protruding from it. Most importantly, he noticed writing near the top of the page, 'High Ground Program/D.O.D.' And down further there was a small box, to the left of the shuttle, which surrounded the words 'IRAN/M-East.' The satellite payload, Tom thought, was apparently intended for an orbital position over the Middle East.

It was clear to Tom that this was the smoking gun he had hoped for. At a minimum, it was enough to corroborate that the person, who was on the recording played for General Kramer, was telling the truth about a covert program at the Pentagon. And the file was certainly enough to prove that Kramer was lying. Tom knew that he had enough information to get started on the story and investigate further. He told himself "maybe this is the big one," then ran his fingers over the diagram as if it were some sort of sacred text.

He looked at the pages for just a few more seconds, then put them back into the manila folder. He leaned down, stretched to his right, and shoved it under the passenger seat. After a quick glance to the rear-view mirror, he put the Jeep in drive and pulled back onto the road. As he accelerated, he cracked opened the window to his left and took a deep breath of fresh air, then exhaled loudly. The windshield became even foggier. He fumbled with some temperature and fan adjustment knobs on the dashboard. More fog. He shook his head a few times, then said, "God, what have I gotten myself into?"

The sky grew cloudy and ominous looking, with swirling purple rainclouds to the west. The severe weather, which had been predicted for days in the D.C. area, compounded the anxiety that was intensifying in Tom's mind and nervous stomach. The act he perpetrated was slowly sinking in. He could feel acid creeping inside his belly and sporadically leaping into his esophagus. It was uncomfortable but, at the same time, told him that he was on to something of international significance. And yet he was concerned that this feeling seemed far removed from that which must come prior to success, fame, or a great story. Perhaps he had simply forgotten what it was like to be on the edge, and taking risks? He hadn't felt such uneasiness in a long time. It was as if his gut instinct had been hibernating for years, only to be jarred back to life all at once. *Hey, remember me? I'm the fire in the belly that made you become a reporter.*

He turned the Jeep into another strip mall on Jefferson Avenue and pulled to a stop in front of a FedEx Kinkos, then jumped out and ran in with the file. He wanted to send a copy of it (addressed to himself) to his office at *The Washington Post*, in case he would have to make up a story about how he received it. "Well, officer, it just showed up in the mail." That sort of thing.

He was sweating like he had just completed a marathon, plus he was still damp from the sprinklers back at the Pentagon. He slowed as he walked through Kinkos to the rear counter, while wiping his forehead on his sleeve.

"Hello, may I help you, sir?" the clerk asked, a girl not older than sixteen.

"Yes. Yes, please. I'd like to FedEx this." Tom set the folder on the counter.

"My, my, did you get caught in a downpour? I didn't think it was raining yet."

35

"Yeah, it's starting to rain out to the West. I didn't have an umbrella."

She offered a consoling smile then asked, "Did you say FedEx?"

"Yes."

"Okay. Do you want it to arrive tomorrow morning, afternoon, or two-day, sir?"

"Uh, tomorrow morning would be good. Thanks."

She reached under the counter and picked up a waybill and envelope. "If you'll just fill this out, please."

Tom didn't want his handwriting to be on the form, so he said, "Would you mind filling it out for me? I sprained my hand playing tennis yesterday. It's still a bit swollen." He grabbed his hand briefly, then shook it a few times for good measure.

"Yes sir." She picked up a pen from a jar next to the cash register. "What's the name of the person you are you sending it to?"

"Lassiter. Tom Lassiter."

"Is there a business name?"

"Yes, The Washington Post Company."

"Okay. The address?"

"1150 15th Street, N. W., Washington, D.C. 20071"

"Phone number?"

"334-6000"

"And your name?"

Tom paused briefly, faking a cough, as he tried to think of a name. He saw a bunch of tourist posters hanging on the rear wall of the store, five dollars each, according to the sign. One of them was of the White House.

"Your name, sir."

Without giving it a second thought, he blurted out, "T. W. House."

"Address?"

"What?"

She looked up at him. "Sir, your address?"

"Sorry, I'm just admiring your cards here," he said, spinning a small rack around. "The address is 0061, Pennsylvania Avenue,

36

Washington D.C. 20500." He had just given the reverse street address of the White House to her, and half expected her to notice. But she just kept going.

"20500?"

"Yes."

"There we go. Will there be anything else, sir?"

"Yes, I need to make some copies before I seal this up."

"Sure, you can use that Xerox over there." She pointed to a copy machine by a display rack of packing materials. "Do you need any help?"

"I think I can manage, thanks." He picked up the folder and walked over to the Xerox, made a copy of all the papers in the Pentagon file, then quickly made his way back. "Okay, I'm ready."

"Yes sir, I'll ring it up while you seal the envelope," she said as she set down a half-finished cup of yogurt. She counted the copies, which he had turned upside down, and moved to the register and punched in the sale.

Tom stuck the originals into the FedEx envelope and secured the flap, then grabbed the copies and put them into the folder. He tucked it under his right arm.

Thirty minutes later he arrived at *The Washington Post*, parked the Jeep in the only available spot, in the last row, and walked briskly through a maze of BMWs, Volvos, and mini vans. He entered the glass, stone and metal monstrosity that was the main lobby. He was fairly dry now, but his clothes were wrinkled and his hair was a mess. Most of his fellow reporters rarely dressed very well since the introduction of so-called business casual attire, so he figured he should fit in fine. But he decided to stop at the nearest restroom and make sure he didn't look too disheveled.

With his hair looking half decent, he tried to make his way to his office but bumped into his boss before reaching cover. "In a little late today, aren't we, Tom?" Thompson asked as he waddled over from his office.

"Yeah. Remember? I had to be at the Pentagon at seven-thirty, to meet that general on the High Ground thing. You know, the call that came in, the recording."

"Oh, that's right," he said in a rough voice, then took a sip of black coffee. In his other hand was a half-eaten maple twist. "Did you turn up anything, or was it a prank?"

"No, it wasn't a prank. But I need to check on a couple things." They walked side by side to the central copy room, and more donuts. It was an unspoken rule in the newsroom to never hype a story. Most of the time you'll embarrass yourself. Better to just surprise everyone, once you're sure of the facts.

Thompson wolfed down the rest of the maple twist, then began pawing a bear claw, the last donut on the tray. "I don't want you wasting too much time on this thing," he continued. "Maybe you should just drop it? You don't have much to go on, aside from that message from the unidentified caller. I've got some other stories lined up that are time sensitive. One of the President's advisors is under an ethics investigation, something involving a call girl."

"Another sex scandal?"

"Yep," he answered, his mouth full and chewing the donut.

Tom rolled his eyes and thought, *Great, another sex scandal.* "I'd really appreciate it if I could pursue this High Ground thing a bit further. I've got more than just the recording from the caller, but I need to flush it out."

"Flush?" he said then took another bite. "That's probably a good word for it. The lead may belong in the can. You know how dependable those—"

"I don't think so," Tom interrupted. "But I need to check it out. Kramer was very—"

"General Kramer?"

"Yeah."

"Good lord. He's still around? Lovable hard ass isn't he. What a piece of work, always has been. I met him, well, it must have been ten years ago," Thompson said, slowly shaking his head. "Most of the senior officers are the same over there—they won't tell you much.

Those guys are very reluctant to provide anything to reporters. Reminds me of a guy I once interviewed." He took another bite, this one of T-rex proportions. "I think it was over at the state department awhile back. He was a former general, brought down by some emails to his mistress." He turned and gazed out a dirty window behind a table with a paper cutter. He swallowed another sip of coffee, then shifted his attention back to Tom.

Tom tried once more. "I've got some information that may point me in the right direction on this thing. But I need to verify it. Just give me a few days. Okay?" He watched Thompson wipe some icing off the now-empty donut tray with his right index finger, then lick it off.

"Okay, Lassiter. I'll give you three days. I don't want to see a grown man cry. But the moment you determine this is a hoax, and I'm sure it is, I want you back here. And I want to see some words flowing out of your computer for a change," he continued as he walked away, moaning slightly and holding his stomach. "I think I'm coming down with something."

Yeah, a triple bypass, Tom thought.

Thompson vanished into his office, which was the third largest on the third floor of the third wing, right next to that of his boss, James Clemens Senior, executive editor, and the father of Tom's assistant, James Clemens Junior. Thompson, and a dozen other editors and vice presidents, had reported to him for two years. Mr. Clemens, in turn, reported to the editor-in-chief, Charles Dupont, a man seldom seen but whose demands on the paper's staff were always clearly felt, even feared. The hierarchy had undergone no less than five reorganizations in four years, yet somehow had managed to end up exactly the same, save the shedding of an international editor whose field research got out of hand, and a vice president of business development who didn't manage to develop any business. He was adiosed by Dupont after thirty-two days and six expense reports and two assistants (one could type and one could screw like a rabbit, according to the rumor mill).

Tom walked to his office, sat down in his cushy chair, and put his feet up. He picked up the phone and called James Clemens.

"Hello," James answered. He sounded more tired than usual.

"Hey James, can you come in here for a sec. I got something I need some help on."

"Be right there." He hung up. Ten seconds later he entered through Tom's doorway, ducking his head.

Tom asked, "How about doing some research for me?"

"Sure. What do you need?"

"Dig up what you can on the space shuttle program, NASA's current involvement with the military, and let's see, perhaps the Defend America Act Dole and Gingrich proposed before they left the Senate. Okay?"

"All right. But why the space shuttle program. I thought they retired the shuttles last summer."

"Yeah, that's the official word. But there's been some rumors about one more mission."

"Okay, is there anything else?" James asked.

"Yeah. Also, give this guy a call." Tom handed over a wrinkled business card. "He's a security expert and private detective. His name is Bill Dunn. He has all sorts of equipment for analyzing video, audio, and photographs. I used him about a year ago on another story. He's a crusty old guy, and big as a house, but he's good, damn good. Ask him to analyze the recording from that caller I told you about yesterday. Here you go." Tom pulled open a desk drawer to his right, removed a memory stick with the recording, and handed it to James. "We need to see if he can determine what the other voice said in the background, just before the caller got cutoff. And maybe he can determine whether the person was male or female, and their approximate age. Okay?"

James nodded.

"All right, well, that'll do for now. The main thing is I want to know what role NASA is currently playing with the military. That won't be easy, but give it a shot. And oh, awhile back the Air Force was working on some sort of missile defense system that uses lasers mounted on military 747's, to shoot down missiles."

"Are you serious? A Laser mounted on a 747?"

"Yes, it was a fairly well-known program, and they did a lot of testing with some sort of high powered laser."

"Lasers for shooting down missiles..." James said under his breath. "Cool."

"So see what you can find out. There's a rumor that the program has been turned back on again, due to concerns about North Korea and Iran."

"Okay," James said as he scurried down a few notes.

"I'll check with you this afternoon or tomorrow morning."

"All right." James turned and walked back to his cubicle, which was located about thirty feet away from Tom's office. Overall, Tom had been pretty impressed with him, so far at least, and he probably would have hired him even if James' dad wasn't one of his bosses. James was a decent writer, good go-fer, and got along well with the rest of the staff. Tom had kept him busy proofreading and fact checking mostly. But he knew James wanted to spread his wings.

CHAPTER THREE

General Kramer walked along Pennsylvania Avenue toward the Washington Monument which could barely be seen due to a low lying mist and drizzle. He had arranged to meet John Broderick and another CIA intelligence officer, Raymond Jones, at noon. Jones served primarily as an assistant to Broderick. He handled any and everything Broderick didn't have time for or felt was "below his pay grade," and frequently served as the designated scapegoat within the department. And that was about the sum of it. He was a good man and had a great wife, three healthy kids. But he, too, had become tainted by several missteps by the CIA, beginning with the agency's failure to prompt action which could have prevented the 911 terrorist acts, or at least limited the damage and loss of life which occurred. Both Jones and Broderick were dismayed when they learned the agency had published a report titled *Bin Laden Preparing to Hijack US Aircraft and Other Attacks*. It was a huge blemish on the CIA which impacted morale across the board, though most blamed politicians and bureaucrats for ignoring the warning. For Jones, the young, patriotic beacon within him was still there, but deep down inside he knew it had grown dim. Slowly but surely he was becoming what he despised, part of the system and the clogged processes which prevent prompt responses to foreign threats.

Kramer had arrived early, parking in a pay lot at the Washington Hilton, a couple blocks from the White House. He was known for frequently asking people to meet him at the Washington Monument—whenever he wanted complete privacy and had to discuss sensitive subjects he didn't want his office cameras and microphones recording at the Pentagon, or over at CIA headquarters. He'd heard from several colleagues that the clandestine meetings away from the Pentagon were a tad too dramatic and unnecessary, but Kramer felt that the monuments and historic buildings of the National Mall, and the proximity to the White House, instilled an atmosphere of patriotism and duty in himself and those he would meet there. Broderick had told him several times that he was just being paranoid, arranging such offsite meetings, but Kramer had spent much of his career helping to deploy increasingly more sophisticated electronic and optical eavesdropping technologies, including reconnaissance satellites which could read the headlines off a newspaper in someone's hands, or pick up the analog or encrypted digital signal from a specific cell phone. He knew firsthand the power of eavesdropping on individuals whether by visual, audio, or electronic surveillance means.

For the past fifteen years reconnaissance and other space-based satellite technology were Kramer's passion, his life really. And few personnel at the Pentagon were trusted with knowledge of, or management responsibility over, such critical and expensive programs largely initiated by the CIA. Modern satellites can cost as much as $800 million or more a piece, a hefty price, especially considering that the average life expectancy of any particular satellite is only five years.

Kramer's relationship and accomplishments with the Pentagon's National Reconnaissance Office (NRO), the agency responsible for the development and operation of all intelligence satellites, was the highlight of his military career. He was widely regarded as a star, someone who could get the job done, and quietly. And being discreet was paramount. Since 1984, when Samuel Morison provided a picture of the Soviet Union's first full-size nuclear-powered aircraft carrier in a port off the Black Sea, security surrounding the Pentagon's satellite operations had tightened considerably. Few details were ever released about the Pentagon's satellite programs. The first satellite to be declassified was the KH-4 Corona, which was first flown in 1960 (the 'KH' stands for 'keyhole'). The craft, rather than communicating electronic images back to the ground, used film which, once exposed, was dropped and picked up by Air Force cargo planes. The next major design change came with the KH-10, touted to the public as a two-person space station and launched by Gemini rockets. The program was abandoned in 1969 due to exorbitant costs and subsequently was supplanted by KH-9 (known as "Big Bird"), which included four film capsules. Nineteen KH-9's were launched from 1971 to 1986. Then, with the KH-11 Kennan satellite, first launched in 1976, design took a giant step forward. Air Force planes no longer had to chase canisters falling from the sky with exposed film and sensitive images. The KH-11, weighing almost eighteen tons and some forty feet long, was the first spy satellite to collect images electronically, then relay the signals to a communications satellite and down to earth. The next leap forward came in 1983 when work started on a satellite code-named Lacrosse. Unlike previous satellites, Lacrosse could see at night by means of its onboard synthetic aperture radar (SAR). The first version was launched in 1988 on a space shuttle, and the second in 1991 via a Titan rocket. At least one of the Lacrosse satellites was used for damage assessment during an early U.S. action against Iraq, an effort Kramer jointly managed.

In addition to the class of satellites primarily dedicated to visual reconnaissance, the U.S. also launched a series of eavesdropping, or signal intelligence satellites (SIGINT). These satellites, such as the "Vortex," are designed to listen to electronic military communications such as troop movement, missile telemetry, and senior leadership commands. They typically have a very large reflector dish of up to 328 feet diameter to collect and amplify signals, then relay them to Earth. An improvement in the SIGINT system was realized when the Navy Ocean Surveillance System (NOSS) deployed not just one satellite operating alone, but groups of three. Differences in the time it takes for the signal to reach each satellite reveals the exact location of the target they are focused on, for example a ship. Finally, the newest satellite reconnaissance technology, supporting the "High Ground" system (code-named KH-30), had been under development for six years with General Kramer deeply involved in the program. From the standpoint of budget allocation and vendor selection, however, some might argue that the system's design work had actually started back in 1960 with the KH-4 Corona program, as the KH-30s borrowed lessons learned from each new and improved satellite since then. Each generation improves upon its predecessors.

Kramer, too, had improved over the years; he knew more about satellites than any of his colleagues at the Pentagon. He was indispensable and this, at least to some degree, offset his personality flaws. Most of his colleagues would tell you that he was known for a wild temper, stubbornness to a fault, and a propensity to shoot-from-the-hip. And since his sons' deaths in Iraq and later in Afghanistan, each of these traits had seemingly intensified.

Kramer picked up his pace, moving steadily toward the monument, his red face catching tiny drops of moisture. It was a typical day in D.C., clear skies one minute and downpours the next. Bureaucrats everywhere. And although the weather had let up, the steady drizzle prompted him to whip out his government-issued black umbrella; it popped open and spit raindrops at his face.

A mile away Broderick and Jones drove as fast as they could in the lunch hour traffic, dodging crazy, or maybe they were just incredibly brave, tourists who crossed streets they shouldn't with eyes as big as the capitol dome. As usual, some were in rental cars, caught hopelessly in roundabouts designed in another era, being circled by yellow cabs like animals preyed and waiting certain death. Broderick was stuck behind one such cabby at an intersection and could see his hairy tattooed arms waving madly in the air, an unfiltered Camel cigarette draped from his mouth and unshaven face, and his curly head leaning out the window as he cursed in some unfamiliar language at the car in front of him. In frustration, Broderick shook his head left and right then stared at a tattered sticker on what was left of the cab's rear bumper—*Welcome to your nation's capital, now go home*. "Obviously a member of the tourism board," he said to Jones as he pointed to the bumper sticker.

The light finally turned green and the swearing and waving arms ceased. They slowly made their way through the intersection. He turned to Jones, whose eyes were fixed on a wet woman riding a wet bicycle and said, "Kramer's in one of his moods. And for good reason."

Jones nodded, not moving an eye from the girl on the bike.

45

"Lucky us," he continued, turning away and adjusting the heater controls. Actually, he was quite used to Kramer. He had worked with the general almost on a daily basis for several months. He now served as his key contact at the CIA, helping with anything necessary to get the High Ground program deployed as quickly as possible which, since Iran's defiance of nuclear facility inspections, had gained an even greater sense of urgency. Having worked with the CIA for over twenty years, he was used to pressure. He had frequently made dangerous trips to the Middle East, including Afghanistan, Iraq, and more recently Iran. Broderick was well respected within the CIA, battle proven, and had seen it all, the good and the bad that was the CIA. And now he was General Kramer's right-hand-man. But since returning from the Erbil fiasco in northern Iraq, where he and his fellow agents were ordered to abandon U.S. sympathizers, he hadn't seemed the same. It had hardened him.

Broderick and Jones parked their government issued car, dropped six quarters in a parking meter, then walked hurriedly toward the Washington Monument. A few minutes later they arrived and sat down next to Kramer on a splintery wet bench facing the White House. Kramer, as usual, ignored them until they were properly seated and composed.

"Good morning, General," Broderick said in a low, burly voice, still breathing fast.

"Good morning, Broderick," Kramer replied, then looked to his left, "Hello Jones. I haven't seen you in a while. How's the CIA treating you?"

"Pretty good, sir. Thanks."

Broderick, who was shivering and wanting to get on with the meeting, turned to Kramer. "I assume this is in regard to that reporter this morning?" He rubbed his hands together, trying to get warm.

"That's right."

"Well, at least we got him on video."

"Yeah, but that's not going to solve our problem. That file he has could shut the program down instantly and end my career, if not

46

worse." Kramer rubbed his forehead hard then wiped the moisture on his pants.

"I know, sir. I've been thinking about that. I don't see any way around it. We might need to scare him into keeping his mouth shut, even if it means roughing him up a bit," Broderick said as he looked nervously around.

"Keep your voice down, damn it," Kramer said as he pulled out a cigar. "You don't need to broadcast to every tourist between here and the oval office. We just need to stay calm, think this thing through. Don't go jumping to conclusions that'll make things worse."

"Sorry, sir."

"Let's take it one step at a time. Tonight, after Lassiter leaves his office at *The Washington Post*, I want you two to follow him and, well, don't tell me how you do it, but get that damn file back, and don't be seen. If we get the file, this whole thing will be his word against ours. Get the file and destroy it, that's our first objective. Agreed?"

"Yes sir."

"I don't have to tell you two about the ramifications if he gets the word out. I can see the headlines now, *Pentagon to bring shuttle out of retirement with plans to launch nuclear weapons into space*. Or worse yet, *General arrested for illegal satellite program*. I'm not going to be brought down by some damn reporter, especially just before my retirement. You know how *The Washington Post* is and—"

"I just can't believe you left him alone in your office," Broderick interrupted. "And with a stack of files on your desk. Stupid, absolutely stupid."

Kramer lit the cigar and stuck it in his mouth. He clenched it between his teeth, breathing hard and puffing mightily. He ignored Broderick's comment. It was, after all, extremely stupid to leave a reporter, any reporter, alone in a Pentagon office, let alone a reporter from *The Washington Post*. No use making excuses about it. He could take it on the chin. He pulled the cigar from his mouth and continued, "I know it was a mistake, believe me I know. What can I say, I screwed up. Look, I want this thing off the ground as much as anyone. Let's just deal with this one step at a time. It's a matter of national security. You have to get that file back immediately."

Broderick turned away.

"There's a lot at stake here," Kramer continued. "And honestly, I think if Lassiter publishes a story on what's in that file, I think everyone will probably think he's crazy, as long as he doesn't have any proof of what we're doing. That's why you two have to get that file. Understand?"

"Yes sir," Broderick replied, then glanced at Jones who nodded.

"We don't need any more of a spotlight on this thing. If word gets out, all hell will break loose in the Mid East. Hell, I don't know, maybe everywhere." Kramer paused to take another puff on his cigar. "Plus, our little covert piggy bank won't be hidden in the CIA budget anymore. I'll be back in the messy business of raising cash for programs and kissing the asses of politicians again, and I just can't stomach that anymore." He took a deep breath and stretched his neck, looking up at the clouds and letting drizzle hit his face.

Broderick and Jones remained quiet, as they always at least tried to do during most of Kramer's sermons. Hopefully he would be done in a minute, if history were any indicator. The weather was getting colder.

"We need to get these satellites launched and launched fast," Kramer continued, then stomped out his cigar in front of the bench. The wet pavement sizzled.

Broderick nodded and stood, looking rather sickly from the smoke, as the general lit up another. "I'm sorry for losing my temper, General. I've been under a lot of pressure lately, as you know."

"Haven't we all, Broderick. Haven't we all."

"You're absolutely right. We just need to stay calm, and get the file back. Sir, we won't let you down."

"Hell, son, screw me. We just need to get that payload launched, and at any cost." He paused, puffing some more. There were several seconds of silence. "Just get me that file back. And quickly. Or all three of us will be wearing numbers on our chests and sleeping on metal bunk beds over at Leavenworth prison for a few years."

"Yes sir. Is there anything else?"

"No, you two better get moving." He stood. "I'll tell you something, gentlemen, we better pray that he doesn't release any story, and copies of that file. This could get ugly. Real ugly. Not just for us, but for the U.S."

"Yes sir."

"Keep me advised. Good day, gentlemen. And good luck."

The general walked swiftly away.

CHAPTER FOUR

Always the procrastinator, Tom reluctantly dedicated some time to trying (emphasis on trying) to catch up on the paperwork that was threatening to overtake the entire surface of his desk at *The Washington Post*. Most intimidating was his in-basket; it was overflowing by several inches, mostly with memos from senior management. There were also a few birthday cards for various staff members soon to log another year. Stacked on one side of the desk there were a few newspapers he hadn't found time to read yet, and pink *While You Were Out* notes were strewn all over the other side. Some, the ones with a check mark in the box next to *Urgent*, were taped to his flat screen monitor.

He was relieved that no calls had come in, no military police were circling the building, and not one of his bosses had come down to ask about the escapade at the Pentagon. He had definitely made the right choice, he thought to himself. Just pretend nothing happened. Business as usual.

With the mess on his desk arranged in slightly neater stacks, he decided to check e-mail, which was the one office task, aside from writing, that he enjoyed getting done. Sure, half the time it was junk mail such as ads for high interest credit cards, or fishing scams from spammers asking to click a link and provide personal information, or invitations from people on Linked-in or Facebook. And, almost on a daily basis, he would receive an email from someone named Candy offering her services via a subscription webcam site. Countless requests to the IT department had failed to stop Candy's emails from invading his inbox over the past year.

Tom clicked on the Microsoft Outlook icon, entered his password, and waited patiently as dozens of emails transferred to his computer. As he scanned the subject fields for any signs of communications related to the Pentagon interview, or the stolen file, his stomach suddenly felt queasy. But as he scoured the emails for signs of trouble, nothing stood out as unusual. Just more junk mail and a few innocuous messages from colleagues. And Candy was apparently fine. Three messages from her. Delete, delete, delete. And there was even one on budget planning and expense report procedures from the head honcho, Thompson, which he promptly saved for later, when he is bored out of his mind and wants to have his ass chewed.

Tom's thoughts turned to the Pentagon file and the allegations about the High Ground program from the caller on his voice mail, and what he needed to do next. He knew he would have to do some research to corroborate the allegations, regardless of the contents in the file. Perhaps he could find someone involved in the program willing to talk, such as an engineer or technician who would be willing to get him up to speed on what NASA and the military were working on together. He rubbed his forehead for a few seconds, then looked up at his monitor and peeled the notes off the top, tossing them into his in-basket. They could wait.

Research was actually a part of the job Tom enjoyed. It kept things interesting, always learning about new subjects and meeting new people. And research was one reason he insisted on having his own stand-alone computer and 4G wireless connection which bypassed the Local Area Network altogether, unlike most of the staff at the *Post*, who were connected to the 'cloud' and a central computer. After losing weeks of research back in 2010, he had quickly decided he wanted no part in trusting his research files and draft articles—some of which would take months to write—to the pale, pimply computer services kid in the basement, who only emerged for the occasional ten-minute birthday-cake-cutting ceremony. He wanted to manage and backup his own work, thank you. Nor did he want his data, his work, to be subject to prying eyes or the so-called *Employee Task and Time Utilization Analysis Project*, one of the more recent brainstorms from senior management. The title of the project alone, he estimated, had to have taken a dozen vice presidents a day to come up with. God only knows how much time they had spent looking at how employees waste time.

Tom settled more comfortably into his desk chair and launched Internet Explorer, which opened with Google as the homepage. He thought about the message from the anonymous caller. Although he had James already doing some research, the reporter in him just had to poke around a bit for himself, maybe take a look at a few NASA and Department of Defense websites. At a minimum, it would keep his mind off this morning's visit to the Pentagon.

Four hours later and the paw on the Garfield clock (a Christmas present from his younger daughter, Emily) was already on the four, and the tail was on the six. Another exciting day in the life of a lonely reporter was almost history, and what a day it was. It could have been worse though. At least he hadn't been arrested. Not yet anyway. He yawned and stretched his arms over his head, then turned toward the window. He knew that his mother had planned a dinner. Nothing too fancy, but she was supposedly going to cook one of his favorite meals, blackened swordfish, red potatoes with butter and chives, corn on the cob, and maybe some apple pie if he was lucky. After a day like this, a home cooked meal sounded good.

He decided to at least try and make a valiant attempt at leaving the office early. He stood, grabbed his coat and briefcase, swatted the light switch off, and made a dash through the land of cubicles. He heard a voice.

"Tom, where the hell are you going?" Thompson yelled out, somewhere over by the copy room. "It's only four-thirty. Are you forgetting something?"

Tom stopped in his tracks, turned around, and walked toward him. Thompson, who had to have been a hound dog in a former life (bags under his droopy red eyes, big ears, loose skin, hair all over) and could smell food a hundred yards or two floors away, approached with a cookie in one hand and diet Coke and some papers in the other.

"Are you forgetting something?" he repeated, this time with his mouth full.

"Sorry, I have to leave early. My mom is preparing—"

"She'll have to wait, Tom," he interrupted. "Remember what I asked you last week? I said there might be a meeting I need you to attend on my behalf and—" He paused, dropping the copies he had just made. "Well, I can't make it. I promise it won't take more than an hour," he continued, looking up with puppy-dog eyes. He stood and began to walk away. "So, you can fill in for me, right?"

Tom followed, trying to come up with a good excuse for having forgotten the request. Thompson was always dropping bombs on him at the last minute. Usually it wasn't anything terribly important, such as a fund raiser, press conference, or just an internal budget or departmental meeting. And this time was probably no different. Knowing that he was already on the hot seat for pursuing the lead from the anonymous caller, Tom decided not to put up a fight. He would go along with Thompson's request, and try to leave as soon as he could.

He called home to tell everyone he "might be" a little late for dinner. As usual, his mother answered the phone (his stepfather stopped answering six years ago after he figured out that precisely ninety-eight point six percent of the calls were not for him). Tom dreaded making the call, but business was business. Being an investigative reporter in Washington D.C. had its sacrifices.

Two hours and a hell of a lot of PowerPoint slides later the meeting was about to end. Subscriptions were up, classified ad sales down, and newsprint costs were rising, seemed to be the brilliant analysis from the accounting department. Productivity was also down which Tom suggested, while rubbing his eyes, was due to too many budget meetings. The sneers and glares from several of the bean counters were numerous in response to the comment. He thoroughly enjoyed the reaction.

The joy of victory was short-lived. He glanced at his watch and realized he had been at the meeting longer than expected. He groaned slightly and shook his head as the director of finance proceeded to discuss the four scenarios of the five-year forecast—worst case, probable case, best case, and complete wet dream. Tom was convinced that monkeys with darts could do just as well.

A few minutes later he reclined in his chair and pushed back from the conference table, staring deadpan at the pie chart being projected on the wall, which he envisioned as his mom's apple pie, with steam rising toward the ceiling tiles above. He contemplated whether he should simply walk out of the meeting. Missing a family dinner, a birthday or a holiday dinner was always tantamount to treason as far as his mother was concerned. It would surely be a cold night in the Lassiter home.

Finally, the meeting ended and he made it out to his Jeep. Rain was streaming down and puddles were forming in the parking lot, which was almost empty. Most of *The Washington Post* employees were already home. He fumbled for his keys then unlocked the driver's door and jumped in, soaking the leather seat. He reached for the ignition, turned the key and the engine started. Even in the worst weather, the Jeep had never failed him over the years, though it wasn't the best looking vehicle anymore. Its dark green paint had faded and there were rusted brown areas around the fenders from road salt. He couldn't see spending the money to fix them, and it appeared that the rust was the only thing securing the right front fender to the chassis at this point. Although he never used it, the Jeep had four-wheel drive. The closest it had ever been to being useful was in the dark parking lot of a Wal-Mart when he accidentally backed over a rogue shopping cart.

He moved the transmission lever into drive and headed to the parking lot exit, hitting the brakes just before reaching 15th Street, then turned right and cruised toward home with the radio blaring a Maroon 5 song.

Several minutes passed.

"What the hell?" he whispered under his breath, staring at the rear-view mirror. He realized that a van had made several identical turns, and was following at a distance. His heart sunk and he knew the morning's chaos at the Pentagon was probably about to catch up to him. Ahead, the light at Lincoln Avenue turned from green to yellow, then to red. Cross traffic made it impossible for him to run the light. The van slowly pulled closer (almost touching his rear bumper). He could see there were two men inside, but couldn't make out the details of their faces. And it appeared they had pulled down the sunshades. He started to breathe faster and the windows of the Jeep became foggy, like in the morning but even worse. Images of the day flew through his brain. The Pentagon file. The meeting with General Kramer. His taking the file in front of that damn camera.

The light turned green. He punched the accelerator and contemplated whether he should just make a U-turn and head back to the office. But then what? The men in the van hadn't done anything to him. He decided to continue driving straight ahead. Maybe he could lose them.

The van kept following. And suddenly, as Tom stared at the rearview mirror, he saw the van's driver jerk the steering wheel and move almost completely to the shoulder of the road, as if he wanted to pass. The van's tires kicked up a stream of gravel and debris, as it swerved back and forth, and at one point the van's front bumper clipped the rear of the Jeep.

"They're crazy," Tom said just over the sound of the Jeep's engine.

He again floored the gas pedal. After briefly falling behind, the van gained ground then followed even closer. The van was now moving radically from side to side in the lane, intermittently hitting the little bumps that are supposed to wake you up before being hurled into oncoming traffic. The man in the passenger seat seemed to be trying to get Tom's attention. Tom could see him waving his arms, motioning to the side of the road as the van continued to sway back and forth. "Jesus, they're going to kill themselves."

He decided to call the police on his cell phone, but it was in the side pocket of his laptop case, which was resting on the backseat. He couldn't reach it. As he contemplated what to do, the van rammed the rear of the Jeep hard, whiplashing his neck backward to the headrest and making him momentarily lose his grip on the steering wheel.

He figured that if they were so intent on violently running him off the road, his predicament could only get worse if he pulled over. He knew his only option was to try and lose them. The Jeep's speedometer read 70, 80, then 85 miles per hour. Still, the van continued in pursuit, at times literally pushing the Jeep.

Not wanting to expose his family to whatever the two men planned to do, Tom turned left, rather than making a right (which would have taken him home), and instead headed down a rural road, just barely wide enough for two-way traffic. He'd been down the road before and knew it was a dead-end, but it was the only alternative he had. He thought that he might be able to get off the road and lose them in the hills, the trees.

Tom again looked in the rear-view mirror, scanning to see if he had lost them. A few seconds later the van skidded around the same turn, sliding off the road. "My god—" The van appeared to almost tip completely over, then ran over a mail box. He could see the post snap, and the top half smash into the van's windshield.

He nailed the accelerator to the floor again. The transmission downshifted hard and the nose jumped upward, the engine roaring. He remembered that there was a large, sweeping curve in the road about a half-mile further. If he could get far enough ahead of the van, he thought he could whip into the woods just after the curve and, hopefully, the men in the van would speed by without seeing him. Then he could back-track the opposite direction and go to the police station in Rockfish.

He slammed on the brakes just after the curve, then swung to the right between some pine trees, almost hitting one. He switched off the lights and rolled down the window to his left, listening. There was nothing to do but wait for the van to go barreling by.

A few seconds later the van passed by, making a swoosh sound.

Tom figured that by the time the men ascertained what had happened, he would be two miles down the road and going the opposite direction. He threw the Jeep into reverse and punched the accelerator. Not a good idea. The rear tires spun, digging perfect craters. He felt the back of the Jeep sink. He pushed the lever to engage four-wheel drive, then punched the accelerator hard with his right heel. This time all four wheels spun hopelessly, with no rearward movement whatsoever, and it sunk even further into the mud. He let up on the gas pedal and held his head out the window, listening for the van. At first, all he heard were crickets and a dog barking in the distance. But then hc heard an engine revving loudly and a moment later the van passed by again, going the opposite direction back to the main road.

He turned off the engine and decided to just leave the Jeep and walk out, or maybe call someone to pick him up. He reached behind the seat, moved his hand into the laptop's side pocket, and removed his cell phone. Once again he considered calling the police, but given what happened at the Pentagon, he wasn't thrilled with the idea. He'd have to explain everything that had happened in the morning, and why a van—which was apparently long gone now—had tried to run him off the road. He got out and made his way over to a granite boulder near a maple tree. He placed his back against its cool, smooth surface and pulled crisp air into his lungs.

CHAPTER FIVE

Tom knew there was only one person to call, if he wasn't going to call the police. And who better to call than someone who already had started research for the story, and was highly paid to help him however was needed. James was the logical choice. He would keep things confidential, and could be a liaison to the execs at *The Washington Post* offices. Tom had no intentions of going anywhere near the *Post*, and running into the goons in that van again.

Thirty minutes after making the call to James, Tom heard the distinctive growl of a Porsche six cylinder approaching (the car was a birthday present to James from his dad, and did nothing for employee morale at the *Post*). Tom often joked that it probably cost more than he took home a year after taxes. And he wasn't far off the mark. As the car approached, Tom walked out to the middle of the road and waved him down. With Pink Floyd blaring from the red Boxster convertible, James parked next to the curb and turned off the engine, jumped out, and walked over to Tom. "What happened?" he asked.

"Come on, let's get going," Tom said as he patted him on the back. "I'll fill you in on the way. Can we head to your house until I figure out what to do?"

"Sure. But why not your house?"

"I don't want to go home. They might be waiting for me."

"They who?"

Tom and James walked to the Porsche and got in. They did a quick U-turn and headed back to the main highway. Twenty minutes passed as Tom filled him in on what happened, though he didn't immediately tell him about the stolen Pentagon file.

"So what's the game plan now, boss?" James asked as he darted across the dotted yellow line and passed an old Lincoln driven by blue hair and two hands. The vehicle, a tan Continental, seemed to be standing still.

Tom started to reply but paused. He contemplated whether he should trust James completely. After all, he really didn't know him that well, and his dad was a top executive for *The Washington Post*. He wasn't in the mood to trust anyone after what had happened. But then again, he thought, he might need James' help. He decided to tell him everything.

"Hello, anyone home?" James said, staring. "What's the plan?"

"Well, we need to dig into something I, uh, received from the Pentagon."

"What are you talking about?"

Tom cleared his throat. "Well, I obtained a file."

"Obtained?"

"Yeah. You know, at that meeting I had this morning."

Slowly it sunk in. James looked at him. "What? You stole something from the Pentagon? The freaking Pentagon?"

"Yes," Tom answered, pinching the bridge of his nose, "the one and only."

"Are you crazy?" Again, James looked at him in disbelief, while turning off the Porsche's stereo.

Tom took a deep breath, then at length said, "Well, it has crossed my mind. I've never done anything like that before. I was left alone in Kramer's office, and, uh, there was a stack of files sitting there, and, I, I don't know what got into me."

"Do you think the guys who chased you in the van were sent by General Kramer?" James asked with big eyes as he shifted to a higher gear.

"I don't know. I don't know, man. Who else would chase me like that. I gotta think. I gotta think about what I should do now." Tom turned and gazed out the passenger window at the rolling countryside and milky gray sky. He went over everything again and again in his head, walking himself through the meeting with Kramer. He said nothing for at least a minute, then turned to James and continued, "I think I should fly over to London and go to British Space Systems.

59

Maybe I can locate the person who left that message on my voice mail. Maybe he'd be willing to give me some more details of the High Ground program. I think that's the first step. I need to find and talk to that guy. I can be in London by morning."

James downshifted the Porsche then came to a stop as the red lights of a railroad crossing began to flash and a wood arm swung down in front of the car's sloped nose. "Damn, we just missed it." He turned to Tom and said, "What about the Learjet?"

"The paper's Lear?"

"Yeah."

"That would mean I'd have to tell Thompson at least part of what happened today. I guess I could talk to him, and see if he'll let me fly over. I wonder if I could take the Lear tonight."

"I'd imagine so," James said. "Isn't there a crew on call twenty-four hours a day?"

"That's what I've heard. Hell, I don't know. I've only been on the thing a few times. I'm not even sure if it can make it all the way to Europe. It may not have the range."

"Do you know where it's kept?" James asked. "The name of the hangar?"

"Sinclair Aviation, I think."

James picked up his iPhone.

"Who are you calling?"

"Information. I'll get Sinclair's number, so we can check on whether it's scheduled, and what its range is. No use going to Thompson if it isn't available, or can't cross the Atlantic."

"Good idea."

"Do you want to land at Heathrow?"

"What? I can hardly hear you." The train was blowing its horn and passing by in a blur.

"The airport, Heathrow, is that where you want to land in London?"

"Yes, that's fine."

A couple of minutes passed as James called over to the hangar. After bouncing between three different people, he found someone who seemed to know what he was doing. A minute later James finally hung up and turned to Tom, who asked, "So what's the deal?"

"He said he's not sure if the Learjet can make it all the way to London nonstop, and that it might need to make a refueling stop in Newfoundland, something he called the Great Circle Route. The Lear is supposedly a 36A, the long-range model, but he said it'll have to fly a precise profile, with the majority of flight time spent at the maximum cruise altitude, forty-five thousand feet, I think he said, and at long-range power settings."

Tom was impressed with James' getting so much detail.

James continued, "So, under a typical scenario, the flight would be calculated on the basis of eighty-five percent probability winds. On a trip to London the pilot would assume a nineteen knot push from the wind. He said the Lear would land in London with only eighty-five pounds of fuel remaining—ten minutes to dry tanks."

"That's real comforting." Tom was already killing off the entire idea.

"He said most pilots would never make such a risky flight, especially over water. It'll be cutting it close, if you attempt a nonstop flight, but it is possible."

"Okay. What about the schedule? Is it available?"

"Nothing's on the books."

"Good. Good work, James."

"He told me he would make sure it's ready, and that he'd notify the crew for a possible flight tonight. And I told him the clearance was in the works from the *Post*, and that I'd be in touch after I talk to my dad."

"Excellent."

"I'd like to go with you, if that's okay," James asked, looking over.

"Well—"

"I'd really like to help. And it might be safer, you know, having two people on this. This could be huge."

Tom thought for a few seconds then said, "I guess it would be all right."

They both watched in silence as the train passed. It seemed to go on forever. The caboose finally made its way by and the wood arm lifted in front of them just, of course, as the little old lady with the blue hair pulled up from behind in her Lincoln. James put the Porsche in first and slowly drove over the tracks. And then, as if a checkered flag dropped, he floored the gas pedal and they were pushed back into the bucket seats. Tom turned and said, "We need to call information over in London and get the address for British Space Systems, or maybe use your iPhone's web browser. In fact, we should try and set up an appointment with someone. Maybe we could tell them that we're working on a story involving NASA subcontractors, and that it would be a good public relations piece."

"Sounds like a plan."

"Then, after London, we'll fly to Florida and dig around at NASA. We need to find out where the payloads are stored before they are launched. We have to find someone who will talk about the High Ground program and the satellites shown in the file. It's a long shot, but perhaps someone will talk."

"Okay. London, then off to Kennedy Space Center in Florida," James said as he changed gears again, accelerating.

Tom's head snapped back. "What, I can't hear you."

"I said Kennedy Space Center, at Cape Canaveral Air Force Station. That's where they did all the launches of the space shuttles and large rockets, and they probably store the satellite payloads in a building nearby."

Tom nodded. "It shouldn't be that difficult to get access to some engineers or technicians at NASA. Someone will talk."

"Maybe we can even get the story out before they launch."

"James, if I have my way, there won't be a launch. The shuttle program is retired, and I intend to keep it that way—if they are actually planning to launch some sort of illegal space weapon on one last, final mission. In fact, that's the first thing we need to check on. Are they preparing for one more launch at Kennedy Space Center? I mean, launching the space shuttle doesn't happen overnight. A lot of people will be involved for weeks or months, before launch. I don't think they can keep that a secret for long." Tom turned to James and with serious eyes continued, "This is more than a big story James. Such a space-based weapon could spark confrontations with not only Iran, but with Russia, China and probably many more countries. No one wants to see another arms race, and especially not in space."

CHAPTER SIX

When evening came they left James' condo and drove to Sinclair Aviation, where the paper's Lear was maintained, stored, and thoroughly pampered. Tom opened a large metal door and they walked into the hangar. It looked more like a hospital or hotel lobby with a polished white tile floor, massive floor to ceiling windows with tinted glass, some leather furniture over in one corner, and even a wet bar and mini-kitchen with granite countertops and stainless steel appliances. But what really stood out were the three shiny Learjets and two jet helicopters parked in the middle. The Learjets had a blue stripe down their sides and silver foil lettering that said *The Washington Post*. Three men, dressed in pristine white jumpsuits, were waxing the left wing of one of the jets. It was spotless. The thought struck Tom that the lavish image before him was in stark contrast to the doom and gloom budget meeting with Finance he had attended back at the office.

As James and Tom walked toward the plane they heard a man's voice. They swung around. It was the pilot, dressed in a blue jacket and perfectly pressed pants, crisp white shirt, tie and black shoes with thick rubber soles. He even had a hat, and little gold wings were pinned to his chest. "Are you the ones who reserved it?" he asked.

"Yes," Tom answered.

He made his way over. "I'm Paul Reynolds." He extended his hand. Tom thought that he was the same guy he met awhile back, on a rare flight with James' dad out to a convention in San Francisco, but the pilot didn't seem to recognize him. It wasn't as if Tom got to mingle with management and fly around in the Lear that often. James proceeded to introduce himself and they all walked toward the pull-down stairs to the passenger cabin.

"I hear you want to fly nonstop," Paul said, turning to Tom. "Is that correct?"

"Yes, if possible."

"I did some checking. We'll be cutting it very close if we don't stop in New Foundland. It's doable, but I don't recommend it."

"We're really in a hurry. It's your call," Tom continued. "But I'd appreciate it if we can get over there as fast as possible."

"Well, the jet stream seems to be blowing in our favor, according to the latest reports, so let's get her in the air, and see how it goes. My copilot will be here in a few minutes." He paused and looked at James. "You two can climb aboard, or wait out here. There are some snacks and drinks over there." He pointed to the waiting area and kitchen.

James and Tom walked over and grabbed a couple of turkey sandwiches out of the refrigerator and some water bottles and potato chips from a counter, then boarded the Lear.

After instrument checks and taxiing to the main runway, they took off toward the west, did a slow sweeping turn, then headed northeast. The takeoff was uneventful but the angle of ascent the pilot managed seemed almost vertical to James and Tom, much too steep than they cared for.

The plane reached an altitude of forty-five thousand feet, according to the pilot's barely intelligible voice from some speaker. They began to level off. "Winds look good. We'll go for nonstop," he added.

For the next two hours James and Tom sat quietly as the jet screamed through the sky, headed for London's Heathrow airport via the Great Circle Route, whatever the hell that was. According to the pilot's calculations, the Learjet would make the trip in seven hours and thirty-seven minutes, assuming no air traffic delays and assuming they would get a fair dose of help from the jet stream gods.

Tom loosened his seatbelt and turned sideways, toward James. "Were you able to dig up anything interesting, you know, on that research I asked you to do on NASA and the Pentagon? I want to get up to speed on the history of the shuttle program." He yawned and stretched his arms.

"Well, I don't know if they'll help, but I downloaded some articles, mostly information on NASA. There's also a transcript of a speech President Reagan gave on the need for an improved national defense, you know, Star Wars stuff from the 80's. It's old info, but it's interesting."

Tom nodded.

"Everything's in my briefcase. Do you want to see it now? You look like you need a nap."

"I know. I'm tired. Yeah, let me take a look," Tom said, rubbing his eyes.

James reached below his seat and pulled out a tan leather case. He set it on his lap and snapped open the latches, then lifted the lid. He reached across the aisle and gave Tom a stack of papers. "Here you go."

"Great." Tom began flipping through the articles. His eyes were immediately drawn to a page that described the history of shuttle missions. He held it up so he could see better. "Where did you find this?"

"NASA's website on Kennedy Space Center. It had a ton of information. I printed out just a fraction of it."

Tom's eyes we're watering and his eyelids were heavy. He reclined the seat and tried to study the printout. The inky black words were suddenly blurry, the bleached page washing everything out.

The list of past shuttle missions identified many of them as classified. The numerous classified designations made Tom's mind race. His stomach felt nervous, from the turbulence the Learjet was now going through, more than anything.

An hour and forty-five minutes passed in silence. Conversation returned after the Learjet began descending to a lower altitude, becoming quieter with the reduced thrust of its two engines. James stretched his neck left and right. A short while later, after small talk, they were both asleep.

CHAPTER SEVEN

The plane descended over the lush green checkerboard landscape of farms surrounding the suburbs and outskirts of London. The air was void of morning fog. Only a billowing power plant, far below, and the vaporous silver-grey geyser from an old locomotive disturbed the stillness, stealing the serenity and indicating life. Tom moved closer to a window near his seat, and looked down. The train below seemed to move far too fast. It looked like a giant, yet in every way graceful, snake meandering purposefully through the English countryside, occasionally burrowing into the earth, then emerging unexpectedly. Tom had traveled extensively in the states and throughout Canada and Mexico, and a few countries in Continental Europe, but he had never been to the British Isles.

The pilot's voice crackled on the speaker again. "Gentlemen, we're about ten miles from Heathrow. Please prepare for landing."

Tom watched as the sun started to rise above the rolling hills to the east. He could see the outline of London as the Lear began to bank to the left. He glanced over at James, who looked half asleep, fading in and out.

Twenty minutes later and they had landed, proceeded through customs, declared their baggage, and made a quick stop at a restroom. They followed a mass of tourists and business travelers down a hallway and toward a huge red sign, *Transportation*.

Tom turned to James and asked, "Do you want to get a cab, or rent a car?"

"Well, we don't want to rent a car in London. That would be suicide. You know, the whole driving on the left side thing, and heavy traffic downtown. Let's take the Tube into the city."

"The Tube?"

"Yeah, you know, the Underground. That's what they call the subway over here," James said, then stopped and turned to an old man who was reading a schedule. "Excuse me, sir. Can you tell me where you picked that up?"

"I got it over there." He pointed to a ticket booth. "But you can have this one. I'm done with it."

"Thanks."

James handed it to Tom. "Here. It's the schedule."

Tom opened it and studied a map of railway lines and stations, and operating times. There were ten or so basic train lines, plus the East London line, which ran from Shoreditch and Whitechapel across the river Thames, and south to New Cross. From Monday to Saturday trains started running just after five A.M. and went until midnight. On Sundays they started two hours later, and stopped running about an hour earlier.

They approached the money exchange booth with the shortest parade of people in line, then slowly made their way to the window. There was a girl with long brown hair working inside. James forked over some greenbacks of U.S. presidents, and she returned queens and kings. After being shocked by the exchange rate they stuffed their pockets full of pounds, then walked over to another booth and purchased two tickets to London.

The fifty-minute ride from the airport, on the Piccadilly Line, was relaxing. Not too crowded either. The train rode above the land as it made its way through farmlands and small blurry towns of red brick and stone, then darted back into the ground in some of the more populated areas. The fluctuation between darkness and daylight was mesmerizing, especially since they were tired. As the train rolled toward London, a brief stop was made at Barons Court, then a change of trains at Earl's Court, and on to High Street Kensington. The hotel James made reservations at was supposed to be only a quarter-mile from there.

They moved in unison with the crowd to the High Street Kensington station exit and out the turnstiles, two cattle in a herd. They soon arrived at the Royal Kensington Hotel, practically dead on their feet; the long flight across the Atlantic had taken its toll. They checked in and decided to get a couple hours of sleep, then freshen up before heading over to British Space Systems. Prior to leaving the U.S., James had made arrangements with the company's director of communications, who said she would be willing to provide a tour of some of their facilities. Although James hadn't asked her over the phone, he hoped that he and Tom might even be able to interview a few engineers, and at least try to locate the caller who left the message at the *Post*.

James was obviously proud of his work. He rattled on incessantly about it as he and Tom walked through the hotel lobby and toward the mirrored doors of the two elevators. James had told his contact at British Space Systems, Victoria Brookshire, that there was a big story on U.S. government contractors coming up, and that it would be a great public relations opportunity for any defense related company with sales to the states. Ms. Brookshire had agreed wholeheartedly that it sounded like a great opportunity, especially after James not so shyly stated that the story would be positive and would surely reflect kindly upon British Space Systems' stock price, which he then pointed out was at an all-time low of forty-five and an eighth. And that was that. She bought his justification for the story, hook, line, and sinker. Or so he thought.

They reached the hotel's elevator waiting area and James hit the up button. The doors of two elevators opened simultaneously (one for floors eleven through twenty, and one for floors one through ten). James made a beeline for one, and Tom the other.

"Give me a call when you're ready," James said over his shoulder.

Tom nodded. "Just meet me in the lobby cafe in two hours." Tom disappeared into the elevator with an attendant who looked like Ichabod Crane and wore a long black coat and smelled like Old Spice cologne circa 1970. He asked Tom what floor then pressed the button for the sixth floor with his right index finger, which resembled a knotted twig of crackled pale wood. The doors closed with a thud.

Tom's stomach rose to his throat as the elevator came to a herky-jerky stop. He watched as the doors parted and the man's fingers crawled around the rubber stops and held them open. Tom nodded politely, then exited swiftly and walked down the hall to his room, 6-17, non-smoking. He inserted the key into the lock, twisted the brass knob, and opened the door. As he walked in he hung his garment bag on a hook. The door swung shut behind him. He kicked off his shoes and promptly fell to the bed as his mind flipped through ideas of what he and James needed to do. He knew they didn't have much time to find the person at British Space Systems who had left the message at *The Washington Post*, get him to talk, then head to Florida and find an engineer or other employee at NASA and see if they would corroborate the allegations. All this—while hopefully evading anyone searching for him due to the Pentagon incident.

CHAPTER EIGHT

The hotel cafe was filled with heavenly Colombian coffee aromas and the strange syncopating music of clanking china, shuffling pinkish-yellow Financial Times pages, and sipping, slurping, serious people. Tom walked in and immediately noticed James over at a small round table, near a foggy and curtainless window. He had made a little porthole in the moisture and was staring down at the street with a blank look on his face, slouched over a cup of coffee and inhaling its apparently miraculous healing mist. But he looked none the better, no more rested than when he and Tom arrived.

They ate a small, overly expensive breakfast consisting of cold wheat toast, a piece of fruit they believed to be orange, and some rare and hopefully near-extinct species of nasty, runny scrambled eggs. But the coffee, thank god, leaned toward satisfying, aside from the primordial muck at the bottom of the cups.

They paid the bill, then walked into the lobby and toward the huge rotating glass door, the exit. Tom stopped suddenly and looked in a gift store, which was conveniently and strategically located next to the cafe. He leaned over, resting his palms on his knees, and peered into a display case crammed full of goods (you know the sort, Rolex and lesser watches, boxes of candy, china plates with various tourist attractions stamped upon their shiny surfaces, a beer stein shaped like Big Ben, a few paisley silk ties, assorted wool scarves, and a collection of current novels). There was also a wide selection of, according to a small sign, various "authentic" gifts from England. And indeed there was, both inexpensive and overpriced, mostly the latter.

"Come on," James said, turning. "What are you looking at?"

"I've always wanted one of these," Tom replied, pointing.

James walked over to see what he was admiring then inquired, "The chocolate Shakespeare head, silk Monty Python underwear, or the spoon and thimble collection?"

"You're a riot, James. No, over there. See? The wooden ship model. See it?"

James moved forward and looked in the case.

"Great, isn't it. Check out the sails, the rigging. And it's real wood. Hand-carved, I think."

"Yeah, by child labor in some former British colony."

"No, look, it says *Made in England*. See the little sticker." More pointing. "I wonder how much it is," Tom continued, then paused for a few seconds, squinting. "Too much, I'm sure, with the exchange rate the way it is. Oh well, come on." He straightened his back, then started to walk away.

"Why don't you run in and check it out," James said. "I'll wait. You won't find one like that in the states."

"Well, we aren't here for shopping. It can wait."

"Ah, live a little for god sakes."

"You don't mind?"

"No, go ahead," James replied, then watched as Tom went into the store. He approached a pretty and plump lady who was dusting a display case in the middle of the store. "Excuse me, ma'am. Would you tell me what the price of the wooden ship is?"

"Certainly, sir. It's seven hundred pounds. Would you care to inspect it?"

Tom raised his eyebrows and shook his head left and right a few times. "Uh, no thanks. That's a little over my budget."

She nodded and smiled, then promptly returned to dusting coffee mugs. Tom walked back to the lobby.

"Well, how much?" James asked.

"I was right. Too much, seven hundred pounds too much."

"You're kidding."

"Nope, that's what the lady said."

They exited the hotel. There were three cabs by the curb ready and waiting, their drivers dressed in black, all proper like. They jumped in the first car and gave the driver the address for British Space Systems' corporate headquarters. "It's supposed to be on Knightsbridge Road, about five minutes from here," James told him. "Just past Harrods department store." This, according to the directions he was given by Ms. Brookshire. The driver seemed perturbed. He obviously knew exactly where it was. The ancient looking but clean black cab began to chug along, merging into traffic.

Tom hoped that, once they arrived at British Space Systems, Ms. Brookshire would take them to the company's labs and manufacturing facilities in Reading, which was supposed to be about thirty minutes to the west of London. He presumed that the person who left the message on his voice mail back at the *Post* would have likely been calling from there, rather than from corporate headquarters in the city, as it would be more likely for a technician, engineer, or factory worker to purport something negative about the company's projects than an employee in senior management. And the caller mentioned that he had "just learned the full scope" of the High Ground program, so he'd obviously been kept in the dark for some time. Thus he was probably not a senior manager, as one would assume that management would be intimately familiar with the entire program from its inception, or at least from the point British Space Systems received the contract for their portion of the satellite work.

The cab slowed and pulled up to the side of the road. The company, it turned out, was located in an old yet well-preserved five-story building. It was made of gray stone and looked more like a cathedral on the outside than a divisional headquarters for a major multinational corporation. It appeared to be at least three hundred years old.

They paid the driver then walked up some slippery granite steps and entered through thick glass doors. The lobby was thoroughly modern, with large leather couches on each side, black marble tables, and glass brick walls. It all seemed rather out of place, given the exterior of the building.

They continued toward the center of the room, where several small crystal sculptures were placed. One of them was of the space shuttle, and it sat prominently on a granite pedestal. "Beautiful, isn't it," James said, leaning forward and admiring it. The miniature shuttle had its cargo bay doors open (also made of crystal) and a satellite of some sort dangled from the robotic arm, which appeared to be made of silver. They both stared at the sculpture for a few seconds, then looked about the lobby. To the left there were six or seven men in suits talking, shaking hands, and schmoozing each other. To the right there were large color photographs (floor to ceiling) of the shuttle and various indistinguishable rockets. They hung behind a reception counter, which was made of glass brick, and were illuminated by small halogen lights concealed in the dark blue ceiling high above. One of the lights also shined a bright, highly focused beam on the crystal shuttle sculpture, making it sparkle from every angle. There was to be no doubting what buttered this company's bread—the United States defense and space budget.

Tom and James approached the receptionist.

"Good morning," James said with a hesitant, jet-lagged smile.

"Good day to you gentlemen. How may I help you?"

"We are here to see Victoria Brookshire. We're with *The Washington Post*. I called and spoke to—"

"Yes indeed, Mr. Clemens," she interrupted, then looked down at a note taped to one of the three phones before her. James cringed, obviously realizing he had forgotten to not use his real name when he had called. Rookie mistake. The last thing they needed was someone from British Space Systems calling a Pentagon official or *The Washington Post* to verify the purpose of the visit.

The receptionist looked up and said, "Victoria gave me a ring a few minutes ago and told me to expect you. She'll be out in just a moment. Please sign in and," she said then handed him a clipboard and pen, "if you would be so kind, please put one of these on." She set two name tags on the counter.

They were obviously some sort of electronic tracking devices, much too thick for just run-of-the-mill name tags, and were probably used to make sure visitors stayed only where they were authorized to be in the huge building.

Tom watched James scribble his signature, then grabbed the pen and wrote down something resembling letters and a name and handed the clipboard back to the receptionist. She smiled and said, "Thank you. You can have a seat, but I'm sure Victoria won't be long."

Tom nodded and turned away from the counter, walking a couple steps away as James followed.

"We're about to be tracked," James whispered as he handed Tom a name tag. "I sort of forgot to use different names when I called here and—"

"Yeah, I noticed, James," Tom said, staring at his name in bold black letters across the name tag.

As they put the name tags on, a woman approached and exchanged hellos with the receptionist, and handed her some files. Tom briefly glanced over at her, then did a double take and fumbled with the name tag. She was truly striking. She had long gorgeous red hair, fair skin, blue eyes, and an exquisite body. *Wow, absolutely gorgeous*, he thought to himself.

She walked toward Tom, apparently seeing his feeble attempt to clip the name tag on straight.

"Let me help you with that, sir," she said with a soft smile.

Suddenly it slipped through his fingers and dropped to the polished marble floor. They both bent over to pick it up, almost hitting their heads.

"Please sir, I'll get it. I do apologize. These things are indeed difficult. Absolutely impossible to clip on straight," she said, reaching for the name tag with her slender left hand and holding her dress to her legs with her right. She slowly picked it up then, being careful not to hit Tom's head, began to stand.

Tom watched her as she stood, with nary a blink. Her elegant red dress was loosely fastened with large black buttons. They led up to her perfect porcelain neck which appeared soft and untouched by sun, a benefit of living in rainy London, he thought. She reached toward him and clipped the name tag on his jacket. His eyes followed her hourglass figure downward to her white silk stockings (those kind that have a lacy floral texture). His heart beat faster. He hoped she wouldn't detect it, but even he could see his chest moving slightly. The rush of excitement felt foreign to him, like a friend who had been gone for years, was forgotten, then returned only to be appreciated more than ever. Her rare beauty caught him off guard. He hadn't been this attracted to a woman since his wife. It felt comforting, exciting, and yet unsettling at the same time. He almost felt guilty, as if he was somehow cheating on Helen by even looking at this woman; he tried to console himself that it had been years since her death.

"There we are now, sir," she said as she straightened the name tag, leaning toward his shoulder to get a better angle.

"None the worse for wear. Right sir?"

He nodded, relishing in the perfume she was wearing—fine, sweet perfume.

"Amazing devices, but impossible to put on. On humans anyway. They apparently shoot smaller versions of them through an animal's ear in the wild, you know, for tracking. We stopped doing that to visitors years ago," she said with a comely smile.

Tom nodded some more and returned the smile and a nervous laugh.

James kept quiet and looked on in amazement, realizing that Tom was somewhat taken with Ms. Brookshire. He couldn't blame him, really. Her delicate face looked like it belonged on a magazine cover. Her eyes were a deep shade of blue. They almost matched the sapphire stone that was draped graciously from her neck, attached to a rope of gold. And her long red hair was incredible; it wasn't the bright sort, it was more reddish-auburn and entirely uniform and very rare, and impossible to derive from a bottle. It was also curled slightly.

She finally introduced herself. "It's a pleasure to meet you, gentlemen. I'm Victoria Brookshire, director of communications," she said as she extended her hand.

"Hello," Tom replied. He quickly noticed that she wasn't wearing any rings. He also noted that she had carefully manicured fingernails and bright red nail polish. They were just the right length, he thought. Not too long. He shook her hand gently but firmly. It was soft and felt almost hot compared to his hands, which were practically frozen from riding over in the freezer that had masqueraded as a taxi. He was just barely beginning to thaw. "I'm Tom Lassiter. Thanks for meeting us on such short notice," he said.

"My pleasure," she replied with yet another warm smile. "My, my, rather nippy out there isn't it," she continued, feeling the coldness of his hand.

"Yes, but not terribly colder than where we flew in from."

"D.C. area, correct?" she asked, then briefly looked over at James.

"Yes," Tom answered, "D.C. Oh, I'm sorry, this is my assistant, James Clemens."

"Pleased to meet you." James shook her hand.

"My pleasure. Would you gentlemen please follow me to our main presentation and meeting room. It's on the second floor."

"Sure."

"We'll take the stairs, as the elevator is currently at the top of the building," she continued, staring up at the red LED floor indicator, "and we can climb a floor faster than it can get down here." They walked over to a large metal door, what appeared to be the fire escape. She opened it and they followed her into a stairway chamber. Tom tilted his neck back and stared upward as her long legs climbed each step, her hips swinging smoothly left and right, but not deliberately or flauntingly. Her dress wavered back and forth in perfect cadence, and her taut, well-defined calf muscles bulged, even through the stockings. He couldn't take his eyes off them.

James followed, close in tow. Tom glanced back at him and saw that he was struggling to see Victoria, his view partially blocked. The stairway was narrow. Victoria's stride produced a wake of perfume. It floated down the steps and into Tom's lonely mind.

They reached the second floor much faster than either Tom or James wanted. Victoria swung open another large door and held it open for them. They proceeded to walk toward the first door on the right of a long hallway and entered a dark theater-like room. She touched a flat control panel on the wall and a few blue-colored sconces slowly came on, bathing the room in a cool glow. The lights revealed a huge presentation screen at the far end of the room, a granite conference table, and an HDTV projector which was suspended from the ceiling. Above the table, modern-looking halogen lamps hung from slender chrome rods. They began to glow and shed white light upon the glossy granite. The soft radiance also spilled onto the room's walls, which were covered in fabric panels, the kind used to keep sound from annoyingly bouncing all over. They sat down in large, very cold, black leather chairs. Fortunately, the heat began to come on.

"So, what do you use this room for?" James asked. "I would never have expected a government defense contractor to have such a flashy conference room. This place is incredible."

"Yes, it is nice, isn't it. We use it primarily for presentations to prospective clients. It's also used for meetings, mostly when the bigwigs fly in, and for new product or design unveilings," she said as she crossed her legs, then discreetly tugged on the end of her dress. "I'm glad you like it, Mr. Clemens. So tell me gentlemen, why did you fly all the way over the Atlantic to visit our rather obscure company? We generally stay out of the limelight. Isn't that a rather expensive trip just for a story?"

"Yes, it's a long flight, but not too expensive," Tom replied hesitantly, then tried to think of something to say that would make the trip seem less important. "James just joined *The Washington Post* and, well, we're putting him through the paces. He's going to be a foreign correspondent. This is just the first leg of our trip. I'm introducing him to key people at our offices in Europe," he continued, then turned toward James. "Right James?"

James nodded obediently.

"I see," Victoria said.

Tom pressed on. "So, Ms. Brookshire—"

"Please, call me Victoria," she interrupted.

"Certainly. And you can call me Tom."

"Very well." She paused, waiting for Tom to finish what he was going to say, but he was obviously waiting for her to continue. "Now, I normally start visitors off with a short video on British Space Systems.

We created it to acquaint visitors with our products, our mission, and that sort of thing. It may help with your story."

Tom nodded. "Sure, that sounds like a good start."

"Great, just give me a second," she continued, then stood, and walked over to the control panel again.

They watched her every move. She pressed a few buttons and a motor hummed to life. The noise lassoed their eyeballs back to the front of the room, where the HDTV projector over the table lowered about a foot and a half. The lights dimmed. An image of British Space Systems' logo appeared on the screen.

She returned to her chair. "Sorry I don't have any popcorn, gentlemen," she said loudly. Music blasted from every wall and vibrated the room. Suddenly the logo disappeared with a swooshing sound and in its place a face appeared. The man introduced himself as "Ted P. Hampton, managing director of British Space Systems." After a few more swooshes, and a few aerial shots of corporate headquarters and the rolling English countryside, he proceeded to provide an overview of the company's "sweeping and proud" past accomplishments. His face then dissolved into the image of a bronze plaque that had inscribed on its shiny surface the letters BSS, and British Space Systems underneath. Then a jumbled mission statement scrolled onto the screen, obviously intended more for investors than anyone else—maximize this, profit from that, penetrate markets here and there and everywhere. *BS indeed*, Tom thought to himself.

The baritone voice of a narrator took over for Mr. Hampton and, in extremely happy fashion, said, "Well, thank you, Ted."

British Space Systems, it turned out, had been one of the manufacturers of the "heat dissipation tiles" used to protect the space shuttle and "other aerospace devices" from the severe temperatures of re-entry into the Earth's atmosphere. The company's roots actually went back two hundred years. One of the company's commercial ancestors was the largest manufacturer of stoneware and glass products in England. The narrator said that this early expertise, transforming silicon and other materials into usable household products, provided the foundation for the company to launch a new division. The new division's entire purpose was to create products for the military and the aerospace industry, as they were increasingly requiring materials that could withstand extremely high temperatures and adverse operating conditions, so the narrator said anyway. The narrator finished, again in dramatic fashion, "And back to you, Ted."

Mr. Hampton went on to say that thirty years ago the company sold off its consumer products division to focus on the more profitable commercial and industrial applications sector. Later, the core company was taken over by a U.S. holding company and, shortly thereafter, it went public. The video went on to say that NASA and U.S. defense contractors were its largest customers the past fifteen years. The space shuttle program was mentioned extensively, and there were dozens of images of workers gluing on tiles to the belly of the spacecraft, like a big jigsaw puzzle. The video also mentioned that British Space Systems had provided technology for use in the intercontinental ballistic missile programs of the U.S., though no specifics were given as to the exact application.

Another swoosh. The image of British Space Systems' managing director dissolved again and the video presented an animation sequence that showed one of the space shuttles back during its production. Although production and flights of the shuttle were over, the video was apparently a couple years old, Tom thought.

The voice of the narrator continued, "When the space shuttle re-enters the Earth's atmosphere after a mission, friction between its external surfaces and the atmosphere produces temperatures above the melting point of steel—over three thousand degrees Fahrenheit at the point twenty-five minutes before landing." The animation illustrated the shuttle glowing bright orange, barreling through the atmosphere. "NASA developed the heat tile system to provide adequate protection of the shuttle over recurring missions. Previous spacecraft dissipated heat by shedding portions of a thick heat shield, a process called ablation." An Apollo landing capsule appeared on the screen. "The coating vaporized slowly, carrying heat away, and leaving the core of the spacecraft safe and relatively cool. The shuttle, however, is a different animal altogether. It was created to be reusable. NASA required a system that could survive a hundred flights or more." The animation stopped and video footage of the shuttle was shown (takeoffs, satellite releases from the cargo bay, landings, and more takeoffs). You'd think every ounce of the shuttle had been made by British Space Systems.

The company, the narrator continued, was contacted by NASA early in the design process of the shuttle and actually had to invent an entirely new material for the heat tiles—a gray substance called "carbon-carbon composite." Another animation sequence showed how workers created the tiles by laminating graphite cloth and treating the cured material to convert the resins to carbon, then protecting it with something called silicon carbide. Each shuttle apparently required over thirty thousand tiles. The video concluded with some descriptions of other past accomplishments of British Space Systems, including work on missile enclosures and on the Joint Strike Fighter, the U.S. military's latest advanced jet.

The video ended, finally, and Tom half expected one Ted P. Hampton to mosey into the room with one last swoosh and try and sell some stock in the fine company.

Victoria stood and walked over to turn the lights back on.

"That's remarkable," Tom said, turning toward her. "It's amazing that such small components, the heat tiles, were so critical to the shuttle missions." He wanted to ask about the other applications mentioned—the missiles—but was concerned he might tip her off as to the real purpose of the visit, researching the military work of British Space.

"Yes, British Space Systems, still today, plays quite an important role with NASA and its subcontractors. We're rather proud of that fact," she said as she sat down. "Although the shuttle program has wound down, our engineers have a full plate of projects these days ranging from satellites to missile enclosures, and various heat-protective components for commercial and military aircraft. Improving heat shield technology is an ongoing effort, as manufacturers are constantly pressuring our engineers to create lighter, longer lasting materials. That's the main focus of our engineering and operations team out at our Reading labs."

"Victoria, do you think it would be possible for us to visit the labs, perhaps take a look at your manufacturing facility, and maybe talk to a few engineers?" Tom asked, then heard a voice in his head continue, *You know, get one of your engineers to admit that he called the Post and reported your company's involvement in a nuclear weapons program for space, that sort of thing, no big deal, then maybe we could have some tea in the afternoon...*

She hesitated for a couple seconds. "Well, yes, I suppose. I'm allowed to take the press to a few areas out there. Some buildings, of course, are restricted. You understand I'm sure. It's a requirement of NASA and the U.S. Department of Defense." She reached up with her left hand and pulled some hair to behind her ear. "If you gentlemen are ready now, we can head over. There's really not much to see here at corporate. I'll just need to call for a limo," she said, tugging on her dress again.

"We don't have to have a limo, Victoria."

"No, really, it's quite all right. It's a corporate limo, always on duty. It rarely gets used during the day. It mainly just picks up Mr. Hampton in the morning, then drops him off at home at the end of the day. Must be nice, huh? I just have to make sure it's nearby."

"Well, that would be great of you. Thank you."

"Before we leave, can I use a phone to call the U.S.?" James asked. "I'll reverse the charges or use a credit card. With the time difference, if I don't call now it will be the middle of the night back home."

"Yes, by all means. You can use the phone right over there." She pointed to one at the end of the table. "And please, you mustn't worry about the charges. Just dial nine to ring an outside line."

"Thank you." James stood, almost hitting his head on one of the halogen lights above the conference table.

In the taxi coming over, James had told Tom that he needed to follow up with Bill Dunn, the electronic surveillance and security expert Tom had asked him to contact. They needed to know whether Dunn was able to determine what the voice at the very end of the phone message said, just before the call was cut off. Tom wanted to know whether a superior or perhaps a colleague at British Space Systems had caught the caller as he left the message on his voice mail at *The Washington Post*. On the other hand, Tom also wondered whether the person who caused the interruption might simply be someone in the caller's family, maybe his wife or one of his kids. Whatever the case, he hoped that if Dunn had figured out what was said, which made the caller hang up, it might provide a few clues as to who the caller was, clues that would help them track him down over at the labs.

After standing, James pushed his chair forward, under the conference table, and walked over to the phone, pulled his wallet from a back pocket, then removed Dunn's business card. He also pulled out a gold MasterCard. Good thinking, Tom thought, James doesn't want the call (the phone number) to go on British Space Systems' billing records. Tom's only concern now was that James was about to talk to Dunn while standing just fifteen feet or so away from Victoria. *Surely he wouldn't do that, would he?*

Victoria and Tom chatted about the weather, and even lesser things, as they watched James enter a string of numbers, the phone cradled between his ear and right shoulder. Tom tried to force conversation to distract Victoria's attention, and simply to fill the cavernous conference room with noise.

But a few seconds later James changed his mind. He hung up, it suddenly occurring to him that Victoria might overhear the call with Dunn. She seemed to be paying far too much attention to him.

CHAPTER NINE

They arrived at British Space Systems' labs and manufacturing facility. As the limousine's tires crunched atop the serpentine gravel driveway, James and Tom noticed that the modest-looking building was strictly utilitarian, made of homely gray tilt-up walls of cement. There wasn't a single curve or ornate feature, not even a window. The grayness engulfed and camouflaged the unassuming building, making it blend perfectly into the gray English sky.

Tom became concerned. Surely, he thought as he peered out the dark windows of the limo, nothing significant could be going on within such a low-tech, run-of-the-mill industrial park setting. There wasn't even a fence around the place. He wondered whether the frugal, plain design was an attempt to downplay the building's importance out of concern for security.

The limo pulled to a stop and everyone got out. Tom and James watched as Victoria walked over to some sort of electronic device, which was mounted on the wall to the right of the lab's entrance, and placed her chin on a small plastic ledge protruding from the bottom of the strange machine. She appeared to look into a small lens in front of her right eye. About two seconds later a monotone electronic voice emitted from a panel and words scrolled into an LCD display, *Clearance Confirmed, Welcome Victoria Brookshire, You Have Five Seconds To Proceed Through Doorway.*

A large metal door swung open. "Okay, Gentlemen, please follow me. Quickly now."

They followed her through the doorway and into a small lobby.

"I didn't know devices such as that really existed," James said, turning to her. "I've seen them in the movies a couple of times." The door slammed shut behind them and James felt like he had just been tossed in a jail cell, almost expecting to be strip-searched any second. He was surprised at the high level of security.

"Yes, quite amazing isn't it," Victoria continued. "The device actually took a picture of my eye, then compared it to another picture on file. You know, sort of a fingerprint, only using the unique patterns of one's eyes. Your Department of Defense required us to install them a few years ago. I understand they use them at many government facilities and subcontractors. Gentlemen, if you will excuse me for a moment, I need to go find out what areas of the building are off-limits to visitors today. I'll be right back, okay?"

They smiled and nodded like good tourists. Victoria turned and walked over to a small reception area, about thirty feet away. James glanced at his watch, then asked Tom, "Should I try and call Dunn again?"

"Go for it. We're shooting in the dark here without his analysis. You better hurry though."

James pulled out his cell phone and tapped Dunn's name in his contact list. A woman came on the line, saying she was with his answering service. He told her he didn't want to leave a message and hung up, then called his voicemail at *The Washington Post*, remembering that he had asked Dunn to leave a message immediately after he completed the analysis of the tape. James entered his password to access the first message. It immediately began to play. It was Verizon asking him to switch from AT&T for the third time this month. He hit the pound key and skipped to the next message.

"Hello Mr. Clemens. Bill Dunn here. I'm calling with the results of the analysis on the tape you provided a few days ago. I'll try to be brief. My assistant took the recording of the message left at the Post and digitally enhanced it. This provided us with the ability to electronically separate, if you will, the frequencies that represent various sounds on the tape. This also enabled us to eliminate unwanted noise. For example, ninety-five percent of the hiss and crackling, caused by such a long distance call, was eliminated. We then boosted the frequencies of the voice that appeared toward the end of the recording, apparently of the person who prompted the caller to cut short his

85

message to you. The voice in the background said, '*Jonathan, the spec on the drawing looks good, so go with—*' At this point the caller abruptly hung up. Now, you also asked whether the voice was male or female, and their approximate age. We determined that the background voice is definitely that of a male, approximately forty years of age. And he is British, probably upper class. I hope this helps you. If you have any questions, please give me a call. I'll put a bill, and of course a copy of the enhanced recording, in the mail to the Post, marked to your attention. Well, I'll talk to you soon. Bye now."*

James ended the call, then thumb-tapped a few notes about the message on his phone's notepad.

"Did you get through?" Tom asked.

"Yeah, good news," he whispered, holding his phone up to read. "Dunn left a message on my voicemail with the results of his analysis. Here's the deal. The person who interrupted the caller was a British male, about forty years old. He said, *Jonathan, the spec on the drawing looks good, so go with*— And at that point the caller hung up."

"Okay, good. Dunn never ceases to amaze me. I knew he could decipher what was said in the background. And he even gave us the caller's first name—Jonathan. Okay, okay, let's see. The person who interrupted the message must have been the caller's boss, or supervisor, because he was commenting on his work—the drawing. And since they were talking about a drawing, the caller must be an engineer. Or maybe a draftsman, or CAD designer." Tom paused, rubbing his chin and thinking. "No, probably not a designer, because they were referring to a spec, which one would assume would be created by a more senior engineer, you know, rather than just a computer-aided design person. The engineer had to be senior enough to create a spec of some sort, a spec for one of British Space Systems' products, a spec that NASA would have to rely on. Yep, he has to be a fairly senior design engineer. Right? What do you think?"

"That makes sense."

Tom looked away, noticing that Victoria was talking to a security guard in a hallway near the lobby. She would surely return soon. He turned to James and quietly said, "There can't be that many

86

people named Jonathan working here. We need to get a list of employees, maybe a phone directory or something. Then we'll weed out the Jonathan's in the departments and positions which aren't a good fit. We're going to find this guy, I just know it."

James nodded.

Victoria approached, and she didn't look happy. "Gentlemen, I apologize for the delay." She took a deep breath. "I wasn't expecting to run into objections to our visit. It seems that one of the higher-ups has put a damper on our plans to see the facilities. I can't tell you how sorry I am. This is the first time I've been turned down on a request for a tour of even the low-security areas. I, I just don't know what to say. After you've come all the way over and—"

"Well," Tom interrupted, then paused for a couple seconds, pinching the clef in his chin, "what if we were to simply talk with an engineer or two. You know, to help give a personal angle to the story. Would that be possible? We could even meet here in the lobby. It wouldn't take more than twenty minutes or so."

The plea worked. "Well, I suppose that would be fine. What kind of engineers do you have in mind?"

"If we could see a list, perhaps a company phone directory, we could scan down and pick out a couple people to talk to from different areas."

"Okay, well, let me get the list from the receptionist. Fortunately it's broken down by department, so it should be pretty easy for you to choose who you would like to interview. I will, however, have to get approval for the specific engineers you decide upon. Okay? They might be occupied in a meeting, or with something important."

"We understand."

Victoria turned away and walked over to the reception area. She asked for the company phone directory. A woman behind the counter pulled a laminated piece of paper from a drawer and handed it to her. Victoria returned to the waiting area and gave the list to Tom. "Here you go. Again, I apologize for not being able to give you a tour, but perhaps an interview or two will help your story."

"Thank you." Tom flipped through the directory, trying to find anyone named Jonathan. He quickly found two listings under the Mechanical Engineering subsection: Jonathan Gilmour and Jonathan George. Not knowing which Jonathan was the probable caller, he just picked one by chance. "How about this guy, Jonathan George, a mechanical engineer." He pointed to the name, holding the list so Victoria could see. She moved a bit closer. The scent of her perfume floated toward him again and he discreetly inhaled the fragrance, trying to memorize its bouquet. Heaven, pure heaven.

"Very well, he's a good choice. I've spoken with him a few times. He's a very nice fellow. He actually just joined us a few months ago, from India, believe it or not. His real name is Ashok, but he changed it because no one pronounced it correctly."

Tom's shoulders slumped and his forehead wrinkled. He knew the caller did not have an Indian accent, and he knew he had picked the wrong name, the wrong Jonathan.

"Let me see if Mr. George is in," Victoria said, then went and asked the receptionist to ring him. Tom could see the receptionist say something to her, then Victoria frowned and placed a hand on her hip. She turned toward him (an even bigger frown) then walked over shaking her head. "I'm afraid we're not having much luck today. Mr. George apparently left last week on vacation, home to Bangladesh. Here," she said as she handed the directory back to Tom, "give me your second choice."

"Okay." He pretended to search down the list, even though he already knew who his second choice was. "How about this guy?" he said innocently as he pointed to the listing for Jonathan Gilmour.

Victoria checked to see if he was in the office today. He was. She obtained approval for the visit then called Gilmour's office. Three minutes later he entered the lobby.

"Jonathan, I'd like you to meet Tom Lassiter and James Clemens. They are with the highly respected U.S. newspaper *The Washington Post*," she said with a slight brushing movement of her hand, politely motioning Gilmour to come over. He slowly approached, quite awkwardly, and not even looking up, as if he had just been summoned to the warden's office (we're talking dead man walking). Tom studied him. He was the sort of person every school and every corporation had at least a few of. Nerd was written all over his face. Tom was convinced he was a member of the rare species who, as kids, had to have had the living crap beaten out of them left and right. But somehow they survived as some form of bizarre social mutation, avoiding extinction, yet never adapting to their environment. He had come across many over the years. These animals didn't say much, but you could bet your ass that what they did say was important.

Gilmour sauntered over with his tail between his legs. He was a tall, slender, dark-haired man. He appeared as if he was ready for anything, even a flood. He wore black pants, which didn't quite reach his well-worn wing tips, but showed off his white socks admirably. His monochrome look also included a white long sleeve shirt and a coffee-stained striped gray tie (yes, you guessed it, polyester). A miniature black-anodized space shuttle served as tie tack and complemented his large, black digital watch, which had an incredible number of buttons protruding from it. As he moved closer, Tom noticed that his wrinkled shirt was partially covered by a pocket protector. Letters were written boldly across it in bright red, *British Space Systems*. It cradled and safeguarded all sorts of stuff that was no doubt, literally and figuratively, close to his heart (three different pens, two of those impossible to load mechanical pencils, a small plastic ruler, and a statistics calculator half the size of an iPad). Everything was poised for some sort of emergency engineer action.

Gilmour finally looked up and smiled ever so slightly, then moved forward a bit to shake Tom's hand, who was surprised to feel something unusual being pressed into his palm as they shook. It felt like a small piece of paper, folded perfectly into a crisp rectangle (about one by two inches) as only an engineer would fold. Tom was startled and almost pulled his hand away, but Gilmour anticipated the reaction and squeezed firmly, keeping Tom's arm from retracting and hand from dropping the piece of paper. Tom didn't know how to react. The handshake seemed to go on forever but Victoria and James didn't notice the slight struggle. Gilmour looked straight into Tom's eyes, still shaking his hand, and said, "Welcome to England, Mr. Lassiter. Picked up any souvenirs yet?"

"Yes, yes indeed," Tom answered. "I've picked up a few things." He pulled his hand away from Gilmour's, being careful not to drop the piece of paper. He slid it into his pants pocket as Gilmour turned to James and introduced himself. They said something trivial to each other, then glanced at Victoria who said, "Gentlemen, might I suggest we have a seat in the conference room, right over here." She pointed while walking to a small room adjacent to the reception area.

Tom realized that it would be impossible to talk openly with Gilmour, with Victoria also in the room. He desperately wanted to take the piece of paper from his pocket and read it as they walked toward the conference room, but it was too risky. But then he got an idea. "Victoria, is there a restroom I can use before we get started?" he asked.

"Certainly. Straight ahead," she answered, tilting her head forward. "You can meet us in this room on our right, by the soda and snack machine, okay?"

"Thanks."

Tom strode quickly down the hall, paying no attention whatsoever to what he was doing. He was only thinking about the piece of paper. He swung the door open to the restroom—the women's restroom—and his attention suddenly improved. He bumped into a young woman, who was obviously a former member of Cirque du Soleil, as she was bent over in an impossibly contorted fashion, either adjusting her pantyhose or possibly performing a tubal ligation, Tom wasn't sure which. He scared her. She scared him. Then he exited, turned to his right, and pushed open the door with the icon of a male figure for a change of pace. He entered and went into one of the three stalls, then pulled the piece of paper out of his pocket and unfolded it. It was a hand-written note, barely legible.

Mr. Lassiter: I was just told that you are in the lobby. There's not much time. Yes, I'm the caller to the paper. I don't know how you found me. You shouldn't have come here! But it's too late now. I'm probably making a big mistake, but I'll fill you in on what I know about the High Ground program. And this is ALL I know. Don't approach me ever again. Understand? And if I see my name in print, I'll personally sue you and the Post. I have a family for god sakes, so please leave me alone, or there will be bloody hell to pay. The Pentagon requested special tiles for some missiles. BSS made them, and several nose cones. I think they will be deployed soon (CIA involved). That's all I know. You must promise not to release my name or that a BSS employee leaked the info. I'll deny everything! I'm trusting you with my life. J.G.

Tom folded the note back into its predefined shape and stuck it in his wallet, then walked quickly to the conference room.

The talk with Gilmour didn't take long. Tom kept the meeting to only twenty minutes, not wanting to make him any more nervous. He also made sure the topics discussed were very general, mostly information that was openly presented in the video they had seen at corporate headquarters. Gilmour was, in fact, quite nervous, at least at first. But he soon realized that Tom and James would play by his rules. They would leave him alone, at least for now.

About an hour later the limo, which had waited outside the labs, delivered Tom and James back to British Space Systems' headquarters just as the rain began to dissipate. It had pounded unceasingly all afternoon.

"Here we are," the driver said over his shoulder in a rough cockney voice, then turned the engine off. "One moment. I'll get the doors." He got out, made his way around the front of the car as he tapped his knuckles on the hood, then opened the door Victoria was sitting next to. She stepped carefully out and walked around to the curb. James and Tom slid across the seat and climbed out the same door. This seemed to irritate the driver, as his lower lip stiffened and he subtly shook his head left and right.

Victoria straightened her collar, and checked a couple buttons fastened at her chest. "Well, gentlemen, we made it. Care to come in, perhaps for a spot of tea? Or maybe you'd like to make a restroom stop before you leave?"

Tom closed the limo door and nodded a thank-you to the driver, then turned to her. "Sure, that would—"

"Tom, don't you think we should get going?" James interrupted. "You know, we should get some rest before we fly out. And we were thinking of taking in the National Gallery this afternoon, if we had time." James didn't seem to feel even slightly guilty about trying to disrupt the mating rituals of a lonely reporter. Tom was speechless for a couple seconds then said, "Oh, that's right." He knew that James was probably correct. If they were to go in and visit some more with Victoria the day would surely be shot.

"Yes indeed, we have some fine museums," Victoria put in, looking at James. "Don't miss the Victoria and Albert. It's absolutely wonderful, and huge. I've been meaning to see it again myself. I just haven't had anyone to go with." She turned and looked at Tom, and then James, who nodded innocently with a forced smile. James was obviously hoping that Tom didn't recognize or act on the opportunity Victoria was presenting. James thought to himself, Maybe the day, and probably the night, won't be shot. And besides, he had seen every square inch of the Victoria and Albert museum, twice. He wanted to head over to the National Gallery. He had only toured a portion of it, on a previous visit to the UK. But a third-wheel feeling was clearly forming in James' gut, rolling toward him in one massive, empathetic, guilt-provoking motion. Even Tom could see the change. James suddenly decided to do him a favor and leave him alone with Victoria. He cleared his throat. "Hey, I know, why don't you two take in Victoria and Albert, and I'll just head over to the National Gallery by myself?" he said, almost enthusiastically. "Can you take the rest of the day off, Victoria? I wouldn't want to leave Tom alone in London. He keeps trying to kill himself crossing streets, you know, looking the wrong way."

"Well, I guess I could take a couple of hours off. What do you think, Tom?"

"That would be great. But I wouldn't want to get you into any trouble. Are you sure?" He took a step toward her, though for a split second he really wanted to hug James, or slip him a hundred pounds.

"Oh yes. It's not a problem, really. I often show visitors around the city. It's part of the job. Tough, huh? I just need to run in and tell the receptionist that I'll be out for the rest of the day, okay?"

Tom smiled and nodded.

"I'll be right back." She turned on one heel and climbed up the granite steps to the building entrance.

Tom watched as she disappeared through the glass doors. He thought, *God, what a woman*. Still smiling, he turned around to James and said, "Thanks."

"For what?"

"For leaving us alone."

"It's no big deal."

"It is to me."

A minute later Victoria pushed open one of the glass doors with her right shoulder, then paused as she carefully pulled gloves on over her nails. Tom's eyes followed her as she gracefully floated down the steps. He glanced at James and with a whisper said, "I owe you one."

"No you don't. Just go have some fun," he quietly said as she approached. "With what you've been through the past few days, and what's ahead of us, you deserve a bit of a break."

CHAPTER TEN

The Victoria and Albert museum was on Cromwell Road in South Kensington. "It's the world's largest museum of the decorative arts," Victoria told Tom as they wove in and out of traffic, their bodies shifting left and right in the back of a taxi. She added that the museum was founded in 1852 as the South Kensington Museum, and in 1899 renamed the Victoria and Albert Museum in honor of Queen Victoria and Prince Albert. The Victorian and Edwardian buildings housed one hundred and forty-five galleries containing some of the world's greatest collections (sculpture, furniture, paintings, silver and glass). The permanent galleries included the largest collection of Constable paintings, an extensive collection of European fashion, Far East and Indian collections, and a furniture display featuring pieces from Chippendale and Frank Lloyd Wright, as well as many plaster casts, the most impressive being Michelangelo's towering David.

The driver pulled cautiously up to the curb, avoiding a group of people departing the C1 bus on Cromwell. The rain had ceased, yet again, though clouds loomed on the horizon toward the east. Tom leaned forward, removed his wallet and paid the driver fifteen pounds, then pulled a shiny chrome handle to open the door.

"I'll get the door," the driver said, counting the money and not moving an inch.

Tom was already standing on the sidewalk, holding the door open.

Victoria scooted across the well-worn green vinyl and carefully stepped out, smiling and peering upward with glistening eyes. "Well, here we are."

Tom closed the door and offered a quick wave at the driver, who beeped his way back into traffic, clearly irritating several commuters, one of them even tossing a finger up.

They ambled up the steps to the museum entrance.

"Careful, Victoria. They're slick," Tom warned, briefly touching her back with his palm. She reached the entrance first and extended her right hand toward the large brass handle, but he quickly moved closer and pulled it open.

"Thank you, Tom."

The central hall was massive and dwarfed the people standing in line to buy tickets and souvenirs. Large columns shot to the ceiling from bases of marble. Skylights emitted a misty, delicate light to the right. The only sound present was from clicking heels on the shiny stone floor. Mustiness hung in the air. They made their way to the ticket line.

"This place is incredible," Tom said, tilting his head back and staring upward.

"It is, isn't it. Quite large, indeed. And this is only a fraction of the building. I hope you have comfortable shoes on."

He looked down at his feet. "Yeah, not too bad, I think."

"So tell me, Tom, what's it like living in the nation's capital? Do you like D.C.? You have some nice museums there too, right?"

"Yes, we have some good ones. The Smithsonian. But actually I don't care much for D.C. Crime can be pretty bad at times, and traffic is miserable. It's next to impossible to navigate. I actually live out in the country a ways, in Virginia."

"Oh really? That sounds nice. Do you have land?"

"Not a lot. My family used to own quite a bit, but not in Virginia. We had a farm up in Vermont. We sold it when I was, let me see, about ten."

"Vermont? Really? I love Vermont. Where did you live? I'm quite familiar with the state."

"You're kidding."

"No, really. I go skiing there at least every few years."

"We lived in Waitsfield. God, I can't believe you've been—"

"Waitsfield?" she interrupted, smiling and touching his arm.

"Yes, right next to—"

"Sugarbush Ski Resort."

"Right!"

"I've rented condos there and stayed many times at a small inn. The Wild Rose Inn, on Route 100."

"Good lord. I know the people who run it, or at least used to run it. The Vandross family. They were nuttier than fruitcakes. They used to run around killing raccoons as if their life depended on it, trying to stop some imaginary coon plague, or something. I remember them tossing the furry little things in the back of their old Chevy pickup, then driving around, drinking Budweiser and bragging about the kill. God they were crazy. The husband has to have ended up in an asylum by now. The last thing I heard, he'd blown up their maple sugar boiler and plastered half the mountain with syrup, like a big pancake I guess."

Victoria laughed. "I don't think they own it now, thank goodness."

"You'd remember if they did, believe me."

"I've also stayed at the Waitsfield Inn, in the village," she continued.

"I know the people who run it too. Nice folks. I saw them about five years ago. The place looked the same. In Vermont, nothing changes and everyone knows everyone, whether you like it or not."

They reached the ticket counter. Tom handed a lady thirty-one pounds and she slid back two tickets. He smiled and thanked her, grabbed tickets, and they walked to the entrance to the casting exhibits. He turned to Victoria and said, "I can't believe you're familiar with Vermont. Small world, isn't it?"

She nodded. "So where did you live in Waitsfield? On the mountain?"

"More in the valley, really," Tom answered. "But we faced the mountain. From our front porch you could see four of the slopes. You know that covered bridge, about a mile from the Waitsfield Inn?"

"Oh yes."

"We had a farm on that street, just a half mile or so east of the bridge. There was a huge red barn on one side of the road and a big white farm house on the other side with black shutters and a granite foundation."

"Near the Round Barn Inn?"

"Yes, how do you—"

"I know the exact house. The cross country ski trails for the Round Barn Inn are right next to it, right?"

"Yeah. God, that's amazing. You know where I spent the first ten years of my life."

They handed the tickets to a leathered-skin man in a tweed coat, then entered the exhibit hall. "So why did your family move from such a lovely area?" Victoria asked.

"Long story. My dad worked over in Burlington at the University of Vermont, he was a professor. He got offered a job in Florida, left my mother and I, and they had to sell the farm, you know, to split up assets. Plus, my mom wanted to move back down to Virginia, where she had lived until getting married. In our family, she was the least appreciative of Vermont's long winters and solitude. She didn't ski, and she didn't like boating. My dad spent half his time on Lake Champlain in the warm months and lived on the mountain every weekend in winter. We barely saw him. Gosh, I haven't thought about that in a long time. In the warm months, he brought home more fish than we could eat."

Victoria nodded. "It's a Shame, I mean, not only your family breaking up, but having to leave Vermont and a farm. It must have been hard on a young boy."

Tom raised his shoulders slightly then looked down briefly, not replying. His silent answer was quite clear to Victoria. She shifted gears. "So was it a working farm?"

"No, not when we had it anyway. They used to grow hay on it, I think. We just had a couple of horses. I remember getting up every morning and feeding them in that cold barn. God how I used to love to play in that thing. Then, in the afternoon, I'd go canoeing on the Mad River, and roam the hills. It was just beautiful, especially in the spring, or after a light dusting of snow." He turned to her, worrying that he was talking about himself too much. "It sounds like you really love to ski."

97

"Yes, I'm afraid so. It's quite an expensive habit, unfortunately. But it's one of my few vices. I manage to visit a different ski area almost every year. Last year I went to Switzerland. Do you ski?"

"Oh yes. In the Green Mountains, kids are born with skis. I even have a scar to prove it. See?" He showed her his wrist.

"That looks like a nasty one."

"Yeah, I hit a tree. Broken in three places."

"The tree or your wrist?" she said, then laughed. "I'm afraid I have a similar record of my skiing ability." She paused, checking to see if anyone was watching, then pulled her dress up just a couple inches and pushed her stocking down slightly. Tom's heart sped up a few notches. "See?" she said, pointing. "Somehow I managed to stab myself with a ski pole, during a bad fall."

Tom nodded and tried not to appear too mesmerized by the sight of her thigh. He thought to himself, *She skis, she's funny, she's intelligent, she's beautiful, and she seems to like me. Not to mention her legs which are absolutely to die for. What planet is this?*

She pulled her stocking up and tugged her dress down, then began to walk down an aisle, toward the casting of the statue of David. "Let's head down here, Tom."

Her wish was his command. He followed closely. "So where did you spend your childhood, Victoria?"

"Well, several places really, but mostly in and about London. We also, for a short time, owned land north of here. We had two barns, a dozen horses or so, a couple dairy cows, and some chickens and goats. I loved it."

"Come now, you don't strike me as a farm girl."

"Nor you a farm boy."

"Touché"

"I haven't always worn dresses and high heels, Tom."

"I haven't always worn them either," Tom joked.

Victoria laughed some more and said, "You wouldn't have recognized me as a kid. I was the biggest tomboy in England, literally. I was overweight, had braces on my teeth, wore jeans almost every day, and tromped around in the mud with the animals much more than I played with dolls or played house."

"No way."

"Yes indeed. My mum used to say I was more like a boy."

"So how does one go from being a tomboy to being drop dead gorgeous?" Tom continued, the words leaping from his mouth before he could think about how they would be taken.

"Drop dead gorgeous? Well now, thank you. I don't think I've ever been called that before. You know how to make a lady blush. Maybe you should visit England more often."

Actually he was the one blushing, but he was proud of his comment. Victoria was now on notice. He liked, no he loved, the way she looked, talked, and moved. And something inside him was screaming for joy, something that had been missing for too long.

They finally reached the statue of David, or the casting of it anyway. Tom tilted his neck back and stared up. The 14.2-foot male frame almost reached the lights above. "Wow, I didn't know it was this big."

"Impressive isn't it." Victoria walked completely around the cast, running her eyes over the musculature. "Have you seen the real one, in the Gallerie dell'Accademia in Florence?"

"No. I haven't traveled out of the U.S. much. I'm always working."

"Well," she said, looking at Tom, "I'm just glad you came to London." She rubbed his arm for a couple seconds.

The thought entered his mind that he couldn't remember being touched by such a woman in a very long time. "Me too. I'm glad I came over."

They strolled around the castings and sculptures for a while, then walked over to the museum's cafe and ordered a couple of black coffees. They sat side by side at a small square table, off in a quiet corner and away from a troop of rambunctious school kids. Tom quickly lost track of everything, except the beautiful woman before him.

CHAPTER ELEVEN

Victoria chose the restaurant, Elizabeth's, just off Knightsbridge and about a block from Hyde Park Corner—only a few minutes away from the Victoria and Albert museum, and her flat. The ambiance was stately British. The foyer had polished marble floors of emerald green with wispy white swirls. On the left side there was a massive stone fireplace (the kind you would expect to see in an old Vincent Price or Boris Karlof movie; you could essentially walk into it). Fine wood paneling, which looked to be of the vanishing rain forest variety, covered every wall and supported numerous gilt-framed mirrors and paintings of stoic and well-dressed Britons atop equally statuesque and elegant horses. They had long chins and held long rifles, but the sharply tailored individuals appeared to be headed to some sort of royal ceremony for the queen, rather than embarking on a treacherous hunting expedition.

High above the paintings, the rain forest, and the marble there was a metal ceiling that was stamped into sweeping renaissance floral patterns. Some of the flowers appeared to be gold plated. Clearly, not a single natural resource had been overlooked or spared. This was a serious restaurant for serious people.

"It seems uncharacteristically slow this evening for some reason," Victoria said as she looked around. "I usually have to wait at least a half hour for a table, even in the noisy main dining room."

Tom nodded. The fewer people the better, as far as he was concerned.

A man approached, apparently the maître d', wearing a black and white penguin suit. "Sir, madam, we have your table ready."

They followed him to a room on the right.

"Here we are. Is this table okay, sir? It's the finest and most private in the restaurant."

"Yes, it's perfect." Tom walked over and helped Victoria with her chair.

"My name is Malcolm. If there's anything I can help you with, please let me know. Your waiter is Charles and he'll be right with you," he said under his breath, then moped away.

Tom turned to Victoria. "You would think he was heading for the gas chamber."

"Well, I guess if my name was Malcolm, and I had to wear that ridiculous coat and tails all day, I'd probably be depressed too."

The table was indeed nice. It looked out over the sparkling city lights of London and was out of earshot of the other tables. By the time they were just about finished with dinner, Tom was thoroughly relaxed and in heaven. The food was excellent and the wine exquisite. He had spent one of the best afternoons in his life with a kind, lovely, and elegant lady—a perfect woman in his mind. He slowly raised a glass of Chardonnay to the warm air above the flickering candle, which was casting a glow upon Victoria, making her red hair even more breathtaking.

"To a wonderful day, a great museum, spectacular city, and a beautiful lady. Cheers," he said slowly, as she also raised her glass. The lips of the delicate glasses gently touched. They each took a sip then set them down.

Victoria smiled and softly said, "Lovely evening, isn't it." She turned and gazed out a misty window, focusing on the horizon.

"Yes, almost as lovely as your eyes," Tom replied, feeling the confidence of three glasses of wine. At least he thought it was three at this point. He wasn't used to drinking more than a beer now and then, and it was starting to show. "I can see the reflections of the city lights sparkling in your eyes. Absolutely gorgeous," he continued, surprising even himself that the words had just come from his mouth, but they felt right nonetheless. He hadn't spoken with such romantic fervor in many years.

She looked down at the candle for a couple seconds, then up at his face. "That's so sweet of you to say, Tom." She caressed his hand with light strokes of her fingers.

They finished the last few cold bites of dinner and the remaining sweet drops of Chardonnay, paid the penguin, then walked out of the restaurant and into the brisk London air. He helped her with her coat as they made their way down the steps to the sidewalk. "Do you know what time it is Victoria?"

"Gee, usually I at least get walked to my door after a dinner. Ditching me already?"

"No, absolutely not. You'll be the one to ditch me, I promise."

"Good. I also promise not to. Shall we shake on it?" She held out her hand and he shook it gently, then raised it to his lips and kissed it softly.

"Well, I guess after that, I can tell you the time." She looked down and turned her wrist and said, "It's about seven. I suppose at midnight you'll turn into something else and vanish from my life forever. A real heart breaker, right?"

"Not a chance, and that's a promise too." He looked away, a bit nervously and sighing.

"What's wrong, dear?" Victoria asked with concerned eyes, seeing Tom's suddenly sad expression as he turned to her.

"Well, the thought just struck me that I've just met a wonderful lady, and I have to go back to the U.S. soon."

Victoria's face revealed that she was equally depressed at the notion. "Well, what about tomorrow? Can I see you then, before you go?" she asked, touching his arm. "I'm supposed to go to Frankfurt for the day, but I can cancel."

"I'd love that. I really would. But I'm afraid I can't. James and I are flying out in the morning to Florida, to do some research and more interviews. We're already behind schedule. If we don't publish a story in the next day or two, I'll be looking for work."

There were a few seconds of silence. She turned away, staring blankly across the street. Tom's sad expression again moved to her face. Victoria looked at him and said, "Well then, we still have tonight, don't we. That is if you think James won't mind being left on his own."

Without hesitation Tom replied, "James said he would be fine tonight. I'll make it up to him when we get to Florida. Take him to a nice dinner or something."

Victoria smiled. "Good. Well, let's make the most of our time. What would you like to do? Perhaps a stroll down to the river for some people watching and fresh air? Though, it is still drizzling a bit." She glanced up at the sky.

The voice in Tom's head said, *Yeah, a stroll, a river, people watching, that sounds real exciting. There's only one person I want to watch.*

She continued, "Or we can be to ourselves. Maybe go to my flat for a bit of dessert and tea?"

Bingo, Tom thought, be to ourselves, that sounds promising. With that, the decision was made. "Okay, that sounds nice. I'd love to see your home."

Ten minutes later they arrived at her flat. It was small but elegantly decorated in hues of rose and light yellow, and that blue—the blue of her eyes. He could practically see every square inch of the place immediately upon entering the front door. An antique baby grand piano occupied most of the living room. The kitchen was really more of a hallway to a small nook, which had a round cherry table and a few chairs with plaid cushions. A window behind the table looked down over the street. Empty flower pots sat perched upon the ledge, just outside the window sill. As did a cat, staring curiously at the distance, back arched, tail swinging happily and brushing the glass of the window like a windshield wiper, leaving arched streaks of moisture.

Victoria asked Tom to sit down on the loveseat, next to the piano. The only other place to sit in the living room, other than the piano bench, was a large high-back chair with carved ball and claw legs. It, too, was rose, yellow, and blue.

As Victoria walked to the kitchen Tom said, "Your home is really nice. Did you decorate it yourself?" He watched as she began to make some tea. He could see her shuffling around, opening and closing cabinets, and adjusting a prehistoric stove.

"Yes, I'm the guilty party. Most people seem to like it. I'd like to do more, but I can only afford to do so much at a time on my salary. Things are very expensive here in London. You Americans are very lucky. More selection, and better prices."

A couple minutes later the kettle screamed to be picked up from the burner. Tom watched as she turned the stove off, poured the water into an elegant china teapot, then carried it in atop a silver tray, along with two cups, saucers, cream, sugar, and a couple of mints. She handed him a cup and saucer, then poured the tea. "Cream or sugar?" she asked.

"No thank you, this is fine," he answered as she finished pouring, leaning toward him. He could see slightly down her dress, as he had earlier at British Space Systems when she bent over to pick up his name tag, only now he felt a little guilty as he admired her. Just a little, and not enough to make him stop looking. He tried not to stare but couldn't stop himself.

She carefully placed the teapot on a small table and sat next to him on the loveseat, moving a pillow out of the way so they could sit more closely. She crossed her long legs and turned to him. The bottom of her dress pulled up slightly, revealing the top of her white thigh-high silk stockings. As Tom sipped his tea, he looked down and noticed the small white fastener that attached a lace strap leading up over her perfect skin, then under her dress. She either didn't notice the dress pulling up, or she didn't care. Perhaps, he thought, because of the wine earlier?

He set the cup and saucer down on the table, and looked up at her eyes. "I had a wonderful afternoon with you at the museum, and at dinner. You—" he said, then paused, searching for the right words.

"Yes, Tom. Go on."

"You make me feel so good, so alive. You're—"

She held two fingers up to his mouth, preventing him from finishing his sentence, then moved her hand to the right side of his face, holding her palm gently to his cheek. She scooted closer, squeezed her eyes shut, then kissed his lonely American lips very

104

slowly, and very gently. He had wanted to feel her lips since the toast of Chardonnay at dinner. They kissed for several minutes.

"Tom, what are we doing?" she finally whispered.

He didn't reply. The last thing he wanted was for his lips to leave her. And hell, he didn't know what they were doing either. Nor did he care at this moment. He kissed her cheek and worked toward her earlobe then slid his hand over her left leg, atop her stocking. She kissed harder and moaned just slightly as he slowly moved his hand up further, over the fastener, then under the strap securing her stocking. He caressed her leg, upward and downward, ever so gently. Her skin was supple and smooth, just as he imagined it would be.

She kissed even more passionately. Their breathing intensified, becoming rhythmically as one, her exhaling became his inhaling. She stretched her arm downward and removed each of her high heels. Tom reached behind her right leg and slowly slid his hand up her dress, to her rear. His heart felt like it was going to jump from his chest as he caressed her baby-soft skin.

They continued kissing. "Tom . . ." she said in a whisper that trailed off. His name never sounded so good. He moved his hand further up. She seemed to be wearing silk, or satin panties. But his first thought was that she wasn't wearing anything (they were the kind that hardly covered an inch; just a vertical strap that disappeared down between her rear, moved between her legs, then up over her pelvis).

Victoria moved her lips to his right ear, his weak spot. She licked his earlobe, then nibbled on it just a bit. He could hear her deep, excited breathing. It made him want to burst. She then lifted her right leg over his lap, revealing her entire hip, and accidentally knocking over one of the teacups on the table. The tea streamed all over the silver tray, then dripped onto the polished wood surface, but she didn't seem to care, not pausing for even a second.

As they continued kissing, Tom reached behind her back and slowly unzipped her dress. He rubbed her lower back briefly and then she made the next move. She slowly pulled away and slid her arms out of the sleeves, letting the top of the dress drop to her waist, and revealing the entire red bra he had fantasized about seemingly all day.

He admired her, unabashedly, staring at her perfectly white breasts, which bulged somewhat from the top of the bra, and underneath slightly. He then looked up at her inviting eyes. "You're gorgeous," he whispered.

Victoria tilted forward and kissed him even more passionately, then paused for a second and again said, "Tom, what are we doing?"

"I know, I know. I—"

She gently bit down on his bottom lip, then let go and licked both lips ever so slightly with the tip of her tongue. She pulled away a couple inches and said under her breath, "We're moving too fast. You're going to get the wrong," another kiss, "impression of me. I swear I've never done this on a first date. Never felt this way," she said slowly, again in a whispery soft voice. "We can't make love. I don't even know you. I may never see you again."

He held both his hands to her face, looked her straight in the eyes, and said, "No, I promise I'll come back. And you can fly to the states, okay. We'll see each other, all right. I promise." Hell, at this moment he wanted to tell her he would quit his job, move to London, become an English citizen, never see the sun again, and take piano lessons. And that was just for starters. But he restrained himself.

He moved closer and gently kissed her chin for a couple seconds, then found his way down the side of her neck, exhaling loudly. "I've never had this happen either." He was almost out of breath. He reached around her back and felt for the snap.

"It's in the front," she said softly. She pulled away a few inches. Tom moved his hands up between her breasts and unhooked the bra, then slowly peeled away each cup, revealing the whitest and purest skin he had ever seen. "You're so beautiful," he continued, then moved his mouth down through her cleavage, kissing lightly. He could smell, almost taste, her perfume. It was exquisite. He moved to the right, his mouth not leaving her, and swam in her curves. Several minutes pass.

She again pulled away. At first Tom thought he had gone too far. She was calling off the fun and probably giving him the boot for moving to second base too fast, though he couldn't remember what, exactly, second base was anymore. She stood before him, then grabbed her bra from the couch and tossed it onto the baby grand piano. She reached behind her back, and Tom assumed she was about to pull her dress zipper back up. But she didn't. Instead she moved it lower, to her rear, then slid her dress downward over her thighs and to the floor. She stepped out of the dress, balancing on one leg at a time, then slid her panties off and tossed them away.

Tom thought he had died and gone to heaven. He leaned back, licking his lips subtly, and just stared at her, admiring her beauty—the voluptuous curves, the silky smoothness, the firmness and tone, and the perfect proportions from her head to her toes. She seemed to like his gaze, as she moved slowly and purposefully. She bent over and slipped her high heels back on. He watched her every move as she reached over to a lamp and turned it off. The light from the kitchen continued to paint most of her skin with a faint warm glow. And he could still see her entire silhouette against the brighter background. A few rays flickered and danced around her body, under and over her arms, and in-between her legs as she moved gracefully toward him. This was not an image Tom would soon forget.

CHAPTER TWELVE

Morning came earlier than either James or Tom cared for. Both were dead tired, especially Tom. He and Victoria had barely slept two hours before he had to get dressed, then kiss her goodbye and head to the hotel where James was awaiting and ready to head to Heathrow airport.

They were kept waiting for a runway for almost an hour, yet the air traffic didn't seem terribly heavy. But eventually the pilot received permission to takeoff. The tower aimed the Learjet toward the mouth of the Seine River and seaports at Le Havre, France, then put them on course to the northwest, crossing near Edinburgh, whose castle's spires and 11th-century Chapel of Saint Margaret pierced a low slithering fog. The haze also lingered along the serpentine streams and nearby valleys. It was gorgeous, Tom thought. The view, and James' description of the countryside (he had traveled to Scotland a few years back) soothed Tom's mind.

Tom loosened his seatbelt and stretched his arms forward, yawning. He thought about how he hadn't slept more than a couple of hours. After Victoria had dozed off, he had lain awake, restless, thinking about his evening with her, and going over the meeting yesterday afternoon with Jonathan Gilmour, and specifically his reluctance to provide more information.

Tom turned to James and said, "We just have to find out what the payload is which Gilmour described. I want to know exactly what he thinks they are launching. And I mean exactly what it is, and before they launch."

"But how? If those guys back home were crazy enough to chase you, practically killing themselves and you in the process, they're definitely not going to let us get close to any of Kennedy Space Center's high security areas."

"James, you're exaggerating just a little, no one practically got killed."

"Judging by what you said happened, I think their intentions were pretty clear. I just don't see how we can possibly get close to someone who will talk."

"Well—"

"Even with the confusion of the crowds and the press corps, we'll never get near the sensitive areas within NASA. And that's probably where anyone who is familiar with the so-called High Ground program is going to be this close to a launch of any kind."

Tom scratched the back of his head, thinking. "Yeah, I know. It won't be easy."

James loosened his seatbelt and arched forward like a cat, scratching his lower back. He turned to Tom. "Can't we just run with what we have, and get a story out?"

"What story, James? That I stole a file from the Pentagon? That I've seen a few memos and a little diagram of a space shuttle—which isn't even supposed to be flying anymore—with a couple of vague objects shown in the cargo bay? That two unknown men chased me while I drove home one night? Where's the evidence that anyone did anything wrong or illegal, except me? I could have made up everything in that file with a three hundred dollar computer and color printer, right? No, we definitely don't have enough evidence yet. If we just run with an unsubstantiated story right now, it would be a journalistic disaster, at least for me. *The Washington Post* doesn't publish hearsay. Trust me. We need a witness, or some sort of hard proof. Something that proves Gilmour's allegations about a space weapon of some sort about to be launched over the Middle East. And, obviously, Gilmour will never corroborate anything. He's too scared."

"I guess you're right," James said with a hesitant nod.

Tom took a deep breath. "We just need to come up with a plan, our own little covert operation. We need to get into Kennedy Space Center and find someone who is as concerned about the High Ground program as Gilmour was when he called and left that message. There's bound to be someone, you know, a technician or engineer. Who knows, maybe they can get us some sort of clearance, perhaps some badges that can get us in so we can snoop around a little. Or maybe our press credentials will be good enough."

At nine-thirty PM they landed at Orlando International then rented a car and drove to a motel, the Floridian Shores & Tennis Club, in the mecca that was Titusville, Florida. The pilot had stopped just once, in Newfoundland, for refueling. Kennedy Space Center, according to the girl at the Hertz rental car counter, was supposed to be just minutes away.

They walked into the hotel lobby, zigzagged their way through a maze of plastic plants and fake palm trees, and aimed for the front desk. A barrel-bellied clerk was talking on a phone and somehow managing to pick his sizable nose at the same time.

The clerk hung up and asked, "Can I help you?"

James hoped he wouldn't want to shake hands, and Tom kept his distance. "Yes," James answered, moving forward cautiously. "We'd like a room, please. Twin beds, non-smoking."

"Yes sir." He looked down at the sophisticated inventory control system, a battered Rolodex of cards. "We're out of non-smoking rooms, but we have smoking."

He said this much too quickly. James had a hunch that there weren't any non-smoking rooms. Not now, not ever.

"That'll have to do," James replied much too politely.

"It's seventy-nine dollars per night. Or you can rent it by the hour."

"Fine, we'll be spending at least one night. And I'd like to just pay in cash, if that's all right." James pulled out his wallet.

"No problem." The clerk seemed quite used to this sort of thing, two people showing up for an hour, the day, whatever works. "But it'll be an extra thirty bucks per night for the security deposit. You'll get it back at check-out."

James told him that would be fine then filled out the obligatory name-address-phone-how many nights card with completely false

110

information, just in case those maniacs who chased Tom back home would want to try and find him in Titusville. Normally they'd never stay in such a rundown motel, but they wanted to pay with cash, and assumed this place wouldn't be too picky about that.

They left the lobby and went quickly to their assigned room—first building, first and only floor, luxury suite 12 (according to the hand-written receipt). As they walked toward the room, Tom thought to himself, *luxury suite*?

"God, I'm beat," Tom said as he glanced at James. "I just want to crash. Then get a fresh start tomorrow. How about you?"

"That sounds good to me," James answered with a drawn-out yawn. Holding the huge plastic key ring in his left hand, he inserted the key into the lock with his right and opened the door. The room was every bit as atrocious as they thought it would be. Maybe even worse. They walked in. Tom promptly closed the door, which revealed a large sign scotch taped to the back side, *Hourly Rates Available*. They ran their eyes around the room. Bars covered the one window. It was cracked open, yet the place still smelled of cigarette smoke and what seemed to be pesticide. The place was decorated in lime green, brown, and orange.

Tom went over to the two beds. "Hell of a suite, huh. Welcome to 1973."

James shook his head slowly, gazing about, then finally said, "Lovely."

In ten minutes they were both asleep.

Morning arrived with the grinding sound of an eighteen wheeler firing up its diesel engine. Tom looked over at James, who was tossing and turning. Some light was leaking in through the window. He figured he may as well let James get some more rest, so he let him sleep. Tom turned to his side, away from the window, and his mind shifted to more pleasant thoughts which slowly coerced him back toward sleep. He reminisced about Victoria, and hoped he would see here again soon. A couple more minutes passed and he decided that he had better get up

111

before snoozing off again. He stared at the yellowed popcorn ceiling, stretching and taking deep breaths, then glanced over at James again in the other twin bed. James was still jostling around, apparently restless. "Are you awake, James?" he whispered.

"No. I'm asleep," he uttered. He rolled over, facing away from Tom. "Wake me in an hour."

Tom's voice became louder. "We need to get going."

James moaned then grumbled, "Come on, just a bit longer."

Tom sat up, leaned against the headboard, and looked around the room. A dispenser, the condom variety, was mounted conveniently above a small sink, to the right of a cracked mirror. The sticker on it said, *Only One Dollar*. Tom rolled his eyes then looked over at James again and saw that he was slowly showing signs of life, very primitive signs.

James turned to his left, swung his feet to the floor, and said, "Man, what a night. This bed sucks." He rubbed his face. "Damn, this place looks worse than it did last night."

They both looked around the room, amazed that such a motel could stay open and apparently be profitable. Tom stood and leaned against the wall next to his bed, stretching some more. The wall made a crackling noise and greenish pieces of something fell to the floor. He realized that some type of reed-like wallpaper was in various stages of peeling off from several areas. His attention shifted to his right, to a piece of not-so-fine art that was literally bolted to the wall facing the beds. God only knows what a covered bridge and maple trees at the peak of autumn had to do with Florida.

James sat on the end of his bed. It instantly bowed three inches and let out a spine-tingling squeak. He put his best scowling face on and said, "What an absolute dive!"

"Don't hold back, tell me how you really feel, James." Tom looked to his left. He was so tired when they arrived he hadn't noticed it, but there was a small television hanging from a corner of the room. Surprisingly, it looked fairly new. He noticed that its remote control was chained to a nightstand, which was sandwiched between the beds. He just stared at the room, speechless. Certainly anyone wanting to track him down would never expect him to stay in such a motel. It was that bad.

They took turns at the bathroom (it was even smaller than the one in the Learjet) then tried to pry their eyes open a bit further. Tom parted the curtains a little, then kicked back on the bed again. He opened the drawer to the nightstand, pulled out a phone book, and thumbed through it looking for a map of the area. He found one and began studying it.

James leaned back in a vinyl chair near the window, clearly needing to go back to sleep. His jaw dropped and his eyes glossed over. Several minutes passed, then he suddenly sat straight up, cleared his throat and said, "I've been thinking about our plan, you know, snooping around at Kennedy Space Center."

"Yeah, thinking about what?" Tom asked.

"Well," he continued, staring at the ceiling, "aren't you worried about those guys, who chased you, finding us and locking us up, especially before we get the story out?" He yawned some more then looked over at Tom.

"Well, I think the safest place in the world for us is right under their noses at Kennedy Space Center, with swarms of other reporters. There's an Atlas V launch scheduled, or at least that's what they show on their website. And there's the opening ceremony of the space shuttle museum. So there should be a lot of reporters covering all that, and we can blend in with the crowds and activities. They won't touch us as long as we're with other reporters. It would cause too much of a commotion. Right?"

"Yeah, I guess so."

Tom continued, "They can't risk having anything strange happen, not during preparations for the museum opening, and not just before a critical launch, whether it is that Atlas V or, as Gilmour said, one more shuttle launch. Plus, trying to arrest two journalists from *The Washington Post* would be very strange and very high profile." Tom paused to rub his eyes. He set the phonebook down. "Don't you agree?"

James nodded.

"But just to be safe, maybe I should disguise myself, at least to some degree. Perhaps I could wear some glasses, and maybe cut my hair a bit. If we do get stopped and questioned, or worse, I don't want to look like I'm purposely disguising myself. I saw a Wal-Mart about three blocks down the road. Maybe you could run over and pick up some glasses for me—fairly clear ones, not too dark—and maybe you should buy some food, you know, to keep here at the room. And buy some scissors too."

"Okay, I'll run over." James stood and arched his back, stretching.

Tom reached over to the one bag he had brought, which was sitting on the dresser. He opened it and pulled out the Pentagon file which he had, well, let's just say 'borrowed' from General Kramer's office. He studied its contents for a few seconds, then closed it. He walked back over to the bed and dropped his knees to the floor.

"What are you doing?" James asked.

"I want to hide this," Tom replied as he lifted a corner of the top mattress, then moved the sheets and bedspread out of the way. He used the room key to cut a slit in the musty fabric then rolled the file into a tubular shape and stuffed it into the slit.

"You look like you've done that a hundred times," James said as he sauntered over, peering down at the operation.

Tom tucked everything back in the way it was, then slowly stood up. "What did you say?"

"Oh, nothing important. Who's first in the shower? Do you want to go ahead?"

"Okay, thanks," Tom replied, already heading for the bathroom.

"While you're getting cleaned up, I'll go on my little shopping spree to Wal-Mart. But first maybe we should call and check in at the *Post*, and touch base with Thompson."

"Good idea."

"Do you want to call, or do you want me to?"

Tom grabbed a towel hanging near the sink. "You can go ahead. Just try and buy us some more time. If he gives you any trouble, tell him your dad is up to speed on what we're doing and we'll check in later. If history is any indicator, Thompson will leave us alone then."

"Alrighty." James grabbed is wallet from the nightstand and tucked it in a back pocket. "Back in thirty minutes or so."

Tom nodded, and has he headed into the bathroom, said, "You're the best, James."

He shut the door and twisted on the unlabeled shower knobs, not knowing which was hot and which was cold. He half expected nothing to happen, but faintly warm water began to emit from the small rusted nozzle above.

CHAPTER THIRTEEN

The drive from the motel (ignoring a stop for gas at Chevron and ten bucks worth of Egg McMuffins, pancakes, coffee, and hash browns at McDonald's) took only fifteen minutes. Real big spenders.

They approached the main entrance to Kennedy Space Center. Ahead, Tom could see a guard standing in front of a gatehouse. He was checking cars through one at a time, with lots of nodding and shaking of his head, waving of his arms, wiping his brow, and glancing at some all-knowing clipboard. He appeared to be alone. A couple cars in line were honking occasionally, trying to get him to hurry up.

James turned to Tom and asked, "Do you think we'll get by this guy?"

"I'd bet money on it. It looks like he's about to have a nervous breakdown. And I don't see him turning anyone around. Get your press credentials out, just in case, and a business card."

James removed his wallet and a card. "There sure are a hell of a lot of cars."

"Yeah, probably tourists. And TV and newspaper types like us."

They finally made their way to the guard.

Another wipe of his forehead, and the guard said, "Good morning. Purpose of your visit, please."

"We're *Washington Post* reporters, covering the Atlas launch and shuttle museum ceremony," Tom answered, mustering up as much of a sincere smile as he could this early in the day. "Would you like to see some ID's, or business cards?"

The guard's eyes moved from Tom to James, then someone in the long line of cars honked again, as if on cue (Tom thought it was the Winnebago with the tons of kids inside pressing their noses and hands to the windows). A few more cars and trucks joined in, horns being tapped just enough to be irritating. And that was that. The guard nodded quickly and said, "The press center is straight ahead, about a mile. Good day."

"Thanks." Tom smiled some more and pulled away from the gatehouse. He drove toward the press center.

James turned to him and asked, "What's with offering ID's and business cards? A little bold, aren't we."

"Nah, I've used that line a million times. No one ever asks, as long as you offer first."

Tom saw the sign for the press center, slowed down, then hung a right into the first entrance.

"The place is crowded isn't it," James said, craning his neck. "I don't see any parking spots."

Tom looked left and right. He proceeded to snake back and forth through four different rows.

"Wait. I think that guy's pulling out." James pointed.

"Where?"

"Over there. First row."

"It's not handicapped?"

"I don't see a sign." James leaned forward, rubbing his lower back. "After that wonderful bed last night, I think I qualify for handicapped."

They parked the car then walked along a rusted and partially fallen chain link fence toward a gate, which was propped open with a brick. Everything very high-tech. People were streaming in and out, moving between the press center and the parking lot. Television reporters, the ones walking around with the big hair and perfectly chiseled features, were everywhere. Even a few radio types were stalking about.

"This must be the place," James said.

"Yeah, look at all these people."

James turned to Tom and continued, "You know, you look pretty hip with those glasses I bought for you."

"Hip? Gee, thanks. That's the look I'm after alright," Tom said sarcastically. "And what's with these glasses anyway? Couldn't you

117

have found any better looking ones?" He reached up and pushed them further back on his nose. "These things barely cover my pupils."

"Ah, what's wrong with them? They make you look European."

"They're goofy as hell. That's what's wrong."

"I thought they'd look good on you. I mean—"

"Yeah, yeah, yeah," Tom interrupted, then pointed off to the distance. "I wonder what's up over there." He could see a group of people carrying signs and slowly walking back and forth over near a gate.

"Looks like picketers. I can't believe that guard let them on the base."

"I doubt they asked for permission," James. "They probably just came in with everyone else, as tourists I guess."

"I wonder what they are protesting."

"I don't know. Let's check it out," Tom said then began walking faster, "let's see what these radicals are up to before they get booted out."

As they got closer to the gate they saw what was printed on the signs the protesters carried, *NASA + Pentagon = Star Wars!*. They approached a lady, thirtyish, wearing jeans, a white cotton blouse, baseball cap, and dark glasses. She was at the rear of the line of people. She carried a sign in her left hand and a can of Diet Sprite in the other. As they neared her, Tom recalled that one of the articles he read before they left D.C. mentioned recent protests at NASA facilities. It said that NASA officials had become used to occasional picketers. They generally showed up prior to the missions designated for the Department of Defense. For the most part they had been peaceful, but the protesters had recently become more and more vocal. They were apparently getting to be a headache for the Pentagon, NASA, and even the White House. Much of the success of the D.O.D. launches depended, obviously, on absolute secrecy as to the nature of the payload and the missions. This secrecy, according to the article Tom had read, was threatened by an increasingly aggressive and well-organized group of individuals. Neither NASA nor the Pentagon knew quite how to handle the situation. The basic position taken by the protesters was that NASA should be focused on exploring space and enhancing scientific knowledge—searching for extraterrestrial life, getting a manned mission to Mars, conducting medical research, and training astronauts for prolonged space travel (you know, the basic Star Trek stuff, going where no man has gone before). They believed that the agency should have nothing to do with the Pentagon, or with any military activities.

Tom approached the woman and said, "Excuse me ma'am, may we speak with you for a moment?"

She stopped, turned around, and inquired, "Are you talking to me?"

The other protesters wandered further away, like ants in a perfect line.

"Yes, sorry to bother you. We're reporters and we were just wondering what organization you represent and—"

"Sorry, I don't speak to the press."

"But if we could just—"

She started to turn and walk away.

"Ma'am—"

She paused. "Look, I wish I could talk to you, but I'm not supposed to be here. I'm supposed to be at work. Understand? I called in sick so I could be here, and I don't want to be quoted in any papers, or be seen on the local news. Okay?"

Tom nodded.

The woman continued, "Our spokesman will be here any minute." She looked down at her watch. "He should have been here thirty minutes ago. His name is Nevsky, Dr. Nevsky. He looks a little strange, so you'll know him when you see him. I really have to go." She turned quickly to her right and jogged back to her position with the others.

Tom and James kept walking. As they got closer to the entrance gate they saw a large round sign, more of a logo really, *Kennedy Space Center Press Center*. They moved through the gate opening, down a few steps, then followed the sidewalk to a gray building made of cinder block. It had no windows, just a couple large glass doors. They followed the sidewalk to a door on the right, where most of the crowd was coming and going. There was another sign, much smaller than the first one, hanging above the door, *Press Must Sign In*.

They entered the building. Inside, dozens more television, newspaper, and radio reporters were scattered about. Many were standing in a long winding line, guided by a serpentine path outlined in plastic chain attached to chrome posts. There were tired frowns and jet-lagged faces everywhere.

James turned to Tom. "What's with all the commotion?" he asked, gazing about the room.

"They're probably waiting to receive press passes."

They both moved away from the door.

"Are we going to risk checking in under *The Washington Post*?" James whispered.

"I don't know what choice we have. Man, I didn't think it would all be so formal. Look, I think they're asking each person for ID."

"So now what?"

"Well, I don't know what else to do. Let's get in line."

Thirty minutes later they exited the cool air conditioning of the pressroom, badges in hand. As they made their way down the sidewalk and through the gate opening, one of the protesters (a white-haired man in a tee shirt and jeans) pulled out a can of spray paint. He then ran over to a sign on the fence and sprayed it with a vengeance.

"This is interesting," James said as they watched him shake the can, apparently trying to make more paint come out. They could hear the little ball inside knocking around.

"Uh-oh." Tom noticed a couple of security guards running over from the press building. "We better get further away, James. Come on."

They exited the gate and walked to the parking lot, all the while twisting their necks to see the big bust of the crazy guy with the spray paint.

Tom paused and looked back. "Here, this should do it. I wonder if he's the spokesman that lady said we should talk to. I don't remember seeing him when we came in."

They watched as the guards stumbled to a stop and grabbed the man by his arms. They pulled him away from the fence. But it was too late. He had already sprayed his message, *No Weapons In Space*. He struggled to swing his arms free.

Tom and James heard him scream, "Let go of me! This is U.S. government property, paid for by U.S. citizens. I'm a citizen of the U.S. I have a right to be here. It's called free speech."

They moved a little closer and saw the guards try to take the spray can from his right hand. He aimed it at one of them. His arm was batted down just as the paint emitted from the nozzle. The can fell to the ground and for some reason just kept on spraying, straight up into the air.

"You sonsabitches," the man continued.

One of the guards removed some handcuffs from his belt and slammed them on the man's skinny little wrists, but he still jumped and jostled about, screaming and yelling things no one could understand. He was beet red and looked like he could have a stroke any second.

Tom noticed a television news crew approaching. The larger of the guards also appeared to see them, as he started shaking his head. He then pulled a walkie-talkie from his belt, apparently wanting to radio security headquarters for instructions.

The old man also saw the news crew, and this obviously pleased him. He immediately stopped jostling about and turned directly toward a bearded gorilla of a man, who was holding a camera and half a ton of other equipment, and said, "We must stop the Pentagon from launching weapons into space. It's the—"

His moment of glory was brief. The guards yanked firmly on his right arm and swung him to the gate. They searched his baggy pants, apparently for weapons, then began moving him away. But he didn't budge more than a foot or two. He made his body go limp and let his scrawny legs drag across the asphalt, like a puppet whose strings had been cut.

The female reporter with the gorilla, a perky blonde who looked like she was from Entertainment Tonight and had silky legs up to her neck, yelled as if possessed, "Tape running, Harry? Is it?" Her

121

eyes were wide and she was almost out of breath, as if she was witnessing the last landing of the Hindenburg.

Harry answered, "Yeah, hit it."

She ran over to the old man, turned and said a few words to the camera all sweet like, while flashing her pearly whites, then pushed a microphone in front of his face. The guards continued dragging him away. "Sir, sir, what's your name?"

James and Tom watched from afar, not wanting to be caught on camera.

"My name is Dr. Nevsky. I'm executive director of Citizens Against Weapons In Space," he yelled frantically. The soles of his shoes had to have been getting hot from the friction of being dragged. Tom thought he could even see a little smoke. Or maybe it was just dust. He continued to let his frail match sticks drag along behind his body.

Tom turned to James. "Did you hear that?"

"What?"

"He said his name is Nevsky. It *is* the guy that lady said we should talk to."

"Yeah, but it doesn't look like we'll have a chance now. Damn, look at him. He's just about kicking their ass, and the little guy is handcuffed. Just look at him."

The television reporter, her cameraman in tow, struggled to keep up with Nevsky as the guards continued pulling him away, even faster. She walked as quickly as she could, heels clicking noisily, skirt fluttering about like a square dancer, and somehow managed to push the microphone back in front of Nevsky. "I spent more than twenty years with NASA, and this is how they treat me!" he yelled as he latched onto a post near the gate opening.

"How long ago did you leave NASA?" she shouted back.

"Ten years ago."

"Do you have proof of your allegations? About plans to put weapons in space?"

"Huh?"

"Exactly what weapons are being put in space? Do you have proof? When were they—"

Her diligent line of questioning was promptly cut off as one of the guards moved in front of the microphone and also blocked the camera's view. He then tried to pry Nevsky's fingers from the gate post.

The reporter rested her smile, even frowned a bit, and scurried around to the other side, yelling at Harry to follow. And follow Harry did.

"My god," James said. "They're being kind of rough with the old guy, don't you think?"

Tom nodded without saying a word.

Once again the microphone flew back in front of the leathery and flaming face. The reporter turned her smile back on and asked him once more, "When did you say you left NASA, Dr. Nevsky?"

"The day they got into bed with the Pentagon, and launched the first D.O.D. mission. That's when," he yelled, spit shooting from his mouth. His eyes seemed like chalk-white cue balls from a pool table. The guards yanked harder, placing their feet further apart and putting some body weight leverage in for good measure.

If Nevsky lets go at this precise moment, Tom thought as he looked on, *they'll fall on their ass in front of three hundred people.*

Nevsky let go. One of the guards fell to the ground and the other just barely stayed afoot. The one on the ground dusted himself off and leapt to his feet almost faster than the blink of an eye, as if nothing had happened at all.

Again, the guards started to pull Nevsky away from the gate area. They whisked him off toward a small building near the press facility, but suddenly stopped in their tracks and stared down at the walkie-talkies clipped to their belts.

Tom and James heard a crackling noise and a faint voice emitting from the walkie-talkies. The guards then looked over to the parking lot. Tom turned around. Behind all the protesters, onlookers, and news chasers, a black and white police car pulled up, lights flashing but no siren blaring.

"They're actually going to arrest him," James said.

A wonderfully tanned officer got out of the car, adjusted his mirrored RayBans, then waddled awkwardly over to the guards and

Nevsky as if he had just ridden a horse for far too long. He looked pretty pissed off, turning redder by the second.

Everyone watched as the guards offered their version of what happened, each of them occasionally pointing over to the damaged Kennedy Space Center sign for added emphasis. The officer took down a report. And slam bam, the guards handed Nevsky over to him. The officer escorted his dangerous criminal to the police car, opened a rear door, and held the top of Nevsky's little gray head down as the rebel climbed in and sat down. Five seconds later and the car sped off. The entire apprehension had happened very swiftly. The streets of Kennedy Space Center were once again safe. And it was all, of course, recorded on videotape for the five-thirty, six, and eleven o'clock Channel 10 News, according to the tee shirt Harry the cameraman was wearing.

The other picketers continued to walk back and forth in front of the gate area, their leader gone but their spirit not broken. The guards seemed to be heading back over to them. So they moved slightly away from the gate, toward the parking lot. But the guards walked right on by. They made their way over to the damaged sign. The tallest guard pulled out a Swiss Army knife from his pocket, then pivoted a tiny screw driver out from the red handle. He reached up with every inch of his frame and removed the four screws that were holding the sign to the fence. He pulled it down, picked up the washers and nuts that had fallen to the grass on the other side of the fence, then calmly walked away. All in a day's work.

CHAPTER FOURTEEN

Just minutes behind the squad car carrying Dr. Nevsky, Tom and James arrived at the police station on John Glenn Boulevard in Titusville. Since they had heard several of Nevsky's statements to the television reporter back at Kennedy Space Center, they wanted to talk to him about his allegations. Tom hoped that Nevsky might even know about the High Ground program, although he worried that too many years had passed since Nevsky actually worked for NASA. At this point how much could he possibly know about a current, clandestine program? And given the behavior he exhibited at the press center, Tom wondered whether he might be just slightly off his rocker.

Forty-five minutes passed as the sun loitered in the hot Florida sky and Nevsky was searched, fingerprinted, and booked for vandalism of the sign, disturbing the peace and resisting arrest. Tom stayed in the rental car, just in case an all-points bulletin was out for his arrest due to the Pentagon fiasco, while James waited inside the station. They thought for sure that Nevsky would be released on his own recognizance, but that wasn't what ended up happening. A few questions from James to the arresting officer revealed that Nevsky had damaged NASA facilities more than once. In fact, this was his fourth violation in two years. And he had refused to pay the fines each time. In the past, according to the officer at the front desk, NASA officials had decided that it would be less provocative and make less news if he was just let go after committing the violations. So they had dropped the charges.

But this time was different. This launch, and the museum ceremony, was far more critical and they didn't need some old-timer chaining himself to fences, or being interviewed before the launch and making seemingly outrageous claims. So the charges were not dropped. NASA and Pentagon officials wanted him to stay put, behind bars, completely secure and silent. But what they didn't know was that James was about to bail Nevsky out.

Once the paperwork was completed, James was asked to have a seat while an officer left the front desk and disappeared into the back of the jail, where the cells were. Nevsky was in the first one, wearing a striped, numbered jumpsuit, and lying somewhat comfortably upon the slouching mattress of a well-worn metal cot, his arms folded under and supporting his head. His bare feet were propped up against the wall, and he was scratching and manicuring his somewhat yellowed toenails back and forth across the rough surface of the bricks.

The officer approached the cell with a large key and said, "Nevsky?"

"Yes."

"You're being released. Get up," the burly cop said as he unlocked the latch to the cell and swung the door outward and to the right. It let out a screech and banged into the vertical iron bars.

"Already?"

"Uh-huh."

"But I haven't even had lunch yet."

"Sorry to disappoint you. Your Jane Fonda sixties-thing is up for today. Someone paid your fines. He's sitting out in the waiting room. Says he's a friend of yours."

"A friend?" Nevsky sat up, almost looking sad.

"Here." The officer tossed a plastic bag to him. It contained his clothes and personal effects (a key chain, cherry flavored Chapstick lip balm, his wallet and a tattered comb).

"Get dressed and sign this form saying that I gave you everything back. I'll come get you in a few minutes." The officer set the form on a chair next to the bed.

Nevsky looked in the bag, then got dressed.

After just an hour and fifteen minutes of fairly pleasant incarceration, Nevsky was released. He was brought to the waiting area and told, "That man over there paid your fines."

Nevsky walked over with a thoroughly confused look on his face. "Who the hell are you?" he asked, looking up at James. His eyes squinted from the light.

"Clemens is my name. James Clemens, I'm with *The Washington Post*," James replied, after waiting for the cop to disappear over to a soda machine. "Let's go outside."

They exited through a pair of doors opposite the front desk.

"Finally..." Tom said to himself as he watched them approach. He reached forward and turned the car radio down. He stretched his neck as James and Nevsky made their way. He was hoping they could get some information out of him then, either this afternoon or in the morning, join all those reporters they had seen for a scheduled tour of Kennedy Space Center, which he overheard a couple people talking about back at the press center parking lot. NASA provided such tours for the press before each launch. Tom knew that the tour, and whatever information Nevsky could provide, would likely only provide background information for the story, but it might just help, and it would surely give them a good feel for how the base was laid out. In the past, Tom had seen stories come to life from sources in the least likely places, and allegations were occasionally corroborated by some pretty bizarre people, many initially appearing unbelievable and even downright demented.

At first, Nevsky seemed reluctant and wary of them, but then they told him that *The Washington Post* would like to buy him lunch and hear all about what he and his fellow picketers were protesting about. He was in the back seat of the rental in a flash, directing Tom to someplace called the Rocket Cafe.

They were seated promptly (it was too late for lunch and too early for dinner). A waitress approached. Her hair was strawberry blonde and it was curled to the hilt. It dangled to her shoulders and over the collar of her white and black checkerboard blouse, which was tucked neatly into a pleated black skirt.

"How y'all doing? Something to drink gentlemen?" she asked, as James, Nevsky, and Tom looked at the one-page grease-covered menus.

"Yes, water for me. And I think we're ready to order, too," Tom replied. He and James ordered cheeseburgers and seasoned fries that, judging by the picture on the menu, would surely clog the largest arteries in their tired bodies. And Nevsky ordered just a plain green salad with low-cal Italian dressing. "Make that dressing on the side, okay. And no bacon bits, please," he said firmly, scratching his nose. "No pieces of pig, or any other bits of dead animals," he added for good measure.

The waitress nodded, grinning. "Anything else?" she said to no one in particular, chomping her gum.

"No, that'll do it," Tom replied, then waited a few seconds for her to walk away. He turned to Nevsky. "So you're a strict vegetarian?" This was as obvious as the red nose on Nevsky's face, but at least it would get a conversation going.

"That's right, twenty years now," he answered, then picked up his glass and gulped down some water. "Ah, that hits the spot." He set the glass down precisely on the water ring from which it came then said, "I like to eat healthy, boys. I'm fit as a horse. Hell, I've never felt better. Didn't you see me wrestling with those morons back at the press center? I could've taken them both on if I'd wanted to. I run two miles a day and fornicate three times a week. How about you two?"

Tom wasn't sure how to respond. "Uh—"

"Yeah, I thought so. You two seem like city boys—no time for life," he continued as he again picked up his glass of water, then made marks with his index finger in the condensation. He held the glass to his lips and gulped down every drop. The empty glass went promptly back to the ring and he said, "My only health problems are the headaches I get from NASA. That's why I resigned."

"So you really did use to work for NASA?" Tom asked.

"That's right. You two won't believe it, no one ever does, but I have a Ph.D. in nuclear engineering and an MS in aeronautical engineering. I spent almost thirty years working for the government."

Tom wasn't sure if he believed him, but he nodded then looked at James, whose doubt was written all over his face. He turned back to Nevsky as James asked, "So why did you resign?"

128

"Because I refused to remain quiet about my objections. You know, my objections to NASA turning into a damn branch of the military."

They both nodded then Tom asked, "Dr. Nevsky, have you heard of a program called High Ground at NASA or the Pentagon?" As he said this the waitress walked over with their food atop a tray. He looked up at her. "That was fast."

"Yep, we guarantee that the food is ready in five minutes or less, except at lunch hour." She put the plates down on the table. "Anything else for now, gentlemen?"

"No thanks," Tom answered as he cleared the table a bit, moving a napkin dispenser toward the window.

Nevsky stared at him, saying nothing, as the girl arranged the plates in front of them. He was clearly waiting for her to leave the table before answering Tom's question.

After the waitress was about fifteen feet away, Nevsky leaned forward and whispered, "You boys know about High Ground?"

"Yes, that's why we're down here."

"How'd you find out?"

"Someone who works for a defense contractor called into *The Washington Post* and left a message. He sounded very concerned about the program. He told us we should look into it right away, before the next launch." Tom purposely avoided too many details, wanting to hear Nevsky's version of what was going on.

Nevsky shook his head slightly then took a big bite of his salad. After he swallowed he said, "It may be too late, Mr. Lassiter."

"What do you mean?"

"The satellites are about to launch. The preparation countdown has started."

James moved forward. "Just what exactly are they launching?"

Nevsky hesitated for a moment then answered, "Two satellites. One is some sort of space platform for nuclear weapons and—"

"You're sure it's nuclear?"

"Yes, I'm positive. And the other one is a command and communications satellite, used for targeting." Again, he shoveled a couple fork loads of salad into his mouth as if he hadn't eaten in days.

Tom cleared his throat. "Dr. Nevsky, I don't mean to sound like I don't believe you, but how exactly did you find out about these satellites, considering that you're no longer with NASA?"

"I have my sources."

"Inside Kennedy Space Center?"

"That's right."

"And they are reliable?" Tom asked.

"Oh yes, my primary contact is absolutely credible. I would trust him with my life. I've known him and his wife for ten years at least."

"Is it possible for us to meet your friend?" Tom asked, though he presumed the answer would be no. "We wouldn't, of course, quote him in the story we're working on."

Nevsky took a big gulp of water, which was freshly refilled by the waitress, while shaking his head left and right. "Absolutely not, he hasn't talked with anyone but me. I've tried to get him to meet with reporters down here before, but he's too worried about his job. We agreed that I would be the fall guy, if it comes to that. I'll never rat on him. He's a good man. He has three kids in college right now and his wife has a heart condition and isn't doing too well. So he needs his job and insurance. Plus, he doesn't want to screw up his retirement."

Tom nodded sympathetically. "But he was concerned enough to contact you, right. So he obviously wants to get the word out."

"Yes, he does. But he didn't contact me just out of the blue. Actually, we contacted him and hundreds of engineers we thought might be involved in the program."

"How?"

"A couple of my buddies—in fact, they were out there protesting this morning—sent out seven hundred and fifty emails directly to NASA employees, and its subcontractors' employees. The message asked for someone, anyone, to anonymously come forward

130

with any information pertaining to D.O.D. payloads that might be illegal, you know, any sort of space-based weapons."

"How many leads came back?"

"Two. One from my friend, who knew I was involved in trying to get the information, and one from some employee of a NASA subcontractor."

"Someone from British Space Systems?" Tom asked somewhat hesitantly.

Nevsky choked slightly as he tried to swallow, and his face blushed. He grabbed a napkin then said, "That's right, how the hell do know that?"

"Because he's the one who called *The Washington Post*," Tom answered, suddenly getting an adrenaline rush from knowing that the pieces were starting to fit together. "Dr. Nevsky, I assume that he didn't tell you his name, when he responded to your email blast?"

"Nope, he just said he worked for British Space, that's all. The email reply came via a Google account, with no name. Do you boys know who he is?"

Tom questioned whether he should say yes, but decided to go ahead and be straight with Nevsky, thinking it would make him more comfortable in talking about his friend. "Yes, we know who it is. But we agreed never to divulge his identity."

"I should hope not." Nevsky pushed his salad away and suddenly appeared more serious, his eyebrows lowering and eyes becoming intense. "I'll tell you what gentlemen, if this launch goes forward, it could start a whole new weapons race in space, and it could very well trigger conflict in the Middle East, at least between Iran and Israel." He paused for a second or two. "You two seem like honest, straight forward types, so I'll tell you a bit more." Again he paused, to blow his nose in his napkin. "The protestors and I, well, we have a secret weapon of our own that might enable us to stop the launch. I was sworn not to say anything though, and I have to ask you for your word to not repeat this to anyone until we agree on how to proceed. Okay?"

"Yes, yes of course," the words flew from Tom's mouth. And James nodded and leaned forward.

"Here's the deal. My friend called me at lunch and told me that he got access to the satellites this morning. We've been trying to get him close for two months now, but he is only involved in preparing satellites just prior to launch. Anyway, he told me he took pictures of both satellites and—"

"God, that's great," Tom interrupted. He almost wanted to reach over and hug Nevsky.

"I'm supposed to meet him after he gets off work, and take a look at the pictures, make some color copies."

"Did he tell you anything about the satellites? Are they being launched on the Atlas V?"

"No. They're being launched on the space shuttle. The Atlas V is just a diversion and—"

"But the shuttle program is retired," Tom interrupted. "Are you certain those payloads are going to be launched on a shuttle?"

Nevsky cleared his throat. "Yes. I'm sure. You see, boys, NASA has kept one space shuttle in near-ready mode since the so-called last flight. It's not on the schedule. And it's not on any NASA website. We're talking top secret defense related mission here."

James leaned forward and asked, "It's a bit hard to believe that NASA and the U.S. would state that the shuttle program is over, then suddenly a launch occurs. You, know, it is just a bit out there."

"I know, I know it is. But do you really think the Department of Defense would trust Russia, or private industry to launch a top secret nuclear weapon into space on behalf of the U.S.? That would be impossible."

James nodded. "I see your point. So *this* is the last mission for the space shuttle program?"

"I would assume so, but I really don't know. There are conflicting stories on that," Nevsky replied, then turned to Tom.

Tom took a drink of water then asked, "But why not just launch those satellites on the Atlas or another U.S. rocket?"

"Because those satellites were designed for the shuttle's cargo bay, years ago, and require the use of the arm. You know, the robotic arm that Canada made for the U.S. which can pick up a payload from the shuttle's bay and carefully deploy it. And it can also serve as a work platform for astronauts, if a satellite requires post-deployment adjustments or repairs. The two satellites they are getting ready to launch require the space shuttle. Those birds were designed during the Bush administration, before the shuttle program was cancelled, or at least publically terminated."

"Then why weren't they launched back then?" Tom asked, as he rubbed his forehead. "Why wait until now?"

"There's a couple of reasons, from what I understand. First of all, there were some technical problems which delayed the program. And then, when Obama came into office, the administration put the whole thing on hold."

"So why now? Why would the administration want them launched now?"

"Well, either they believe that Iran's threats against Israel justify the deployment of such a space-based weapons platform, or maybe the administration doesn't even know that the launch will occur. I don't know. Or maybe the satellites are due to North Korea's threats toward America and South Korea." Nevsky again blew his nose in his napkin, and looked back and forth at James and Tom.

"I don't see how such a major program could go forward without the administration knowing it."

"You may be right, Tom. I really don't know who is behind the program. But as we both know, a hell of a lot of illegal activity goes on within the CIA, which never comes to light. And if they don't get those satellites up soon, it may be too late."

"Too late for what?" James asked.

"Too late to deter or do anything to stop Iran, if they continue with their nuclear weapons development and, god forbid, take any action against Israel or the U.S. And too late to launch the satellites on a space shuttle. NASA can't sustain such an aging program forever, even it if is just keeping one shuttle on standby, such as for this launch.

They either launch those satellites now, or never. Like I said, there's no way the U.S. can contract with Russia or with a private company to launch something so sensitive. And illegal."

Tom and James nodded in concurrence. Nevsky was making sense. The U.S. Department of Defense could never subcontract the launch of a space weapon to the Russian Federal Space Agency or even a private space company. Aside from the technical considerations Nevsky pointed out, it simply wouldn't be possible to secretly launch a space weapon unless the operation was one hundred percent controlled by the Pentagon and CIA.

Nevsky, Tom, and James sat in silence for a moment, finishing their meals.

"So your friend just got the opportunity, today, to take pictures of the payloads?" Tom asked.

"Yes. He just got them. He actually called me just before I was arrested, which is one reason I flipped out. Everything we suspected is true. I sort of lost it over there."

"I understand," Tom said empathetically. "I can totally understand."

"So anyway, my friend told me he was calling from a restroom over at Kennedy Space Center's employee cafeteria. Said he had finally gotten a chance to take the pictures without anyone else around, and told me to meet him after work. That's all he said."

Tom exhaled loudly and there was a long pause before he whispered, "This could be huge. You know that, right."

"You're damn right I know that. That's why I'm telling you boys. *The Washington Post* has a pretty good record in dealing with government cover-ups, right?"

"Yes, yes we do."

Nevsky leaned forward again. "Well boys, this will make Watergate look like child's play. This is bigger than that. And it's bigger than the warnings before 9-11. Look at me in the eyes right now, Tom. You have millions of lives in your hands because of what I just told you."

"I, I don't know about that," Tom replied nervously.

"Tom," Nevsky said seriously with a piercing glare, "I'm not kidding. You have to get the word out on what they are launching. If they get those satellites up over the Middle East, there's no telling what could happen. Even if they don't even intend to use the space-based nuclear weapon, it will no doubt spark tensions which are already on edge due to Iran's nuclear development program. Hell, you two see and live the news every day. Iran's leaders are talking about eliminating Israel altogether, and they make threats against the U.S. all the time. This is very serious. And it's in your hands to get the word out and stop the High Ground program, before it even starts."

Tom nodded. His stomach was starting to feel queasy.

"As you know, the P5+1 talks haven't exactly been going well. I'm sure you two follow P5+1, right?" Nevsky asked.

"Yes, I know. The negotiations are all but stalled," Tom answered.

The P5+1 Nevsky referred to was the group of countries attempting to hold discussions with Iran regarding its nuclear program. The group includes the U.S., Russia, China, France, Britain and Germany. But Israel had held out no hope for success of the talks, and the Secretary of State was on record stating that the talks had not achieved any substantial results. Iran still wasn't fulfilling its obligations under the IAEA (International Atomic Energy Agency) and the UN Security Council. And Prime Minister Binyamin Netanyahu had recently stated that "the current rounds of talks with Tehran leadership hadn't stopped the regime one bit, not an inch, and that Iran had enriched material for five nuclear bombs."

Nevsky took a last sip of water, cleared his throat, then continued, "I think you two gentlemen are about to become heroes. That is, if you can stop what they are about to launch. This is *your* 9-11. Now go stop it."

CHAPTER FIFTEEN

As the sun sank lower in an orange-yellow sky, then disappeared entirely beyond the edge of the shimmering Atlantic, James and Tom were parked at 1172 South Palm Drive, in front of Nevsky's condo. It was almost eight o'clock. He was supposed to be there any minute with the pictures, if he followed through with what he told them earlier. After lunch they had dropped him off at Kennedy Space Center, where his van was still parked. He was almost surprised to see it, thinking that perhaps the police had impounded it when he was arrested.

James rolled down his window and fanned his face. It must have been a hundred degrees, and the humidity was making it feel even worse. Beads of sweat were pouring out of him, and the cheap vinyl seat of the rental car was sticking to his skin. Tom was equally uncomfortable. He was tempted to turn on the engine and kick the air conditioning on high, but didn't want to draw any more attention to them than they already seemed to be getting. Since they had arrived, a kid had walked back and forth on the sidewalk, staring as if he was completely invisible. And a gray-haired lady had peeled her drapes back every five minutes or so from inside one of the nearby condos, only revealing half her sun-crinkled face and spidery fingers which held the drapes open just slightly.

Finally they saw Nevsky's van pull up behind them. His tires screeched as he slammed on the brakes and jumped out. Tom thought he hadn't even turned off the engine, nor had he bothered to shut his door. This, Tom thought, would surely give the kid and the old lady plenty more to contemplate.

As Nevsky ran up to the window, Tom turned his head toward him and said, "We better not stay parked here. Your neighbors seem to be a little nosy."

Out of breath, he nodded and without saying a word opened one of the rear doors, then flung himself in and slammed it hard.

"I think you better run back and turn off your engine and shut your door, don't you?" Tom asked.

Nevsky's head swung mechanically around, as if mounted on a tripod. "Damn, I'll be right back, boys."

James turned to Tom. "I'm guessing he has the pictures."

"Yeah, I'd say so. Either that or he has just robbed a bank."

When he returned and climbed back in, Tom decided to come right out with it and asked, "Did you get them?"

"Yep. And you're not going to believe your eyes." He wiped his face on his shirt.

They headed to the nearest parking lot they could find, two blocks away at a strip mall. Tom figured that if Nevsky didn't calm down he could always run into the nearby liquor store and buy something strong to soothe his nerves. He found the most vacant corner of the lot available and turned off the engine. He and James swung around toward the back seat in perfect sync. Nevsky was already pulling the pictures out of a manila envelope. His hands were shaking and the pictures were falling out all over the back seat, turning like leaves catching an autumn breeze.

"Careful," Tom said as calmly as he could, as the wind blowing in from a window continued to scatter them across the hot, sticky vinyl.

Nevsky frantically grabbed at them. Tom hoped that his fingerprints wouldn't screw them up too bad before they could get them into print at The Washington Post. Nevsky collected the pictures and handed them over the seat, to Tom.

Tom's mouth dropped open slightly when his eyes hit the first one. "This is incredible."

James leaned over, also staring at the first picture. He uttered beneath his breath, "My god. It's true."

Tom held the picture closer. "This is big, gentlemen. This is real big." There was no doubting what he was seeing. There were two satellites sitting next to each other in what appeared to be a huge warehouse, or a clean room where satellites are protected from dust while in storage. One of them had what looked like missiles sticking out from it. Tom couldn't tell how big they were, as there wasn't anything nearby to give him an idea of scale, but a total of four missiles seemed to be aimed outward from a large cylindrical structure. As he looked closer he saw some sort of an ID (KH001/HG342) and he could see that there were small squares and rectangles covering the entire surface of the central structure. Looking at the missiles again, he realized that their nose cones were also covered with them. They were obviously heat dissipation tiles, just as Gilmour claimed, and just like that video at British Space Systems showed on the shuttle. The missiles were obviously designed to launch from space—the ultimate 'high ground' of any battlefield—without burning up on re-entry into the Earth's atmosphere.

"Can you believe it?" Nevsky said, hanging his neck between the two front seats.

Tom continued to flip through the pictures. Nevsky's friend had taken ten pictures, and there were at least a dozen different angles. Most of them were of the satellite with the missiles, but there were a few of the control and communications satellite, which resembled the pictures Tom and James had seen of typical commercial satellites for television, telephone, and internet transmission. It's surface was covered with a material resembling aluminum foil, and there were various appendages attached to it, including two large solar collectors with those little wafer squares that collect light.

Tom asked Nevsky, "Is this the only set of pictures?"

"No, there's one other. My friend wanted to keep a set. He said he was going to take them home, and put them in his safe."

"And what about the digital versions. They're in a camera?" Tom asked.

"No. Well, yes. They were anyway. He took the pictures with his smart phone."

Tom wanted to get a copy of the digital versions, which could be printed in better quality and transmitted to *The Washington Post* easier. "Why didn't he just email or text them to you then? Can we get digital versions?"

"I asked him about that, before I went to meet him. But he said he didn't want a record of transmitting them, you know, on his cell phone account, or through his email."

Tom nodded. "Okay, that's okay."

As Tom went through the pictures one more time, holding each one closer to his eyes, he noticed something he hadn't seen when he quickly flipped through the first time. He could just make out some additional lettering and a logo on one of the missiles, on its nose cone. It was a bright orange rectangle with white letters across it: Caution, Radioactive. And below this, he recognized the symbol used to warn of radiation risks, its three swirling circles, one positioned above two, also painted in orange. A shiver went through his body as he absorbed the fact that the missiles indeed had some sort of nuclear warheads. And when he brought this to James' and Nevsky's attention they both grabbed at the picture and nearly tore it in half. "Easy, easy, I'll hold it," he told them, shaking his head.

CHAPTER SIXTEEN

The mustiness seemed to intensify as the Florida sun began to peek through the motel's lime green drapes, which hung over most of the window and just above the noisy air conditioner and heater (you've seen them before, those ancient combo types). It had rattled incessantly all morning. But the noise hadn't stopped Tom and James from falling asleep when they got back to their room. It had, however, taken awhile for their adrenaline to wear off. After Nevsky showed them the pictures (he ended up giving them the entire set he had), they took him out to dinner at Landley's Bar & Grill on Tenth Street. They stuffed him full of caesar salad, sourdough bread, and two pieces of apple pie, along with three glasses of Chardonnay, trying to convince him to ask his friend to meet with them so they could get some details about the satellites. But Nevsky stood his ground, god bless him; he said there was no way he would push is buddy any further. It was, it turned out, Nevsky's idea to take pictures of the satellites and it had taken quite a bit of convincing to even pull that off. There was no way his friend would talk. And Nevsky wasn't about to ask him.

Tom continued to stare at the streams of light flickering in from the window, then turned and looked at the clock radio on the night stand. It said 7:50 AM. He had called the front desk when they returned, asking the clerk for a wake-up call at six-thirty, but the phone never rang, or maybe they just hadn't heard it. Fortunately, the sound of the maid's squeaky cart, and someone yelling something about soap and towels, caused Tom's weary body to reanimate. He glanced over at James in the other bed. "James, are you awake?" he asked in a crusty morning voice. This was turning out to be his standard daily greeting.

"I guess you could call it that," he replied, his bare feet hanging a good ten inches off the end of the bed. "The bathtub would have been more comfortable than this mattress. It's lumpy as hell."

"We need to get moving. We over slept."

"Go ahead. Move," James said, then mumbled something else while pulling what had to be the world's thinnest pillow over his head.

They had both agreed that they would get up bright and early and take half the pictures to the airport and fly them counter to counter, so they would be ready at *The Washington Post* once the story was written and sent in.

Tom decided he should go ahead and jump in the shower and get dressed, which would give James a few more minutes to sleep. He switched on the television and turned it to CNN, with the volume just a tad too loud, then went to run the water.

By ten-thirty they had dropped half the pictures off at Delta, eaten breakfast, and driven to Kennedy Space Center (the airport was one big traffic jam, kids with Mickey Mouse caps running around everywhere, and sunburned parents in tow, all looking completely traumatized from their wonderfully relaxing vacation to Florida).

When Tom and James arrived at Kennedy Space Center's press center, it seemed to be equally busy. There were hundreds of rental cars and six or seven television broadcasting trucks. Their generators were noisily chugging and puffing smoke skyward. Large uplink satellite dishes were aimed at the southern horizon, already beaming pre-launch test signals skyward. Tom wasn't sure if the media were there for the shuttle museum ceremony or to watch the scheduled Atlas launch, or both.

Somehow they managed to find a parking space. They locked the car and began to walk to the press center. There were people everywhere.

Tom shifted his attention to James and said, "This is good, we should blend in with all these reporters."

James nodded. "Yeah, if they only knew the story we are working on. Speaking of which, when do you want to release it anyway? We don't have much more time, if we're planning on trying to get them to stop the launch. Do you think they are going to launch the

141

Atlas and the shuttle at the same time, or is the scheduled Atlas launch just to throw everyone off."

Tom lifted his shoulders slightly and said, "I'm not sure. But I doubt NASA would have the resources to launch both an Atlas and a space shuttle simultaneously, or even quickly back to back. So maybe the Atlas is just serving as a decoy, and won't even be launched."

James nodded once and said, "Assuming they launch the shuttle, I mean, if we can't stop the launch, I wonder what they will tell the world. You know? Suddenly the shuttle is brought out of retirement for one more launch? It's going to be big news."

"Well, it will be even bigger news when our story hits the *Post*," Tom said, then looked down at his watch. "But as for another, unannounced space shuttle flight, it's not exactly huge news. They only recently announced the end of the program. And everyone knows there are a number of top secret *Skunk Works* projects in the military which never see the light of day, or only after they are deployed or declassified."

In 2008 Tom had written an article for *The Washington Post* about the history of various "Skunk Works" projects. The term originated at Lockheed Martin in 1943, when the Air Tactical Service Command of the Army Air Force met with Lockheed to express interest in a new jet fighter, the XP-80. Over the years since then, Skunk Works projects had included the U-2, SR-71 Blackbird, F-117 Nighthawk, F-22 Raptor and various top secret military satellites. Skunk Works projects were known for their autonomy and were generally unhampered by bureaucracy and oversight, which is essential for top secret projects. Tom really wasn't surprised that the government was able to keep development of those two satellites confidential for so many years.

Tom continued, "I'm planning to get the story out this evening via a special update of the web edition, which will be promoted by a Breaking News Alert email to subscribers and other media. Those pictures we dropped off with Delta should arrive in D.C. about three hours before all that."

Tom knew that the print edition of the newspaper was increasingly taking a backseat to the web edition, which is updated throughout the day by teams of editors whose job is to provide fresh content. The peak times for online reading were early morning and early afternoon, right after lunch. But in the case of a news alert, swarms of online readers could be drawn to the paper's website with the simple press of a button to send out an email blast. As for the print edition, the story would likely come out first in a regional edition that hits newsstands before midnight and go to the far outer provinces, then release to suburban and metro editions that come off the press between midnight and 3:00 AM for close-in circulation errors.

Tom continued, "I think we are fine on the timing. The news alert can get the word out whenever we are ready."

"And what about writing the story?" James asked. "When will we have time?"

"This afternoon. Don't worry, I already have most of it in my head." Tom tapped his right index finger on his temple a few times.

"That makes me feel a whole lot better."

Tom smiled slightly. "James, we have time. I write fast, and you are great at editing. We'll email or fax it to the *Post* this afternoon. But first, I'm hoping this press tour will give us some filler information that we can put in," Tom replied as he opened the door to the press building, then ushered James in with his palm.

Tom's eyes darted about the pressroom. People were scurrying all over the place. He turned to James and said, "A couple hours after breaking the story in the *Post*, and giving it a few moments of glory for our hard work, we'll phone it into CNN, Atlanta. I have a buddy there who can probably get us a phone interview immediately. Or, if they have an uplink truck down here, we might even go on live. Maybe we can time it for prime-time, at least on the west coast."

Tom craned his neck and tried to read a schedule that was written on a blackboard near the line for press passes.

"So, anyway, after CNN, we'll give the story to all these talking heads. Many of them will want to interview us."

He looked toward the entrance. More reporters and cameramen were rushing in. "Once all these mouths get word of the payload, NASA and the Pentagon will have to call off tomorrow's launch."

Twenty minutes later, NASA personnel divided everyone into herds of thirty-five, then corralled them into what looked like rented school buses. As James and Tom waited for their bus to fill up, they perused the press kits that were handed out with the badges. Inside the bright blue folder was a brochure touting the importance and value of having a space station, a NASA fact sheet, a history of the space shuttle program, and a couple of White Papers about the Mars *Curiosity* rover mission. Also inside the folder, tucked into the left interior pocket, was a map of Kennedy Space Center. It looked similar to the one in the file Tom had taken from General Kramer's office. He immediately recognized a few of the areas depicted—the D.O.D. Staging Building, a runway or taxiway, and the launch pads. He studied the map for a while, then examined the itinerary for the tour, which was stapled to the front cover of the folder.

* PRESS TOUR ITINERARY *

WELCOME TO KENNEDY SPACE CENTER

(The following itinerary is subject to change,

depending on launch preparations and weather conditions)

EVENT #	EVENT DESCRIPTION	LOCATION
01	Bus ride to VAB	Press Build.
02	Shuttle Program Overview	VAB
03	Tour VAB	VAB
04	Bus ride to LCC	VAB
05	Partial Tour of LCC	LCC
(access restricted due to Atlas launch prep.)		
06	Bus ride to Crawler	LCC
07	Visit Crawler & Pad	L. Pad
08	Bus ride back to Press Build.	L. Pad

The bus fully loaded, the driver walked up the steps and took his seat, then reached over and pulled a handle to close the bi-fold doors. He moved his eyes higher and smiled to the mirror mounted above the windshield, making sure everyone was seated and not pulling hair or shooting spit wads, then turned the key in the ignition and started the old diesel engine. The bus immediately began vibrating, and it felt rather nice on Tom's lower back. He twisted left and right a few times.

The ride to the first stop took just a few minutes. They exited the bus and were quickly escorted into a massive building, then entered a large room that had at least a hundred folding chairs set up, all facing a wood podium and a pull-down slide presentation screen. They chose a row and sat down.

A well-dressed woman, wearing a white silk blouse and a pleated black skirt, strolled to the front of the room and stepped up to the podium. Her brunette hair was woven into a neat bun and secured with a tortoise shell clip. She smiled at the audience, then angled her head down and with the red-painted nail of her index finger poked at the switch at the base of a microphone, trying to turn it on. She then tapped its foam top and an annoying reverberation immediately echoed through the room.

"Sorry. There we go. How's that? Loud enough?"

The crowd nodded approvingly.

"Good. Ladies and gentlemen, welcome to NASA's Vehicle Assembly Building, or VAB as we call it. My name is Dawn Miller and I'll be your host for the tour. I want to thank all of you for coming. This is the first stop on our tour of Kennedy Space Center. This is also the point of the tour at which we provide a general slide presentation of both the Atlas and other current rocket programs, and the history of the space shuttle program, in order to familiarize you with many of the things you will see later."

She pointed to some empty chairs.

"I believe we have some seats available right up here in front, if some of you standing in back would like to sit down," she continued, then looked over to a security guard near the entrance. "If I could have the lights dimmed please. Thank you."

"I apologize for the temperature. This room is usually used for storage. There's no air conditioning or heater." She glanced at her notes. "As you probably gathered when you came in, this is an amazing building. The VAB is the core of what we call Launch Complex Thirty-Nine. It was used to accommodate the pre-flight assembly of the shuttle's primary elements. Previously, the VAB was used for working on the Saturn V and Saturn 1B launch vehicles, seen in this slide." She motioned to her left, to the screen.

"The VAB is the world's largest single-story building, standing over five hundred feet and occupying over eight acres. It is here that the space shuttles were carefully hoisted almost two hundred feet into the air and moved into place next to the large external tank and solid rocket boosters, as this slide shows." Again, she looked at the screen.

"Now, after our presentation, we will enter this room," she said, pointing to a door on her right, "and see where the shuttles were readied for their missions. Next slide please."

"In this picture we see the Orbiter Processing Facility, or OPF. The OPF is essentially a sophisticated aircraft hangar where special platforms can roll up to a spacecraft, enabling crews to check the entire craft for cracks or other problems. Furthermore, as this slide shows, payloads capable of being stored and handled in a horizontal position are loaded in the OPF. Some payloads, however, must remain in a vertical position and are mated with a spacecraft out at the launch pad."

"Tom," James whispered, turning his head sideways. "You're supposed to be watching the slides, not the—"

"Yeah, yeah. I know," He whispered back. "She reminds me of Victoria. Don't you think she looks like her?"

James shook his head and with a hushed voice answered, "Sure, she's a spittin' image, except for a few things—wrong color hair, a bit heavier, and wire rim glasses. Aside from that, she looks just like her."

The spokeswoman paused to adjust her glasses, then continued, "So, you may be wondering how in the world we transported huge satellites to the space shuttles, or to a rocket today? Well, we do it with this." She pointed to the screen. "This slide shows the Payload Transporter Vehicle. As you can see, it has wheels all along its bottom—forty-eight to be exact. This enables it to transport

146

extremely heavy payloads in either vertical or horizontal orientations. In fact, you may see this vehicle today as it transports a communications satellite, or Comsat, this afternoon for an important Department of Defense mission."

James tilted his head toward Tom's ear and quietly said, "Yeah, right. Communications satellite my ass."

Tom nodded once but didn't shift his attention; he was still staring at the spokeswoman, and dreaming about Victoria while trying to pay attention.

James looked back at the screen. "Oh yeah, I can see that this entire exercise is really going to help the story."

"Now," she continued as she reached up, checking her hair, "before a shuttle mission, and after the satellite would arrive at the launch pad, the payload canister doors would be opened. This was done only after a tight seal was made with the launch pad's Rotating Service Structure, or RSS, seen in this slide. The RSS accommodated the loading of vertical payloads at the pad. It's mounted on a semi-circular track that allowed it to rotate through an arc of one hundred and twenty degrees. It would pivot until fitting flush with the shuttle's cargo bay, thus allowing the satellite to be installed close to launch time, and under contamination-free, clean room conditions. Next slide, please."

Tom turned to James and whispered in his ear, "Yeah, it also enables them to hide nasty little secrets, like nuclear-armed satellite platforms. The two satellites in those pictures Nevsky gave us must be vertical-oriented. That's why they've been in storage, and why they aren't in the shuttle yet. And that's probably how the Pentagon has kept most of NASA's personnel from seeing top secret payloads. They'll just transfer the satellites directly to the shuttle, completely sealed in that transport thing. No one will even see them."

Suddenly the microphone freaked out again, sending an excruciating shrill through the room. The entire audience cringed in unison. Tom thought to himself, *Land men on the moon—no problem. Make a public address system that works—mission impossible.*

"I'm sorry," she said. More tapping of the microphone. "Goodness, we'll have to get that fixed. Okay, hopefully if I stand further back. There we go. Now, in this slide we see another amazing vehicle built especially for NASA. This may look like a strange building of some sort, but look closer. This is one of our Crawler-Transporters. We like to call them the Mighty Tortoises, because they only move at about one mile per hour. Can you guess what their fuel mileage is?" she said smiling, gazing out at a sea of blank-faced reporters.

The pop quiz wasn't appreciated, as no one said a word. And there were a handful of contemptuous looks that seemed to say, We're reporters for god sakes. We embarrass, incriminate, and generally pester others by asking questions—not answering them.

"No guesses?" she continued. "Well, believe it or not, they only get twenty feet to the gallon."

After a few "wows" rippled through the audience, she pressed on. "Ladies and gentlemen, these massive vehicles can support the incredible weight of over eleven million pounds—the space shuttle, two solid rocket boosters, external tank, and the launch platform."

"Not to mention the warheads," James said beneath his breath.

Tom bumped his leg. "Keep it down. I think the suit next to you heard you. He keeps staring."

After a few more slides of the VAB and the space shuttle, the lights came up and everyone was escorted into what she called the Main Chamber. She explained that this was where the shuttles for future missions would be mated to two solid rocket boosters and an external tank. During the peak of the shuttle program, the mating ritual apparently occurred about every two or three weeks, just before each four hundred million dollar launch (you read right, four hundred mill).

As the hour clicked by, they were guided outside and immediately blinded by the sun, which was hovering almost directly above at this point and staring down intensely. Everyone piled into the bus and sat down like good little reporters. The old gears ground as the old driver released the old clutch, causing every head to bop forward and backward a few times, perfectly synchronized. Unlike the gears.

They headed toward what the spokeswoman called the Launch Control Center, but first did a loop around the south side of the base, for no apparent reason other than to see just how sprawling Kennedy

148

Space Center really was. The bus continued on, chugging noisily along a small two-lane road.

James looked at his watch and said, "Shouldn't we be getting back? It's already ten after one. The tour is running long."

"No, we're okay. I was thinking about the timing of the story back at that slide presentation. I think it makes more sense if we get it out closer to launch—sometime tomorrow morning."

"Why?"

"I want to make damn sure that those two satellites get out to the launch pad and into the shuttle. If we blow the whistle before they're moved, the Pentagon will deny everything and take them out of the Staging Building before anyone can verify our allegations. They'll disappear, and we'll look like idiots. Right? They can't haul them away if they're already on the pad, not easily anyway. And not without being seen. And they can't claim that there was no intention of launching them, if they are already on the shuttle."

"But what about the pictures and the file? We have proof," James continued, bouncing up and down in the seat as the bus driver ground a couple more gears and drove over a speed bump.

"I thought about that too. I don't think they are enough. The Pentagon could just claim that they were faked. You know what can be done with photo retouching, on even a home PC, let alone with the equipment and software we have at the *Post*. The pictures and file are obviously important, but they're not enough to make sure we're taken seriously." Tom paused, glancing out the window to his left. "They might even say that the pictures are just of scale models, or something. No, we need to catch them with their hands in the cookie jar—with those satellites out at the launch pad."

James gave a quick nod. Tom was making sense.

Tom continued in a hushed voice, "The Atlas launch is scheduled for eleven o'clock tomorrow. I assume they will actually launch the shuttle at that time, instead. So we can work on the story tonight. Then, in the morning, we'll email or fax it to the *Post*. After that, we can meet with the other press here, say two hours before launch. I want to make sure that the launch is looking certain. You know, sometimes they get up to T-minus-whatever, then delay the whole thing for hours or even days. We can't have them taking those satellites back to the Staging Building or, obviously, anywhere else. If things go right, all these reporters will demand that the Pentagon, or maybe even the President, halt the launch and allow a press contingency, and perhaps some representatives from the United Nations or something, to open the shuttle payload doors and take a look. Does that make sense?"

"Yeah. Amazingly," James answered.

"Scary, huh? I guess we're starting to think alike. We've probably been together a bit too much."

"Probably?" James replied in a higher voice than normal.

"Ah, come on. Not having fun?"

James just stared straight ahead, deadpan, and watched the beady eyes of the bus driver dart about in the mirror above his head. How he managed to drive and keep an eye on the passengers at the same time was a mystery. It suddenly struck James that everyone seemed to be beady-eyed and watching his and Tom's every move. He was feeling more and more paranoid by the minute.

Tom continued, "We don't really have a choice anyway."

"Of being together?"

"No. Of staying on the tour. Do you need a nap, James, or what? What I'm saying is that they aren't going to run us back to the press building in the middle of the tour. So we're stuck here for probably another hour."

CHAPTER SEVENTEEN

As British Airways flight 2037 began its descent to Orlando International, Victoria (yes, this was when things got real interesting) reached down to the armrest on her right and pressed the metal button to recline her seat a few notches. The last two hours of the flight had been rougher than she or any of the passengers cared for. The turbulence had made several of the three hundred and thirty-eight weary travelers airsick. A massive storm was to blame, some three hundred miles to the northeast.

A young flight attendant, who looked just as fatigued, sickly, and pale as everyone else, leisurely made her way toward first class from the galley near the cockpit. She grasped at the tops of the leather seats on either side of the aisle, being jostled left and right. She paused at each row, collecting empty glasses, used napkins, and the obligatory puny peanut bags.

The attendant motioned to Victoria and said, "Ma'am, we're about to land. Would you please pull your seat-back forward and fasten your belt?"

"Certainly."

"May I take your glass?"

"Please."

"Would you like anything else before we land?"

"Uh, no, I'm fine." Victoria uncrossed her long, silky legs, leaned to her left, and looked down at the armrest and pressed the button to bring her seat-back forward. She fastened the belt, then said, "Unless you have some antacid, something for my stomach."

"Yes, ma'am. Would Rolaids be okay?" The attendant picked up a napkin and empty peanut bag and stuffed them into the glass, then folded the tray into the armrest. "Or I think we may still have some Alka Seltzer."

"A couple of Rolaids would be splendid."

"I'll bring them right away, ma'am. I'm sorry that you're not feeling well. It was a rough flight wasn't it," the flight attendant continued with a slightly strained but pleasant smile.

"Oh, the flight didn't bother me. I'm afraid it's what is waiting for me in Florida that has my stomach upset."

"I hope it's nothing serious, ma'am."

"Quite serious, I'm afraid. I have to do something I don't really want to do."

The flight attendant felt it best not to inquire further. "I'm sorry. Well, I hope things go well for you. I'll be back with your antacid in just a moment. Okay? Are you sure you wouldn't like some 7-up or something to wash it down?"

"No thanks."

Victoria reached below the seat and grabbed the high heels she had taken off almost five hours ago. She adjusted the seams of her stockings around the tips of her toes, then slipped each shoe on.

The flight attendant moved away and collected some trash from a gentleman dressed in a suit across the aisle, then turned back. "I'll just be a moment, ma'am," she said, smiling again, then walked to the front of the plane, disappearing behind a curtain.

The sound of the flaps extending was heard, then the landing gear cranking down and locking into place. The plane's angle of descent became steeper. Victoria crossed her legs, leaned over and lifted the sunshade on the window to her left, then stared blankly at the sky and the scratch patterns in the Plexiglas window panel, which almost looked like snowflakes. Her eyes became glassy. She followed the shapes with the tips of her fingernails, thinking and worrying.

CHAPTER EIGHTEEN

Tom wiped his forehead and gazed at the wispy clouds that streaked through the sky like twisted taffy. The air was thick and sticky, a radical change from just two hours earlier. But according to one Raúl José Capablanca, a chronically gregarious five-foot-three Cuban reporter for the Miami Herald who had talked constantly the entire tour and walked off the bus just in front of him and James, the semi-pleasant weather would be short-lived. "The National Weather Service predicts the storm will hit sometime late tonight, or maybe mid-morning tomorrow," he'd said in a thick Cuban accent. "They might not even launch tomorrow." He then proceeded to provide the average rainfall and temperature statistics for Florida, and rambled on about various topics to which he was apparently an expert on (something nonsensical about the tide coming in, global warming, banana and sugar cane imports, and the Princess Cruise he'd recently enjoyed absolutely free, claiming to be a travel writer). Eventually Tom and James managed an escape from Mr. Capablanca.

Tom stretched his arms and asked James, "Does something seem strange to you?"

"Aside from Raúl?"

"Yeah. Look around."

"You're right. No picketers, no Dr. Nevsky. I thought he said he would be here this afternoon."

"I wonder if they arrested the whole bunch this time. Look over there." Tom pointed to the press building. "Aren't those the signs they were carrying?" There was a stack of them leaning against a chain link fence, upside down and turned away from the parking lot. "Strange."

They continued walking toward the rental car. Tom wanted to head to the motel and work on the story, but he stopped suddenly and turned to James. "I don't know about you, but I could use a restroom after bouncing around in that bus."

"Me too."

"There must be one inside somewhere," Tom continued, motioning to the press building.

They walked over to the entrance. As James started to open the glass door, he froze and did a double take. "What in the world. Why is—"

"What?" Tom interrupted, standing off to one side and seeing James' surprised expression. "Is it the police?" He asked nervously.

James shook his head. "No. It's not the police. Come on. Let's go in." James pulled the door open the rest of the way, then held it so Tom could go in first, and see what he had noticed on the other side of the glass door.

Tom walked through the doorway and his heart seemed to skip a beat. It was Victoria Brookshire.

She immediately noticed them and walked over. "Tom, James, great to see you."

"Victoria, what are—"

"I wondered whether I would run into you two down here," she interrupted as she made her way over to Tom and gave him a tight hug, then kissed his cheek.

James thought that Tom looked like he could knock him over with a feather. Tom was glowing.

Victoria turned to James. "And how are you, James?" She extended her hand to his and shook it firmly.

All three exited the doorway and stood outside the press center. "I can't believe you're here," Tom told her as the redness slowly dissipated from his blushed face.

"I know. I know. My boss, god love him, did it to me again. He asked me just last night to take his place and come over for the launch. Something about a luncheon tomorrow afternoon for NASA subcontractors. I guess he wants someone from British Space Systems to at least show their face."

Tom nodded and thought, *And what a face to show*.

154

She held the palm of her right hand up to his cheek and caressed it a couple of times with a slow downward motion, then moved her nails over his temple and into his hair slightly. "You cut your hair, didn't you. Looks good."

"Yeah, just a bit. Thanks." He was relieved that he had decided not to do too dramatic of a change, such as dye his hair.

"So where are you two headed?" she asked. "Do you have any free time over the next twenty-four hours?"

Tom glanced at James. James' face seemed to say, *Here we go again*. Tom then answered, "Sure. Uh, well, are you done here?" He motioned toward the press center entrance.

"Oh yes. I have my pass to the so-called VIP viewing area for the launch," she answered as she glanced down at a gold-colored ticket dangling from a loose string tied around her neck. She held it up for Tom to see.

Tom scratched the nape of his neck a few times then asked, "Well, would you like to go grab something to eat?"

"Yes, that would be nice. I didn't eat on the plane. The flight was so turbulent they didn't even attempt to serve lunch. I don't think anyone felt like eating anyway."

Tom shifted his attention to James. "Are you hungry?"

"No, not really," James replied. "You two just go on without me and I'll—"

"Are you sure, James?" Victoria interrupted. "Just a drink maybe?"

"No thanks. I think I'll head back to the motel and work on the story. I'm really not that hungry."

He was lying and Victoria and Tom knew it.

"Okay," Victoria said softly. "Well, I promise to have Tom back early enough to help you. All right?"

James nodded politely as if he believed her. He knew that if he saw Tom before midnight it would be a miracle of the first order.

Victoria turned her head and yawned. "Please forgive me, I'm rather tired from the long flight," she said as her palm rose to her mouth, covering those ruby red lips Tom remembered so well. Jet-lagged or not, she looked incredible.

"That's right," James said to her. "You're not used to this time zone are you?"

"No, I'm not, unfortunately."

Tom glanced at his watch. The afternoon was slipping by quickly. "All right then. Well, shall we go?" He looked at Victoria.

She nodded. "We can take my rental car if you like." She pointed toward the parking lot.

"Okay, that will help," Tom replied, then gave James the keys to their car and said, "I won't be too late. Go ahead and get started on the story and I'll take a look at the draft tonight. Okay?"

"Yeah, that's fine. You two have a good time."

"Thanks James."

"It was nice seeing you James," Victoria said as she and Tom began to walk away.

They made their way to her rental car. A few minutes later they drove south on highway 1, toward Cocoa Beach, and found what looked to be a decent restaurant, The Lighthouse Grill. Large wooden decks adorned every side of the building, which was made of weathered boards; a few overlooked a wide sandy beach. There were Mercedes, Porsche, Lexus, and Range Rover vehicles everywhere—even a flaming red Ferrari that looked like it needed a speeding ticket just sitting still. And, of course, there was valet parking. Tom turned in the driveway and pulled up near the front door. Two surfer types, sporting tuxedos and earrings, immediately opened the doors to the stripped-down and dented Ford Taurus rental. Tom got out and handed one of them a five-dollar bill.

"Thank you, sir," the kid said, then mumbled something unintelligible about the car keys and handed Tom a piece of paper with a number scribbled on it. God only knows how they managed to rally enough brain cells to keep the toys before them organized and safe. Tom handed him the keys somewhat reluctantly, then the other kid whipped his blonde curls over his shoulder and held open the large front door of the restaurant, which was carved into the shape of a

156

dolphin (its fin serving as the handle). Tom ushered Victoria inside with a light touch of his fingers to her lower back. They were promptly seated near a large window. They sat on the same side of the table, so each could see outside. This would, Tom thought, also provide at least some degree of privacy.

The view was spectacular, the waves crashing upon the beach, and mist flying upward then disappearing. They could even hear the water as it slapped at the shoreline and could feel its vibration on the old wide-plank floor of the restaurant. And, Tom noticed, the air was crisp and smelled of salt and seaweed. "Gorgeous, isn't it," he commented, gazing out.

"Yes indeed," Victoria answered then turned toward him and said, "Would you excuse me, Tom. I just need to freshen up and check my messages."

"Sure. I'll order wine, okay."

"Great."

He helped her pull out her chair. She grabbed her purse and left the table.

Victoria wasn't sure her phone, which was with British Telecom, would work in Florida. So she found the hallway where the pay phone and restrooms were, but she couldn't use the phone—a cocktail waitress from the restaurant was on her break, making love to the receiver and some guy named Fernando—so she entered the women's restroom. She felt fatigued, still not over the long flight. She retouched her makeup, washed her hands, and walked out the exit just as the waitress approached her all aglow, the steamy conversation with Fernando apparently over. They squeezed by each other and Victoria quickly made her way over to the pay phone. She nervously set her purse on a metal shelf, then opened it and pulled out a piece of paper. Written on it was a cell phone number. She picked up the phone receiver and set it on the small metal shelf below the phone, then removed her pocket book from the purse and a Mastercard. She slid it through the magnetic reader slit, then picked up the receiver with her right hand, which was starting to shake. A dial tone came on and she punched in the number. She turned to make sure no one was around, her blue eyes darting about. With the exception of Fernando's significant other, who was now dropping quarters into a candy and gum machine fifteen feet away, the coast was clear.

The phone rang and was quickly answered by General Kramer's CIA liaison. "Hello. Broderick here."

"Broderick, it's agent Brookshire."

"Victoria! Good. You landed already?"

"Yes sir."

"Where are you?"

She held the receiver, which reeked of smoke and even worse things, closer to her mouth and spoke as quietly as she could. "I'm in Florida," she answered purposely vaguely. "I made it onto the first flight out of Heathrow, right after I got your call. I've tracked down Tom Lassiter and we're at dinner. I can't talk long. He thinks I'm in the restroom, and calling in for messages. What are my instructions, sir?"

"I want you to find out how much he knows about the High Ground program, and how much he's passed on to his colleagues at *The Washington Post*. I can't say much more than that at this point, but it's extremely critical that you get him to talk. It's possible that he knows about the payloads. He was able to get one of General Kramer's files at the Pentagon."

"Files? But how did he—"

"That's not important right now," Broderick interrupted briskly. "Listen carefully, Victoria. If you can get him to show the file to you, immediately call me for further instructions. Understand? If we can't keep him under control before the launch, and get that file back, I may have to consider a much more serious option. I've been told to do whatever it takes to make sure the launch and payload deployment goes smoothly."

Victoria was silent. She again looked around the restaurant's hallway. There was no one around. She felt dampness on the back of her neck and under her arms and her eyes were getting watery. Sure, she'd heard that things like this went on within the agency, but she had never been confronted with a fellow agent actually alluding to so-called *serious options*. Never. Her mind raced with images of what Broderick might consider doing to Tom.

"Are you there, Victoria? Do you understand?"

"Yes. Uh, I understand, sir." She paused to clear her throat. "Shouldn't you tell me about the payload now? You know, so I can ask targeted questions that'll get him to talk, and see what he knows."

"No, I think it's better that you don't know. It's too risky. You might inadvertently pass on more information to Lassiter. It's a need to know basis, and you don't need to know. I'm sorry, but you understand, I'm sure. Just find out how much information he has as soon as possible, who he's told it to, then check back in. Kramer is on his way to Kennedy Space Center right now, so I want this resolved before he arrives. I'm counting on you."

She felt what seemed like all of her blood draining from her head, then some dizziness. She again looked around the hallway, and over her shoulders left and right. Still not a soul around. She whispered into the receiver, "What do you mean by more serious options, sir? That seems very drastic and unnecessary. He's just a reporter and—"

"That's not for you to worry about, Victoria. And it's out of my hands. I know you aren't used to this sort of thing, but you were bound to run into it sooner or later in your career. It's just part of the job. I don't like it either, but our national security is at stake. It's a very serious situation."

"And taking serious action, perhaps even taking out a reporter will make everything all better?" she said with a quivering voice. Her hands were shaking severely now; she could barely hold the phone steady. "I'm sure the payload on this launch isn't that sensitive to U.S. security and—"

"It is, Victoria. It's that important. And headlines in *The Washington Post* are that important."

She cleared her throat once more, which was suddenly incredibly dry, then continued, "Sir, I'm afraid I must get back to Lassiter. I'll try to find out what he knows and check in after dinner." She paused. "Uh, someone's walking over, I have to go." She abruptly hung up, fearing that Broderick might again ask where she was. She didn't want to tell him. Not yet anyway.

Broderick tucked his cell phone away. He was perturbed that Victoria cut their conversation off. He turned to his sidekick, Jones. "She didn't tell me where they're at. Damn it!" He took a deep breath, blew his cheeks outward, and exhaled loudly. "God, I'd love to get my hands around Lassiter's neck. All this for a newspaper story, can you believe it?"

Jones shook his head obediently.

Broderick decided to call Kramer back, who was sitting at an airport tarmac at Andrews Air Force base in Maryland in a fully fueled C-20 Gulfstream IV, one of the 89th Airlift Wing's planes. Located just outside Washington D.C., the 89th Airlift Wing provides global Special Air Mission (SAM) flights, logistics and aerial support and communications for the President, Vice President, Combat Commanders, and senior military officials, such as General Kramer. Not all of the military's 900-plus generals had access to a jet, but Kramer was one of a small percentage who could schedule a plane at will.

Broderick again pulled out his cell phone, unfolded it, then punched in some numbers and waited to be connected. He thought he could hear someone answer. There was static on the line, a weak digital connection.

"General?" Broderick asked.

"Yeah, Kramer here. Speak up. Is that you, Broderick?"

"Yes sir. Good news. Agent Brookshire has made contact with Tom Lassiter."

"Excellent. Can we trust her? She didn't get too close to him over in London did she? I mean, emotionally involved? You know very well what can happen when an agent gets too close and—"

"I think we can trust her, General," Broderick interrupted. "She's never let me down before. She's the best agent for the job. I'm sure she'll find out what he knows and who he's communicated with, and I doubt—"

Kramer interrupted, speaking more loudly, "What's that? The plane must be shielding the signal."

"Lassiter would never communicate what he knows to anyone else," Broderick continued, also raising his voice. "He may not even tell her, but she's our best shot."

"Okay, sounds good. Well, I should be down there in a couple of hours, assuming we don't have to fly around too many Florida thunderstorms. Use the number for the plane's phone until I arrive."

"Yes sir."

"Fine then," Kramer said, his voice breaking up.

Broderick spoke even louder, "You have nothing to worry about, sir."

"Good. Maybe we're getting hot in the britches over nothing, huh?"

"Perhaps, sir."

"Anything else, Broderick?"

"No sir. Please call me when you land. Have a good flight."

"Thank you," Kramer replied, then ended the call.

Broderick glanced at his watch then folded his cell phone and put it in his pocket. "Just one twist of Lassiter's scrawny neck . . ." he said with a hushed voice. "That's all I will need."

Jones, standing nearby, asked, "Did you say something?"

Broderick rubbed his forehead briskly, pinching the skin above his eyebrows. "No. Come on, let's get moving. We only have a couple of hours before Kramer gets here. We need to find Lassiter ASAP. It's payback time."

CHAPTER NINETEEN

Victoria Brookshire (that was, in fact, her real name) had joined the CIA in 1995, fresh out of graduate school at the University of Oxford, not far from Swindon, England, where her American father and British mother had lived since she was in elementary school. She had been the perfect female recruit for the agency. She had a BA in Political Science and MS in International Relations. She knew some Spanish and spoke Russian fluently, and had even studied Farsi and Persian culture. She'd been a "military brat," the daughter of an Air Force general who had served as commanding officer of several bases in Europe, mostly in England. She was well accustomed to the sacrifices of serving one's country, including uncompromising commitment, low pay, frequent relocation, and personal sacrifice. She was also beautiful, and this uncommon beauty had served her well in the CIA, both domestically and as an international operative working on several of the agency's most clandestine activities.

Her first couple of years with the CIA had focused on learning how to create Analytical Estimates, the carefully prepared assessments and forecasts of future activities of both friendly and hostile countries around the world. And after just three years with the agency, she had become a highly respected operative and member of an elite group of agents—what the CIA refers to as "Gray Men." Gray Men are dedicated and well-educated. On assignment, they draw little attention to themselves and complete their missions with precision and discreetness at all costs. In short, they can be trusted to accomplish what they are ordered to do, even under the most trying circumstances.

Her early success in assisting with the creation of Analytical Estimates, and her experience living overseas, prepared her for a highly critical position with the CIA, on a Special Collection Element team based in London. Special Collection Elements are groups of three to four CIA and National Security Agency personnel. They're positioned in U.S. embassies around the world and are critical to America's intelligence operations. In some countries, they are essentially the only means of collecting solid information on a continual basis. For this reason, when relations are strained with a country, the embassy is usually the first thing to be closed. Thus, intelligence gathering becomes extremely difficult at the most critical times.

The National Security Agency also praised Victoria's work. In recent years she had spent much of her time in support of the NSA, working with a select inner circle of intelligence officers. She was exposed to extremely sensitive secrets and plans of the U.S. and other countries. NSA operatives are responsible for breaking communication codes and intercepting foreign intelligence critical to the President's ability to staying a jump ahead. They're capable of deciphering most of the sophisticated coding methods used by other countries. To accomplish this, the NSA employs over thirty thousand people, spread around the globe at listening posts and in the Fort Meade headquarters in Maryland, where Victoria occasionally worked. She'd recently been told that, even with the cold war long over, there were still more than a thousand personnel dedicated to Soviet intelligence at Fort Meade alone, armed with listening equipment aimed from orbiting satellites, which intercepted communications and relayed them for processing. Hundreds of people were also dedicated to intercepting communications in the Middle East.

The CIA's recruitment of Victoria had largely been driven by her academic studies in the area of international relations and nuclear arms proliferation. Her college thesis had, in fact, fallen into the hands of the CIA well before she was ever recruited—*Nuclear Weapons Deployment and Control: Past, Present, and Future*. One area of the thesis, which received considerable attention at the CIA, was a section in which she correctly predicted the downfall of the Soviet Union before 1993. Of particular interest was a section in which she discussed the ramifications and risks of such a major historic event on the proliferation of nuclear weapons. She described the danger of strategic weapons located at sites in Russia, Ukraine, Kazakhstan, and Belarus, and warned that there would be considerable risks if the Soviet Union broke up. She wrote that this would hasten the spread of sophisticated weapons to the Middle East, the Indian subcontinent, and other world trouble spots. Her thesis also clearly demonstrated to the CIA that she had a solid understanding of nuclear arms limitation treaties. One of the most important agreements on arms control, which she wrote extensively about, was the Nuclear Nonproliferation Treaty of 1968. Signatories pledged to restrict the development, deployment, and testing of nuclear weapons to ensure that weapons, materials, and technology would not be transferred to non-nuclear states.

She also described, with perfect accuracy, the Limited Test Ban Treaty of 1963 that banned the United States, Great Britain, and the Soviet Union from testing nuclear weapons in the atmosphere, underwater—or in space. And she discussed at length the Outer Space Treaty, signed in 1967 between the same nations, which was supposed to limit the military use of outer space to reconnaissance only. In this treaty, the deployment of nuclear weapons in orbit was expressly prohibited (such as military installations or weapons on celestial bodies, such as the moon, and the placing in orbit of objects carrying nuclear weapons of mass destruction). Even a completely defensive implementation of the Strategic Defense Initiative, as was touted to the American people in '83, or the more recent Defend America Act (introduced in the Senate by Bob Dole as S.1635 shortly before his resignation), which mandated that a national missile defense be deployed by the year 2003, violate the treaty. In recent years the United States, Russia, France, India and Israel have all developed missile defense systems, with none of the systems providing adequate protection from an incoming long-range ICBM. Instead, most of the research and development has concentrated on creating "theater missile defense" systems to defend a country against short and medium-range missiles, such as Israel's Arrow system and Iron Dome.

Victoria, in her thesis and numerous times since becoming an agent, had made her opinion of the U.S. disregarding treaties widely known. She deplored the U.S. breaking agreements at will and feared that it would lead to other countries tossing their agreements and commitments aside. It was for this reason that her superiors had kept her in the dark in regard to the nuclear-armed satellite. If deployed, it would be completely illegal and in violation of the treaties.

No one knew quite how she had obtained much of the information for that college thesis she had written. Most astonishing was the section in which she provided details of the CIA's ongoing effort to refine the highly sensitive Single Integrated Operation Plan. SIOP serves as the ultimate war plan for the Department of Defense—nuclear war with the Soviet Union. Victoria didn't know it, but SIOP had recently been expanded and revised—nuclear war with Iran or North Korea.

CHAPTER TWENTY

Tom finished his first glass of '87 Beringer White-Zinfandel and started on a second. Victoria must have a hell of a lot of messages, he thought as he gazed out the window and watched the surf pound the beach. The rhythm of the waves rushing in, then slowly retreating, seemed to relax his mind. Spotlights, mounted atop the restaurant's wood-shingled roof, were aimed at the beach and made the tiny bubbles and sea foam sparkle in the evening air.

A few minutes later Victoria finally rushed back to the table. "Sorry I took so long, dear. I had a rather long-winded message from my boss, and there was quite a line in the restroom. I sincerely hope that someday a woman will design restrooms, for women," she added as she squeezed behind his chair, rubbing his shoulder. Her touch sent a chill down his spine.

"I hope you don't mind. I've been hitting the wine without you," he said as he reached over and pulled the chair out for her. The legs of the chair skipped across the floorboards, making a stuttering sound.

"Of course not. California wine? I don't drink that often," she said as she read the foil label, then hung her purse on the back of the chair. She carefully sat down, holding her skirt against her legs as she rotated toward the table, then moved forward a few inches.

"Care for some?" Tom reached over and picked up the bottle.

"Yes, that would be nice. Thank you, Tom." She pinched the stem of her glass and moved it closer. He poured it to within a half-inch of the brim and said, "So tell me, is this the first time you've been to Kennedy Space Center?" He set the bottle down.

"No, I've visited a couple of times before, but I've never seen a shuttle or rocket launch. I'm really looking forward to it. It's supposed to be a spectacular sight."

166

"I've heard the same. They say the entire sky turns a pinkish white and there's an eerie crackling noise for several seconds. It's too bad—" he said, then abruptly paused, realizing that the wine was making him a bit too loose-lipped. He was about to say that it's too bad there wouldn't be a launch to see. He fully intended for it to be called off after news of the High Ground payloads hit televisions and newspapers around the world. He hesitated for a second or two, feigning the sudden need to clear his throat, trying to think of something suitable to finish his sentence, then he continued, "It's too bad that more people can't see such a technical achievement, though the glory days of NASA seem to be in the past now. At least in regard to manned space flight."

"Come now, Tom. That's not what you were going to say, now is it?"

He lifted his glass and took a long thoughtful sip, trying to buy time, then swished the wine around his mouth like a connoisseur in deep analysis. He wondered whether he should trust her with what he and James knew. He thought that her company, British Space Systems, would probably be directly impacted by their blowing the lid off the High Ground program. He assumed that, at a minimum, British Space Systems would lose its Pentagon and NASA contracts for at least the near term, and maybe even forever. He thought to himself, *What if she tells someone before we get the story out and blows the whole thing?*

She watched him as he swished the Zinfandel about some more and turned away, staring out at the waves. She knew he was stalling; his performance, the wine aficionado routine would be pitiful even to a lesser-trained eye.

"Tom, what were you really going to say?" She reached over and touched his hand, rubbing slowly. It was still damp from the wine bottle.

He exhaled loudly. The touch of her soft skin weakened him. Everything about her weakened him. He rotated himself toward her. The sparkle in her eyes put forth the final blow. Perhaps he could trust her.

167

"You're right, that's not what I was going to say," he finally confessed.

She gently stroked his arm. "Go on, dear. What's the matter?"

He looked around the restaurant thinking, *Damn, where's a waiter when you need an interruption.* "Well, Victoria, what I'm going to tell you is highly sensitive and—"

"Tom, I think we know each other well enough, don't you?" she said coyly, apparently referring to their escapade in London. They had made love for three hours, ending up strewn across the top of Victoria's baby grand piano. Tom's knees and back were still sore, and he could still hear the piano occasionally playing its own music, the piano strings randomly vibrating with his and Victoria's movement.

"Yes," Tom replied on cue, agreeing with her that they indeed knew each other quite well. And he wanted nothing more in this world than to get to know her even more, piano or no piano. He sipped some more wine into his big reporter mouth. His lips were beginning to get even larger from the wine's acidity. He was trying to anesthetize his concerns about telling her what he knew.

"Yes. Yes of course." He put the glass down and looked her square in the eyes. "And I trust you with my life. But what I know involves a very serious situation. I don't want anything to happen to you, you know, with British Space Systems and your position there. And I want you to be safe. You're really better off not knowing anything about what James and I have gotten into."

"Tom, I insist. I'll be just fine. You'll have me wondering all evening what you were going to say. That's not nice now, is it? Let's focus on each other tonight."

With that, his decision on whether to spill the beans was made. "All right, but just promise me you won't repeat what I'm about to tell you. Not to anyone."

"Of course," she said, then touched his cheek with the back of her hand.

He poured more wine (if this kept up he figured he would need to check into the Betty Ford clinic by Saturday). He took a deep breath then said, "Well, you obviously know that tomorrow's launch is for a Department of Defense mission."

"Yes."

"Do you know what is being launched?"

"No. Only that it's some sort of satellite for the military."

Tom continued, "But you don't know what it is for?"

"No, Tom. I swear, I don't know anything about the mission."

"Well, what they are launching," he continued, then looked around the table to make sure no one was staring or listening, "are two satellites for the Pentagon."

"Two?"

"Yes. And we think that one of them is some sort of advanced spy satellite, capable of seeing objects, or perhaps targets, through any weather, day or night."

She nodded. This wasn't news, it was just another spy satellite. "And the other?"

"The other," he answered in a whisper, "and I know this is hard to believe, is a weapon, a space weapon, armed with nuclear missiles of some sort." He rubbed his forehead then gulped down some more wine.

There was a long pause. Victoria thought to herself, *Could he be right?* She then said in a hushed voice, "My god, Tom. Nuclear?"

"Yes. It's all part of a program they're calling High Ground."

She suddenly became pale. She placed a hand over her mouth and shook her head slowly left and right.

"Are you okay?" Tom asked with concerned eyes.

"Yes. I, I—"

"I know this must be a shock, since your company is involved in the program."

"What?"

"The tiles. The heat tiles. They're all over the satellite and the missiles."

She nodded slowly, her head tilted down as if ashamed. She stared at her glass, thinking. "Good lord," she uttered under her breath.

"You swear you don't know about this?"

"I swear, Tom. This is the first I've heard about the payload. It's, it's hard to believe. I'm shocked."

"I wouldn't believe it myself, if I hadn't have seen the pictures with my own—"

"You have pictures of the satellites?" Victoria interrupted as she turned to him with big eyes.

"Yes. James and I are going to release them with a story tomorrow, a few hours before the launch. You can't say a word, Victoria. Promise me."

She ignored his request and immediately asked, "But how in the world did you get pictures? You know, with all the security." She finally picked up her glass. She almost swallowed its pink contents in one gulp.

"Want some more?" he offered.

"Yes. Lots."

"You're better off not knowing where we got them, believe me. I don't want you knowing anything else. It could be used against you."

She pressed on. "So where are the pictures? May I see them?"

Finally, a waiter approached. "Ready to order?"

They hadn't even looked at the menus. Tom's appetite seemed to have escaped all at once. He told the waiter, "Just bring a couple of dinner salads, for starters, oil and vinegar dressing is fine. We haven't decided on the main course yet."

"Very well."

This, Tom hoped, would at least keep them from being kicked out of the restaurant, and buy some more time.

The waiter jotted down the order as if it was so complicated he would forget it, then flipped his braided ponytail over his shoulder and walked away.

Tom turned to Victoria. "Well, the pictures are hidden away, in my motel room," he continued, intentionally not mentioning that some of the pictures had already been flown to D.C., given to a courier, and delivered to the *Post*. The plain brown envelope was probably already sitting on his desk, waiting for him to call and direct someone to open it in the morning.

"Tom, you're absolutely positive it's a nuclear-armed weapon?"

"Yes, I'm positive."

There was almost a minute of silence as his words sunk in. Victoria peered out the window and watched the waves with glassy, still eyes (we're talking no emotion whatsoever, an absolutely perfect and gorgeous mannequin). She eventually turned toward Tom and picked up her glass again. She took another sip. A spray of dappled light filtered down upon her face from the halogen lamp high above the table.

"Victoria, I don't have to tell you what it could mean if the shuttle gets those two satellites launched, and the rest of the world finds out that we're placing nuclear weapons in space, especially over the Middle East."

"You are sure they are going to be placed above the Middle East?" she asked. "How do you know?"

"I just know. We have sources. Those satellites will be hovering over Iran, if the launch proceeds. And you know what could happen. That could be the match that lights the fire. Iran will take some sort of action, probably retaliating against the U.S. and Israel."

"Publishing a story will surely alert them, Tom. It could make matters worse."

"Not if James and I stop them from launching. And frankly, there's no way the government can keep a secret like that for very long. It will come out sooner or later. May as well be sooner, before they are launched."

The waiter brought the salads over. He set them down and walked away without a word.

Tom continued, "That's why James and I flew over to London. There's really no story on NASA subcontractors," he said at length. "I'm sorry we lied to you, Victoria. We were there for one reason, just to get more information on this launch. And I had to disappear for a while, out of the U.S., out of D.C. especially."

"Why?"

"There was an incident, at the Pentagon. I was interviewing a General in charge of the High Ground program and, well, I'd rather not

171

tell you the details right now about what happened. It will all come out in the story."

She scooted back from the table, not looking well, then moved her right hand to her stomach. "Tom, do you have any other proof?" She pushed her wine glass away and grabbed the ice water. "You know, aside from the pictures?" She took a drink, and nervously chomped on a couple of ice cubes.

"Yes, I have a file, also hidden back at our motel, that I, well, let's just say I borrowed it from the Pentagon," Tom answered, then immediately realized he had said more than he wanted to. He figured he may as well tell her all the gory details at this point.

"Borrowed?"

"I stole it."

"I see," she said in disbelief. "What's in it?"

"Some sort of map of Kennedy Space Center, an illustration of the shuttle Atlantis, and—"

"What kind of Illustration?" she interrupted.

"We think it's intended to show where the two satellites are to be placed inside the payload bay."

Victoria rubbed her forehead hard then asked, "But the shuttle program is over. As you know, all the shuttles are at museums in the U.S."

"Not the Atlantis," Tom continued. "The Atlantis is right here at Kennedy Space Center. And it was the last shuttle to fly, back in July of 2011. So it's the most flight-ready shuttle in the fleet. Yeah, it's for the Kennedy Space Center museum alright, but it is clearly on standby for this flight, and perhaps for future emergency missions to the space station. I think that Atlantis is NASA's backup plan. Something to call on if needed for a special payload, or astronaut rescue from the space station."

"But how can the Pentagon keep a shuttle launch secret?" Victoria asked. "That's impossible. Once it is launched, everyone will know what it is."

"Of course. But they won't know what is in it. And the government can just say it is just one more highly classified launch."

172

Victoria nodded. "Was there anything else in the Pentagon file?"

"There are a few letters, or memos, but most of the information is blacked out." Tom poured another glass of wine.

"Was there anything written on the illustration? Anything else to corroborate that they will launch the satellites for placement above the Mid East?"

"Yes. There was a bunch of numbers. Drawing numbers, or document control numbers, I guess. But what really got our attention was a small box to the left of the illustration. It said *Iran/Geosynchronous*, and I forget what else."

"Iran? It actually stated Iran on the payload illustration?" she asked, then inhaled and exhaled deeply.

"That's right."

"Geosynchronous, geosynchronous" she repeated slowly, then gazed out the window again.

Tom continued, "It's apparently an orbital position, twenty-four thousand miles up. Satellites at that altitude apparently stay over the exact same geographic location, even as the Earth rotates."

She turned to him and nodded. She, of course, was intimately familiar with such satellites.

"Are you okay?" he asked, then reached over and caressed her back lightly while staring into her glistening, damp eyes.

She didn't answer with words. She looked down for a few seconds, sniffling and shaking her head slowly, then once more raised her eyes to his.

Before she could say anything to him he whispered to her, "You know, I think I could look into your eyes for the rest of my life."

She blushed and attempted to smile, then wiped a tear from her left cheek. She could tell that Tom desperately wanted to kiss her.

Twenty minutes later, after much lighter conversation, she looked at her watch. Her face immediately dropped, and her forehead wrinkled. She drank some more water then turned to Tom, who was attempting to eat at least some of the salad he had ordered. She cleared her throat and said, "Tom, would you excuse me again?"

"Do you want to leave?" He poured the last drops of Zinfandel into his glass, then looked at her. Both of them had all but lost their appetite.

"No, please, you keep eating. Finish your salad," she answered as she stood and pushed her chair in. "I just want to freshen up again."

He wiped his mouth with a cloth napkin, wondering how much freshness she could possibly obtain from a restaurant bathroom, given that this would be her second visit of the evening. She seemed pretty darn fresh already, in his opinion. He folded the napkin and placed it back on his lap.

"I'll just be a minute."

"Okay." Tom watched her walk toward the restaurant lobby and the restrooms.

The cocktail waitress, thank god, wasn't talking to Fernando as Victoria approached the pay phone near the restrooms, then pulled the piece of paper with Broderick's cell phone number from her purse. She nervously slid her credit card through, punched in the numbers, and waited for him to answer. Her hands began to shake again.

"Hello. Broderick here."

"Broderick, it's Victoria," she said as she put the piece of paper and credit card back in the purse, then looked behind and all around her.

Broderick got right to the point. "What does Lassiter know?"

"I'm fine. How are you?"

"Uh, sorry. It's just that Kramer has been calling me every thirty minutes for an update. He's on his way down there. I'm a bit jumpy."

"Yeah? Me too." There was silence for several seconds. "Well, I'm afraid you won't like my news, Broderick."

"What? What did he say?"

More silence. Her heart was pounding and her hands were becoming clammy. She knew that what she was about to say would forever change her life. She could either lie, and protect Tom, or she could tell Broderick the truth, do her job, and save her career—business as usual, and another step up the slippery CIA ladder.

"Are you there, Victoria?"

174

"Yes, sorry. Someone walked by," she replied, her voice noticeably shaky. She swallowed another breath, trying to calm herself, and said, "Lassiter doesn't know anything."

"What? He has to know something?"

"Well, he just said that his paper received a prank phone call a few days ago. And he mentioned that he obtained a file that, at first, he thought was significant—I think that's how he said it—but he determined it wasn't anything earth shattering after all. He said he was almost fired for running off to Europe, and chasing false leads. Broderick, I think he's a bit off his rocker, as he said he believes the government is trying to get him. He seems very frightened. Says he just wants to go home to D.C., or maybe take some vacation time, something about a condo in Hawaii. I think he mentioned Maui. Anyway, I don't know what you were worried about. Lassiter's afraid of his own shadow."

"You think so?"

"Yes. Definitely."

"That's all he said?"

"Well, he did mention that he and his assistant Mr. Clemens are looking forward to seeing the rocket launch tomorrow, and that he'd never seen one before. And he talked about his two daughters throughout most of dinner. Broderick, I don't think he knows anything about what is being launched. I think we've just got a nervous reporter who did something he regrets, and thinks everyone's out to get him now. I don't know how anyone could take him serious. He's really quite bizarre."

"Okay, Victoria," Broderick said, then paused for a couple seconds. "All right. Good job. I'll let Kramer know right away."

She thought his voice sounded hesitant. "Anything else, Broderick? I really should get off here," she continued, again wanting to cut him off before he could ask what restaurant she and Tom were at, though she assumed he was tracing the call. She needed to get away from the phone, and fast.

175

"Uh oh, Lassiter's walking over. I need to go," she whispered, then thought, Lord, surely he'll realize I used the same interruption routine twice this evening.

"All right," he replied. "Check in tomorrow morning, in case we need you."

Indeed, the call was definitely being traced, she told herself. This was too easy. "Right, sir. Goodnight." She hung up then leaned her head against the wall to the left of the phone. She managed another deep breath and wondered whether she had just jeopardized her entire career, and maybe even her life. She tried to calm herself, *Okay, it's over. Maybe he believed me. I did the right thing. I know I did the right thing. We have to get out of here.* She snapped her purse shut and lifted it from the shelf.

Tom watched as she barreled around a corner and almost knocked over a waitress. He could see that she was upset as she approached. Her eyes were reflective, face blushed, and she was wearing a frown. He looked up at her and asked, "What on earth's the matter?"

"Tom, we have to go. Hurry." She reached behind him and grabbed her jacket from the back of her chair, then slipped it on.

"What's wrong?" he asked as he stood.

"No time. Come on, I'll tell you outside. Please hurry."

He pulled his billfold from his back pocket, then removed two twenties and threw them on the table. When he turned, Victoria was already halfway to the restaurant exit, looking back at him and motioning with her left hand. He caught up with her and they walked outside.

"How was dinner, sir, ma'am?" valet boy number one asked.

"Just great," Tom replied.

"Good. Could I have your claim check please?" he said, as if he didn't already know that the rusted rental Taurus was theirs.

Tom searched his pockets. "Um, where the hell did it go." He looked up at the kid and said, "It's that Taurus right there." He pointed. "Next to the Ferrari."

"Which one?"

"Hell, I don't know. That one, right there." More pointing.

"I gotta have the ticket, sir."

"Hurry," Victoria said again as she searched the parking lot with a roving stare. She seemed to be checking each car, to see if anyone was watching.

Tom finally found the claim check and handed it to the kid.

"It will just be a few minutes, sir."

"Just give me the keys."

"I can't—"

Tom grabbed him by his shirt and pulled him closer. "Keys. Now."

"Okay, dude. Chill." He turned around to a pegboard with dozens of keys and scavenged for the matching numbered tag. "Here they—"

Tom took the keys from his hand and batted him out of the way. Victoria ran to the car. He followed right on her heels. He stuck the key in the lock and opened the doors. They jumped in, started the engine, then sped out of the parking lot.

"What the hell's going on? What're you looking for?" he asked, seeing her twist to the left, looking out the rear window. He felt like they had just robbed a bank and bullets were sure to spray the rear window any second.

She turned around then placed her left palm over Tom's mouth. At first he struggled to speak, but then realized what she was doing. She slowly pulled her hand away and held her right index finger up to her lips. Under her breath she said, "Shush ."

He nodded his silent response, looking completely confused and rattled, and continued driving straight ahead, toward the south. He didn't say a word, but kept glancing over at her.

They approached what appeared to be a parking area, or possibly a viewpoint for the beach. Victoria pointed toward the entrance and Tom pulled in. He swung into a parking spot next to an overflowing trash can. He couldn't see any cars or people around. Victoria opened the passenger door and got out before he had even turned off the engine. She slammed the door and walked away from

177

the car and down a steep dirt path. Tom got out and had to run to catch up with her. He could hear waves crashing on the beach. He waited for a few seconds, wanting her to say something first and let him know it was okay to talk now. But she remained quiet and kept walking briskly to the beach, not even looking up.

She stopped for a moment and pulled her high heels off. Tom couldn't wait any longer. He gently reached for her arm and asked, "What was that all about?"

She glanced over her shoulder, to the parking lot. No one seemed to be following. "Here. Let's sit down over here." She ambled over to what appeared to be an area of clean, dry sand, about twenty feet away.

"We need to talk, Tom." She sat down, then reached up to him with her right hand. "I'm sorry for all that. I thought someone might try and follow us, and that the car might be bugged. I'm sorry."

He sat down next to her, speechless and breathing hard. "Car bugged?" He looked her straight in her eyes and, although it was quite dark, saw an intensity that hadn't been there earlier. He became even more worried.

She squeezed his hand more firmly. "Tom, I'm trusting you with my life, and my career, though I'm not sure if it really matters to me at this point. You must promise not to tell anyone what I'm about to tell you."

He watched as she set her shoes down on the sand to her left and turned more directly toward him. He nodded, not blinking even once.

"But first I want to tell you why I'm trusting you."

She paused and gazed out at the waves apparently, Tom thought, trying to think of the right words for whatever she was about to drop on him.

"Yes, go on," he told her. He saw a tear roll slowly down her cheek. It sparkled, catching a sliver of light from the evening sky. He let go of her hand, reached up, and gently wiped it away.

"Tom," she continued as another tear formed. "I, I believe I could fall in love with you," she whispered just over the sound of the waves. "I'm developing very strong feelings for you, and within a very short period of time." She turned and looked at him. He started to open his mouth and tell her that he felt the same way about her, but she continued.

"Please, dear, let me finish," she said, looking into his eyes. "The day at the museum, and evening with you at my flat in London, was magical. I know this sounds strange. We hardly know each other. It's crazy really. I can't explain why I feel this way. Only that I do. I've never felt a connection like this with anyone before. And I've never felt like you make me feel."

He gently picked up her hand and held it to his lips, then kissed gently. "I feel the same way about you. You know I do. *That's* what you feel." A few more kisses. "But why are you crying? And why did we have to rush out of the restaurant? Why would anyone follow you?"

There was silence as she again searched for the right words. None came. Just more tears.

"Please, go on, Victoria."

"I've betrayed you, Tom."

"What?"

"I've lied to you, and probably jeopardized everything we could have had together," she said, wiping her eyes.

"What are you talking about?"

The tears were now streaming down. Her chin quivered as she said, "I'm with the CIA, Tom," then stared at him and waited for his reaction, some clue as to whether he would still care for her, trust her, and believe in her.

He said nothing at first, then said, "CIA?" His eyes, too, became moist. He turned his head away and faced the ocean. He couldn't believe what he was hearing. Here he was, with the first woman he had let himself get close to in years, and she worked for the CIA. Apparently, he assumed, for or with the nice folks who chased him the other night back in D.C., trying to run him off the road.

He turned back to her, his mind racing through the past few days. "So this is all just a game to you?" he said slowly, shaking his head. "I'm just part of the game? Part of the job? London, it was just an act?" He turned away again.

She tried to pick up his hand but he pulled it sharply away. "No, Tom, you're not just part of the job. I meant every word I said, that night, and just now. I care deeply about you. I want to spend time with you, and get to know your heart. I would never do anything to hurt you. That's why I had to get you away from that restaurant, in case they're trying to find you and—"

"So the CIA is behind what happened to me?"

"What are you talking about? What happened?"

"A few nights ago, after I took that file from the Pentagon, a couple guys in a van followed me from work and ended up chasing me. I swerved off the road and lost them, almost hitting a tree head on."

"My god." She touched his hand again.

"Who knows what they would have done if they had caught me."

"I know nothing about that, Tom, I swear. Please believe me."

He shook his head and again said, "CIA? But you're British. How can you be an agent?"

"I'm a U.S. citizen. I've lived in the UK for most of my life. My father was in the Air Force. We were stationed over there." She paused, wiping her eyes with the back of her hand. "The CIA has sent me on several assignments to the UK recently, and they—"

"So you have nothing to do with British Space Systems?" he interrupted.

"No. Nothing. They arranged for me to act as the Director of Communications, just for your visit." There was silence again as they stared at the waves. She continued, "Tom, I never expected to get close to you." Another tear rolled down her cheek. "And I had no idea about what they tried to do to you, or how serious the situation is. I'm so sorry."

He turned toward her. "So you know all about the High Ground program—the satellites, the missiles? You were just pretending not to know back at the restaurant?"

"No, Tom, I swear I knew nothing about it until you told me. I know that tomorrow's launch is a D.O.D. mission, but they refused to tell me what the nature of it is. They were afraid to tell me. You see, I'm regarded as, well, somewhat of an expert on nuclear weapons proliferation."

Tom thought, *Wonderful. Girl of my dreams. CIA. Nuclear weapons. What's next?*

"I think they were afraid I would be opposed to the launch, and probably to the entire program."

"And are you?" he asked.

"Yes, I'm scared to death about what will happen if that launch goes forward. They're right, I would have been against it."

"It's just hard to believe that you wouldn't know anything about High Ground," he continued, again looking her straight in her eyes, trying to detect any sign of hesitation.

"I know it is. It's hard for me to believe that they've kept me out of the loop on this whole thing. But I'm telling you the truth, I've had nothing to do with the program. Please, Tom, you must believe me."

He thought she seemed sincere. Why else would she be telling him all this? He asked, "What about other D.O.D. programs? Are you aware of other projects?"

"Yes. I'm sure you've heard about the Defend America Act from a few years ago, right?"

"Yes. But I thought that program was dead, or on hold?"

"No, it's downsized and not spoken about, but not dead. And that's the only program I know about. And I'm only familiar with a few details of what is planned. I know about the laser-armed 747 aircraft they've secretly been working on again. It's supposed to be for defensive purposes only. And I think they're working on some ground-based lasers, as well as some sort of conventional ground-to-air missiles."

"That's all."

"Yes." She shifted her eyes, gazing at the sea, then moved her hair over her right shoulder and looked down at the sand. "I'm so sorry,

Tom, for having to put on that whole act at British Space Systems, and for lying to you. Will you forgive me? I was just trying to do my job."

Another touch of her hand revealed to him that she was shaking now. He put his arm around her and pulled her close, then kissed her forehead. She trembled slightly. He took his jacket off and spread it out on the sand next to her. They positioned their backs slowly down against the cool sand and stared up at the stars. The sky had suddenly become remarkably clear. Victoria then sat up for a second and slipped off her coat and placed it over them like a blanket. They turned to their sides and held each other tightly. Neither uttered a word. The rhythmic sound of the waves—the water cascading forward over the beach, then retreating into the sea—eventually calmed their minds.

CHAPTER TWENTY-ONE

Tom twisted the key in the lock and pushed the door open to the motel room. The rusty security chain James had fastened, apparently in a feeble attempt at peace of mind, pulled free from the drywall and swung away, its two retaining screws dropping to the carpet in a cloud of white dust. He looked over at the TV. It was blaring some HBO boxing promo. Then he glanced at James, who was sound asleep, a pen resting loosely in his hand. James was hunched over and drooling out of the corner of his mouth, and his head and arms were draped across the pressed-wood desk before him. Tom wondered how he could possibly sleep through the noise of the TV.

Tom closed the door and walked over to the TV to turn the volume down. Somehow James sensed the sudden quietness. He jumped up and the chair flipped over backwards. Not seeing Tom yet, he moved his eyes over to the door and to the broken chain. His heart seemed to skip a couple of beats.

Tom started to speak, "James, I—"

James swung around. Tom thought he looked like he would have a heart attack any second. While tossing the pen at the desk, he yelled, "What's going on?"

"Calm down. All I did was walk in and—"

"And the chain just flew off, all by itself."

"Yeah. Pretty much," Tom answered as he made his way over, kneeled, and picked up the screws (they were only about half an inch long). He set them on the desk. He couldn't help but laugh. Regardless of what happened from here on out, the motel from hell would not soon be forgotten.

"Where have you been anyway? I thought you were coming back early to work on the story," James asked as he rubbed his eyes, then stretched his arms above his head.

"Something came up."

"Yeah, I bet. How is Victoria anyway?"

"Fine." Tom slipped his jacket off and shook it near the sink. Sand fell to the carpet.

"Sand? I'm here working my ass off on the story, while you're on some beach with a redhead?"

Tom hung the jacket up on one of those permanently attached clothes hangers, then turned around. "Working? You write in your sleep? Interesting." He grinned, sat down on the bed, and watched as James reached over to the desk, picked up three hand-written pages, then tossed them over.

"I guess you have been working," Tom continued as he picked them up and scanned the first page. A minute later he said, "Looks like a good start."

"Start?"

"Yeah. You need a little stronger lead-in, but it's pretty good."

James just shook his head and bent over to pick up the rickety chair he had knocked over. He sat down.

"Careful with the fine furniture. You'll lose our deposit."

"Yeah, whatever," he replied as he rested his elbows on the desk and rubbed his forehead with both palms. His heart rate was slowly returning to normal.

Tom softened his tone. "Are you okay?"

"Just tired, that's all." James coughed slightly, clearing his throat.

Tom rested himself on the bed. His thoughts turned to his daughters and his mom and dad back home. He reached for the telephone.

James asked, "Who are you calling?"

"Do we still have credit on this thing?"

"Yes, I gave the guy at the front desk another forty bucks."

Tom held the phone to his ear. "I'm calling home."

"This late?"

"My mom has trouble sleeping. She usually stays up until at least one every night." He looked down, hit 9 for an outside line, then punched in the number. The phone rang four times then, just before the answering machine would normally come on, the line clicked a few times.

"Yes," a male voice said.

Tom didn't recognize who it was. He asked, "Have I reached the Lassiter residence?"

He knew he had the right number, but he didn't know what else to say.

"Yes. Who's calling, please?"

"Who is this?" Tom couldn't hear anything. The person on the line was obviously stalling. "Hello?"

James walked over and Tom turned to him and pointed to the phone's speaker, urging him to listen in. James moved closer, placing his left ear near the handset.

"Hello, is anyone there?" Tom said into the receiver.

Finally, a voice came on, "Mr. Tom Lassiter, I'm afraid that your family is not available. But they are safe."

"Who the hell is this?"

"No one you know."

"I'm calling the police if you don't put them on immediately," he threatened, again not knowing what else to say. "You understa—"

"Mr. Lassiter, we know what you are trying to do. You will not be permitted to interfere with the national security of the United States. Do you understand?"

"If you even touch them, I swear I'll—"

"Come now, Mr. Lassiter. If you'll cooperate, no harm will occur. Not to anyone, I assure you. I must say, you have two very lovely daughters, especially the older one. Hayley is her name, right? Did her mother have such lovely red hair, and exquisite body? Quite a temper though and—"

"Look, asshole," Tom yelled into the phone, then became beet red and breathed even harder. "Just one finger on her and I swear I'll kill you. I'll find you and I'll kill you."

James moved a few feet away, staring at Tom and rubbing his forehead hard.

Tom continued, trying to control his emotions, "You can tell the CIA, and whoever else is involved in this, that *The Washington Post* is going to—"

"Mr. Lassiter, do you want to see your family again?" the voice interrupted.

"Do you want to see your colleagues at the CIA, NASA, and a general or two at the Pentagon brought down? Do you? Who do you work for? General Kramer?"

"That's not important right now. Mr. Lassiter, you and your associate are to meet two men in a tan Ford Explorer at the corner of Tropic and Hoover tomorrow at nine-thirty A.M. You will then be taken to your family and held until after the launch. A decision will be made at that time as to whether you can be trusted and let go, or incarcerated. Or perhaps other measures might be taken. Have I made myself clear?"

Tom noticed James motioning downward with his hands. In response, he nodded and immediately pulled the receiver away from his face, then carefully covered it with his palm.

James whispered, "I'm sure they're tracing the call. You better hang up. And I mean now."

"Are you there, Mr. Lassiter?" the voice blared from the speaker.

Tom held the phone up and said, "And if we don't follow your instructions, then what?"

"Quite simple. You will not see your family again. And you and your associate will also be disposed of. Now do you understand, Mr. Lassiter?" His voice seemed much too calm.

"Yes."

"Splendid, Mr. Lassiter. I hoped you would see it my way. Splendid. Now, do you realize the significance of—"

Tom slammed the phone down and turned to James, who looked like he was going to have a nervous breakdown. "The bastards have my family."

"I heard, I heard," James replied as he held a hand over his stomach. He started pacing.

"Do you think they were able to trace the call?" Tom asked.

"I don't know. But I'm not staying around to find out," James answered as he began to get his things together. He folded the draft of the story and stuck it in his pocket. "We need to get the hell out of Dodge. Maybe go to the FBI, I don't know. That guy was probably lying about wanting to meet us tomorrow. Why would they wait until then, so close to the launch? Why not meet us now? He was just trying to make us stay put, make us think everything is okay."

"I know."

Tom walked over to the closet and grabbed his jacket. He ran back over to the bed and lifted the corner of the top mattress. He stuck his hand in the hole he had made and pulled out the Pentagon file. "You have the pictures of the satellites, right?" he asked over his shoulder.

James nodded. "Yes."

Less than a minute later they drove out of the motel parking lot. They headed west, snaking in and out of traffic as fast as they could for three miles. "Okay, slow down. I don't see anyone behind us," James said, twisting his neck sideways and looking out the rear window. He turned forward, fastened his seat belt, then took a deep breath. "My god, they have your family. Maybe we should just turn ourselves in, you know. This has gone too far."

Tom didn't say a word. He made a sharp right and entered the onramp for 408. They drove for a while, continuing westward, then he broke the silence and turned to James. "I have to tell you something."

"Great, now what?"

"It's about Victoria."

"I'm listening."

"I learned something about her tonight."

"Yeah, yeah, I saw the sand . . ."

"James, she's with the CIA. She's an agent."

James turned slowly to his left, raising his eyebrows. "This isn't a time for joking around."

"I know, James."

"You're serious?"

"Yes."

"You have to be kidding. What about her position at British Space Systems? What about the—"

"I know, I know. It was all a setup."

"But how?"

"They obviously found out we were heading over to British Space Systems. Hell, I don't know how."

"So she's been feeding them information, working against us?"

"No. I don't think so."

James turned away and mumbled to himself, shaking his head slowly left and right and looking out the passenger window. "Of course she's an agent. Why not? What else would she be? Of course."

"James, I'll think of something. Don't worry," Tom continued, changing lanes.

"I'm telling you, we need to go to the FBI, man. You hear me?"

"Quiet, I'm thinking. Give me a minute." He leaned forward and looked up at a sign, *Orlando/West*. He made another lane change, then heard a horn honk. Then another, but longer.

James jerked his head left, trying to see who it was.

"Is it a cop?" Tom asked as he also twisted his head to the left. He couldn't see the car. It was in a blind spot.

"I don't know. It could be. Looks like a black Mustang 5.0."

Tom slowed a bit and glanced at the speedometer (they were only doing sixty) then looked out the window to his left. He could see the car now. The driver was waving his right arm up and down and yelling something. Tom's heart sunk further into his chest and his nerves seemed to fire all at once. But then he realized what the driver was yelling—"Lights, lights, lights." He reached forward and rotated the knob on the control stalk to the left of the steering wheel and turned them on. Then he waved and feigned a courteous smile at the man. He inhaled deeply and stretched his back as he watched him pull away and disappear into traffic. He moved his eyes to James, who was speechless.

Moments later, James reclined his seat, trying to get more comfortable and calm his nerves. He then looked at Tom. He could tell that he was deep in thought and apparently trying to come up with a plan. Finally, Tom turned to him and said, "James, you're somewhat of a computer expert. Right?"

"Expert?"

"You know, your degree in college, and you said you did some programming."

"Oh yeah, just call me Gates. Bill Gates."

"Tell me, is there some way you could set up a computer to automatically transmit an electronic message, unless a password is entered periodically, like once a week or something? You know what I mean?"

"Yeah, of course. Good god, what are you up to now?"

"What if we create a file?" He paused, passing a Shell fuel tanker, then glanced down at the gas gauge. It was half empty. "You know, a software file, which would include the story, details of everything that's happened, a copy of the papers in Kramer's file, and the pictures of the satellites. You can scan them in, right? Could you do that?"

"Yes. You just need a scanner to digitize the pictures and Kramer's stuff. And we could scan in the hand-written draft of the story too."

"You can do it fairly quickly?"

"Sure. It's no big deal."

"Could you put copies of everything on several computers, or servers at the *Post*, and setup a program that would automatically transmit the information to sites we designate? You know, like an email blast or fax broadcast to multiple numbers."

James nodded. "We just need to designate the host computer, or as many as you want. The designated hosts could fax or E-mail everything over the internet. No problem. In fact, I already have an eFax account which can do it, or we can use the servers at the paper."

"That's it then."

"That's what?"

"Our safety net. At least until we file the story, and become the world's most famous whistle-blowers, which is the only thing that will keep us safe long term. If you set up such a program and make it so a password—like an ATM password—has to be entered, say, once a week, they might just leave us alone. Are you following me?"

"Not really." James shook his head.

"If they lock us up, or worse, the password won't get entered, and the file will automatically be transmitted. Get it?"

"Yeah, I get it," James replied, rolling his eyes. "We might be in jail, or possibly even dead, but the story will come out anyway. That's your plan? Maybe you should keep thinking."

Tom slowed down for some traffic merging from an onramp. A Volkswagen Bug on a suicide mission darted over.

James continued, "I don't see why we can't get the story out right now, just fax it to UPI or Reuters or something. Then they won't have a reason to mess with us, right? It'll be a done deal."

"No. Like I said earlier, I want to announce everything just before the launch tomorrow. We don't know whether the satellites have been moved from the Staging Building and into the shuttle. We have to make sure they've been transferred to Atlantis before we break the story."

"I say we cover our ass right now, get it over with. I mean, what if they find us before your little live press conference."

Tom shook his head no. "We will just tell them about the file you'll have created. They may hold us, but I don't think they will hurt us, or my family. If they do, everyone will find out."

"Uh-huh, like I said, dead but famous."

Tom changed lanes. "Could you make it so we both have to enter passwords, say, by each Monday at noon, or the file gets transmitted?"

"Yeah, I think so. But where are we going to get access to a computer and a scanner at this hour?"

"I, I don't—"

"Wait, take the next exit," James interrupted, tilting forward and staring at a sign ahead.

"What? Why?"

"Hurry, just get over. University of Central Florida, next exit. We just need to find an office supply store or uh, you know, a FedEx Kinkos. Some of them have computer stations setup. They rent them by the hour, mostly to students. They're always near schools. We can scan everything in, and probably even get access to the internet. I'll set the file up remotely, on the mainframe at the paper. I have my access number right here in my pocket." James pulled his wallet out and removed a piece of paper.

Tom put the blinker on and moved to the right lane, then exited the freeway. The brakes squealed as the car slowed. "It's almost midnight. Do you really think something is open this late, especially a copy store?"

"Yeah, there has to be one around here somewhere. A lot of them are open twenty-four hours a day, the ones near colleges. How long has it been since you were in college anyway?"

"Too long, James, too long. Seems like another lifetime." Tom slowed some more and turned right at the light at the end of the exit ramp, then headed toward what appeared to be a main thoroughfare. He could see lights and signs a mile or two away. His thoughts shifted to his family, and for a moment he actually wondered whether it really would be better to just go to the FBI.

"James, do you think they'll hurt my family? They're all I've got."

"I doubt they'd do anything to them. They'll be okay," he replied, almost convincingly. "They know that your family is the only control they have over you right now. They'll be all right. In the morning we just need to get the word out on what's happened, and before the deadline for turning ourselves in, assuming that jerk on the phone was telling the truth. What time did he say to meet tomorrow, nine-thirty?"

"Yes."

"That gives us a little time anyway." James reached forward and shut off an air conditioning vent. "And if they try to pull something before then, we'll just tell them about this little file I'm going to setup. I have to admit, it's a pretty ingenious idea."

"Well, I hope so. We just need to get through the night, and get this whole thing over with," Tom said, looking over his shoulder and changing lanes. "I couldn't live with myself if something were to happen to my girls, or parents."

James nodded and his face suddenly became more serious.

Tom asked, "Do you want to call and check on your mom and dad?" He could tell that James was thinking about his family.

"You read minds, too?" A small smile appeared on James face.

"Occasionally."

"It's okay. I'll check on them tomorrow. I just remembered that they were going to head up to the vacation house in Nantucket. They should be okay there. I don't think anyone knows they're going."

"Good. Say, why don't I pull into this gas station. You can run in and ask if there's a copy store around here."

"Okay."

Tom swung a right and parked next to a glowing Chevron sign. He left the engine on as James walked over to the cash register booth, near a car wash.

"Excuse me, sir, are there any copy or office supply stores in the area?" James inquired.

In barely recognizable English, the gas station attendant answered, "Yeah, there are two, only a mile or so away. The closest is on the corner of Jefferson and Ninth Street, next to a McDonald's," he continued, then immediately looked down at a school textbook, flipping a page with a highlighter in his hand.

"Thanks." James went back to the car, got in, and shut the door. He said to Tom, "There's one down the street, next to a McDonald's."

"Now there's a landmark. We've only passed ten or twelve of them since we left Titusville."

The directions ended up being spot on. They found the copy store, parked, and quickly ran in. A kind-eyed Asian man greeted them wearing a red and blue Hawaiian shirt, brown polyester pants, and sandals that showcased his too-long toenails. A real GQ type.

The man said, "Evening, may I help you, gentlemen?" he set down a magazine.

"Yes, do you rent computer-time?" James inquired.

"Yes sir. We have two Dell workstations and each has an eight-core processor, scanner, and black and white laser printer. They are loaded with Word, Excel, Photoshop, and Internet Explorer. We have color printers for rent as well, ink jet or laser."

"Thanks. We don't need a color printer, but we'll rent a workstation."

"Very well. They go for ten dollars an hour."

"That's fine," James replied.

"Just follow me, right over here."

James and Tom walked behind their new friend Ralph Lauren to one of the two cubicles setup next to a storage area crammed with boxes of paper and envelopes. James gave him the money and they got to work.

Just ten minutes later and they had already scanned in the contents of the file, the draft of the story, and a few pictures of the satellites. James grouped everything into one PDF file, then asked Ralph how to log onto his internet service provider.

He replied with a frozen smile, "That'll be three more dollars, sir."

James forked over three bucks, and the man gave him the WiFi password to get online.

James launched Internet Explorer and made his way to a *Washington Post* web page, entered the employee access area, then typed in his password. He uploaded the PDF file to the mainframe computer, then set up some instructions that would fax and email the file to the newsrooms at the *Post*, UPI, and Reuters at exactly noon on each Monday, unless two six-digit passwords were entered. If anything happened to either James or Tom, the file would automatically be transmitted and the entire world would learn of the High Ground program. Not the greatest insurance, but better than nothing.

James hit a few more keys, smiled slightly, then moved his eyes to Tom, clearly proud of his work. "Okay, there we have it," he said, beaming. "You just need to type in a six-digit password, hit return, then re-enter it for confirmation." He moved away from the computer, wanting to avoid seeing the password Tom would type in.

"Six numbers, or letters?" Tom asked as he hunched over the keyboard.

"It doesn't matter."

Tom paused, trying to think of something to enter that he wouldn't forget. He typed in the name of the restaurant he and Victoria ate at in London, hit the return key, and re-entered it. "Okay, James, it says it's confirmed."

James turned around and entered another password, for his use. "All right, that's it. Do you want to try and put the file on any other servers?"

"Well—"

James interrupted, "I can upload it to my website server. But it might take a while to set it up there."

Tom thought for a few seconds and answered, "Well, the *Post* should be enough, don't you think?"

"I'd say so. I set it up on two different servers, located in two different buildings." James stood and looked at Tom. He immediately knew something was wrong. Tom was pacing back and forth, scratching the back of his head, obviously deep in thought.

"What's the matter?" James asked. "Now we've got something on them. They can't touch us without everything coming out."

Tom stopped and said, "Yes, but they may still launch."

James looked perplexed. "Even after we release the story in the morning?"

"It's possible," Tom replied, then paused for a few more seconds. "I'm concerned that we're cutting it too close, James." More pacing. "They might still go through with the launch, even with the story out. And by the time even a few politicians in D.C. get the word, and the importance of the whole thing sinks in, the shuttle might already be in orbit."

This wasn't news to James. He had made his opinion quite clear all along—that they should just get the story out ASAP.

The pacing again stopped. Tom turned to James and said, "Wait. Way, way, wait. Maybe we can make sure that they won't launch."

"How?"

"With a little help, a little pressure. Give me the file and the pictures."

James handed them to him.

Tom walked over to the store clerk and asked, "Do you have a fax machine we can use?"

The clerk nodded and pointed toward the front of the store, then strolled away, motioning for Tom to follow. Tom could see a combo copier-fax machine on a metal stand next to the window, just below a neon sign. "How about a phone?"

"Use this one," the clerk answered, then picked up a phone that was built into the fax machine and handed it over to Tom. "I'm afraid that will be three more dollars for domestic or ten more for international, sir. Sorry." He held out his hand, palm facing up.

Tom looked at James. "Do you have ten more bucks on you?"

James handed over the money. The clerk walked away, still smiling. Tom punched in a phone number.

"Who are you calling," James asked as he tucked his wallet away again.

"Information. International information."

Tom held the phone's receiver closer to his face. An operator came on. "May I help you?"

"Yes, please. May I have information in Moscow, Russia?"

"Yes sir. One moment."

James looked at Tom with a confused expression. "Russia?" he whispered. "What in the world are you—"

"Shush . . ."

The line connected and the operator came on with a thick accent, "Moscow information. May I help you?"

"Yes, operator, I'm trying to get the number for the Kremlin. Perhaps a Press Bureau or a main number."

"Please hold."

"Thank you."

A few seconds passed and the operator came back on. "Are you ready, sir?"

"Yes, go ahead." Tom grabbed a pen from a display rack nearby.

"Where are you calling from please?"

"The United States."

"The number is 495-771-81-00."

Tom scribbled down the number on the back of his hand. "You're sure this is for the Kremlin?"

"It's for the Ministry of Communications and Mass Media, sir." she replied.

"Thank you." Tom hung up and quickly called the number. A woman answered and he couldn't understand a word she was saying. He asked, "Have I reached the Ministry of Communications?"

She, thank god, said "yes" and switched to some resemblance of English.

He then asked, "Do you have a main fax machine?"

"Yes sir. The number is 495-771-81-21."

"8121?" Tom repeated.

"Yes sir."

"Thank you." Tom hung up and looked at James. "Okay, I have a number. It is supposed to be a fax machine at the Ministry of Communications and Mass Media in Moscow. I don't know if the fax will make it to the top, but it's worth a shot."

"Would you mind telling me what you're doing?" James asked.

"If the Pentagon doesn't stop the launch because of the story, maybe they'll stop it for Russia. I'm sure our Russian friends will be interested in what's being launched tomorrow. Right?"

James nodded. "Does your brain ever rest?"

"Okay, okay. Here we go." Tom pulled the Pentagon papers and pictures out of the folder and stuck them in the machine, then punched in the fax number.

James straightened them as they waited for the call to connect then said, "I don't know how well these pictures will come out on the other end though. And they may not even feed into the machine."

"Here, we'll use the gray scale mode." Tom pressed a button on the control panel. "That should help. And we'll just feed them in one at a time." He heard some clicking sounds, then the screech of the other fax machine. He hit the start button, set the phone down, and exhaled loudly as the first page began to pull in. Then another page. Moments later all of the pages, and two of the pictures, had been successfully transmitted to some machine in the Kremlin's Communications Bureau.

"All right, just to be safe, let's send a copy to the Editors' desk at the *Post*, to Tanya. It'll be waiting for her when she comes into work in the morning." Tom began to enter the number.

James was confused. "But we already sent pictures to the *Post*, via counter-to-counter service."

"Yeah, but she doesn't have the story yet. This is just to be safe, and make sure the *Post* gets the story directly from us. Here, I'll write a note and tell her to hold the story until one of us calls in." Tom removed the first page and wrote down some instructions to Tanya.

James placed the first page back into the machine, which Immediately started beeping. An LED flashed on the control panel. "Uh-oh."

Tom peered down at the paper feed. "Damn it, looks like it's jammed."

James shrugged his shoulders and said, "All I did was stick a page back in."

The store clerk seemed to appear from nowhere, as if this was the standard routine, and they half expected him to slap them with a ten dollar un-jamming fee, to which James fully intended on responding by slapping the little twit upside the head.

But the little guy just smiled and said, "I have to unplug the cord and reset the machine. Just a moment." He bent over in front of the machine and unplugged the electric cord from a power strip on the floor, then quickly stuck it back in. He began to stand up, moving slowly and mumbling something about his bad back.

And then It happened.

They heard a gunshot. Just one gunshot.

The store window before them shattered to a million shards of glass. Then more shots.

Tom yelled, "Down!"

They dropped to the floor and covered their heads. Glass was flying everywhere. The neon sign above them swung sideways, then fell to the floor. Bullets rained into the store from somewhere outside.

And then, just as abruptly, the gunfire stopped.

Tom looked up and discovered that the store clerk had been hit and was draped over the fax machine. He immediately knew what had happened—the clerk had taken a bullet intended for him, his body serving as a shield. With his heart pounding, Tom tried to think of what to do, then looked over at James. He was curled up in a ball, hands covering his head, and glass all over his back and sparkling in his hair. But he appeared okay. Tom reached up and lifted the clerk off the fax machine and carefully moved him to the floor. He had been hit in his left arm and, surprisingly, he wasn't bleeding very much and his eyes were open. "You're going to be okay, we'll go call for help," he told him. The clerk nodded slightly. Tom grabbed the papers and pictures from the fax tray.

James finally raised his head and looked over. He whispered, "Stay down!"

"Come on, let's head to the back of the store." Tom crawled to his left, over to a wall and away from the window. James followed, trying to keep from cutting his hands and knees on the glass. They both looked to the rear of the store and saw a door with an exit sign hanging above. They crawled toward it. Reaching the door, they stood, pushed it open, and ran outside.

"Which way?" James yelled over his shoulder.

"The right. Come on."

They ran down the alley, making it about ten yards, then a voice shouted from behind, "Freeze!"

They swung instantly around.

"Put your hands up."

Tom and James threw their hands high and watched as two men approached. They were dressed in dark suits and had guns drawn. Behind them, they saw another man exit the back door of the store. Several onlookers from the McDonald's next door walked over.

At least there will be witnesses, Tom thought, his heart still pounding mightily.

"Face down on the ground!" one of the men yelled as he moved closer. He seemed to be just as nervous.

James and Tom dropped to the pavement.

"Spread your arms and legs!" he continued, then tucked his gun in his shoulder holster and turned around. He said to the man approaching from the store exit, "Do you want us to take them, or put them in your car?"

"My car," Broderick replied, pointing down the alley. "And hurry, before the local donut munchers get here." His voice lowered. "Christ sakes, did you two really have to shoot through a damn window on a downtown street? I thought you had put a beacon on their car? They wouldn't have gotten far."

"Well, we saw them using the fax machine and—"

"Okay, okay. Just get moving," Broderick said as he approached. He seemed to study James and Tom. They were panting and out of breath and Tom's left knee was bleeding, creating a small puddle on the asphalt. "I guess your fun is up, huh boys," he said, peering down with satisfaction.

Handcuffs were slapped on tightly and they were jerked to their feet and pulled away by the other two men.

"Wait!" Broderick yelled, then walked over to Tom. "I believe you have something that doesn't belong to you. Where is it?"

Tom turned around. The file and pictures were tucked into the back of his pants, hanging halfway out.

Broderick grabbed them. "Here we go," he said calmly as he flipped through each one. "Pictures even? Lord, how the hell did you get these?"

Tom ignored the question and said, "You need to call an ambulance. The clerk inside the store was hit."

Broderick nodded once. He rolled the file and photographs up and stuck them in his coat pocket, then looked over to one of his men. "Okay, take them to my car. I'll be there in a second." He made his way back to the rear of the store, opened the door and went inside.

James and Tom were promptly escorted to the Ford Explorer and locked in the back seat. Tom turned and said, "We'll be okay. There were witnesses. Don't worry, James."

"This is insane, man. I don't want to end up like that clerk."

"We're not going to. Just stay calm." He thought James would pass out any moment.

Inside the store, the glass crunched below Broderick's shoes as he neared the fax machine. He stopped and looked down at the store clerk, who was holding his arm and staring upward. "Stay still, mister. We have help coming." He then moved closer, peered down at the control panel of the fax machine, and was immediately relieved to see that just an area code was showing in the small LCD display, 202—Washington D.C. The fax hadn't gone out to the *Post*.

"Got here just in time, just in time . . ." he whispered to himself. Then he pressed the re-dial button. A long string of numbers scrolled into the display. "Sons of bitches."

He immediately recognized the city and country code for Moscow, Russia.

"God help us." Broderick continued slowly, his words trailing off. The last thing the CIA or Pentagon needed right now was to explain a *Washington Post* reporter's allegations about a nuclear-armed space weapon about to be launched.

CHAPTER TWENTY-TWO

The first thing Tom noticed was the vibration beneath his feet, then the glow that illuminated the entire room where he and James were tied to two chairs. Quickly following the vibration, they heard a bellowing roar, which was almost deafening. Tom immediately knew what was happening. He swung himself around toward a window facing the launch pad. He could see a space shuttle, just barely moving away from the launch tower releasing it, skyward. The tower swayed back and forth as if it would self-destruct. Yellow, orange, then blue flames blasted down from the huge propulsion nozzles. They blew away from the platform in every direction, slowly dissipating into a black haze, then muted gray. Tom and James watched as the shuttle began to lift upward in a tug-of-war with gravity into the dark skies above Kennedy Space Center, hours before the previously announced launch time of the Atlas V rocket the public was expecting.

Tom yelled at the top of his lungs, "They can't be launching! It's not time," then stared through the window and watched the shuttle rise, higher and higher. The black sky transformed into pinkish-yellow and it seemed as if the sun had just risen.

"Is it the shuttle?" James asked, though he already suspected that it was Atlantis space shuttle, and not the Atlas rocket. He was sitting on the opposite side of the room, next to a metal table. He tilted forward, stood, and walked over to Tom with a folding chair dangling from his handcuffed arms, behind his back.

"The bastards launched early," Tom continued, his words immediately being swallowed by the noise.

The room vibrated and windowpanes rattled noisily in their old frames. Lights barely clung to the ceiling, swaying and flickering.

"But it's not supposed to go up until tomorrow," James said as he turned from the window, toward Tom.

Tom shook his head. "They actually got the satellites launched. They got the damn evidence up—my god, nuclear weapons in space. We didn't stop the launch, James." His eyes dropped to the tile floor in defeat. He sat down next to the window. The room was still aglow and shaking.

Suddenly Tom and James could hear a door fly open behind them, slamming against an adjacent wall.

"Going somewhere, Mr. Clemens?"

It was Broderick. He looked at James, who was still standing, then slammed the door and pulled a gun from his shoulder holster.

"Please sit down, Mr. Clemens."

He aimed the gun at James, then shifted his attention to Tom. "Is your boy here trying to escape, Mr. Lassiter? We can't have that now, can we?" He held the gun outward and slowly approached with a slight limp.

James placed his chair next to Tom and sat down. They watched as Broderick made his way over to them; he stopped just three feet away. His twisted face and intense eyes looked down. They could smell his breath and hear his breathing. He said nothing for several seconds. He just stared, coldly. Then he raised his arm and held the barrel of the pistol to James' head, between his eyes.

"Is this how the CIA operates these days?" James asked, his eyes fixed on the barrel of the gun.

"Shut up, boy."

"Don't call me *boy*, you son of a—"

Broderick turned to Tom. "What, you can't control your assistant, Lassiter?"

"I suggest you put your gun away," Tom replied, trying to stay calm.

"I *suggest* you go to hell, Lassiter."

There were a few seconds of silence then Tom continued, "Don't even think about messing with us any further. Understand? You'll all be exposed, from Kramer on down. You see, we have a little backup plan. Something to keep you in check."

Broderick's left eye twitched a couple of times. "Okay, Lassiter, I'll bite. What the hell are you talking about?" He pulled the gun away from James' head, but just a few inches.

"I'm talking about our insurance policy," Tom continued, weighing his words carefully.

"I'm listening."

"We've setup six computers—servers in different locations—to transmit the contents of the file you took from us, including pictures of the satellites the Pentagon just launched, and extremely thorough details of all the corrupt things you and your CIA friends have been up to," Tom continued, purposely lying about the number of computers James had setup.

"Sure you have."

"You better take it seriously, Broderick, if you want to avoid federal prison for the rest of your life. Unless we enter passwords into the computers once a week, everything automatically gets sent to *The Washington Post* and several news wire services."

He seemed remarkably unimpressed. He pondered Tom's words for a few seconds, then again moved the pistol closer to James' head. "And I'm supposed to believe you, huh?"

"That's your decision, and your risk. If you want to go to jail, see the CIA turned into a cold war relic, maybe even be closed down, then don't believe me. It's that simple," Tom said, staring up at Broderick's face and not blinking once. "Launching nuclear weapons over the Middle East? Is General Kramer crazy or what? Do you really think the American public would support this? Do you think they will support their government's decision on this, the President's decision? You may have just started world war three and—"

"First of all," Broderick interrupted, "don't assume that the President knows what was just launched, or understands what we are trying to do with those satellites. We're trying to prevent a nuclear war between Iran and Israel, not start a war."

"And you think that violating a long-standing treaty banning weapons in space, and placing nuclear-armed missiles above Iran is not going to ignite, at a minimum, a nuclear arms race over there, if not direct retaliation at the U.S.? It's absolutely insane," Tom said, his voice cracking a bit with emotion. He paused for a couple of seconds then asked, "So, were you in that van which chased me home the other night, and nearly ran me off the road?"

"We just wanted the file you took, Lassiter."

"And you would have let me be? Just taken the file and let me go?"

"Possibly."

"Sure you would have."

"Lassiter, you couldn't have proven anything without that file. Not in time to stop the launch anyway."

"Look," Tom continued, "I guess we both made some mistakes here. Right?"

Broderick nodded. "You could say that."

"But you can still save yourself, Broderick. You didn't pull the trigger back there at that copy store. I know that. But there were a lot of witnesses back in that alley who saw James and I get arrested and thrown in your car. If something happens to us, everyone will know you were involved, especially after the file is transmitted. And do you think *The Washington Post* will ever let this whole thing die down? I'm telling you, you can still save yourself. It hasn't gone too far yet, not for you anyway."

It had, of course, gone way too far. Tom was lying and he knew full well that Broderick probably wouldn't buy what he was saying. He had every intention of burning the bastard at the stake for what Broderick and his CIA and Pentagon colleagues had done. As far as he was concerned, when the shuttle took off a whole new nuclear arms race started. And maybe even worse. God only knows what the response would be from Iran's government, or from North Korea, which was also trigger happy and had threatened South Korea and the United States repeatedly. No doubt, North Korea's leadership would assume that the Pentagon was placing such satellites over their country too, and not just Iran.

Broderick licked his lips, subtly flared his nostrils a few times, and appeared to become more nervous, his eyes darting around the room. His breathing grew labored. After a few seconds he looked down, staring squarely at Tom's face and searching for any sign of hesitation. "An electronic file, huh? And it will automatically be sent out?"

"That's right."

There was another long pause then he said, "Well, I don't believe you, Lassiter."

His cell phone rang and he backed away quickly, stuck his pistol under his left armpit, then pulled the phone out and answered as he leaned against the metal table.

James and Tom listened as Broderick took the call.

"Broderick here. Yes, General Kramer, I saw the launch. Congratulations, sir. Yes sir, I have them at Kennedy Space Center. No, we're in the D.O.D. Logistics Facility, the main conference room. No. No one is around, and no one saw me bring them in. The place is empty. Yes, I know we'll have to get them out before morning. Well, I'm not sure what I'm going to do with them, sir. Like you said earlier, they're my problem. Uh-huh. Hang on, let me see."

Broderick leaned forward and peered out the window. Only a small spot of reddish light could be seen, high above the Atlantic.

"Yes sir, I can barely even see it. Looks like a perfect launch. The air control tower should let you land any time now. Yes, it is a big relief, sir. Uh-huh. Okay. Do you need me to meet your plane? Are you sure? I can just lock them up here. Okay, I'll wait for you. I really don't know why you came down, sir. You can head back while I finish up here. No, I'm not telling you what to do, sir. Yes sir, I'll stay put. All right, thank you sir. Good bye."

Broderick pressed a button and tucked the phone back in his pocket, then stared down at the floor. A few seconds passed. He removed his gun from under his arm and turned around to the table. He mumbled, "Just fifteen minutes. Damn it." He knew he didn't have much time before Kramer's plane landed nearby.

Tom and James watched his every move, wondering what he was going to do. Broderick sat down, then slammed the pistol onto the table. He was clearly contemplating his options. He toyed with the gun, spinning it in a circle with his right hand, and held his forehead with his left, elbows resting on the table's shiny stainless steel surface. He seemed to talk to himself, nod a few times, then shake his head. He finally looked over. The gun continued spinning, making an annoying scraping sound.

"Expecting company?" Tom asked. "How is General Kramer anyway? It sure doesn't sound like he treats you very well, ordering you around and all."

"Shut up, Lassiter," he replied, then shifted his eyes to James.

"You know, I can't stop thinking, you seem to act awfully damn important for someone who gets bossed around so much, ordered to chase people, putting your ass on the line all the time. Perhaps being the *fall guy* for this entire mess. And all for a General who will either be retired or dead in a few years. And where will you be, Broderick? Maybe you should ask for a promotion, huh? What do they pay thugs these days anyway?" Tom continued, trying to divert Broderick's attention and hoping he wouldn't go back to threatening James.

James turned toward Tom and offered a stern look, apparently trying to convey that maybe they should just keep quiet now. No matter what would happen from here on out, he would never forget the feel of the cold tip of that pistol's barrel on his skin. This memory would no doubt forever be etched in his mind.

Broderick didn't respond, but all of the sudden he looked angrier; his forehead wrinkled and his eyes appeared as black dots (no color nor movement, just a steady glare). His brow lowered and he stopped spinning the gun, then slammed his fist on the table. His face turned red as he got up and walked halfway back over to James and Tom. He stood, dead center in the room, with the pistol draped from his right hand. He raised it, this time pointing at Tom, and said, "I want to know the truth."

Tom's heart quickened as he said, "I just told you everything."

"No, I want to know the *whole* truth. There's no electronic file waiting to be transmitted," he continued slowly, then paused with mad eyes, "is there."

"Yes, I swear to you there is. And we also faxed everything to Russia—"

"Oh, I know all about that, sending the information to the Russian Ministry of Communications. I'm surprised you even found a fax machine that works over there. Did you really think that would help?" Broderick said confidently. He moved closer to Tom. "There's no electronic file, now is there? I'll tell you what. I'll count to three. I suggest you give me some answers. Understand?"

Tom swallowed hard, staring at the gun.

"One."

"Two."

"Three!"

Broderick's face turned brighter pink and some spit flew from his mouth. He swung the gun away from Tom, aimed at James, and instantly squeezed the trigger, firing one shot at James' chest. James flipped backward in his chair and fell hard to the floor, hitting his head hard.

Tom screamed something incoherent and watched in horror. He jumped to his feet, the chair he was tied to dangling awkwardly behind him. His ears were wringing painfully from the blast. He looked at James.

Broderick shouted, "Lassiter, shall I give him another one?"

"No!"

Tom moved closer to James, who was staring up at the ceiling, clearly in tremendous discomfort. He set the chair down next to him.

Broderick backed away a few feet, exhaling loudly, as if he'd just released a mountain of tension. "Don't worry, he may live. For a while anyway. I hit him an inch or two to the right of his heart. Now, you tell me the truth and we'll get your boy here some help, okay."

Tom ignored Broderick, focusing on James. "James, James," he said, looking down at him, at a man who had grown from being just an assistant, to clearly becoming a very close friend.

Suddenly the door to the room opened.

General Kramer walked in with two men. "What the hell is going on here?"

Broderick swung around and said, "He, he tried to escape, sir." Broderick quickly tucked the pistol into its holster.

Kramer pushed him out of the way. "Escape? Tied to a chair?"

Broderick's eyes lowered.

Kramer made his way over to James, placed a knee on the floor, and felt his wrist for a pulse. "Are you all right, son? Your pulse feels strong."

James looked up at him, wincing in pain as blood poured from his chest. He couldn't speak. Kramer turned and glanced over at Broderick. "Get these handcuffs off him," he barked, then looked at one of the other men who had accompanied him. "You, call an ambulance. No, wait. Get an air ambulance, a helicopter. Go on." Kramer shifted his attention back to James, whose hands were now free and holding his chest.

Tom moved closer. "James, you're going to be okay. Just hang in there," he said, his eyes swelling with moisture.

James tried to nod, but it was barely detectable.

Tom shifted his attention to Kramer. "Get these handcuffs off me so I can help him."

Kramer stood, looked over at Broderick again, and nodded once. Broderick reached down behind the chair and inserted a key into the handcuff around Tom's right wrist. It snapped open, releasing one arm from the chair backrest. Then he inserted the key into the other handcuff and it too opened with a click.

Big mistake.

Tom leapt from the chair, pulled his right arm back while making a fist, and swung hard at Broderick's face with every ounce of his being. The impact was solid and a cracking noise could be heard as the burly man flew backward and landed on his ass. Tom shook his hand, which was stinging and throbbing, and then tried to dive for Broderick again, but Kramer secured his arms and swung him to the floor.

Broderick rose to his knees and lunged forward, reaching for Tom's neck. His face was boiling. "I'm going to kill you!"

"No!" Kramer yelled. He let go of Tom and pushed Broderick away.

"He broke my fucking nose. He broke my—"

"I suggest you get out of here before he rips your head off too," Kramer continued and pointed to the door. "Or before I rip it off."

"But, I—"

"Now!"

Broderick moved away with his head hanging down, both hands holding his nose. As he neared the door he glanced over his shoulder in disgust, then left the room.

Kramer exhaled loudly and adjusted his belly under his belt, shaking his head left and right as two men approached and lifted Tom to his feet. They held his arms for a few seconds, but he sprang loose and moved over to James.

"It's all right. Let him be," Kramer ordered. "Just check on the helicopter."

"Yes sir," one of the men said, pulling out a cell phone.

Tom dropped to his knees, then took off his jacket, rolled it into a pillow, and stuck it carefully under James' head. "You're going to be all right," he said as he rubbed his palm over James' forehead. It was sweaty but oddly cold. James' eyes looked okay though, and his pulse was still strong. *If he doesn't lose much more blood he should be okay,* Tom tried to convince himself. "This is all my fault. I'm sorry, James."

Finally, he spoke, his words barely escaping his lips. "No, it's not your fault. I'm the one who asked to help on the story, and it was my decision to stay involved and come down here."

Tom shook his head a couple of times then asked, "Does it hurt?"

"No, it feels good. Tell him to shoot me again."

"You still have your sense of humor anyway, huh?"

James nodded slightly.

"The bleeding is letting up. You'll be okay, James," Tom repeated, though he knew it was letting up because James' blood pressure had probably dropped significantly.

"I want you to tell my family," James said faintly, then paused for a breath, "that I love them."

Tom choked up a bit then said, "No, you're going to tell them yourself." He patted James's arm.

The door opened to the room and two paramedics rushed in with a gurney. "Excuse me, sir," one of them said to Tom, ushering him out of the way.

"Is the helicopter here?" Kramer asked one of the paramedics. "I didn't hear it come in."

"No sir. It can't land here," the man answered as he dropped to his knees and opened a yellow plastic case which looked more like a fishing tackle box than medical kit. "There are too many trees and electric lines. We've been told to do what we can for him, and then take him to the runway. The med-evac helicopter will be there in about ten minutes."

Tom stood next to Kramer and watched as the paramedics checked James' pulse and ripped his shirt open to look at the area where the bullet entered. They then shuffled through the yellow case and pulled out a vial and syringe. The plastic wrapper was removed from the syringe, and the needle was carefully poked through a rubber membrane cap in a bottle of hydrocodone pain reliever. One of the men held the syringe up to the light above his head and filled it.

James squeezed his eyes tightly as the needle slid into his arm. The injection was over in three seconds. The paramedics then cleansed his chest wound and applied a white gauze bandage. He was lifted to the gurney and tied down with straps.

"Am I going to be okay?" James whispered to one of the paramedics.

They either didn't hear him or simply didn't want to reply. They quickly rolled him toward the door. Tom walked alongside.

Kramer followed and said, "I'm sorry, but you can't go with him, Lassiter. We need to have a little talk. But don't worry, they'll take good care of him." The gurney was pulled through the doorway. "I give you my word. They'll take good care of him," he repeated.

210

Tom froze and yelled at the paramedics, "Wait," just as the door was swinging shut. He moved closer to James' head and looked down at his eyes. "You'll be okay." He picked up his hand and squeezed it. It felt clammy and lifeless.

James nodded once.

"They won't let me stay with you," Tom continued, "but I'll get over to the hospital as soon as I can. Okay?"

"Remember, Tom, tell my family. Tell them all."

The paramedics pulled Tom away a few inches and said to him, "Sorry sir, but we have to get him to the runway. The helicopter should be here any minute."

Tom released James' hand. "Hang in there, okay. You'll be all right." He then turned to the two paramedics and thanked them. They offered a consoling look, and moved James quickly away. Tom watched the gurney roll down the hall to an elevator. The doors had been propped open with a trash can. The paramedics opened them a bit further and rolled their patient in.

As the doors slid shut, Tom wondered whether he would ever see James again. If he could change places with him right now he would.

CHAPTER TWENTY-THREE

The thumping rotor noise of a Bell 430 air ambulance filled the air and a halogen light, mounted beneath its chin, pierced the pre-dawn sky which was slowly revealing itself as an amber ribbon on the eastern horizon. The noise became intense as it approached, swooping in from the north, seemingly out of nowhere. It circled once, then swiftly landed on the white circle that was painted on the asphalt next to the main runway, about a thousand yards from Kennedy Space Center's control tower, and less than five hundred feet from where General Kramer and Tom were standing. They were side-by-side and leaning against the handrail at the bottom of the stair platform of the General's Gulfstream jet. Tom was tired yet wide-eyed, not quite understanding how he had managed to get himself into such a mess.

He had insisted on seeing James transfer from the paramedics' van to the air ambulance. And although his nerves were still raging, and the image of Broderick squeezing that trigger was playing repeatedly before him, indelibly engraved in his mind, the sight of the emergency personnel rushing about the tarmac provided some sliver of relief. Maybe James would be okay.

"I told you we'd take care of him," Kramer said, then exhaled cigar smoke over his left shoulder, downwind.

The paramedics slid James out of the van, carried him to the helicopter, then transferred him to a smaller gurney. Rotor-generated wind hitting hard on his face, he was carefully lifted up and into the right side of the helicopter. His substantial frame barely fit and his feet, one of the men mentioned, would surely touch the door when it was closed. He looked at James' face. "Have you ever played basketball?" It was the standard question James had heard a million times since junior high.

James didn't reply.

The paramedic turned to his partner and whispered, "The eyes are dilating."

Over at the Gulfstream, Kramer yawned and looked directly toward Tom. "Okay, Lassiter, he's in. We have to go now." He tossed his cigar down, smashed it with his right foot on the tarmac pavement, then nudged it off to one side. A man holding a large fuel hose to the Gulfstream's wing quickly offered a scathing look.

The way things are going, Tom thought, the plane will blow up any second. Handcuffed, he took a few cautious steps toward the Gulfstream's forward doorway, all the while staring in the distance at the air ambulance helicopter as James was secured. Tom saw one of the paramedics slowly slide a large door shut. He watched as one of the ground personnel backed away from the helicopter and gave the pilot a thumbs up. The engine, which hadn't been shut down after it landed, began to scream again. The craft tilted forward, then lifted quickly and turned to the north.

Tom continued to watch and felt a blast of air hit his face as he stood halfway up the Gulfstream's stairs. It faded as the helicopter moved away, as did the glow of the blinking red light on its tail. And just like that, James was gone.

"Come on," Kramer said from above, standing in the Gulfstream's doorway. "We gotta take off, Lassiter."

Tom walked the rest of the way up and entered the plane. Inside, it resembled an average civilian aircraft, only everything was military gray and shades of muted blue, and much smaller.

Kramer pointed and said, "Head back to the third row, or so, and sit down."

"With handcuffs on?" Tom asked.

"All right, hang on." Kramer motioned to some men who were standing in the aisle at the back of the plane, looking totally confused as to who Tom was and what the hell he was doing on their airplane. One of them made his way over and removed the handcuffs. Tom sat down and leaned back in a leather-covered seat. He looked down at his arms. His wrists were sore and all red, from the handcuffs. For the second time in the last few days, he felt like a fugitive—and perhaps he was at this point—being transferred somewhere no doubt terrible.

"Put your seat belt on, Lassiter," Kramer said as he too sat down, in a seat directly across the aisle.

Tom reached for the seat belt and said, "Now you're concerned about my safety?"

Kramer didn't reply.

"So I guess this means we're adding kidnapping to the list of crimes you've committed in recent days," Tom continued, looking across the aisle and waiting for an angry reply.

But Kramer was perfectly calm. He almost seemed like a different person, compared to how he was when Tom met with him at the Pentagon. His face was less red, and his forehead seemed to be less wrinkled. He had even slipped his tie off and loosened his collar. Tom watched as he crossed his legs, pressed the button on the side of the seat, and reclined. The General appeared to be ready for the in-flight movie and maybe a gin and tonic.

"You're not being kidnapped, Lassiter. But we—"

"Sure feels that way to me," Tom interrupted.

"You'll be released soon enough. We just need you to stay quiet a bit longer."

"Why? Your satellites are up. Or should I say, the evidence is up. And you have your file back. The whole story's going to come out Monday, no matter what. Neither you nor I can stop it. What's the reason for detaining me?"

"That story is the least of my problems, Lassiter. We may be headed for an international crisis. If you flap your gums to the *Post* within the next few hours, it's possible that you could jeopardize the safety of millions of people. In fact, you may already have," he said slowly, his words measured.

Tom reclined his chair so he could see him easier. "I haven't jeopardized anything."

"Guess again. You know that little fax you sent to the Russian Ministry of Communications?"

"Yeah. Your thug Broderick told you about it?"

214

"No, the Secretary of Defense told me."

Now Tom was the one looking confused. "How did he—"

"The Secretary got a phone call," Kramer continued as he reached over to his jacket. It was draped across the seat to his left. He pulled out another cigar and seemed to scavenge for matches or a lighter.

"From Russia?" Tom asked, his voice pitched higher than usual.

"No, not Russia." He found some matches and struck one. "Iran."

"Iran? But how—"

"Their Deputy Prime Minister called." Kramer lit the cigar, inhaled deeply, and shook his hand to extinguish the match. He tossed it on the floor and blew a cloud over the seat in front of him.

"It appears that someone at the Kremlin got their slimy arms-trading hands on your fax, and was kind enough to forward it to Iran."

"I don't understand."

"Lassiter, Russia is one of the largest exporters of military and nuclear technology. You did a very stupid thing. That fax you sent landed on the wrong desk. And, well, whoever it was must have gotten pretty upset. See, you let the cat out of the bag that one of their biggest customers might be at risk." The General paused to cross his legs the opposite direction then continued, "I'm sure you recall that there was an illustration depicting a space shuttle in that file you stole from me."

Tom nodded.

"Well, do you remember what was written on it?"

Tom's back stiffened and he turned to his right and looked out a small window. His memory of that illustration—the shuttle, the two satellites—was still clear, as was the small box to the left of the payload bay rendering that, among other things, said *IRAN*. He moved his eyes back to Kramer. "Yes, I remember."

"Well, figure it out, Lassiter. You're a smart man." Another puff on the cigar.

"So the payload *is* being placed over Iran?" Tom asked. He wanted confirmation of what he and James had been told by Dr.

Nevsky, that the nuclear armed satellite and spy satellite were intended for placement above Iran.

Kramer didn't immediately reply but then said, "Before I tell you more, we need to come to a little understanding. Broderick told me about your so-called backup plan—the electronic file that will automatically get sent out."

Tom nodded. "He didn't believe us. But trust me, it exists."

"Oh, he believed you. I believe you too. It seems that we are stuck with one another, aren't we? I must say, that was very clever. I like that, I like your spunk, Lassiter."

There was silence for a few more seconds. A young woman approached from the galley near the cockpit. About twenty-five years old, long brown hair, cute freckles. Tom thought, *They even have flight attendants on military aircraft?* He watched her walk down the aisle.

"Would you gentlemen care for something to drink before we takeoff?"

"Yes," Kramer answered as he held the cigar away to his left, looking up at her chest. "Coffee, and make it strong and black. It's going to be a long night, or I guess I should say morning." He turned to Tom. "Do you want anything, Lassiter?"

"Coffee, please."

"Yes sir," she replied. "Cream and sugar?"

"Please." Tom watched her walk away, then looked at Kramer. "So now what, General?"

"Like I said. We need to come to a little understanding."

"Understanding? I'm not exactly in the mood for negotiating. At least not until you release my family, and unharmed, of course. Until then, I don't intend on making any deals," Tom said firmly.

"First of all, I had nothing to do with those idiots messing with your family, and I'm sorry they were brought into this whole thing. Secondly, you'll be happy to know that they were released, oh, about an hour ago," Kramer said, angling his watch.

"And they're okay?"

"That's what I'm told."

"And I'm supposed to trust you now? Believe this? After everything that has happened—"

"Look, Lassiter," Kramer interrupted, "Now, I know things got out of hand, but I had nothing to do with it. I'm sorry for what happened. Things got way out of control."

"And you aren't to blame for any of it?"

"Oh, maybe some of it. But I'm just a patriot trying to do his job," Kramer said, staring at the end of the cigar with glassy eyes. "And that's not always easy. You see, when the CIA gets involved, things always seem to get a little crazy."

Tom raised his brow. "A little?"

"You don't know how serious this whole thing is, Lassiter. Extreme situations call for extreme measures."

"Well then, why don't you enlighten me. Just how serious?"

"Okay, I'll tell you. And then you can call your family and verify that they're all right." Kramer paused to yawn. "I've got nothing against you personally, Lassiter. I know that you're just trying to do your job, just like me." Another yawn.

"General, you don't seem to be too nervous. I mean, if what you said is true, and millions of lives may be in jeopardy."

"My mission is accomplished, that's why I'm relaxed. I got that payload launched and in orbit. Hopefully we can keep an eye on Iran now, and they won't do anything stupid to their neighbors, or the U.S. And if they do try something, we'll be able to respond—and before they can strike Israel or anyone else. That's why I'm relaxed," the General repeated, then scratched his nose vigorously, causing it to redden. "Look, Lassiter, I did what I was told to do. I served my country well, and I always have."

"Putting nuclear weapons into space isn't serving anyone. And I'm sure you know that it's also just a tad illegal. You're violating at least two or three international treaties."

He hunched his shoulders. "I'm no lawyer."

"Well I am. Or was, and—"

Kramer grinned slightly and interrupted, "Good, maybe you can represent yourself soon."

Tom's mind raced at this possibility. He swallowed hard.

"Sorry, I couldn't resist," Kramer continued. "Go on."

"You know damn well that the U.S. is violating the Limited Test Ban Treaty and the 1967 Outer Space Treaty, agreed upon by over a hundred countries. And that's just for starters. I don't know how you could go along with this whole thing. You've had a distinguished career. Why would you screw up the record and get involved in such an idiotic plan as High Ground? Hell, you could be retired by now and—"

"It's not idiotic. Like I said, Lassiter, you don't know the severity of the situation. Sure, I could have retired years ago. But I wanted to go out with one last bang. A last hurrah, you might say."

His words hung in the thick, smoky air which now filled the Gulfstream's cabin. Tom noticed that the flight attendant was approaching with the coffee. She set the styrofoam cups down in the recesses of the chair armrests.

"Careful, they're very hot," she said.

"Good, keep it coming. Thank you." Kramer offered a quick smile and nodded, again to her chest, then exhaled loudly and stretched his arms. He cracked his knuckles then turned to Tom.

"You know, once we get through this crisis, I'm going to retire and finally move down here to Florida. The wife and I have already bought a condo, a real nice one, half-mile from the beach, and a mile from an eighteen-holer." He sipped his coffee, then looked at his watch again. "I wonder what the hell is taking so long," he continued as he leaned to his right for a second and peered forward, toward the cockpit. "It's a beautiful course, one of Arnold Palmer's designs. It has a great big clubhouse."

Tom nodded slightly, pretending to care about the General's musings about retirement, and picked up the cup of coffee.

"No more snow for me," Kramer added, then stretched his back. "Yep, out with a big bang, then out to play golf till I buy the farm, probably from smoking these damn things. That's my plan."

"That's probably a good way to put it, General—out with a big bang, the nuclear sort."

"Yeah, maybe, maybe so Lassiter. And if it comes to that, it'll largely be because of you."

Tom didn't reply, but his eyes revealed the impact of Kramer's words.

"Perhaps I should give you a little lesson about the world we're living in now, Lassiter," he continued slowly with a low crusty voice, suddenly the professor and not the Florida tour guide. His spine stiffened slightly. "I remember you saying that the cold war is over, you know, back at our fun meeting at the Pentagon. Remember?"

Tom nodded. How could he forget.

"You're right. It is over. But do you have any idea what America is facing today? Do you have any clue as to how many nuclear weapons there still are? Or where they are located, or who's controlling them? Do you?"

"No, not exactly but I'm sure—"

"Well, I do. Let me tell you about this so-called safer world you and the rest of the liberal press write about so proudly, as you condemn the military for wasting billions of dollars. We now have Pakistan, North Korea, India, China, France, the UK, Israel and of course Russia with nuclear weapons. Let's start with Russia," he said, as if talking down to a naive little kid. "Now, I know all of you think that the threat of nuclear war is gone, since the Soviet Union collapsed twenty-odd years ago. But nothing could be further from the truth. Russia, including its offspring—Ukraine, Kazakhstan, and Belarus—still possess thousands of strategic warheads. You see, they don't even know how many weapons they have. Some reports put the number as high as forty thousand."

"But they're destroying them as we speak, right?"

"Sure. They've started. Or I should say, we've started."

"We?"

"That's right. You see, we don't trust them, so, under the so-called Swords for Plowshares agreement, we're purchasing uranium and plutonium from them. The bad news is that it will barely make a dent in their stockpiles." He took another sip of coffee. "It helps, and keeps us involved, but there are literally thousands of surplus weapons and raw materials floating around over there. And what scares me to death, more than this, is that there are also surplus nuclear scientists— a hundred thousand unemployed or underpaid designers, technicians, and machinists. Now that their country doesn't need them, many of these people can barely afford to put food on the table for their families. We think there are well over nine hundred of them in China alone. And there are reports that North Korea and Iran have also employed thousands." He squashed out the remainder of the cigar in the armrest ashtray. "It scares the hell out of me."

"So you're saying that officials, or companies in Russia or China, may be selling nuclear material, or missile components, perhaps even ICBM's? And their scientists are helping other countries deploy them?"

"That's right."

"Including assisting Iran?"

"Yes. Well, we have some pretty convincing evidence anyway. We know where the research and manufacturing sites are in Iran. And if we confirm it with the help of the new imaging satellite just launched, we'll pound them into dust once and for all," he said, then clenched his jaw. "I'll take their so-called leaders out too, if it's the last thing I do. They aren't going to threaten any more neighbors, or invade any other countries. I guarantee it. We're not going to allow another Holocaust."

Tom immediately thought about Kramer's late son; he recalled the article he'd read from the paper's archives, describing how the young soldier died in Iran. High Ground obviously wasn't just a cold military exercise for the general. It was clearly personal, something he had to do, illegal or not. Tom hesitated for a second or two then said, "Those are strong words, General."

"Yep. Strong feelings too."

"Are you sure they aren't colored by one of your sons dying in Iran? Colored by a desire for revenge?" Tom knew he was pushing it, but he had to at least test the waters. He told himself that if this man's feelings, pain, and desperation had somehow influenced the decision to implement the High Ground program, or had influenced the space weapon's design, God only knew what he was planning to do. Tom's mind was a jumble of thoughts. *Could Kramer have driven the entire weapons development portion of the launch, without senior U.S. leadership knowing? Maybe the U.S. government only approved launch of the imaging satellite?*

With the mention of his son, Kramer's face grew grim and he clenched the cigar harder. His eyes became reflective, then he looked away and said nothing, absolutely no response to Tom's question about whether he was driven by his son's death in Iran. And the silence said everything. A couple of minutes passed, both of them not saying a word. Tom almost felt guilty for bringing up the General's son.

Finally, Tom cleared his throat and continued, "All this because of purported nuclear weapons development in Iran? Amazing. Just amazing. Just like back with Iraq, we have no clear evidence that Iran is building a nuclear weapon."

Kramer glanced over. "'Purported, my ass. We know damn well they are intent on building nuclear weapons, and they may even already have nukes."

"How do we know?" Tom asked.

Kramer took a sip of coffee. "The CIA has had people planted inside Iran, in very senior political and technical roles, since Reagan was President, Lassiter."

"Moles?" Tom asked. Tom had casually read about the CIA's alleged methods over the years, since moving to Washington D.C. In the world of espionage, a mole, also referred to as a penetration agent, sleeper agent, or deep cover agent, works as a long-term clandestine informant. They are often born in or educated in the country they spy on, and slowly infiltrate deeper and deeper into government and business activities, thus avoiding suspicion. Usually.

Kramer nodded. "That's right. The CIA has been in Iran for years."

"And why are you telling me all this?"

"Like I said, Lassiter, I'm retiring. The payload is up and I'm calling it a day. And you know half the story already anyway. You may as well know the rest, the motivation for all this."

"And it doesn't bother you that I'm going to publish all of this? You could be incriminated," Tom said, purposely softening the statement. Could be? Hell, he was already visualizing the general and his sidekick Broderick in those bright orange prison jumpsuits with numbers written boldly across their chests, stamping license plates at Langley Federal prison.

"Go ahead," Kramer replied confidently, "incriminate the hell out of me. I'll deny everything. There's no solid evidence. And just keep in mind, I have a videotape of you stealing that file from my office at the Pentagon. Just keep that in mind. I wonder how many years in jail you could get for something like that? You could be locked up for the rest of your life, Lassiter. So maybe you should just let bygones be bygones, you know. And rest assured, the folks who committed any sort of crimes are being taken care of." He looked at his watch again.

"What do you mean?"

"Broderick was arrested, about forty-five minutes ago."

Tom sat up straight from the Gulfstream seat, turning toward Kramer. "Arrested?"

"That's right. He and his CIA colleagues can't go around shooting civilians, now can they. Though the thought, I admit, has crossed my mind a few times." He rubbed his eyes and scratched his nose. "It's a shame. He was a good man. They just pushed him too far. Then he got out of control and they couldn't rein him in. He did some crazy things recently, damn crazy. Like orchestrating the shooting back at that office supply store. Of course, every country needs a few men they can count on to—"

"Do their dirty work?" Tom interrupted.

"That's right. Like it or not, arms-for-hostages, assassinations, and maybe a *coups d'état* now and then sounds terrible, but they make the world a safer place for every American."

"That's sick," Tom said as he turned away.

"You print what you want, Lassiter. Call it sick. I don't care. I'd just like you to print the whole story. What we are doing is valiant. You have to print the whole truth, when the time is right, of course."

"And when will that be?"

"Soon. Very soon." The General stood and walked toward the front of the plane. "You stay put," he said over his shoulder as he made his way. "God sakes, what's the damn delay? We should have taken off by now."

Tom watched as the General tapped on the door to the cockpit, then opened it. He leaned his head in and said, "Gentlemen, what's the delay? I saw the fuel truck pull away ten minutes ago."

"Sorry, sir, I should have told you. We've been ordered to stay on the ground."

"What?"

"Apparently the Secretary of Defense called the Chairman of the Joint Chiefs of Staff, who had someone get an order to the tower that we're to await further instructions. The tower also said that Military Police are on the way to take Mr. Lassiter."

"Christ, now what," Kramer said, then slammed the cockpit door and walked a few steps to the galley. He grabbed a phone hanging on a wall and hit a few keys. "This is Kramer. Patch me through to the Secretary of Defense, ASAP. I'll hold the line."

About ten seconds passed. He heard a clicking noise, the line being transferred. A voice came on, "General Kramer?"

"Yes sir. I was just told that you've requested that we stay on the ground at Kennedy Space Center."

"That's right. I was about to call you, but I'm still waiting for some final instructions from the President."

Kramer's heart sank to the bottom of his stomach. "The President, sir?"

"That's right, General."

"But why is the President—"

"No time to explain. Now, I want you to get on board the Boeing YAL-1. It's flying down to you right now."

"The 747 Airborne Laser, sir?"

"Yes, I'm sending both of them to Iran. General Lansing is already on the other. It's just precautionary at this point, but it looks like we are moving to DEFCON 3 very shortly. The bottom line is Iran has demanded that we bring the shuttle and its payload down immediately. If we don't, they are threatening to destroy Israel, New York, and the Washington D.C. area with ICBMs."

223

"My God," Kramer said under his breath, suddenly feeling weak.

The Secretary of Defense continued, "The President is handling the situation personally. I talked to him about five minutes ago. I'll be in touch with you shortly with more information. I better get off here for now."

"Yes sir. I'll be waiting."

"Bye General, and good luck."

"Yes sir." Kramer hung up. "I can't believe this. DEFCON 3?"

Tom watched as Kramer walked back down the narrow aisle, shifting back and forth like a penguin making its way across ice. He looked different, not as calm as before and his eyes were intense. "Is something wrong, General?" Tom braced for the response.

Kramer ignored the question at first and made his way back to where he had been sitting. He reached over and picked up his jacket.

"Understatement of the decade, Lassiter," he finally replied. "Looks like you may have gotten the world into a bit of a mess. I just got off the phone with the Secretary of Defense. He had just spoken with the President." He slipped the jacket on. "Iran has demanded that we bring back the shuttle and the two satellites, and destroy them in front of their representatives. Things are heating up."

Tom slid down in his seat slightly. He was speechless.

Kramer reached in a pocket and pulled out a roll of antacid, then popped three in his mouth and chomped noisily.

"This could be a nuclear standoff, Lassiter. Is that story of yours worth all this?" Kramer asked, looking down at Tom with piercing eyes. "God help us." He then turned and started to walk away.

Tom's pulse quickened. "And if we don't bring back the shuttle and destroy the satellites?"

Kramer stopped and looked back at Tom. "Well, they are threatening to destroy Israel, New York, and Washington D.C. For starters, of course," he said way to calmly. "Or at least that's what they apparently told the President. Who knows. Last year Iran threatened to wipe Israel off the map. And they're still there. Maybe they're bluffing again."

Tom cleared his throat nervously then asked, "So now what?"

"Well, there's a plane coming to pick me up." He pulled out another Tums antacid and seemed to swallow it whole. Not even one chomp, just straight down his windpipe.

"What's wrong with this plane? Is it broken?" Tom asked.

"No, it's fine. They have a special plane coming, an experimental 747 armed with a missile-killing laser, and surveillance equipment. It'll be here shortly."

"You're kidding, right?"

"I wish I was, Lassiter. I wish I was."

"But I thought the Airborne Laser program was put on hold, or terminated."

"That's what we wanted everyone to think, Lassiter. Well, I guess we'll see if they work, huh? Time for a little beta testing, in the field."

"Good god." Tom paused, raking his fingers through his hair. "And what about me."

"MPs are on the way to pick you up. You'll probably be detained here at Kennedy Space Center until we take care of this little situation you got us into. Charges will probably be brought against you, and you might even do some time for taking that file from my desk. Then you'll be let go, I'm sure, under some whistleblower law. You'll go home and write a five-part exposé about this whole mess, and then there will be the book, of course. You'll probably become rich and famous—all because of a little file. Pretty amazing, isn't it."

Kramer paused and opened an overhead bin to remove a small suitcase. "Yep, this is one helluva way to go into retirement. Thanks a lot Lassiter."

Tom watched him, then turned to his right and stared out the window. He saw a plane approaching from afar. He turned back to Kramer. "That must be it."

Kramer set the suitcase on a seat, then bent over and looked out the window. "That's it all right. And there's another one too, apparently already in the air headed to Iran airspace. We'll probably fly them all the way to the Mid East, nothing will happen, and we'll fly them all the way back."

"Do you really think it's just a false alarm?"

"Based on Iran's past rhetoric, yes."

"I want to go with you," Tom blurted out without the slightest hesitation, and without thinking. His words slowly sank in, then he continued, "I want to record what happens."

"You've lost your mind, Lassiter. This isn't some run-of-the-mill military exercise. You're staying here at Kennedy. Now come on." He picked up the suitcase. "I'll turn you over to the military police. They've already been called." He moved to the front of the plane, holding his bag outward in one hand, and clutching his lower back with the other.

Tom followed, nipping at his heels. They departed the plane and walked down the steps, then made their way around the Gulfstream's nose. Tom looked off in the distance, thinking. He decided to give it one more shot. "General, you said you want me to get the whole story. Right?"

"You know I can't take a civilian on a military mission. Especially on an experimental plane. Christ, Lassiter."

They watched as the 747 landed. Tom heard the engines quickly reverse and the brakes screech. He didn't know they could slow down so fast. Seconds later it was rolling to a stop adjacent to the Gulfstream. A mobile stair platform immediately drove up to it. The door just behind and below the cockpit opened before the steps were even completely in place.

Kramer nervously looked at his watch. "Damn it, where are they? The MPs should have been here ten minutes ago." His head and eyes darted around the airport taxiways and toward the hangers, three hundred sixty degrees. Kennedy Space Center was completely still, no movement whatsoever.

Tom continued to try, "General, I insist on going."

He laughed. "You're a real piece of work, Lassiter."

"Look, I don't want to be left here with Broderick's goons."

"Lassiter, as I told you, Broderick was arrested, and his—"

"He's got friends."

"News to me."

"Please General, I want to see this miracle of technology—the Airborne Laser. It'll help the story, and perhaps sooth some nerves that the U.S. has at least some means of knocking down missiles."

Tom watched as Kramer rubbed his forehead, apparently actually considering the request. Tom continued, "We'll probably go up for a little ride and be told to land shortly thereafter. Right?"

Kramer nodded, "Yes, probably."

There was silence for several seconds.

Kramer continued to look about the tarmac. Still no military police. "Okay, okay, what are they going to do, fire me. Come on, Lassiter."

They ran toward the 747. They reached the stairs and Kramer looked around once more, then quickly ascended the steps. Tom followed, tripping twice, as he stared at the strange aircraft. There were hardly any windows, and the nose was covered with what appeared to be a glass shell, which was bulbous and detracted from the otherwise clean aerodynamic lines of the plane. They walked in, went up some more stairs, and made their way to what would usually be the first class section, the upper lounge.

In the cockpit, the pilot, Major Bill Sutton, gazed down from the window to his left. His headset clicked a couple of times and a voice came on.

"Major Sutton, this is KSC Control."

"Go ahead KSC Control."

Static, then, "We were just notified that you are to wait two minutes for the arrival of additional personnel."

"More personnel?"

"Yes sir. Two minutes only. Then you are to depart immediately."

"Roger. Standing by." Sutton looked at his watch and then notified Captain Leckart, who was standing in the galley.

One minute and fifty-five seconds later Leckart closed the door, just as a car screeched to a stop at the base of the stairs. Major Sutton again looked down from the cockpit. He watched as the driver's door swung instantly open as if it would tear off from its hinges. A woman stepped out then ran up the steps to the 747's main door. She pounded furiously on the door. Captain Leckart quickly opened it.

"Just made it," she said, completely out of breath. She flashed an ID and walked in.

"Yes, ma'am, just in time."

The 747's door slammed shut, was secured, and the mobile stairs were pulled away.

CHAPTER TWENTY-FOUR

Tom noticed that the first class cabin of the 747 Airborne Laser aircraft was separated into two main areas. One section, near a spiral staircase, had two rows of average-looking airline seats. They even had the familiar blue fabric he had seen on older American Airlines' planes. Tom also noticed that there were doors flanking each side of the cabin. One looked like the typical emergency variety (a handle, small porthole window, and bright orange warning stickers everywhere). The other door was twice as large and he could see the guts of the latches and mechanisms that held it in place, as there wasn't a plastic panel concealing its internal works. It looked like it was custom created for the aircraft, or perhaps not even completed. Real comforting. It had just one large round industrial-looking aluminum handle, a wheel-like locking mechanism. A red line had been painted or taped on the floor, two feet away from the bottom of the doorsill.

In front of the seats, and just before the forward galley and cockpit door, was an area that looked very different from a typical Boeing 747. The focus of this section seemed to be a large platform of some sort, about four feet wide and six feet long. It sat in the middle of the cabin and simply appeared as a large black box, standing about three feet off the floor. It resembled a table, except there wasn't room to scoot chairs underneath, though there were leather chairs placed around it at a distance. The sides of the platform, which were made of sheet metal, dropped straight to the floor and had small vents in several areas; there were no legs.

Above, suspended from the ceiling, was a similar box-like structure. It hung down about two feet, directly over the surface of the bottom unit. It too was black and made of metal, but it didn't have vents. The two units were perfectly aligned with each other and there was about four and a half feet of open space between them.

The strange device in the center of the cabin, and the fine high-back leather chairs surrounding it, were in sharp contrast with the rest of the forward area. In fact, the walls and most of the ceiling of the plane appeared unfinished, or taken apart. Most of the ivory-colored plastic panels, which usually cover the aluminum structure of a plane and the maze of hydraulic pipes, electrical lines, and air circulation ducts, were missing. The very guts of the aircraft were visible and, most unsettlingly, the thin aluminum outer skin could be seen in several spots. Some areas of the walls, however, were covered with control panels and orange-colored metal boxes.

Near the galley there was a workstation of some sort and two swivel chairs that looked like they belonged in a bar, not in a military aircraft. They were mounted on single posts that were bolted to the floor, and faced a myriad of switches, buttons, computer screens, and red, green, and yellow LEDs.

The aircraft was a 747-200, the Air Force's second choice for the ABL prototypes, according to an article Jake (the *Post* reporter who covered military technology) had given Tom on the Airborne Laser program; he'd written a story on the ABL about a year ago. The Air Force's first choice had been the newer 747-400. But since a used 200 can be purchased for under thirty million, and a new 400 would have cost almost one hundred and fifty million, the Air Force succumbed to budget pressures. The 747 family of aircraft had been an easy decision. The plane was thoroughly proven (over 1,400 units delivered, accumulating twenty-five billion miles) and had a long history going back to 1966, when Pan Am ordered the first configuration. The first flight of a 747 was on February 9, 1968. A year later it was put into service between New York and London. It proved so safe and reliable that the Air Force ordered two specially equipped 747-200s to transport the President, the first of which was deployed in August of 1990. The plane was available in three maximum gross weights up to 875,000 pounds. Except for a larger wingspan and six-foot-high winglets at the wingtips, and the added twenty-three feet of upper deck, the newer 747-400 and the older 747-100 could be twins. The original design was that good, that timeless.

Tom walked further into the cabin and turned to General Kramer. "What's all this?" he asked.

Kramer tossed his jacket onto the back of one of the seats. "It's the control room for some special imaging equipment. Now look, Lassiter, I don't want you moving beyond here." He pointed to the second row of seats. "You're to stay away from all equipment and remain seated in one of these rows. Understand?"

Tom nodded twice.

"And if you move, I'll tie you up myself. If you talk too much, I'll tape your mouth shut. Got it?"

"Yes."

Tom sat down near one of only a handful of windows and watched as Kramer made his way to the 747's cockpit. Several uniformed men emerged from the galley and its elevator, having just risen from the bowels of the plane. Tom heard some sort of motor and saw another man emerge, wearing jeans, a polo shirt, and tennis shoes. He had long unkempt hair and looked completely out of place.

Kramer approached the men and said, "Good morning, gentlemen. At ease. Is everything ready?" he asked as he offered his hand, first to the man with the most medals on his chest.

"Yes sir," Lt. Colonel Flemming answered as he shook firmly. "Ready as we can be, given the short notice."

"Good."

Flemming continued, "I'd like you to meet our crew today, General. This is Captain Leckart."

"Good morning, General Kramer."

"And this is Major Rodriguez."

Rodriquez replied with a rigid salute and, "Sir."

Flemming turned around and ushered the long-haired man over. "And this is Mr. Goldstein, our civilian computer and software consultant."

"I gathered that much," Kramer quipped, running his eyes from head to toe, clearly not approving of Goldstein's attire which resembled the stereotypical Google or Facebook programmer look, rather than a military contractor.

Goldstein came over and they shook hands for a split second. "Nice to meet you, General."

"Uh-huh, pleasure."

Attempting to interrupt the awkward introduction and Kramer's rudeness, Flemming continued, "Goldstein worked on NASA's Mars Curiosity mission recently. Do you recall the panoramic 3-D images that were sent back?"

Kramer nodded once.

"That was his work. And now he's one of the brains behind the imager," Flemming added, motioning with his left hand toward the black box with the chairs sitting around it. "He's from M.I.T. and has two Ph.D.'s, computer science and physics."

"Yeah, I know. I've read the memos," Kramer replied, then looked at Goldstein. "So, does it work?"

"Yes sir, at least in the lab simulations. I haven't tried it on board yet. And we obviously don't know whether it can receive real-time data from the new satellite you just launched. I'm pretty sure it—"

"You better be more than pretty sure, son."

Goldstein raised his eyebrows, not knowing what to say.

Again, Flemming interjected, clearing his throat somewhat nervously. "We better get moving, gentlemen. Shall I tell the crew we're ready, General?"

"Why not."

"Yes sir." Flemming started to turn toward the cockpit but paused. "Who's the passenger, sir?" he asked, briefly glancing at Tom then looking at Kramer.

"Oh, he's a *Washington Post* reporter who wants to make us famous. I need him to keep his mouth shut until this blows over, so he's along for the ride."

A concerned look moved to Flemming's face as he said, "I don't have to tell you that this is very unusual and—"

"I know, I know. But trust me, we're better off having him where we can see him. And don't worry, I'll take personal responsibility for bringing him aboard." Kramer turned away, ending the conversation.

232

Flemming walked to the cockpit and opened the door. "Gentlemen, we're ready."

The pilot said over his shoulder, "We're just waiting for them to move that car, sir."

"A car?"

"Yes sir." He pointed out the window to his left, down at the ground.

Flemming crouched down and peered out. "What on earth?" He turned and walked back to Kramer, who was now in the galley drinking a glass of water. "General—"

"Clear to takeoff, Flemming?"

"Uh, not quite sir."

"What do you mean not quite?" He set the cup down.

"We're waiting for a car to be moved. It's next to the nose of the aircraft, sir," he continued, pointing downward and to his right.

"Whose car?" Kramer went over to one of the windows and looked out. "Who the hell—"

"Good morning, gentlemen," a soft voice suddenly interrupted from the area near the staircase landing.

The British accent startled Kramer the most. He swung around and moved his eyes to the rear of the cabin. Tom got up from his seat and also looked over.

"Victoria Brookshire?" Kramer asked.

"Yes sir," she replied. She couldn't see Tom yet; he was blocked by the other men.

Tom turned away and his pulse quickened. *Why is she aboard?*

"What are you doing here?" Kramer inquired, then walked sternly toward her.

"You mean you don't know?

He shook his head.

I got a call twenty minutes ago from Langley headquarters, sir. They ordered me to meet you here. They said that you might need my help."

"Help? What sort of help?"

233

"With the missile assessment and damage estimates, sir, if Iran gets a missile off at us, or Israel, and—"

"Good god." He turned around and walked back to the galley. "Now we have a woman on board too," he mumbled, just barely loud enough for Victoria and everyone else to hear. He picked up the cup of water he had left on a stainless steel counter and gulped it down as if taking a shot of whisky in one swallow.

As the other men introduced themselves to Victoria, Tom sat down and slid low into the seat. He didn't want to startle her. He shielded his face as best as he could with his hand, and rotated toward a nearby window. But it didn't work.

A few seconds later she walked over. "Tom? Is that you?"

He turned to her.

Her eyes became bigger as she said, "My God. What are—"

Kramer came back over, interrupting her, "I believe you two know each other," he said sarcastically, then leaned over and again peered out a window to check on the car that had brought her. He yelled over his shoulder, "Her car is gone, Flemming. Let's get this thing in the air."

"Yes sir," Flemming answered instantly, as he walked quickly toward the cockpit.

Seconds later the 747 began to roll and headed to the largest runway at Kennedy Space Center.

Flemming returned from the front of the plane. "We're cleared for takeoff." He handed Kramer a thick procedures notebook and they walked over and sat down in the leather chairs.

Rodriguez and Leckart were seated near the control panel which was attached to the black platform, going over a checklist. Tom could just barely hear them. The engines were getting louder.

Victoria turned, such that her back was to Kramer and the others, and faced Tom. "What are you doing here?" she whispered, gazing down at him with warm curious eyes and total bewilderment.

"It's a long story. They tracked us down. And, and, James has been shot."

"What?"

"A maniac named Broderick and his henchmen did it. Your CIA associates, apparently."

She held the palm of her right hand up to her lips. "My god. Is he all right?"

"I don't know. They life-flighted him out of here, supposedly to Florida Hospital in Orlando. They wouldn't let me go with him." Tom paused for a couple seconds. "Do you have a cell phone with you?"

"Yes."

"Don't give it to me now." He paused again. "Just, um, hide it in the restroom somewhere." He looked around the cabin. "There must be one up front, or in back. Hide it in a cabinet or something, or maybe in the tissue box holder in the bathroom. Okay?"

She nodded.

"I want to check on my family, and at least try to see how James is doing."

"All right. I'll leave it in the restroom."

"Victoria, I don't think you should be seen talking to me."

Another nod. Her face became more serious, forehead wrinkling slightly. "Are you okay, Tom?"

"Yeah, but James looked pretty bad."

She shook her head, then walked quickly over to a restroom near the galley. A few minutes later, after Tom noticed her coming out, he told Kramer he needed to get up and use "the latrine" and Kramer grunted "yes, help yourself."

Once inside, Tom found Victoria's cell phone and called home. A few wrings and he soon heard his mom fumbling with the phone, her arthritic fingers trying to pick it up in the dim light from the alarm clock no doubt. He was relieved that she was home.

His mother cleared her throat and said, "Hello, Lassiter residence."

"Mom! Thank God."

"Tom, are you all right?"

He heard the bed creak as she sat up. "Yes. Are you—"

"I'm okay now, son, but I have a pounding headache. Some men came to the house and said we had to go and—"

"But everyone Is okay?" Tom interrupted. He didn't want to be in the restroom too long, plus he was concerned that the cell signal might soon be lost once the 747 was airborne. He was also concerned that his voice might be heard in the galley.

His mom replied, "Yes, we're fine now."

"Good. I can't talk for long, mom. I just wanted to make sure you were released and are okay. Please listen carefully. I want you to wake everyone up and leave the house."

"Leave? But those men said we should stay here, or else you'd be hurt."

He paused for a few seconds, thinking. "Mom, I still want you to leave. I'm okay. Nothing will happen to me. I want you to get as far away from Washington D.C. as you can. Understand? Maybe, uh, go to aunt Diane's farm in Kentucky. Okay?"

"Now?" the pitch of her voice raised.

"Yes, right now. I'm sorry I can't explain. Go there and wait until I call you again. Go, okay, just go. I have to get off here. Tell everyone I love them. Everything will be fine soon, I promise. I have to go now. Bye Mom." He hit the end button, then frantically called for operator assistance.

"Operator. May I help you?"

"Yes, information for Orlando please."

"One moment and I'll connect."

"Thank you."

The line clicked a couple times. "Information, may I help you?"

"Yes, the number for Florida Hospital in Orlando."

"One moment, please."

Tom could hear people talking outside the restroom door.

"Still checking," the operator continued.

Tom whispered, "Thank you."

"The number is area code 407-894-6585."

"6585?"

"Yes sir. Would you like me to connect you?"

"Yes, thanks," Tom answered, then turned around and flushed the toilet, just to make some noise for whom ever was standing outside the restroom, or in the galley.

A few seconds later, he heard the line connect and ringing. A lady answered. "Florida Hospital. How may I direct your call?"

Tom cleared his throat and said, "I'm calling about a patient who was brought in tonight, I mean, this morning. He has a gunshot wound."

"Yes sir. I'll transfer you to emergency. One moment, please."

He could feel the plane moving faster. The thin stainless steel and plastic panels that made up the walls of the restroom were creaking and the door was rattling.

A voice came on, "Emergency room, admissions desk. May I help you?"

"Yes, I'd like to check on a patient who was brought in early this morning."

"May I have the name please?"

"His name is James Clemens. He probably arrived about an hour ago by helicopter. He has a gunshot wound."

"Can you hold, sir?"

"Yes, I'll hold, but I'm in a real hurry," Tom answered. "My cell phone's about to go dead."

"Yes sir. Just one second, please."

Suddenly someone knocked on the restroom door and jiggled the handle. Tom covered the phone's receiver and said, "Just a minute."

"You need to take your seat, sir. We're about to takeoff." It was the voice of Flemming. "And I need to use the latrine, sir. Quickly now."

"Okay, I'll be right out," Tom said, then flushed the micro toilet again.

A few seconds later the lady came back on the line. "Sir?"

"Yes."

"Mr. Clemens is in surgery."

"How bad is he? Will he be all right?"

237

"It's too early to tell, sir. I'm sorry. The doctors haven't come out yet. I don't have a way of knowing just yet. Maybe if you call back in thirty minutes or so, we'll know something."

"Okay. Well, can you give Mr. Clemens a message from me, once he is stable?"

"Certainly."

"Please tell him that Tom Lassiter called, and that I'll be there as soon as possible, but had to leave town for a bit."

"Tom?" she asked. "Lassiter?"

"Yes ma'am."

"Very well, sir. I'll give him the message. But you're welcome to call back."

"I'll try. Thank you, ma'am."

Tom disconnected the call and stuck the phone in his pocket, then opened the door and walked out. Flemming squeezed by in the hallway, appearing nervous and slightly sweaty, and made a beeline for the restroom. He entered and slammed the door shut.

Tom went back to the main cabin. He heard a voice come on over some speaker overhead, "Prepare for takeoff."

CHAPTER TWENTY-FIVE

Tom noticed that the sun was starting to come up. The reddish glow was incredible. The 747 reached thirty thousand feet, according to another announcement by the pilot, and began to level off. The storms that loomed off the coast of Florida at takeoff had moved on. The sky was clear for as far as the eye could see, at least on the left side of the plane. Tom stared out a window, his chin resting on his palm. His eyelids felt like bricks were tied to them and his face had over a day's worth of stubble. He looked, felt, and smelled terrible. But the sunrise was indeed spectacular. He knew the serenity was misleading.

As the plane banked to the left he saw some islands below, probably the Bahamas, he thought. He peered down at the silhouettes of their white beaches, which separated the ocean from the dark green inland areas. He hoped that the alert would be called off and that the pilot would turn around and head home. Maybe life would get back to normal. Perhaps he'd take a vacation to the Caribbean after the story was out and things had died down, possibly even to one of those beaches down there, with Victoria by his side.

Kramer unfastened his seat belt and stood. He walked over to Goldstein and Flemming. "Goldstein," he said gruffly.

The kid jumped three inches from the cushioned chair he was sitting on. "Yes sir."

"When can we get something on the imager?"

"It should be just a few minutes, General. Ten at the most. We have a lock on the relay satellite and data is coming in."

"Good. The new one is up and running?" Kramer asked, referring to one of the satellites just launched.

"That's what we understand, sir."

Kramer let out a sigh of relief and watched as Goldstein turned, leaned forward, and typed at a keyboard like a piano virtuoso. Complete command over his instrument.

"There we go, General. The data rate looks good and the signal's getting stronger," Goldstein said, then looked at Flemming. "I'm ready, sir. May I turn the unit on?"

Flemming's face lit up. "Go ahead."

Goldstein reached over and flipped a switch on the panel to his left. "It should be up in just a moment," he continued as he gazed at an LCD monitor before him.

Everyone walked to the black console in the middle of the cabin and sat down in the leather chairs. They stared at the open space before them as if a miracle was surely about to happen. Goldstein reached down and pressed a button above the vents on the left side. A wide drawer slid out slowly. There were various devices mounted on top of the drawer—another keyboard, a flat panel touch screen, and a small strip of buttons.

Goldstein hit a few keys, then leaned back slightly in his chair, also staring at the blank space above the platform. He turned to each face around the strange machine and said, "It might take a few minutes."

"Goldstein, while we're waiting," Flemming said, "why don't you give Ms. Brookshire a rundown on what this device is, and how it works."

"Yes sir."

"And in simple terms, please."

Goldstein nodded and pulled some of his hair away from his eyes. "Well, let's see. Basically we're sitting at what we call the front end, or user interface, of a C4I system—command, control, communications, computers, and intelligence. The system was designed to be an aid in analyzing and implementing war plans in real-time. Downstairs we have one of the world's most powerful super computers. It has ninety-two hundred Intel processors operating in tandem, you know, simultaneously. It can do several teraflops per second. And can—"

"A teraflop?" Victoria inquired.

"Yes, a trillion calculations per second, about two and a half times faster than the typical super computer. Data is streaming in, as we speak, from three satellites over the Middle East, one of which, as you know, was just launched. Would you like me to describe the satellites, and how they are integrated into the system?"

"Yes, thank you. For some reason I was left out of the loop," Victoria answered to Goldstein, then immediately turned to Kramer.

Kramer turned away, ignoring the jab.

Goldstein continued, "Well, the three satellites and their CCD imagers, essentially high resolution cameras, are capturing live images of the region and, well, they're performing some error correction and A-to-D, or analog-to-digital conversions. They compress the data—which means they throw out redundancy and make it easier to transmit—and then send the data streams to relay satellites, which bounce the signal around the curvature of the Earth to us, another 747 Airborne Laser aircraft, the U.S.S. Stennis aircraft carrier, CIA headquarters, and the Pentagon." Goldstein paused and turned to Kramer. "Am I going too deep here?"

"No," Kramer replied. "But make it quick, Goldstein."

"Anyway, we're basically able to perform a triangulation via the three satellites whereby we receive an image of each side of any object within the theater of operation. In short, we can see in 3-D. The device before us, the imager, takes the real-time data from fiber optic lines coming from the super computer downstairs and, using what we call high definition volumetric display, projects images on this surface."

Goldstein ran his right hand over the top of the platform. "The beamformers are above and below these glass lenses and they project the image using what we call programmer's hierarchical interactive graphics, or PHIG. They form a CGI, or computer generated image, and the—"

"Too deep," Kramer interrupted.

"Yes sir. The bottom line is that we end up with a virtual reality image of the area the three satellites are aimed at."

"Splendid," Kramer said. "It gives us a picture. So where is it?" He pinched the bridge of his nose and tilted forward in his chair.

Goldstein stared down again at the monitor mounted to the drawer. "It should be up any second, sir. It takes a while to warm up, and perform sum-checks. You know, error correction. Wait a sec, here it comes, sir."

Suddenly the space above the imaging platform lit up in a green glow. Goldstein angled further back in his chair and smiled broadly with pride. The entire area, between the unit suspended from the ceiling, to the bottom platform, was shining brightly and pulsating with light.

"It should stabilize in a few seconds," Goldstein continued, then hit a few keys. The pulsating stopped and slowly, near the bottom, an image began to take form.

Mountains.

Desert.

Sea.

The details increased with each second.

Cities, roads, and buildings.

"Congratulations, Goldstein," Flemming said as he stood then walked around the imager and patted him on the back, not taking his eyes off the image.

"So that's what a hologram looks like," the general commented, also staring. "Amazing. M.I.T. huh, son? Amazing. Is this real-time data?"

"Yes sir. All three satellites appear to be working fine."

"My god," Kramer continued, rocking back and forth in his chair while pinching his chin.

Goldstein rotated his chair and looked up at Flemming. "It's a little shaky, I know, but it should stabilize," he repeated.

"Good. Can we zoom in yet?" Flemming asked.

"Yes," Goldstein answered, then hit a few more keys. "What location?"

"Tehran. Downtown."

"Yes sir."

The image shut off entirely and a new one began to be painted, everything in green. Small buildings grew atop the platform, floor by floor, and miniature cars and trucks moved through the streets that came to life, everything in three-dimensional form.

"It's actually working," Goldstein exclaimed, also amazed.

Everyone leaned forward, watching additional details of Tehran filter in.

"My word," Kramer said under his breath, "a live picture of Tehran, in 3D."

"Incredible isn't it, sir?" Flemming added, turning to him.

"Sure is. I can't believe it's really working. Iran's military and nuclear scientists won't be able to take a piss without us knowing it," Kramer replied and even released a slight smile.

"Yes sir, General. May I suggest we test the laser now. We're far enough away from Florida."

"Very well."

Flemming walked to the galley, entered the tiny elevator, and descended to the lower level. There, three men were seated at another control console, what is referred to as the battle station.

"We're ready to test, gentlemen."

"Yes sir," Captain Nelson said, swiveling his chair to the left. He made eye contact with the other two men. "Proceed with test firing." The men were clearly ready, eyes peeled wide open, backs stiff, posture military perfect. It would be the first time the onboard laser was fired in the air with full power.

Nelson again turned and looked up at Flemming. "Where do you want to aim it, sir?"

Flemming moved his attention to a monitor showing a map of the region where the plane was at the moment.

Flemming answered, "Ten degrees nose up, continue steady, eastward, twelve o'clock, level optics and on auto, assuming we get the okay from the cockpit that there are no planes or satellites in the laser's path. I'll tell Major Fletcher to climb, then I'll give you the okay. Go ahead and check for clearance with our friends at Space Command.

243

We don't want to hit something we shouldn't, and knock out satellite TV and telephones for the next five years."

"Yes sir."

Suddenly Flemming became more confident as he said firmly, "Prepare to fire." He then grabbed a phone attached to a vertical column. "Flemming here. We're ready to test the laser."

"Yes sir," Major Fletcher replied.

"Raise the nose ten degrees and maintain course."

"Yes sir," Fletcher replied.

"I'll let you know how it goes." Flemming hung up and turned toward the battle station. Twenty seconds later the plane was climbing at full power, ready for the test. "Are we clear yet?" he asked, bracing himself by means of a plastic handle dangling from the ceiling.

"Yes sir," Nelson answered.

"Okay, give me two seconds on armed mode and then go to standby. On three . . ."

"Yes sir, on three. Going to armed mode." Nelson twisted a key.

Flemming cleared his throat then said, "One. Two. Three. Fire."

"Firing now." Nelson pushed a lever forward on the control console and the laser instantly illuminated the dark sky the plane was aimed at. It fired straight as an arrow for exactly two seconds, then shut off by itself. A buzzing sound emitted from a panel.

Flemming moved closer. "Which alarm is it?"

"Heat, sir. It did the same thing on some of the ground tests, even at half power. It should go away in a few seconds."

"I thought they fixed that."

"Me too, sir."

Flemming's chest bulged as he took a deep breath, shaking his head. "How was the power?"

"Normal sir."

"Deflecting lenses and mirrors?"

"They were right on, from what we can tell here. The system made ninety-five corrections." Nelson said, then looked down at the console again. "No, make that ninety-seven."

"Good. Okay, looks like we're as ready as we'll ever be. Go to safety and standby." Flemming went over to the phone. He picked it up and said, "You can level off. We're done testing."

"Yes sir. How did it go?"

"Everything looks okay now, but the laser, or optics, got too hot. Nelson is looking into it. Stay on course along the Saudi-Persian Gulf coast."

"Yes sir."

Flemming hung up the phone, then entered the elevator and rose to the imager level.

"How did we do, Flemming?" Kramer asked, twisting sideways in his chair. He pulled out a cigar and searched his shirt pocket for matches.

Before Flemming could reply, Goldstein somewhat timidly interjected, "General, I wouldn't smoke. It may interfere with the Imager. It has sensitive optics, sir. Sorry."

Kramer nodded, grinding his square jaw back and forth a few times.

Flemming sat down near the Imager, turning to Kramer. "Everything seems okay, sir. The system got hotter than we like, but it did the same thing in some of the ground tests, without damage. It should be fine, if it's not fired consecutively too quickly."

"Good. Well, hopefully we won't have to use it." Kramer stuck the cigar back in his pocket and stared at the 3D video before him, which Goldstein now had in a wide-angle mode. There was little detail. Only mountains and the Persian Gulf could be distinguished clearly. He started to speak but stopped, leaning toward the image. "What are all those blue dots?" He reached into the hologram, pointing. His arm became green all the way up to his elbow, with swirling and distorted psychedelic images, as if a tattoo had come to life on his skin.

"This thing won't hurt me will it?" Kramer asked, referring to the beam of light hitting his arm.

"No sir," Flemming replied. He paused briefly then turned to his right and asked, "Is that radar data, Goldstein?"

Goldstein cleared his throat and answered proudly, "Yes sir. We just picked up the feeds from the AWACS."

Flemming moved closer to the image coming in. "General, those dots you're pointing at represent aircraft flying over the Persian Gulf. Blue dots are either our planes or allied aircraft, most likely Saudi or British."

"You're serious? Real-time radar combined with the 3D live satellite image of Iran?"

"Yes sir."

"And what are the red dots?"

"Iranian aircraft, sir," Flemming answered then looked at the image. There were currently only three red dots, directly over Tehran.

Kramer was speechless. He just moved his hand through the image and poked at the dots that were slowly moving around in midair, temporarily making them disappear. Most were on an east-west route, south of Tehran. He tilted back in his chair. "Amazing, absolutely amazing. Okay, well, what I want to do is talk about where these bastards might have missiles hidden. Maybe we should start with you, Victoria, since you're the expert." This he said with more than a trace of sarcasm.

But Victoria ignored the undertone. "Very well, sir." She leaned forward, resting a palm on the platform. "If the Iranian military have actually developed or acquired ICBMs to deliver nuclear payloads, they would have probably chosen older, proven Russian-made missiles. Either SS-25 Sickles, SS-24 Scalpels, or the SS-18 Satan." She paused, clearing her throat and coughing. She sounded terrible, no doubt from sitting on the beach last night with Tom in the damp air, after they left the restaurant.

She continued, "Their ranges are ten to eleven thousand kilometers, fully fueled. Perhaps a bit further with a good tail wind. Now, the latest version of the SS-25 is road-mobile, and I'm sure Iran would love to have a few. They could move them anywhere they want, night or day. But if Iran has been sold some of those, I doubt that they have the latest version. It's more likely that they have the leftovers from either the Ukraine, Kazakhstan, or Belarus."

246

"How many warheads are we talking about?" Kramer asked.

"Ten on the SS-24 and SS-18. One on the SS-25, but it's a point-five-five MT, sir. Any of them can wipe out an entire city quite easily. For example, if they have SS-18s, each missile can pack an explosive punch that would be about fifteen hundred times greater than the bomb dropped on Hiroshima."

Kramer nodded a couple of times and Flemming exhaled loudly, rubbing his face nervously. He then looked at Victoria and asked, "Fifteen hundred times greater than Hiroshima? From just one missile?"

"That's right. So," Victoria said, "if we continue our comparison, the Hiroshima bomb completely destroyed five square miles, ninety percent of the buildings, killed almost a hundred and fifty thousand people, and injured about the same number. And all by the end of 1945. The actual impact, of course, was much greater if we factor in cancer and inherited diseases. You see, the radiation not only caused problems for the survivors, but also for their children, since genetic errors occurred and perpetuated some effects. We still don't know the full impact."

Flemming moved closer. "So if Iran were to carry out their threats against Israel, which is relatively close for them to attack, and if they hit even one of the cities there, the—"

"What regions have they threatened?" Victoria interrupted. "Israel *and* others?"

"Yes. Israel, New York, and the D.C. area."

She shook her head slowly. "Gentlemen, if they hit any of those targets, millions of people will be killed. And that's a best case scenario."

"Best case?"

"Yes, the death and destruction could be much worse. You see, nuclear explosions release energy in the form of the blast, direct nuclear radiation, direct thermal radiation, and pulses of electric and magnetic energy, or EMP, as well as the radioactive fallout. Everything from the weather to the altitude of the explosion can change the effects of all these." She paused, pulling some of her hair over her left shoulder. "Also, If one of their missiles includes MIRVs, Multiple Independently Targeted Re-entry Vehicles, then the situation could be even worse, as prior to landing the warheads break off and, in essence, become separate missiles. The damage area becomes immense and rather unpredictable. Gentlemen, we had all better pray that Iran isn't planning on using them."

Flemming held a hand up to his cheek and fluttered his fingers nervously.

Victoria continued, "So, the blast constitutes about fifty percent of the total energy released. You all know what the blast can do. As for thermal radiation, it makes up about thirty-five percent and causes blindness and severe burning for, depending on the strike, seven to forty-five miles away. It also sets everything on fire. I don't mean to be so graphic, but I'm sure you want the facts, no matter how unpleasant they are."

Kramer nodded. "That's right. Please continue, Victoria."

"At the time of the explosion there is also intense ionizing radiation. A dose of one hundred rem causes acute radiation sickness, while a dose of one thousand rem is lethal. The larger the weapon, the more deaths there will be, proportionately, by radiation, as compared to the blast or the thermal radiation. With a one megaton blast, harmful doses of fallout might cover an area of roughly one thousand square miles, but the radioactive particles can spread much further and can last for years. For example, there are still some particles returning to Earth from the stratosphere, where they were thrust after the atmospheric tests in the fifties and sixties. Wonderful things we've invented, aren't they."

Kramer tilted his chair back. "Would you advise evacuating the cities that Iran has threatened? I mean, clearly Iran's leadership will take aim first at Israel. Perhaps people could evacuate."

"No," she answered without hesitation. "The panic that would ensue wouldn't be worth the number of lives you would save. In fact, it's doubtful you would save many lives. There's no way you can move that many people out of a city in time, and outside of the explosion and fallout zone. And if this whole thing is just a hoax, you'll have caused rioting and complete chaos, and probably will have also prompted counter-attacks. Plus, where would people go? They'd have to be moved far enough away to get out of range, then sheltered and fed. The food and water would be contaminated, so there's really no purpose in evacuation."

"You make it sound pretty hopeless," Kramer continued.

"Yes. I'm afraid it is, if Iran truly intends to launch a nuclear armed missile. Even if one survives the blast, there would be disintegration of family life and social context, disorientation, grief, and guilt for the living. Not to mention the uncertainties over the consequences of radiation doses. In Japan, the survivors became known as *Hibakuska*—those who have seen hell. And indeed, living in such an environment would be hellish, if not impossible."

There was silence for several seconds, her words registering.

"And the long-term effects?" Flemming asked.

"Depending on the number of warheads detonated, destruction of the ozone would cause sunburns, wipe out many types of plants, and blind or kill most animals. And, then, you can have the nuclear winter scenario—smoke and debris would throw the planet into a deep gloom, if you will, and lead to a reduction in land and sea temperatures. Temperatures could fall to minus twenty-three degrees Fahrenheit in the center of the continents in the northern hemisphere. Little if any light would get through. Crops and the entire food chain would obviously collapse. People would starve."

"Death of the Earth?" Flemming asked, then cleared his throat nervously.

"Yes. Well, actually, something would probably survive. Maybe some bacteria. But definitely not humans. Life, as we know it, would die. Something else would start over, and evolve into God only knows what, given the ongoing radiation."

"Okay, well, so much for the good news," Kramer said under his breath. "Hard to believe that one or two crazy leaders can kill a planet, isn't it. All right. Thank you, Victoria. That was enlightening." He paused and turned to Goldstein and continued, "Guess this damn thing of yours better work, Goldstein. If we don't find where Iran has their missiles hidden, well, you heard what she said."

Goldstein nodded his head rapidly, his eyes intense.

"Victoria," Kramer continued as he pulled out his cigar, unwrapped it, then chewed on its end for a moment. "Let me ask you another question." He stood and began to walk around the imager.

"Yes sir."

"I want you to put yourself into the frame of mind of Iran's leaders and military, as unpleasant as that may be."

"Okay." Victoria already knew where the general was going.

"Where would you place ICBM launch sites?" he asked, walking over and standing behind the back of her chair. He leaned over, gazing over her right shoulder and at the video coming in. His head was just inches away from hers.

Tom peered over from the back of the cabin, wondering what the hell Kramer was doing near her. He could see that she was struggling to concentrate.

Victoria seemed to hesitate, then said, "Well sir, I'd probably place them in many locations, to prevent destruction of all of them, just like they have spread their nuclear development program across the country. But I'd probably place missile launch sites in Tehran, since it's a big city and would be less likely to be targeted."

In her time at the CIA, Victoria had written many reports on Iran's nuclear development program, including descriptions of the facilities and sites associated with the program. In fact, she was one of the CIA's liaisons to Israel's Mossad, otherwise known as the *Institute for Intelligence and Special Operations*, whose mission is to conduct covert intelligence beyond Israel's borders, prevent development and procurement of non-conventional weapons by hostile countries, and carry out special operations outside Israel. Victoria had cooperated with the Mossad on a recent report which detailed potential sites to target within Iran. The list included the Tehran Nuclear Research Center, Isfahan Nuclear Technology Center, the massive Nantanz Enrichment Facility, Bandar Abbas Uranium Production Plant, and the Keyeh Cutting-Tools Complex where centrifuge parts are made. The CIA and the Mossad had determined that many of Iran's nuclear development sites were built deep underground. The Natanz enrichment facility, for example, is six stories underground. And the Fordow facility outside Qum has centrifuges spinning in a facility built under shelf rock almost three hundred feet thick, which the Pentagon had questioned whether America's Massive Ordinance Penetrator, a 30,000 pound bomb designed to be dropped by modified B-2 Stealth bombers, would even be able to destroy such a facility.

General Kramer scanned the 3D image before them in complete silence for what seemed like a minute. He then turned to Victoria again and asked, "But where, Victoria? Let's focus on Tehran. Where in Tehran would the Iranian government place nuclear-armed missiles?"

Victoria began to speak but Kramer pivoted to Goldstein at the control panel. "Give me another zoom on Tehran, closer this time."

"Yes sir." The hologram vanished and a new image appeared.

Kramer shifted his attention back to Victoria. "Where, Victoria? Where would you hide the missiles?"

"Well, I doubt they would place them at religious sites. That would be too controversial with the Iranian people. They would probably put them near refineries and oil reserve areas which are already protected with excellent security and air defenses. And perhaps they would place them near schools, or hospitals, since Iran would probably think that Israel, or the U.S., would never bomb in those locations."

Kramer made a lap around the imager, viewing each side of the video coming in of Tehran, then walked slowly back to his chair and sat down. "You don't think Iran's leaders would hide missiles near religious sites? I'm not so sure about that. I think the record shows pretty clearly that Iran's leaders could give a rat's ass about their own people. Half of them are practically starving or bankrupt because of the sanctions. If religious sites are at the top of your list of places they *wouldn't* hide weapons, they are probably the best places to hide them."

Kramer leaned forward, placing his face into the hologram. The green light made his wrinkles appear more pronounced, and he

251

suddenly took on the twisted lime-colored face of the *Grinch Who Stole Christmas* peering down at Whoville.

He continued, "Victoria, what religious sites would Iran think we would never strike at, or near?"

Victoria paused for a moment, thinking through the many religious sites in Tehran. But suddenly her mind shifted to a site she had visited. It wasn't even in Tehran. She looked at General Kramer and said, "Actually, the least likely place they would expect anyone to suspect nuclear development or weapons is probably the Imām Reza shrine—the largest mosque in the world. It is the center of tourism in Iran, too."

Kramer's back stiffened, "The largest mosque in the world? So where is it? What part of Tehran? Let's take a look."

"It's not in Tehran, general. It is in Mashhad, Iran. I actually visited there many years ago. It is a vast complex of over six million square feet and has multiple mosques, a museum, library, four seminaries, a university, and numerous courtyards and golden domes."

She turned to her left, toward Goldstein. "Can you zoom in on the city of Mashrad?"

"Sure."

A few seconds passed and the image changed.

"Yes, there it is," she said.

"There what is?" Kramer moved closer.

"Imām Reza shrine."

"Tell me more, Victoria."

"Well sir, it dates to about the 16th century, I believe. It has gold-capped domes and minarets that rise above a central courtyard."

"Minarets?"

"Yes sir. You know, towers. Some are used to call people to prayer. They're all over the Middle East. Many are quite tall and angled, or rather tapered, at the upper portions. Actually, they look a bit like missiles, come to think of it."

"All right then. Give me a close-up of this Imām Reza shrine," Kramer said, turning to Goldstein.

Goldstein glanced over at Victoria. "Where's it at?"

She stood and reached into the hologram. "Right here," she continued as she pointed. "See the outline of the main courtyard? And the domes, over here?"

"Yeah. Give me a sec." Goldstein licked his lips as if he was going in for a kill. He typed new coordinates into the imager.

General Kramer moved over to him and asked, "How close can you zoom in, son?"

"How close do you want, sir? Do you want to see the whole complex? Or be able to count the bricks in the courtyard?"

"You're serious?" Kramer asked, placing one hand on Goldstein's shoulder, suddenly his best friend.

"Yes sir. However close you want."

"Let's start with a shot of the general area."

"Okay." A few more keystrokes by Goldstein and the image again vanished, and was soon replaced by a much closer view of Imām Reza shrine.

"My God," Victoria whispered as the image of the buildings, domes and minarets gradually came in with increasing levels of detail. "You can even see people walking around. Look."

"Pretty impressive," Kramer added, nodding excitedly, and then offering a rare smile which created two rows of vertical canyons on each side of his mouth. "These are the, what did you call them, minarets?" he asked, pointing.

Victoria leaned forward. "Yes sir. Minarets."

"They do look like missiles, don't they."

"Yes sir."

"Okay, where else?"

"Sir?"

"Where else would Iran's leaders likely hide nuclear armed missiles. At other shrines?"

Victoria contemplated her answer for a few seconds, then said, "Perhaps sir, but this is the biggest and I believe the most important shrine in Iran, and closest to a high-population area. I doubt they would expect anyone to possibly imagine that they would hide nuclear-armed missiles at such an historic, spiritually significant site. It's just too

253

important to Iranian history. They'd never expect another nation to take any sort of military action around this site, or even inspect all those facilities. It's the perfect hiding place for weapons, or weapons development."

Kramer nodded then cleared his throat. He turned to Goldstein again. "Okay, zoom out again, to the city view. A wider angle."

Again the image changed and small buildings began to grow atop the imager platform, glowing bright green. Little cars and trucks scurried about the streets as if they were remote control toys racing around a labyrinth of tiny streets.

Kramer looked over at Victoria. "How familiar are you with the government and military facilities in the area surrounding the shrine?"

"I'm afraid I really don't know enough to tell you where they are, sir. Or their purpose. I only visited this city once, and just briefly."

Goldstein scratched his head, thinking. Suddenly his eyes became wide and you could almost see a light bulb go off above his head. Clearly he had an idea.

"What is it Goldstein?" Kramer asked.

"I just remembered that I can overlay the names of streets and major buildings. We did it a few times back at the labs."

Kramer raised his eyebrows slightly. "You can overlay the names of streets and buildings, for Mashrad, Iran?"

"Yes, sir."

"How the hell do you do that?"

"Google maps, sir."

The general shook his head in amazement and said, "Well, do it son. I want to know where any government buildings are in Mashrad. Military or civil service."

Goldstein quickly entered a command into the control keyboard, enabling map labels. Almost instantly, small name tags appeared above many of the buildings and streets, hovering just above them.

Victoria and General Kramer looked at the larger buildings being displayed, and the names above them.

"Victoria," Kramer asked, "do you see any buildings that might be military-related."

"No sir, I really can't tell based on what I see at this zoom level."

Kramer coughed slightly then grabbed a bottle of water from the galley area of the plane. He paced back and forth for a few minutes, as everyone looked on. Finally, he returned to the imager and looked at Goldstein. "Zoom back into the shrine area. I want to take a closer look at those buildings and courtyards. Victoria here seems pretty sure of herself, that the shrine area would be the least likely place anyone would look for weapons." This was said with an air of chauvinism, as if he really didn't believe Victoria could make such an educated guess. Nevertheless, he continued, "If it is indeed the world's largest shrine, and so important, maybe she's right. Maybe the Iranian government is hiding something there."

Once again, Goldstein zoomed in on the vast area of the Imām Reza shrine.

The general leaned over the imager, obliterating almost half of what was projected, and pointed to an area off of the main courtyard. "What's this over here? Can you zoom in closer Goldstein?"

"Yes sir. One second."

"No, that's not it," Kramer barked. "Zoom out again."

Goldstein tapped at the keyboard in a blur.

Kramer backed further away, his face moving out of the green lighted area. "There you go. This building, or whatever it is, right here. Zoom in, son."

"Yes sir, just a second."

"That's it. There you go. There you go." Kramer focused in on the image of a large complex with a couple of buildings in the middle. A fence surrounded them and a gate house was situated on the north side. The complex wasn't more than a football field away from the main courtyard of the shrine.

"Give me a zoom on this, Goldstein." Kramer pointed to a large square object, near one of the buildings.

"Okay." Goldstein hit a couple keys. Suddenly almost the entire imaging area was filled with a huge square object, with no doors or vents or air conditioners on top. There was nothing but a single seam, or a striped dark line, right down the middle of the square and separating each half. Compared to the nearby buildings, which had tiles and air conditioners and all sorts of pipes and wires atop them, the perfectly square and clean-surface of the building they were focusing on stood out like a sore thumb. It simply looked completely out of place at the shrine complex.

Goldstein zoomed in a bit more.

Suddenly Victoria jumped back, startled and almost stumbling over her own high heels. The building, or whatever it was, now covered almost the entire surface of the imager.

"Awesome!" Goldstein pushed his chair back, trying to take it all in.

Kramer stood. He walked around the imager in a complete circle. "Does this look familiar to you, Flemming."

"No sir."

"How about you, Victoria. Have you seen anything like this before?"

"Well, sir, yes. It resembles a bunker or a silo, a missile silo, but I'm sure it's—"

"I agree, Victoria. It does look a lot like a missile silo." His eyes shifted to Flemming. "See the seam on the doors, Flemming? Right here. And the hinges on the outside edges?"

"It could just be a bunker, General. Or some sort of storage facility?"

"With doors that open skyward, Flemming? I don't think so. This just doesn't look right."

Once again the general paced back and forth. He seemed to talk to himself a few times. At one point he glanced over at Flemming and said, "We really can't waste too much time reviewing one particular site. We need to find more sites ASAP and get the coordinates to command, just in case they need to target them."

256

Flemming nodded obediently. The general was stating the obvious. But they were spending a lot of time staring at one building in one city in Iran.

Kramer approached, pinching his chin nervously and continued, "I think Iran's leaders may have indeed placed either missiles or some sort of nuclear weapons development facility in the heart of the biggest damn shrine in the world. That's what I would do, if I were them."

The cabin went silent, except for the sound of the 747's engines and the cooling fans of the imager.

Kramer pointed at the strange building again, "You could put a missile—maybe even several—in such a complex. Right?" He looked at Victoria and then at Flemming.

"Yes sir," Flemming pensively agreed, as he straightened his back. He didn't seem convinced. He looked at Victoria, obviously wanting another opinion on what Kramer was claiming. Victoria seemed to pick up the cue.

She turned to Kramer and said, "General, I don't think this is a missile silo. I'm quite sure it's simply a bunker where the occupants of the nearby buildings can seek shelter. Iran would never put a missile silo out in plain sight like this. It just doesn't make sense."

Flemming appeared relieved. At least someone was making sense and calming the waters.

"I disagree, Victoria," Kramer replied. "I've seen countless intelligence reports on Iran, including several satellite photographs of facilities. This building, whatever the hell it is, is completely out of place for such a religious site. It's modern-looking, and obviously much newer than anything around it. And that's probably why it isn't camouflaged yet. Or maybe Iran just assumes we'd never even consider looking for weapons or nuclear development facilities at a shrine," the general said vehemently, then turned to Goldstein and ordered, "Zoom out ten percent."

The image changed to a wider view of the shrine. "Flemming, I want you to notify Jansen at King Khalid Air Base. Tell him what we've identified, and to add this facility to the potential target list—if it should come to that."

Flemming moved closer, looking Kramer square in the eyes. "But if we're wrong, we may kill hundreds or even thousands of civilians, including tourists visiting the shrine. And we'll surely cause major damage to nearby, very historic buildings at the shrine. If we're wrong, it would be a disaster."

"We're not ordering an attack, Flemming. I'm just being cautious. For godsakes, Iran has threatened to fire ICBMs at America and Israel. *That* would be a disaster."

Flemming said, "Yes, sir. I know but—"

"This looks like it might be a missile silo, right?"

"Yes."

"Now get on the phone and tell Command what we think we've found, and to standby!" Kramer's face turned bright pink. He pointed to the imager. "What the hell good is this thing if we don't communicate what we see?"

A long pause, then, "Yes sir. But shouldn't we notify the Secretary of Defense first?"

"No. I don't want to rile anyone up just yet."

"But the procedure is to—"

"That's an order, Flemming."

"Yes sir."

Tom, who had been listening to every word he could hear over the sound of the engines, was literally sitting on the edge of his seat, in complete disbelief that Kramer was actually considering a strike, apparently with little or no proof of what the facility really was. He could tell that Flemming didn't agree with the general's assessment. Flemming was just following orders, and looked like a nervous wreck, sweating head to toe with perspiration under his armpits and down his back. And Victoria seemed equally anxious. Tom couldn't help but wonder whether General Kramer was just using the strange building they had identified as an excuse for going after Iran. Something to light the match. A reason to initiate an attack on Iran and address all the years of nuclear development.

Flemming hung up a red phone on a nearby wall near the galley area of the plane, then walked back to the imager.

"Did you get through?" Kramer inquired.

"Yes sir, I did. I gave them the coordinates."

"Good." Kramer sat down in one of the leather chairs and took a deep breath.

Victoria glanced at the general, then her eyes moved to Tom. She could tell that he wanted her to come over to him. She started to turn in her chair and rise, but she stopped as Kramer stood and began pacing back and forth alongside the communications console again. He seemed to be weighing his options, and appeared more intense. He paused, looking down at the imager. "What's that, a truck rolling in?" His eyes moved to Flemming for half a second. "It's military, isn't it?"

Flemming moved closer. The image of a large truck with a tarp over its bed was making its way into the shrine complex. "It might not be military, sir. It's probably just a delivery truck."

"No, that's definitely military, Flemming. Just look at it. What the hell is it doing at a shrine? With a truck that big they could hide a missile inside. It's certainly large enough."

Flemming's mouth dropped slightly. "Yes sir, we better keep an eye on it, General. I'll notify the—"

"Notify my ass, Flemming," Kramer snapped. "I want to take this facility out."

"Sir, if I may say, I don't think we have enough evidence to support such a recommendation. I suggest we order a fly-by, you know, get some color photographs and other assessments and—"

"There's no time, Flemming. They've threatened to fire missiles and they know they need to get them off before we take action. I believe this facility may be a launch complex. I'm not going to wait to find out. I want it taken out. That's clearly a military vehicle and it is now within the shrine complex. And look, here's another one. And another one."

Suddenly there were over a dozen vehicles driving toward the shrine from all directions. And most appeared to be military-type heavy-duty trucks, some with trailers in tow.

Flemming coughed slightly, swallowed hard, then said, "I just think we should check with—"

"We're the eyes here, Flemming. The Secretary of State and the Joint Chiefs are waiting for our assessment. We're calling the shots. That's what we are here for," Kramer continued. He suddenly seemed far too calm, like he had rehearsed the entire conversation a hundred times and was just going through the motions.

"General, I suggest we at least check with the other 747 Airborne Laser, you know, have their team verify," he said as firmly as he could.

"We're ordering an attack, Flemming. Period!" Kramer walked over to his briefcase, which was near the galley. He thumbed the two combination locks to the open position, then reached in his pocket and pulled out a key. He inserted the key in the hole between the combination locks and a split-second later the case lid popped open. He removed a brown manila envelope, the standard office variety. The case was promptly snapped shut.

Nearby, Flemming appeared as if he would have a coronary any moment, as he watched the general. His face was shiny, completely covered in a layer of perspiration. His eyes were darting between each of his men. He reached up and wiped his brow on his sleeve, then looked at Victoria, who was shaking her head slowly.

Back at his seat, Tom's eyes were also glued on General Kramer. Kramer was in the galley, grasping the envelope in his left hand and holding a cup of water with his right, drinking slowly, his hands appearing to shake. Then Tom looked over at Flemming, and immediately tried to wave him over without the general seeing.

Victoria noticed that they were communicating and decided to try and keep Kramer occupied in the galley. She motioned to Flemming (by tilting her head two times) for him to go over to Tom.

Flemming swiftly made his way over and sat in the seat next to Tom, trying to stay ducked down behind another row of seats at the front of the 747.

"What is it?" Flemming asked. His breathing was labored.

260

Tom whispered, "You know damn well that may not be a missile silo. I heard everything you and Kramer said. You know we can't let Kramer initiate an attack just because of that strange building, right? I can see it in your eyes."

Flemming nodded twice, and his eyes dropped.

Tom continued, "You have to stop him. He's just out for revenge."

"What do you mean?"

"One of his sons was killed in Iran. You know about that, right?"

"Yes."

"Well, I think it's the General's pay-back time. I think Kramer wants to take out Iran's nuclear development program, at least, and regardless of the consequences. I'm not kidding you. I interviewed him the other day. This is all about vengeance and creating some sort of legacy for himself—something to be remembered by. He even told me that. He wants to be remembered for getting rid of Iran's nuclear program and saving, as he told me, Israel from destruction. He actually thinks he's preventing a 21st century holocaust."

Flemming blew his cheeks outward and inhaled deeply. "He actually said all that?"

"Yes. I swear. Every word."

A bead of sweat rolled down the left side of Flemming's temple. "But he may be right, Lassiter."

"I know. I know," Tom said, nodding his head quickly. "He may be right. But clearly there's not enough evidence to initiate an attack on Iran at this point. You have to go over General Kramer's head. You have to tell them what I just told you."

Flemming's face became even sterner, staring right into Tom's eyes. "If you're wrong, I'll be court-martialed. We're talking mutiny here."

"I know. But you don't have any choice." Tom paused for a couple seconds. "I saw him take an envelope out of his briefcase. What's in it?"

"It could be the codes."

"For ordering an attack?"

"Among other actions," Flemming whispered.

"My god. This is insane." He looked toward the galley. Kramer appeared to be yelling at Victoria. She was standing in the hallway and blocking him, but Tom could see his hands flying to the air and could hear his voice. He turned to Flemming. "You better get away from me. She can't keep him pinned down forever."

He nodded. "I don't know what to do."

"Just stop him. Somehow, you have to stop him."

Flemming rose with weak knees and sauntered back to the imager and sat down. He wiped his face on his right sleeve and loosened his collar.

Victoria glanced over her shoulder and Tom, making an "OK" sign with his fingers, let her know that it was alright to let Kramer return to the imager area. She said something else to Kramer then turned around and went back to the leather chair she had been sitting in. She gave Flemming a piercing look, to which he nodded in silent reply.

Kramer poured himself some more water, swigged it back, then walked over as he crunched another antacid tablet. He still had the envelope in his hand.

Flemming cleared his throat, trying to get Kramer's attention, then asked, "Should we take a look at some more sites, General?" Flemming then looked over at Goldstein. "Zoom out to the city view. I want to see some other areas."

"No!" Kramer yelled. "Leave the imager alone. I don't want to see any other parts of the city!" He then quickly walked over to the communications console and picked up a red phone.

Flemming inched forward in his chair, hesitating, then stood. "General, put the phone down, please."

Kramer swung around, again his face brightening instantly. "What was that, Flemming?"

"I said put the phone down, general. Please." Flemming took a few steps forward. "And give me that envelope, sir."

Kramer tilted his head slightly. He obviously couldn't believe what he was hearing. "Do you know what you're doing, Flemming?"

"Yes sir. The envelope, sir."

Kramer gulped some air and glanced over at the other men, clearly attempting to assess how many people were supporting Flemming's actions. Leckart's mouth was hanging partially open and he was blank-faced. Rodriguez turned and buried his face in a control panel to his left.

"A mutiny for christ sakes?" Kramer said. "Is that what this is, Flemming?"

Flemming remained silent. Tom could see his hands trembling.

"We've been through a lot, Flemming. You're asking for a court-martial, and you know it. Is that what you want?" Kramer asked, staring with intense eyes. "Now get your ass to that chair. I'll deal with you in a minute." He turned to the communications console, raised the phone to his ear with his left hand, then reached to the keypad with his right.

Flemming surged forward and grabbed the phone. Tom was shocked that the old boy had it in him. Tom then looked at Kramer, who appeared just as shocked.

Kramer backed away from Flemming slightly then said, "You're going to regret this, Flemming." He turned to the other men. "Leckart, Rodriguez, I want you to apprehend Lt. Colonel Flemming and escort him to a chair."

Leckart stood and moved his eyes to Flemming, who was slowly shaking his head.

"That's an order, Leckart," Kramer continued. "Off your ass, Rodriguez."

Rodriguez stood up, but didn't move further.

Kramer's eyes moved back to Flemming.

"General, I'm relieving you from duty," Flemming said firmly. "You're clearly violating protocol. You know damn well that any attack has to go through the Secretary and the President. It's my duty to stop you. I'm sorry, General." Flemming then looked at Leckart. "Do we have handcuffs on board?"

"No sir. But there are some nylon restraining straps with the first aid kit and supplies."

Tom noticed that Kramer's chest was rising and falling rapidly.

Kramer looked down at the floor, then up at each of the men. He then turned away and stared at the phone in Flemming's hand and yelled, "Give me that damn phone!" He rushed toward Flemming and tackled him to the floor. They both hit hard, slamming against the communications console. Tom ran toward them. By the time he got close, Kramer was on top of Flemming, punching his face, spit flying from his mouth.

"You bastard, how dare you ignore my orders!" Kramer screamed. He threw a few more punches.

Flemming's mouth was bleeding when Leckart and Tom finally managed to pull Kramer off of him.

"God damn it!" Kramer continued, his arms swinging madly.

"Rodriguez," Leckart yelled. "Get the nylon ties. Hurry!"

Tom finally managed to get hold of Kramer's left arm and Leckart secured his right.

"All of you are going to jail. Hear me? All of you! You have no idea what you've just gotten yourselves into. No idea." Kramer continued to try and pull away.

Flemming gradually rose to his feet. Victoria ran over and handed him a Kleenex, which instantly became soaked with blood as he blotted his mouth. She searched for something else to hold to his face. "Hang on," she said, then moved quickly to the galley.

Rodriguez approached with a nylon tie, about twelve inches long.

Leckart grabbed the tie. "Help me tie his wrists." He grasped Kramer's wrists, squeezing them together. Rodriguez just stood still, completely frozen. Flemming, who continued to drip blood from his mouth and nose, grabbed the tie and secured Kramer's wrists. He then bent over and picked up the envelope, which Kramer had dropped during the scuffle. He reached for Kramer's security briefcase, popped it open, and tossed it in. Victoria walked over with a roll of paper towels. She handed them to him and he blotted his face some more, wincing from the pain.

Leckart escorted Kramer over to one of the blue seats on the right side of the cabin. Kramer's anger somehow shifted to a comatose look. His face was still red, but it was deadpan. Then, just as quickly, it saddened and his eyes became glassy. He exhaled and sunk back into the chair.

"Should we tie him down, sir?" Leckart asked.

Flemming started to say something but Kramer interrupted. "That won't be necessary," he said slowly. A calmness swept over him.

Flemming moved his eyes to Leckart and shook his head a couple times. "The nylon tie should be enough."

"Yes sir."

"Keep an eye on him. I'm going up to the cockpit for a minute," Flemming continued, then made his way to the front of the plane. He continued to blot his mouth and nose.

Tom moved back to the chair he had been sitting in, completely amazed and thinking what a story all of this was going to make for *The Washington Post*. He could see the headlines already.

Victoria approached Tom with a wet towel. "Here, you have blood all over."

"Thanks." Tom took the towel and wiped off his face and arms.

CHAPTER TWENTY-SIX

Everyone, even Flemming who had blotted his face for fifteen minutes with everything from paper towels to folded drink coasters, had calmed down since the skirmish with Kramer. As the shock of the situation settled into acceptance and talk of what to do next, Tom noticed Goldstein getting a soda from the refrigerator in the galley. Goldstein approached him while popping open the can. Fizz shot upward and it started to bubble over the brim. He sucked down what he could then asked Tom, "So you're with the *Post*?"

"Yes, the last time I checked, anyway."

Goldstein turned so his back was facing the area where Kramer was sitting, wrists still tied. "This whole thing should make the front page, huh? I can't believe what's happened."

Tom nodded. "I know. It's crazy."

"Frankly, I never thought I'd even step foot on one of these laser-planes. I've been training two of Flemming's men for the past six weeks on how to use the imager."

"They aren't on board?"

"No. One of them is on the other ABL aircraft. And one is in Europe, apparently on his honeymoon."

"Great timing," Tom said sarcastically, raising his eyebrows slightly.

"Exactly." Goldstein gulped some more soda. "They called me in the middle of the night and said they were sending a plane to get me. They said it was a national security emergency, and wouldn't give me any other information. Try explaining that to your wife."

Tom nodded.

"What do you think they'll do with Kramer?" Goldstein continued, lowering his voice.

"I don't know. Court-martial maybe," Tom answered as he glanced over at the general. Kramer was leaning forward in his seat and resting his forehead on the palms of his hands, a portion of the nylon handcuffs dangling between each wrist.

Goldstein took a long sip of his soda. "Want some, Tom?"

"Yeah, thanks." Goldstein handed over the can and Tom took a long sip. His throat felt raw. He handed it back and wiped the moisture, which the can left on his palm, off on his pant leg.

"Flemming said we're still on alert, heading toward Saudi Arabia, to await further orders," Goldstein continued. He shook his head slowly. "Man, I hope they turn us around." He swigged back some more soda. "So, how the hell does a *Post* reporter wind up on an experimental 747 ABL in the middle of a national emergency?"

"Do you have a couple of hours?"

"That long of a story, huh."

"Afraid so. Well, you've obviously heard of the High Ground program, right?"

Goldstein nodded. "I know of it, but the imaging technology is completely separate from the weapons systems. I'm only involved in the imaging satellites, the computer system, and software design. And the imager itself, of course. This whole thing has been driving me nuts. The Pentagon hasn't said a word about how all this technology interfaces and controls their weapons systems. I can't figure out whether the imaging satellites simply provide data to the airborne lasers and imaging platform, or if there's something else they've developed."

Tom was surprised that Goldstein didn't know more. "They haven't told you anything else?"

"No. Nothing. It's a typical Pentagon trick. Compartmentalize everything so only a few people know the big picture. Do you know what sort of weapons they've deployed?"

"Yes, I know. But not the details," Tom answered.

"How the heck did you find out? What are they—"

"Long story short," Tom interrupted, "I got a tip."

Goldstein nodded quickly, hanging on every word.

Tom motioned to the chair next to him. "I'll fill you in. You might want to have a seat."

Goldstein flopped down in a chair and turned to him. "Tom, whatever they have launched can't be worse than what I've imagined."

"I don't know about that," Tom said under his breath as he also took a seat, then turned to Goldstein and continued, "General Kramer and his personnel managed a weapons development program, a nuclear weapons program. What they've launched is a nuclear-armed satellite, a space-based weapon with missiles capable of launching down at earth, apparently to take the place of a traditional intercontinental launch, which most countries can detect and respond to quickly."

Goldstein was silent for several seconds. He rubbed his forehead hard while shaking his head slowly, realizing that his work on the imaging and positioning system was an integral component of a nuclear weapons platform now hovering over Iran. "My god, you're absolutely sure it's nuclear?" he whispered, just audible over the sound of the plane's engines.

"Yes, I'm positive."

"No wonder." Goldstein looked down, deep in thought, then moved his right hand to the back of his neck, massaging and stretching.

"No wonder what?"

"You saw me enter those coordinates into the imager, right?"

"Yes."

"Well, about six months ago I was asked to provide a high-speed data link, you know, an interface that's separate from the other command channels and bandwidth-intensive video. No scrambling and no compression, just straight kick-ass, ultra-low latency minimal data with nothing to slow it down. They wouldn't tell me what it was for. They just said to output GPS latitude and longitude information of whatever the imager is zoomed in on, in real time."

"For aiming the missiles?" Tom asked.

Goldstein nodded. "That's my guess."

Tom's attention shifted to Victoria, who had been talking with Flemming in the forward galley. She noticed him peering over and approached.

As Victoria sat down next to Tom, Goldstein got up and said, "I'll leave you two alone."

Tom nodded, then turned to Victoria.

She asked, "Are you okay?" She was referring to a small cut on his arm, courtesy of Kramer's stainless steel watch (you know the kind, those big glow-in-the-dark things for skin divers that are rarely even splashed on by a bathroom faucet). It had gouged Tom pretty good during their wrestling match.

Tom looked at his right wrist. "It's nothing," he answered. "I'm fine. So what's the word? Is the alert still on?"

"Yes. Flemming's been ordered to keep us over the Persian Gulf, just off the Iran coast, in case their threats are carried out."

"Do you think they are bluffing?"

"Who knows. We have to take them seriously though. Obviously the United States and Iran relations have been strained for decades. And they know that the US will always be in lock-step with Israel, their arch enemy." Victoria paused, reaching upward and pulling a lock of hair to behind her left ear. "Iran's been in terrible shape since the sanctions were put in place. If they have actually acquired nuclear ICBMs, I'm sure they won't hesitate to use them on Israel, and the United States if they will reach that far." She again paused, looking over at General Kramer, then back at Tom. "He looks pretty bad, doesn't he Tom."

"Yeah, thirty-year career down the tubes, I guess. Maybe they'll go easy on him, because of his previous record of service, and losing two sons in two different Middle East incidents."

"Two sons?"

"You don't know about Kramer's sons?"

She shook her head.

"One of his sons died in a helicopter crash when President Carter sent in troops to try and rescue Americans during the Iranian hostage crisis, back in '79. The other was killed more recently in Afghanistan."

Victoria shook her head slowly left and right then said, "That explains a lot, doesn't it. I wish we could get the General on the ground. He appears as if he's about to pass out, or have a breakdown or something."

"I think we're past that." Tom looked across the aisle. He could see Kramer finally raising his head. The air in the plane's cabin wasn't warm, but he seemed to be sweating and his eyes were darting about. The General appeared panic-stricken all of the sudden.

A terrible thought entered Tom's mind. He thought about a story he'd read about the former head of the Navy who, distraught and embarrassed over a reporter calling into question several of his medals, sadly proceeded to take his life shortly before a scheduled meeting with a news magazine's Washington bureau chief. Everyone at the *Post* was shocked, especially Jake over at the Pentagon. Tom remembered that he even went to the funeral. And now Tom couldn't help thinking that if Kramer had a gun at this moment, he'd probably use it.

"What's wrong?" Victoria whispered.

"I don't like this. Just look at him."

"Maybe there's some sort of sedative we can give him, perhaps in a first aid kit?"

"Can you check? I'll try to—"

Suddenly General Kramer leapt from his seat, arms and nylon handcuffs held straight out, and reached toward the handle to an exit door on the plane's starboard side. Victoria screamed something unintelligible as Flemming and Tom rushed toward Kramer. Kramer grabbed onto the emergency handle and pulled it, but the door wouldn't open. Flemming tried to move him away. Just as Tom made it over, Kramer let go of the handle, grasped both hands together, and swung at Flemming, batting him out of the way with a two-handed fist which was still locked in place with the nylon handcuff tie.

"No!" Tom yelled as Kramer turned then quickly reached for the handle again.

Tom threw himself at Kramer's feet, grasped his legs, and pulled. Kramer wouldn't budge. His hands were firmly latched onto the emergency handle.

Victoria screamed again and backed away from the commotion.

Tom noticed Flemming in the corner of his eye, moving closer again. Leckart was behind him. Then Tom moved his eyes back to the exit door. He heard a loud popping noise and saw the bottom of the door move slightly outward from the 747 fuselage. He heard Flemming yell, "Grab onto something!"

Grasping Kramer's left pant leg with one hand, and lying face down on his stomach, Tom reached with his right arm over to the chair he had been sitting in just seconds ago. He wrapped his arm around a bar (part of the chair's base) and squeezed his fist to his chest, trying to lock himself in place. As he felt Kramer jerking back and forth, continuing to try and open the door, he told himself that the aircraft's engineers surely wouldn't have designed a door that could be opened in flight. Then he looked up at the unusual door before him. It seemed more like an erector set of exposed metal parts, probably designed to allow large equipment to be brought in, such as the imager, he thought. It wasn't a normal 747 door.

A few seconds passed and, all at once, the door shot outward. A deafening swoosh of air exited the plane. Tom felt Kramer, who was now also on the floor, being pulled through the doorway. He looked up. Kramer's head and arms were outside the fuselage. He knew he couldn't hold him much longer. He grasped the General's ankles as tightly as he could. But Kramer slowly moved away from him, sliding out the doorway even more. Pieces of paper, pens, and notebooks flew overhead, then a couple coke cans and an ice bucket. One of the leather chairs from the Imager area tumbled by. Almost everything not tied down was sucked out of the doorway. The noise, the intense, horrible noise. Tom felt like he was being split in two, caught in a twister. He could just barely hear Victoria yelling his name.

The air pressure equalized and the cabin became quieter. Tom's lungs felt empty and his head was dizzy. He couldn't see, he couldn't breathe.

A few minutes later, which seemed like hours, Tom opened his eyes and Victoria's face was staring down at him, tears glistening on her cheeks. He immediately realized that he had been knocked out. He tried to raise his head, but she placed her right hand on his shoulder, holding him down.

She said softly, "Just stay still, Tom. You're all right."

He looked around. He was stretched out on the floor next to the imager. Chairs were strewn around him. A green oxygen canister and clear plastic mask were to his right.

"Is he okay?" Flemming asked, coming into view.

"Yes, he'll be fine. It's just a bump on the head. He'll be fine," Victoria answered, stroking his temple. "A chair or something must have hit him."

Tom tried to get up.

Victoria touched his shoulder once more. "Easy now." She stood and reached down for his hand. "Can you make it to this chair?" She rolled it over.

"Yeah," Tom barely uttered under his breath.

His head aching, he rose to his feet then promptly collapsed into one of the few leather chairs that hadn't flown out the doorway. He looked at the hole in the side of the plane, where the exit door had been, and saw wispy blue-white sky mingled with streaks of sunlight. "My god, did I let go of General Kramer?"

Victoria shook her head. "No, he's downstairs, tied up and sedated."

Leckart approached with a cup of water and a small plastic bottle of aspirin. He handed them to Tom. "Here you go."

"Thanks." He tossed three pills in his mouth and gulped down the water.

Another twenty minutes went by and Tom's head felt somewhat better, the aspirin having a minor effect. He watched as

272

Flemming talked to Rodriguez and Leckart over at the communications console.

Flemming walked over to Victoria and said, "Major Fletcher just got word from the Pentagon. They want us to land in Saudi Arabia and get the door replaced or at least patched somehow, then continue loitering over the Gulf. We should be okay till then, as long as we keep our airspeed down and stay at a low altitude, for oxygen."

The noise from the air blowing in from outside made it hard for Tom to hear anything, but he could just make out the words as Flemming said to Victoria, "I'd still like your help, Ms. Brookshire, if you're up to it."

"Certainly." She stood and moved over to the imager. They both sat down.

"Captain Leckart, would you join us," Flemming continued, glancing over his shoulder.

"Yes sir."

Goldstein was reclined in a chair, feet up on the edge of the imager, and reading an operations manual. He dropped his legs to the floor and scooted forward. Time to get back to work.

Flemming, with General Kramer now out of command, spoke firmly and more confidently, "Although we are heading to Saudi for repairs, we should continue to assess sites in Iran with the Imager. We still need to try and determine where Iran would place ICBMs. I don't believe that Iran would put missiles at that site General Kramer was so fixed on. So let's cross that off our list. What area do you recommend we look at, Ms. Brookshire?"

"Well, as I said earlier, Iran would probably want to hide them near areas with a high concentration of civilians such as large apartment buildings, hospitals, schools, or possibly religious sites such as the site Kramer had us looking at. We could take a look at some of those areas, perhaps near Tehran. But frankly I think we should take a closer look at that site the General had us aiming at before, as some of those buildings indeed looked out of place."

"You're the expert on Iran, Ms. Brookshire. Let's take one more look then," Flemming said, then turned to Goldstein once more. "Give

273

us a picture of the site General Kramer had us looking at. I don't want to spend much more time there, but a quick look is fine."

Goldstein hit a few buttons on the keyboard before him. An image slowly came in, glowing green buildings and cars moving about tiny streets. "How's that?"

"Fine," Flemming replied.

Victoria moved closer to the image. "That's odd. Look at all the traffic over in this area." She pointed to an intersection. "It wasn't like that before. What's this large building over here, with all these cars and trucks and people moving about?"

"Give us a zoom, Goldstein," Flemming said firmly.

"Yes sir. And I should be able to pull up the address information as the GPS data syncs in."

Flemming nodded once.

"Here we go. That building is a hospital," Goldstein continued.

"Goldstein," Flemming continued, "Zoom out a bit. Give us a bigger picture of where all this traffic is coming from and going."

The image changed, all of the buildings getting smaller but more area being revealed.

Victoria said, "Gentlemen, I don't think the cars are heading to or from that hospital. See? They're driving by the entrance. They're moving north."

"Toward the mosque?" Flemming inquired, looking up.

"Perhaps," Victoria answered. "Could we take another look at Kramer's site, but at this zoom level?" She glanced quickly at Goldstein.

"Yes, it'll just be a second. I've got the coordinates stored." He tapped at a few keys and the image disappeared then gradually came up, showing a courtyard, several domes, and a few large minarets.

"What the hell?" Flemming said loudly, moving closer. "Do you see what I see? People are running from the mosque, and out of the courtyard. Get us a little closer, Goldstein. What the—"

"But it looks like some of them are running in," Victoria interrupted. She turned to Goldstein. "Zoom in on these people, the main building, right here."

274

The image changed. Now there were dozens of foot-tall people running atop the imager platform.

"My god . . ." she whispered.

"What?" Flemming asked. "What is it?"

She pointed at one of the people running, then another. "See how they are dressed?"

Flemming moved in closer, "Yes. Are those military uniforms?"

Victoria suddenly became more serious, moving her eyes to Flemming's. "I believe so, sir. It's not right. It just isn't right. These aren't religious men serving at a mosque. These are soldiers."

Flemming walked around the imager, studying the glowing holograms of people running about. He then looked up and nodded a couple times.

Victoria continued, "See? The people who are running away from these other buildings and minarets," she said, pointing, "are dressed appropriately for a religious site. The women are following the *hijab*."

"Hijab?"

"It's the religious dress code for many women in Iran," Victoria answered then paused for several seconds. "Sir, the mosque is being filled with individuals with no interest or respect for this sacred place." She turned to Goldstein. "Zoom out twenty percent please."

The image changed to a wider view.

"What on earth?" Flemming said, raising the tone of his voice. He leaned forward.

Vehicles were pulling up near the mosque. "Those are military, aren't they, Leckart?"

"Yes sir. I believe so." Leckart held a hand over his chin and stared down. "They are up to something. Some sort of alert."

The vehicles continued to pour in. People were jumping out and leaving doors open, then running toward the central dome. Complete chaos.

Flemming swallowed a deep breath and yelled at Rodriguez who was over at the communications console, "Get me the White House, now. The Secretary of Defense should still be there." He paced back and forth, then walked around the imager, doing three laps with his eyes glued to the holograms darting about.

About twenty seconds went by then, "Sir," Rodriguez said loudly. He handed Flemming the red phone. "The Secretary left the White House. He's now on Air Force One."

"Thanks." Flemming turned away and reached for the phone.

Tom stood and moved swiftly over to the imager. He gazed down. "I can't believe this. What the hell are all these soldiers up to down there?"

Suddenly all eyes moved to Flemming as everyone began to listen in, which was almost impossible to do over the sound of air still pouring in from the hole in the fuselage where the door blew out.

Flemming was amazingly calm as he spoke to the Secretary of Defense. "Yes sir, we think they have some sort of military installation hidden near a mosque in the city of Mashhad, the Imām Reza shrine area. Yes, I know this is very sensitive. We could be wrong. But you tell me why they have dozens of military vehicles pulling up to the place, and people scurrying in and out. Yes sir, I know. If we're mistaken, the entire Middle East will be outraged. I'm just telling you what we see, sir. You can confirm with the Joints Chiefs. I understand they have their imager up and running in the War Room. You can also have the other ABL-7-4-7 team take a look. Yes sir, and I—"

All of the sudden, everyone braced themselves as the plane banked sharply to the right, adjusting course. A blast of wind roared through the exit door opening. It lessened as the plane leveled off.

Flemming continued, "Sorry sir, it's a bit hard to hear. Can you repeat? What would I do? Well, I'd stay calm for the time being and just keep an eye on the facility. Like I said, we could be wrong. If we see something to confirm that it's a military site with any sort of nuclear capability, we can hit them with the Stealths using one-ton GBU27 guided bombs. I understand that the Stealths are loitering in the region right now. Yes, that's right. And if it comes to that, we can probably save the mosque, maybe the main dome and sensitive areas. That's right, sir. I know. If they have ICBMs, and if they are planning to launch, there's not much time. But I think the other ABL is getting closer to the area, which will help. Yes, I believe they've tested their laser. Ours is working too, as far as we can tell. Yes sir. One other thing, I assume Israel's military has been informed of potential incoming missiles? Good."

There was silence. Everyone continued to stare at Flemming, who now had his forehead resting against a wall near the galley, rocking it left and right, phone pressed snugly to his right ear. He was listening intently to the Secretary of Defense.

Flemming continued, "Well, if they do launch something, and we can catch them early, there's probably nothing to worry about. One of our lasers should take them out. But if they get them up, well, you know the rest. I doubt that we can intercept them, not with a 747 and not with the range we currently have on the lasers. These are still prototypes, sir. We aren't sure they'll even work as planned. Yes, we might get lucky, knock one or two missiles down, if we can determine their trajectory, which I assume is toward Israel. But these things weren't designed to knock them down once they are out of the boost phase, as you well know, sir. Okay, I'll—"

"Major!" Lockart yelled. He then jumped from his chair and it rolled away and slammed into the cabin's wall. "Look." He pointed at the imager.

"Hang on, sir," Flemming said into the phone, as he walked over with it in his hand, as long as the cord could reach. His attention was fixed on the center of the hologram. "Those sons of bitches."

Everyone focused in on one of the domes. It was opening, right down the middle, almost like one of those massive telescope domes cracking open just enough to let a telescope peer through.

"My god," Victoria said beneath her breath. Her hands began to tremble slightly.

Flemming held the phone back up to his mouth. "Sir, you're not going to believe this, but one of these domes—the gold domes at the mosque—is opening up, you know, like a giant telescope or observatory being opened. And there are soldiers running in and out of nearby buildings. I think they are preparing to launch something. We better hit them with whatever you've got in the neighborhood, sir. Command should have the coordinates from the imager. Yes. Bye sir."

Flemming moved closer, phone still in his hand, staring at the hologram before him. Almost half of the dome roof was now completely peeled away, but the imager wasn't revealing anything within the recesses of the dome yet. He turned to Goldstein and, as he pointed precisely inside the dome opening, with his hand and arm glowing green from the imager, said, "Zoom in as much as you can, right here."

"Yes sir."

Goldstein tapped at the keyboard and the image changed, completely zoomed in on the dome opening.

"My god. They're actually going to do it," Flemming continued. "There they are. See them? Right here." He pointed again. "A few of them anyway." The very tips of several missiles could be seen within the recess of the dome. He looked up. "How many do you see?" he asked to no one particular.

"Three sir," Leckart answered.

"Three sir," Rodriguez followed.

Victoria leaned forward. "Three, maybe more. The dome is still opening. They could be SS-18 or—"

"There's smoke!" Flemming interrupted. The phone dropped from his hand and was yanked halfway back to the communications console by the spiral cord. "See it? Right inside the dome, and some over here. Goldstein, zoom out a bit."

The hologram of the dome was replaced by a large view, with nearby buildings and courtyards.

Flemming aimed his right index finger to a gate area and parking lot. "That must be the exhaust port for the missiles, or some sort of underground tunnel. There's smoke coming from there too." He turned and quickly walked away, bent over and picked up the phone, then entered a number. After a couple seconds he said, "Lt. Colonel Flemming here. Mr. Secretary, they are launching. We see three or four missiles at the mosque, and smoke or some sort of vapor is starting to come from the site. Yes, positively. Okay. Yes, will do, sir. Bye." He tossed the phone to Rodriguez and ordered, "Get hold of Command and make sure they have the right coordinates." He walked back to the imager.

"Jesus, there goes one!" Leckart yelled, pointing.

Everyone watched as the tiny hologram image of the first ICBM emerged from the depths of the mosque and moved upward, seemingly pointed directly at one of the imaging satellites high above. It got larger and larger, rising above the surface of the imager in 3D. Flemming appeared completely stunned; he closed his eyes for a couple of seconds and rubbed hard, then opened them. The missile was still there, this small bullet shaped object rising higher and higher. Then another missile and another. "Zoom out, Goldstein."

Goldstein pressed a few keys. "How's that, sir?"

"Fine."

All of the sudden the entire image became blurred. Tom, who had been standing a couple yards away, moved closer, his eyes wide. He had tried to stay out of the way of the crew as they ascertained what was going on at the site, but could stay away any longer.

Leckart turned to Flemming. "What the hell happened to the image? I can't make anything out."

The hologram was a sea of swirling circles and unidentifiable images.

"They took it out!" Flemming yelled. "The imager can't render smoke, or explosions. "I think they took out that dome at least."

"Already?" Leckart asked.

Flemming straightened his back and rubbed his neck hard, in disbelief that the United States had just destroyed an ICBM complex within Iran, and that some of the missiles had made it up. "The Stealths were probably circling overhead, waiting for confirmation that the site indeed had missiles, or maybe they saw the launch themselves."

The hologram now appeared to be locked up, no motion whatsoever. Then it disappeared entirely. The green haze above the imager surface vanished.

Heads moved left and right, as everyone wondered why the system had crashed. The image was completely gone.

"What the hell's going on, Goldstein?" Flemming asked.

"I don't know. Maybe, maybe it can't handle the data rate. The motion could be too much, you know, with all the smoke and explosions. The compression is probably overwhelmed. Hang on." Goldstein typed in a command and the hologram image reset and slowly came back on, but it was of the entire city.

Victoria moved closer. "Wow. Look at that."

There were blue dots everywhere, swarming like bees over Iran. The imager's green hologram was sprinkled with radar data of every U.S. plane converging on Iran nuclear development sites.

"Our men are going to annihilate every nuclear development and military site they can," Flemming said.

"And then some," Leckart added.

A phone rang—the dreaded red one.

Flemming ran to the communications console and picked it up. "747-ABL-Alpha, Lt. Colonel Flemming speaking. Yes, we see, sir. It's an outrage. I hope we level every single nuclear and uranium enriching site they have."

There was a long pause.

"Yes sir. But you know that the odds of our intercepting them are practically nil at this point. Yes sir. We'll just have to give it our best shot. God bless and good luck to you, too, sir. I assume you'll be on Air Force One until further notice? Good, sir. I'll advise ASAP. Bye sir." Flemming hung up then ran to the cockpit. The door almost came off the hinges as he pushed it with his shoulder.

The pilot twisted his head to the right as Flemming said to him, "Stay on course but await new coordinates from Command. At least two missiles got up, apparently heading toward Israel. One of the other 747-ABLs is trying to knock them down. We've been ordered to shoot down any other long range missiles that are launched. They should give us a location in a couple minutes. If Iran launches from another facility, we need to get in front of the missile's trajectory."

The pilot nodded and said, "Yes sir."

Flemming continued, "Get in touch with Holton. He's pulled together a team to estimate the best interception point and timing." Flemming closed the door and went back to the imager.

Leckart asked, "What are our orders, sir?"

"They got at least a couple missiles up. They appear to be on a trajectory for Tel Aviv. They are too far from us now, but one of the other ABL's will attempt to shoot them down, or hopefully Israel's missile defense can stop them before they hit ground."

"What?" Leckart responded, hoping that he had misunderstood Flemming's words. He looked like he was about to be sick.

"You heard me correctly, Captain. Two ICBMs are heading toward Israel. And there's a good chance that Iran has more than one launch site, so we are supposed to loiter in case they launch more—in any direction."

Suddenly the plane turned sharply to the left and everyone braced themselves. Tom grabbed the back of Victoria's chair to keep her from rolling away from the imager. She latched onto its base with both hands. As the plane leveled off, she felt Tom's hands move to her shoulders, which provided a brief moment of comfort.

The co-pilot emerged from the cockpit and ran toward everyone near the imager. "They just launched more ICBMs. The trajectory could put them on course for New York or D.C."

At first, everyone was speechless. No response whatsoever. Then Victoria said, "My god, they are trying to hit the U.S.?" She reached up to her right shoulder and touched Tom's hand.

Flemming held up his right sleeve and wiped the moisture from his forehead. "Are they positive they're aimed at the U.S.?"

"Yes sir. But we are right in their trajectory, too. They are headed toward us right now. Sir, you have to shoot them down," the co-pilot said then immediately turned and ran back to the cockpit.

There was complete silence. The plane made several minor course corrections and again leveled off. Victoria sat still with her left palm over her mouth. Tom found a chair and sat down next to her. His mind was a jumble of thoughts. He tilted forward, rested his elbows on his knees and covered his face with his hands, rubbing up and down slowly. He felt Victoria's fingers move to his back, gently caressing up and down his spine.

There was nothing they could do but wait for the missiles, which were screaming toward them, to get into range of the ABL's laser.

CHAPTER TWENTY-SEVEN

No one spoke. Whether it was due to an inability to comprehend the severity of the crisis they were in the middle of, or personal reflection, or concern about the potential mass loss of life which could occur if the ICBMs manage to hit their targets—or simply a scarcity of appropriate words to say—wasn't clear. The plane was slowly turning to the left and its nose was pitched upward. It was gaining altitude, heading northwest, attempting to position itself precisely in the trajectory of the missiles apparently aimed toward America, before they gain too much altitude and get out of range of the 747's laser.

Victoria stood and came over to Tom. "Tom," she said softly as she sat down in the seat next to him. He straightened his back and turned toward her. While looking into her eyes he instantly threw his arms around her, squeezing tightly. The hell with what anyone would think.

"Any more news?" Tom asked, then let go of her.

"As far as we know, they got four missiles up."

Tom's eyes widened. "Four?"

"Yes. Two nearing Israel now. And two on trajectory for New York or Washington, D.C. And those two are approaching us right now."

"Good lord."

"You can probably get in touch with your family and tell them to get away from the D.C. area, just in case." She reached over and held Tom's right hand.

"I already did, before we took off." Tom pulled the cell phone, which he borrowed from Victoria earlier, out of his pocket and handed it to her. "We're really going to try and intercept the missiles? Do you think we can?"

"I don't know, Tom. The ABL program, as you know, was de-funded and put on hold for years. No one knows whether these lasers will really work on an ICBM. I hope and pray we can stop them. But we are literally flying in a one-point-five billion dollar experiment that only a few months ago was in storage at Tucson's bone yard."

"Bone yard?"

"It's where old or discontinued planes are stored for parts, or in case they are needed again someday."

Tom nodded. "So what about the two ICBMs headed toward Israel. They should be there already."

"I know. Hopefully one of the other ABL lasers blew them up, or one of Israel's missile defense systems—the so-called *Iron Dome*. It's the best in the world. But it's never been used on ICBMs. We should get some news soon, on Israel."

Tom was quiet for several seconds. He just shook his head and looked into Victoria's eyes. He finally said, "Have you heard them talk about using the nuclear-armed satellite, to retaliate against Iran?"

She hesitated then answered, "You won't believe this, but Flemming said he has no knowledge of such a satellite. He told me that as far as he knows Kramer has been working on a new version of the B-61 bomb, which he believes has nothing to do with satellites. But he said Kramer often referred to the B-61 program as *High Ground*."

Concern moved to Tom's eyes as he considered this, then he asked, "What is a B-61?"

"It's a nuclear weapon designed to destroy underground facilities, such as labs, bunkers, and factories for chemical or other weapons. Iran conducts much of their uranium enrichment, and probably weapons development, underground and out of harm's way of traditional bombs. The B-61 and its newer iterations are the latest versions of the old B-53s, which were deployed in 1962 and are far too destructive for pinpointing smaller targets. They cause too much collateral damage. The B-61s are more precise and can penetrate deep within the earth, to destroy underground facilities."

Tom nodded, vaguely remembering reading about them. "So they can be dropped from high altitude?"

"Yes. They're shaped like a huge needle—very pointed—and their case is constructed of uranium, because it's strong and about

284

thirty percent heavier than lead. They can be dropped without a parachute and—"

"You mean from a plane or even a satellite platform?"

"I don't know whether they can withstand re-entry if launched from a satellite. But yes, they were originally designed for use on aircraft. They are apparently ideal for the B-2 bomber, as they weigh only seven hundred and fifty pounds. The old B-53's weighed nine thousand pounds and could only be carried by B-52 bombers."

"I had no idea that the U.S. was still making nuclear bombs. So they are dropped from high altitude?" Tom asked.

"Yes. And after they hit the ground they burrow down about fifty feet, then detonate the warhead."

Tom nodded. "Amazing. So most of the destruction is underground?"

"Right. There's much less damage on the surface, compared to traditional nuclear weapons. But it's still a crazy weapon. The only way it has managed to go into production is because the Pentagon claims it really isn't a new weapon. They say it's just an updated and safer B-53. Hogwash, if you ask me."

Tom raked his fingers through his hair then rubbed his forehead hard.

"What's wrong, dear?" Victoria asked softly, again touching his back.

"This doesn't add up. The pictures James and I were given showed two satellites, and one of them was clearly a satellite weapons platform, and its missiles were definitely nuclear."

"Well, General Kramer may have been lying to Flemming about the program he was working on. If Kramer really managed a space-based weapons development project, very few people would have had such clearance to know about it. Such a program would be illegal, in violation of international treaties."

Tom paused, thinking. "I guess you're right."

Victoria continued, "I'm just telling you what Flemming said. He told me that the shuttle launch—the very last shuttle launch—only had one satellite for surveillance, as far as he knows. He's probably just out of the loop."

Tom cleared his throat then said, "I guess that makes sense. Flemming's responsibility has been on resurrecting the Airborne Laser program. It's just hard to believe that Kramer has somehow managed to get a nuclear-armed satellite up without a lot of people knowing about it. But that seems to be exactly what has happened."

Victoria nodded then stood. "I better get back over there."

"Do you think we have any chance at shooting those ICBMs down?" Tom asked, looking up at her soft eyes.

"It's possible, but not likely. The laser was designed to fire at them when they're moving relatively slowly, climbing in the boost phase. Even if we can predict an interception point, they'll be flying by us at three or four times the speed of sound, at least. They'll make us look like we're standing still. According to Flemming, the laser optics and steering motors weren't intended to track them at those speeds, or at high altitude. But there's always a chance, especially if we can get in front of them and fire several shots straight on, you know, less targeting corrections. We have to at least try."

CHAPTER TWENTY-EIGHT

The first ICBM, according to Rodriguez and Leckart, who were sitting at the forward communications console, was four minutes away from the interception point with their location. The only good news was that there wasn't a cloud in the sky, three-hundred-sixty degrees around the plane. This, Flemming had pointed out, would greatly help in tracking and locking on to the missiles. He said that although the Airborne Laser had adaptive optics, which were supposed to compensate for phase distortions of the light beam caused by temperature changes, clouds, and even light rain, the technology wasn't proven. Most of the tests had been conducted on the ground, in clear weather, and under ideal conditions in the desert southeast of Las Vegas. Even under these conditions the Chemical Oxygen Iodine Laser failed to fire within tolerance twenty percent of the time. And on several tests the beam control system and steering mirrors, which attempt to compensate for such distortions by means of up to a thousand adjustments per second, failed to accurately pinpoint the intended target, especially on longer-range tests of two hundred and fifty kilometers or more.

Flemming paced nervously back and forth adjacent to the imager. "What's the ETA, Leckart?"

"Three minutes, forty-five seconds, sir. The first one is headed right at us. It's all up to the computers and laser now. There's nothing we can do."

"That's reassuring." Flemming looked down at Goldstein who was tapping at the keyboard again and staring up at the area above the imager platform. It came on slowly, glowing green, but without any distinguishable image. "What are we looking at now, Goldstein?"

"I'm trying to get an image of our location, combined with the incoming ICBMs."

Flemming and Leckart moved closer.

"I can't give you a real visual image, but I can give you—"

"Blue dots, and red dots?" Flemming interrupted.

"Yes sir," Goldstein answered, looking up. "And the terrain below us. This one is us." He pointed at an area about two feet above the surface of the imager. "And this red dot is—"

"An ICBM?"

"Yes sir. Moving like hell isn't it."

Tom stepped closer, behind Victoria. They watched as the red dot raced across a hallogram-generated desert image below, toward the blue dot—their plane.

Goldstein continued, "And there's the other ICBM."

Another red dot appeared, following the first as if it were chasing it.

Flemming looked at the swirling hand of his Seiko watch. "Less than sixty seconds," he whispered, appearing rather queasy. He sat down.

A voice blared over a speaker, "We have visual on the first missile."

Goldstein entered a command into the imager's control keyboard. The imager shut down.

Flemming erupted. "Goldstein, get the damn—"

"Yes sir. Hang on, here it comes."

The image returned. "There we go."

"What in the world? I thought you didn't have video," Flemming said as he stared at the image of a tiny 747 hovering over the platform. He looked at the area a few feet to the right. There was a small hologram of an ICBM moving closer. "You're amazing, Goldstein. How did you—"

"The plane and missile holograms aren't live satellite images, sir. They are simulated in the software and interfaced with the satellite, GPS data, and the flight control system. It's just—"

Suddenly the plane banked sharply to the right. Tom tried to brace himself as a couple chairs rolled and smashed into the right cabin wall. He fell to the floor and quickly moved to his knees and latched himself to Victoria's chair to keep her from rolling away. She barely

288

managed to hold on to the corner of the imager. Tom glanced up at the hologram. The miniature 747-ABL was also banking to the right.

The plane leveled off somewhat.

"We're okay," Flemming said. "The auto pilot is just trying to keep up with changes in the interception point." He tilted his wrist and moved his eyes to his watch, yet again.

Leckart waved his hand through the hologram of the 747, then through the missiles, obviously impressed with Goldstein's work. With the ICBMs now getting into range of the laser, and everyone appearing even more worried, he awkwardly attempted to make small talk, "You programmed these yourself?"

"No, the plane was from Microsoft Flight Simulator. I just borrowed the code, you might say, and wrote the interface. I created the ICBMs though."

It struck Tom that the nervous chatter was completely out of place, given the threat that was screaming toward them, but it appeared to be helping to take everyone's mind off the situation, for a second or two anyway. And there really wasn't anything more the crew could do, according to Flemming. The computers were in charge now. Microprocessors, software code, and a resurrected experimental laser mounted on the chin of the aircraft would decide whether eight million, or perhaps even more people would die if the ICBMs passed them by and actually hit New Your or Washington D.C.

Tom stared at the holograms of the ICBMs. They were getting closer and closer.

Again Flemming held his left wrist up, his watch directly In front of his face. "The laser should fire anytime now. The ICBMs are in range."

A few seconds passed and then everyone could hear that annoying and anxiety-provoking buzzing sound again—the laser overheating as it had done in test firings.

"It's firing!" Leckart yelled.

Flemming moved closer to the imager. Both holograms of the ICBMs were still there, moving toward the tiny 747. "Did it hit the first ICBM?"

Leckart twisted his neck toward Flemming, "I don't know yet sir."

Flemming angled his face up at the intercom speaker. Dead silence. He took a deep breath and finally said, "The flight crew is supposed to immediately announce visual confirmation of any hits. The first shot must have missed."

There were more buzzing sounds, the laser firing again.

Flemming walked back and forth adjacent to the imager, nervously wringing his hands together. "Come on, come on. Hit those mothers."

The laser fired yet again, two seconds worth. Apparently another miss. More buzzing.

Everyone stared at the imager. One of the missiles was clearly starting to pass them by, continuing on a trajectory toward New York or Washington D.C.

"It's moving by." Victoria said under her breath. "My god."

"I think we have one more shot at this first one." Flemming slowed down his pacing.

There were more buzzing sounds from the bowels of the plane.

About ten seconds later, the intercom speaker crackled and popped a bit, then the voice of the pilot came on, "This is Major Fletcher." Everyone looked up at the speaker in the ceiling of the cabin. "We nailed the first ICBM. I just saw an explosion off to our left."

"Yes!" Flemming yelled, eyes intense.

"Thank god," Victoria said, then turned to Tom. "One down."

Tom nodded hesitantly. He wasn't relieved yet. He watched the hologram of the first ICBM vanish from above the imager platform, but his attention immediately turned to the second ICBM approaching their location.

"One more, just one more," Flemming said, wringing his hands together. He seemed to have forgotten about, or was ignoring, the other two ICBMs which had been fired toward Israel as well. His only focus was the hologram of one hovering above the imager platform and closing in fast on the image of the 747. "The second one looks in range."

290

The sound of the laser system filled the cabin again, this time seeming louder. Lots of buzzing noise.

Flemming turned to Victoria. "It's firing."

More buzzing.

The plane, under complete control of the targeting computer, suddenly banked sharply to the right.

Flemming yelled, "Hang on!"

Tom grasped a corner of the imager and somehow managed to keep standing. He saw soda cans and cups flying around the galley, then loose papers, manuals, and a fire extinguisher. Wind again rushed in the exit doorway that Kramer had opened. One of the leather chairs made a beeline for it and rolled right out of the plane.

"Damn it! Missed it on the first shot," Flemming said loudly. "Come on, come on."

The laser fired again.

"It's moving by us, sir." Leckart was shaking somewhat, and his stomach was queasy. The plane leveled off again and he jumped from his chair and ran over to a window on the left side of the plane. "There it is," he yelled, holding the tip of his index finger up to the window. "See the smoke, the vapor trail?"

Flemming moved to the window. "Yeah, I see it. Why isn't the laser continuing to fire?"

"It must be overheating, sir."

Flemming turned around and walked back over to the imager. "It looks like we missed the second one," he announced. He sat, folded his arms, and placed them on the surface of the imager. They were aglow, bright green. He leaned forward and rested his head on the back of his hands, then exhaled loudly as he raised back up and looked at everyone. "God help us."

The speaker above crackled as the pilot said, "The laser missed the second ICBM. We are awaiting instructions from Command."

A minute passed without anyone saying a word, then Victoria turned to Flemming. "There might still be a chance of stopping it."

He raised his head slowly, looking pale. "It's too late, Ms. Brookshire. We're out of range."

"How, Victoria?" Tom asked. "How can we possibly stop it?"

Victoria cleared her throat then answered, "The U.S. can launch, or divert, every military plane possible that's near New York, and has a chance of intercepting the missile. Put every military plane possible in the trajectory of that ICBM—and I mean any plane, armed or not."

Flemming's eyebrows rose. "You mean—"

"Tell the pilots of the planes to fly at the ICBM, head on. Create as much of a wall of aircraft as possible, in the exact trajectory NORAD predicts. For those aircraft with air-to-air missiles, they can attempt to lock on to the heat signature of the ICBM and take it out. If they can't hit it, then all available aircraft need to just get in the way of that ICBM before it hits ground or gets too close to New York, D.C., or wherever it ends up aiming at. It's doubtful, but the ICBM might just hit one of the aircraft, if they can't shoot it down first."

Flemming weighed Victoria's suggestion for several seconds. Trying to shoot down an incoming ICBM, or put an aircraft in its trajectory, was a crazy plan, but it was the only possible way to try and stop the death of literally millions of Americans. The United States had only just begun funding a minimal missile defense program, even in the midst of threats from North Korea and Iran, and was a sitting duck relative to defending itself from incoming missiles. The East Coast was especially vulnerable, as most missile defense efforts had focused on sites in Alaska, to intercept missiles from Russia or North Korea.

Finally, Flemming said, "It's worth a shot, but we better hurry and suggest this to the Pentagon and the President." He stood and ran over to the red phone hanging near the galley. He entered some numbers quickly, then spoke into the receiver as if possessed.

Tom tried to listen but the cabin was too noisy to hear well.

Flemming hung up and walked back over. "They're going to try it."

Nearly a half hour had passed. Everyone had just stared at the imager the entire time. Sure enough, the left side of the hologram, near what Goldstein said was Long Island, began to fill with blue dots—U.S.

292

military planes from every base within a three hundred mile radius of New York, New York. The planes were coming from every direction. Ten, twenty, then thirty and over a hundred. It looked like they would all run into each other, right above Manhattan.

Flemming sat down near the imager, next to Tom and Victoria, and tilted his chair forward. He looked as if he had run a marathon. He was sweating profusely and his face was rosy red. As he watched the hologram of the second ICBM approaching the east coast of America he said under his breath, "Come on. Come on, just knock that thing down." His mind was filled with worst case and best case scenarios. Had Iran actually developed a nuclear weapon capable of flying that far and exploding? If the ICBM hit, how many people would be killed? What would the U.S. response be to Iran, given the fact that its citizens really had nothing to do with the crazy weapons program and attack pursued by a small fraction of their government.

More blue dots appeared, representing everything from Marine Corp Hornets to the Air Force C5 Galaxy to KC-135 refueling tankers and everything in between. They were loitering at various altitudes over and around New York, waiting for precise coordinates from NORAD radar and GPS data which would try to position them in the direct path of the incoming ICBM.

"Those are brave men," Victoria said softly as she too looked on.

Tom wiped his forehead then moved closer. "Look at them. How'd they get them up so fast?"

"I'd imagine they were already on alert. Maybe even in the air when they received orders to head to New York or D.C.," Flemming answered. "And they were probably moving them out of the target zones to keep them from being destroyed."

The hologram of the ICBM was suddenly moving faster in relation to how it had been moving. It was closing on downtown New York. The blue dots—all the planes—now appeared indistinguishable in one area above the city. Only a couple dozen planes were identifiable off the coast of Long Island, maintaining what appeared to be a defined distanced from each other. Tom assumed that they must be the first line of defense, perhaps the planes which are supposed to try and lock onto the ICBMs heat signature with hopes of shooting it down.

Flemming raised his voice, "Okay, guys. Knock that son of a bitch out of the sky!"

"Looks like it got through some of them," Victoria said as she stood and backed away from the imager, suddenly feeling slightly sick to her stomach. The tiny missile hovering above the imager had passed several of the blue dots off the coast.

"Wait, look!" Tom said as he, too, stood up. "Where did it go? Did they—"

"Yes, yes, I think so." Flemming chimed in. "I don't see it. There's no ICBM." He leaned forward some more.

"The imager might be overwhelmed by the number of blue dots," Goldstein said, almost apologetically. "Want me to zoom—"

"Yes!" Flemming yelled.

The image changed. The blue dots became bigger and further apart.

"I still don't see it. I don't see the ICBM!"

The speaker above popped a couple of times and everyone gazed up.

"Major Fletcher here. Confirmation just received." The pilot sounded different than he had before. He spoke more slowly, purposefully. "The ICBM was destroyed by an F-16 from the National Guard out of Vermont. One man lost. God bless him."

Victoria walked over to Tom. She threw her arms around him and squeezed hard. She started to cry, a sudden release of stress.

"Are you okay?" Tom asked. He could feel her body trembling. He backed away from her slightly and raised his hands to her face.

Victoria composed herself and said, "I'm all right. Sorry."

"Maybe you should sit down." Tom motioned to a chair near the imager.

She nodded and walked over and sat.

"Do you want some water?"

"Yes, Tom. Please."

Tom went to the galley. Flemming was there, also getting a bottle for himself. He looked relieved, his face not as red. As Tom picked up a bottle from a box sitting on the floor of a storage bin, he noticed General Kramer's travel bag hanging above. Tom's thoughts instantly turned to Kramer's *High Ground* program, and suddenly the relief he had just felt when the two ICBM's headed toward New York were destroyed seemed distant. He wondered whether Kramer's weapons platform had already been used on Iran, perhaps to destroy the most highly fortified nuclear development sites buried deep underground. Tom decided to try and talk to Kramer. After all, what did the General have to lose at this point? He had already been relieved of command for initiating an attack on Iran on his own. His career was probably over, regardless of whether the *High Ground* program was an approved, sanctioned weapons development effort or not.

Flemming turned to Tom and said, "I guess this will make a hell of a story for the *Post*, won't it?" He paused to sip some more water. "And it ain't over yet."

Tom nodded. "You mean the *High Ground* satellite?"

"Yes. And also Israel's response to Iran's firing two nuclear-armed ICBM's at Tel Aviv."

Tom hesitated to ask, but said, "Did they hit?"

"No. We think one of the ICBMs was damaged by the 747-ABL which was loitering near Israel. They fired the laser at it but it didn't bring it down immediately. But a minute later it self-destructed."

"And the other one?"

"The second ICBM was destroyed by Israel's *Iron Dome* missile defense system—just in time, apparently."

"Thank God," Tom said under his breath.

Tom opened a bottle of water for himself and took a long drink, trying to absorb everything that had transpired the past hour. He changed the subject back to the *High Ground* satellite. "So, has the U.S. used Kramer's satellite yet? Have they dropped any nuclear-armed missiles, or bombs, on Iran?"

"I haven't heard any details yet, but no. That satellite Kramer put up—and its missiles—haven't been used."

Tom took a deep breath, then shifted gears. "I'd like your permission to speak to General Kramer."

"What for?" Flemming asked.

"I want to see if he will talk about that satellite. I want to know whether it was an officially sanctioned program, or if he somehow managed to develop it without approval of the President and Congress."

"I understand that Victoria filled you in, on what we learned at Kennedy Space Center, and the pictures we have, and people we spoke to?"

Flemming tossed his empty water bottle into a nearby sink in the plane's galley and answered, "Yes. But I find it hard to believe. The United States would never put a nuclear-armed satellite into space. That would be illegal. And the program would be almost impossible to keep quiet, even with a limited set of people and military contractors involved. But hell, I don't care. Talk to General Kramer, if he's awake. We knocked him out pretty good with those sedatives."

"Thank you."

"Let me know what you find out. You can use this elevator." Flemming motioned to his right. "The General is tied to a metal cot below deck, near the cargo area."

Tom nodded then walked over to Victoria, and handed her a bottle of water. "Here you go. Sorry. I should have brought this over right away, but I was asking Flemming for some more details."

"It's okay. I'm feeling better. Thanks, Tom."

"I'm going below deck to talk to Kramer. Flemming gave me the okay."

"What for?"

"I want to see if he'll tell me about the weapons satellite. Will you be okay?"

"Yes."

Tom touched her shoulder and said, "I'll be back as soon as I can."

He went to the elevator and began to descend to the lower deck. He heard the hum of an electric motor. Then the door opened and he instantly saw Kramer. He was flat on his back on a cot, just staring at the ceiling of aluminum beams, wiring, and hydraulic pipes that somehow enable the huge 747 to fly. He noticed that Kramer's wrists and ankles were tied with nylon straps still. Tom exited the elevator and made his way over.

Kramer noticed him, but said nothing and looked away.

Tom opened one of the bottles and held it forward. "I thought you might be thirsty."

The General didn't respond.

Tom set the bottle down and opened another, then took a drink. Kramer finally turned toward him. Tom could tell that he wanted a drink, and could see that his lips were badly chapped and cracked. He had to be dehydrated.

Tom set his bottle down and picked up the other one. "Here, tilt your head up." He helped raise Kramer's head and held the lip of the bottle to his mouth. Kramer gulped the water into his parched throat like he had been in the desert for days. Drops rolled across his chin and neck, then wet his shirt. He eventually pulled away and Tom set the bottle on the floor.

"Thanks, Lassiter," he said slowly, his voice hoarse. "So you're my prison guard now?"

A few seconds passed then Tom said, "I guess we both got ourselves into quite a mess."

Kramer coughed and cleared his throat. "Excellent observation. It should make a nice newspaper story for you though."

Tom shook his head no. "That's not important at this point."

Kramer seemed groggy as he asked, "And what is important?"

"I think you know, General."

Kramer turned away, facing the fuselage and some sort of electric panel.

"General, I want to know about that *High Ground* satellite you launched."

His attention shifted back to Tom, as his eyelids grew heavy. "It's just a spy bird. That's all."

Tom shook his head. "No it's not. I've seen pictures of it. Let's stop playing games. You put two satellites up."

Kramer took a deep breath. "And why should I tell you a damn thing, Lassiter?"

"Well, I saved your life, for starters. You were on your way out that exit doorway if it wasn't for my holding on to you."

Kramer slowly said, "No points there, Lassiter. I have nothing to live for anymore."

"Sure you do, General. You have a wife. You have that golf course and club in Florida you told me about retiring to. And you have the obligation to honor the memory of your late sons."

His eyes became wet. "Give me some more water, please."

Tom held up the bottle and Kramer drank some more then continued, "Thanks. No, Lassiter, I won't be moving to Florida. You know that. I'll be lucky if I'm not in a military prison for the rest of my life."

"Not if you cooperate. They'll go easier on you if—"

"Sure they will," Kramer interrupted. "Sure they will."

"Did any of the men tell you what happened?" Tom glanced at several officers seated at a laser control console seven yards away.

"Yeah. They told me."

Tom sipped some water, then wiped his brow on his shirt sleeve. "I want to know about that satellite, General. You told me you wanted to get the whole story out. Right? So I have to know what the hell you launched, and why."

"You already know what it is."

"Nuclear?"

Kramer hesitated, then, "Yeah. It's nuclear all right."

"Who else knows about it at the Pentagon?"

"A handful of people."

"How high up? The Secretary of Defense?"

Kramer promptly turned away again.

Tom pressed on. "Is anyone controlling those missiles right now, or are you the only one who can disable—"

Once again Kramer interrupted, and moved his eyes back to Tom. "Did we nail Ahmadinejad yet?"

Tom remembered reading an interview with the General in which he made his contempt for Ahmadinejad widely known. "I don't know, General. We've had our hands full the past hour."

Kramer nodded once and seemed to be having trouble staying awake. His eyes were closing for several seconds at a time.

Tom continued, "Now tell me about that satellite. Has it been placed over Iran?"

"Yes."

"Who is controlling it?"

Again, Kramer turned away.

"There's no reason to go through with whatever you had planned, General. Iran's uranium enrichment facilities and nuclear weapons sites are being wiped out as we speak. There's no reason to kill thousands, or millions, of innocent Iran civilians over there. They're victims, General. And you know it. Now, you gotta tell me—"

Kramer jerked his head left. "Okay, okay," he said in a low gruff voice, then sniffled slightly.

"Who's controlling that satellite?"

"No one."

"What do you mean? You're the only person who can—"

"No," Kramer interrupted. "I'm not the only one, but that doesn't matter right now. It's on full auto, Lassiter."

Tom's heart began to pound. "What do you mean?"

"It's a ticking time bomb. That's what I mean."

Tom's shoulders slumped. He moved a bit closer, eyes fixed on Kramer's eyes. "You mean, it's set to drop those missiles by itself?"

"Yes."

"When, General?"

Kramer sighed and barely whispered, "Eighteen hundred hours."

"*All* the missiles aboard the High Ground satellite will launch at Iran?"

"That's right. You have to tell Flemming to get all of our men out of the region. They haven't sent in any ground troops have they?"

"I really don't know, General."

"What cities are those missiles going to hit?"

"Top to bottom, Lassiter. The whole fucking country is going bye bye. There won't be an Iran."

"My God," Tom said, then reached up and rubbed the back of his neck which felt like a giant knot. "Can it be stopped? You can disable the satellite and the missiles, can't you?"

"Yes. In fact, I already tried once. I want you to mention that in your little *Washington Post* story. And before they hang me or toss me in the gas chamber."

"I'm not following you. What do you mean you already tried once? You tried to stop their launch?"

"The envelope, Lassiter, in my briefcase. I wanted the code to disable the satellite and missile launch, not the code to order an attack on Iran. But you idiots stopped me."

Tom looked down. His head started pounding. "But why were you going to disable it, after all the work in getting it developed and launched?"

"Because there wasn't any reason to have it go off. Think about it." Kramer paused, coughing. "It was obvious that we were going after Iran *anyway*. I had no way to know that this whole thing would happen, that we'd be swept into a conflict with them. I just wanted their uranium enrichment and nuclear development sites destroyed, one way or another. With Iran launching ICBMs at Israel and the United States, or anywhere for that matter, obviously their nuclear program was going to be destroyed. *High Ground* wasn't needed at that point. If you and Flemming hadn't stopped me, I would have terminated the *High Ground* launch, Lassiter. I just couldn't tell anyone that."

Tom's head swirled with thoughts. Was the General telling him the truth? But he figured at this point it didn't matter whether Kramer had planned to launch the missiles, or terminate their launch. The important thing was they were apparently now set to go off automatically.

300

Tom asked once more, "You swear to me that the satellite is going to automatically launch those nuclear-armed missiles by itself?"

"That's right, Lassiter. We were afraid word would leak out somehow, and we wouldn't be able to control the satellite manually. So I had them design in an automatic sequence. It's going off, Lassiter. Unless we can get the disable code transmitted in time."

"God, I can't believe this. Do you realize how many people could be wiped out with those missiles?"

Kramer said nothing, moving his eyes away from Tom.

"We have to do something, General. We have to—"

"What time is it?" Kramer cut in, suddenly appearing more energetic. "I can't see my watch."

Tom peeled Kramer's left shirtsleeve up a bit, revealing his watch. "It's four thirty, General."

"You better move your ass. In an hour and a half that thing is going to prepare to launch, then go off—dropping *all* those nuclear warheads on Iran—unless the code is transmitted in time."

Tom stood. "How do we—"

"Like I said, Lassiter, you better first tell Command to get our boys out of harm's way, and evacuate any military bases or aircraft carriers near Iran, just in case of nuclear fallout. We should be able to disable the launch, but this entire system has never been tested, obviously."

Tom nodded quickly. "All right, General."

"Now go get my briefcase. And tell Flemming to come down. I'll walk him through the disabling sequence."

"Okay." Tom started to turn around, but paused. "General, those missiles aren't the ones that burrow into the ground, then explode, are they? Like the new B-61's in development?"

"No. That was just a shell program to cover everything up. The missiles on that satellite will explode about a mile above ground. They'll wipe everything out over there," Kramer said far too calmly.

Tom turned on a dime and walked quickly to the elevator. He rose to the imager level, exited, and ran over to Flemming.

Flemming immediately asked, "Did General Kramer talk?"

"Yes, he admitted everything. There's a nuclear-armed satellite set to launch its missiles at eighteen hundred hours."

Flemming looked at his watch.

"Kramer's willing to walk you through the disabling sequence, but he needs the code." Tom turned and looked about the cabin. "Where's Kramer's briefcase?"

"I don't know." Flemming moved away, dragging his eyes across the floor, under seats, behind chairs.

"Is that it over there?" Tom pointed.

"No, that's mine."

Flemming and Tom both simultaneously looked at the exit door opening, clearly wondering the same thing—did Kramer's briefcase get blown out of the doorway like everything else when the cabin lost pressure? They then swung their heads toward each other as Tom said, "Do you think it got sucked out of the plane?"

"Yeah, it looks that way doesn't it," Flemming said frantically as he ran forward toward the cockpit area, looking under chairs and everywhere he could see. "Check the galley, Lassiter."

Tom surveyed the galley. No briefcase. He stopped, out of breath, and yelled over at Flemming. "I don't see it."

"Maybe it's under the seats in back?" Flemming continued.

They moved to the blue chairs, just as Victoria came out of a nearby restroom. "What's going on?"

Neither Flemming nor Tom answered. Flemming looked under the seats on the right side. Tom checked the left. They only saw papers and other debris strewn about.

Flemming paused and glanced over at Tom. "Are you sure he said he has to have a code to disable it? There's no other way?"

"That's what he said. And he told me that you should notify our men over there to get out of harm's way of potential nuclear fallout. Actually you should tell Command that they better inform every country near Iran," Tom continued.

Flemming nodded and headed for the red phone again.

302

Tom made his way to the last row of seats on his side. Lodged underneath one of the chairs, he saw a black briefcase. He turned to Flemming and yelled, "I see something, over here."

Flemming rushed over and they pulled the case out.

"There's a name tag," Tom yelled, then flipped the tag over. *General Kramer* was printed across it.

CHAPTER TWENTY-NINE

Tuesday, about ten o'clock in the morning. It had been forty-eight hours since Tom's flight with Kramer and company. And he was still completely exhausted. The bump on his head had gone down some, though. He parked on 23rd Street and ambled through the parking lot of George Washington University Hospital. He hated hospitals.

He entered the building through glass doors, smiled at a candy striper nurse, then made his way to an elevator. Ten seconds, two stops, and seven floors later he arrived at the upper level of the north wing. The place smelled like rubbing alcohol and disinfectant. An old man in a wheel chair approached, as he had last night when Tom visited James for a few minutes, just after James was transferred from Florida Hospital.

Tom said, "Good day," and the man didn't say a word in reply. Again, just like last night. Tom wasn't sure whether he was grumpy or just didn't have his hearing aid on. Tom continued, toward James' room, 714.

After checking in with Mrs. Johnson, the attending nurse, he made his way down a long hall where there were more unpleasant hospital smells. He passed a young girl on crutches, whose eyes smiled at him. Then his hand met a cold chrome handle and he slowly swung the door open to James' room. Last night he had caught nurse Johnson and her assistant giving James a sponge bath, and he wanted to spare his eyes such a sight today if at all possible.

He walked in. Good news. James was fully clothed and his harem of nurses were gone.

James sat up in the bed and said, "Hey, Tom."

"How are you feeling, buddy?"

"Not bad, not too bad. Just have this little hole in my left lung where those idiots in Florida shot me, that's all."

304

"Well, James, you still have one good one, right."

"Yeah, lucky me. Have a seat." James pointed to a chair by an IV pole.

Tom dragged it over and sat down. "How's the food?" he asked, seeing a partially finished tray on a stand to his left.

"Just great. Want some coconut-lime Jell-O?"

"Uh, no thanks. I'd throw up."

"Me too. Don't touch that bag over there."

Tom laughed.

"Tonight we're having meatloaf and lima beans, if you want to come back."

"Gee thanks."

James adjusted the bed, a motor grinding his tall frame up a few inches. "Man, I still can't believe what happened. We're lucky to be alive, Tom."

"I know. A lot of people are lucky to be alive. Did you see today's front page of the *Post*?"

"No, not yet."

"Hang on, I'll go see if there's a paper in the hall." Tom left the room and found a newspaper in a nearby waiting area. He returned and handed it to James who promptly held it up and ran his eyes down the page. "Man, looks like we made a little news."

"Yeah, just a little. A bit more than we planned, isn't it?"

James nodded then asked, "So they arrested Kramer already?"

"Yes, and I'm sure that's just a start. An FBI agent called me this morning, asking me not to leave town. He said they want to ask me some questions and tell them about Kramer's actions on the plane and, obviously, about Broderick's in Florida. They also want all of the pictures Nevsky gave us of the satellites, and they want the Pentagon file, of course."

"You're going to give them everything?"

"There's no reason not to. I copied everything, and most of it is in print now anyway."

James set the paper down. "Man, what a mess. Not exactly what we were expecting."

305

"No, but it could have been worse. Kramer could have killed millions of people in the Middle East, and if even one of Iran's ICBMs had hit Tel Aviv, New York, or D.C., well, you know what could have happened. We were very lucky." Tom paused and looked at James' face. "James, are you sure you feel okay? You look kind of pale. Do they have you on enough pain killer?"

"That's what they say, but damned if I can tell."

"Why don't I go ask the nurse if she can give you something. All right?"

"Okay, thanks." James again adjusted the bed, appearing extremely uncomfortable, then reached up and tugged on the bandage about his chest.

"Hang on. I'll be right back." Tom stood and walked to the doorway, then made his way to the nurse station. Two men, both facing the other way, were talking to nurse Johnson. Tom cleared his throat and they turned around. He noticed that nurse Johnson appeared nervous, her eyes blinking quickly.

One of the men said, "Well, well, here you are, Mr. Lassiter."

"Who are you?" Tom asked.

Both men pulled badges from their suit pockets and flashed them faster than Tom could read a word. "We're with the FBI. I'm agent Browning and this is agent Rogers. I'm afraid that you're under arrest."

"What?"

One of the men removed handcuffs from a back pocket then said, "You have the right to remain silent. If you choose not to remain silent, anything you say can and will be used against you in a court of law. You have the right to an attorney. If you cannot afford an attorney, one will be appointed to you. You have the right at any time not to answer any questions or make any statements. Do you understand these rights?"

"Yes," Tom answered. The agent said something else, which went in one ear and out the other, and Tom nodded and turned toward nurse Johnson, who now seemed to be in complete shock. He said to her, "James Clemens is in pain. Can you give him something?"

She nodded quickly.

Tom continued, "Please don't tell James about this. He has enough to worry about, and he'll find out soon enough. Just tell him that visiting hours are over and I had to go. Take care of him. Okay?"

"Yes Mr. Lassiter, I will."

Without the agents saying a word, Tom turned around and put his wrists together. They slapped the handcuffs on. This was getting old.

CHAPTER THIRTY

Tom was given a tour of the J. Edgar Hoover FBI Building, lots of gray halls, lots of important people, and lots of heels clicking everywhere. Just like at the Pentagon. Starsky and Hutch took his wallet, watch, keys, and a pack of gum, then listed the items on an inventory sheet. Tom signed it. They walked into a small room and he had his picture taken and did some finger painting.

They headed down a narrow dreary hall with flickering fluorescent lights and locked Tom in an equally dreary room (stainless steel door, metal tables, and an obvious two-way mirror). They told him to "sit tight" and that they'd be right back. He nodded and sat down on a folding chair, next to the largest table.

Ten minutes later they returned. They sat on the opposite side and pretended to scribble notes on their yellow pads. Tom knew they were stalling. They wanted him to talk first. So he kept his mouth zipped shut and tried to drive them crazy.

It seemed to work. Moments later one of the FBI agents twisted his neck, exhaled, and finally looked up. He was breaking. The other did the same and said, "We'd like to ask you a few questions if that's all right."

Tom weighed his options. He could say nothing, or he could make like he had no idea why he was there. The lawyer in him screamed for him to not say a word, but the reporter blurted out, "I believe I have a right to know why I've been arrested."

"Sure," one of them said, then reached down to an aluminum case, popped it open, and pulled out a DVD.

Tom knew exactly what it was. He tried to stay calm.

The agent stood and went over to a TV and DVD player on a metal cart, then slid the DVD in and pressed play. And there Tom was. In living color even.

"This look familiar?" one of the agents asked, real cocky like.

Tom nodded then said, "Yeah, it's my evil twin, Elroy. Where'd you find him?"

One of the agents became obviously irritated at this and the other managed a slight grin, then quickly wiped it off.

They all watched as the DVD video showed Tom taking the *High Ground* file from General Kramer's desk. The camera even caught him adjusting and repositioning the file after he shoved it in his pants, and beneath the elastic band of his underwear. This looked interesting, to say the least. The jury will surely get a good laugh, Tom thought as he sighed, not moving his eyes from the video.

The video ended.

"Do you have any comment?" agent Browning asked.

Tom hunched his shoulders and shook his head, not saying a word. Suddenly he thought that perhaps he should have a lawyer present. The agents stared at him for a few minutes, in-between even heavier note taking activity.

Finally, Tom broke the silence and said, "I'd like to call my lawyer." Actually, he didn't have one to call. But he was optimistic that maybe the *Post* could help, or that one could be appointed to him by the court.

Two hours later and Tom was sitting in the same locked room. All alone. A lawyer, courtesy of the paper, was supposed to show up any minute. And not a minute too soon. His hands and arms were aching from the damn handcuffs, and he could definitely use a restroom break. He assumed that the agents were behind the glass over there to his right, watching him sweat and fidget about. He turned toward the mirror and said, "Hey in there, I gotta take a leak. How about taking these off me. I'm not going anywhere."

Dead silence, but he knew they were there.

Eventually he heard keys jiggling in a lock and saw the knob on the entrance door move. He could also see the tops of three heads through the small glass window at the top of the door. The door opened and his accusers marched in with, he hoped, his attorney.

"Mr. Lasslter?" the man accompanying the agents asked.

"Yes."

Tom turned to the agents. "I'd obviously like to speak to him alone." He then glanced at the two-way mirror. "Do I have your word that no one will be eavesdropping or watching, or recording?"

"Yes," agent Browning answered. "We'll give you thirty minutes."

"That's fine."

The agents left and locked the door behind them.

"I'm B. Jack Slayter," the attorney said with a thick southern accent, turning to Tom. "You can call me Jack." He pulled out a business card and set it on the table. Not very fancy, no gold nor embossing. "One of *The Washington Posts'* in-house attorneys called and filled me in, asked me to come down."

Tom nodded.

"Quite a mess you're in, Mr. Lassiter."

"Yes. Apparently so."

"Have you seen the video they purportedly have of you?" he continued, then glanced at the two-way mirror.

Tom immediately realized that this meeting would be more of a show for the FBI than anything else. He new they must be watching behind the glass. "Yes, I saw the surveillance video."

"And, Mr. Lassiter, at the time the video was taken—in General Kramer's office—did you believe General Kramer was involved in illegal activity that could possibly cause harm to millions of people?"

Tom took his time to answer. He suddenly liked this attorney the *Post* had sent over. He decided to simply answer, "Yes."

"So you thought the file was evidence, and it might help stop this illegal activity that General Kramer was involved in?"

"That's right," Tom answered.

Attorney Jack—Tom's new best friend—cleared his throat and sat down across the table, then leaned back. He crossed his arms, and changed gears to a different subject. He said, "I really liked the article you wrote. It's pretty damn amazing, you know, everything that you and your colleague Mr. Clemens went through. Based on what I've heard and read, you fellah's rights have been violated. This could cost the government a lot of money," he continued, then again glanced at the two-way mirror.

Tom nodded politely.

"So tell me, Mr. Lassiter, where did you get those pictures of the two satellites? Those so-called *High Ground* satellites, and missiles."

"They just, well, came into my possession, that's all. I can't say anything about the source. I've made promises not to."

The attorney tilted forward in his chair. "So you're saying that it is the right of *The Washington Post* to keep its sources confidential?"

"Yes, always. Ever hear of Deep Throat and Watergate?"

The attorney nodded and finally offered a brief smile. "Okay, Mr. Lassiter, that's all of the questions I have for you right now. I have an important meeting in a half hour, on another matter."

"So what's next? Do I have to stay locked up?"

"Yes, for now anyway. We're scheduled for a court appearance on Friday. At that time you'll be charged and asked whether you're innocent or guilty. We can request that bail be set, but they may not go for it. Then a trial date will be determined. We might be able to get it fast-tracked, so you can get it over with as soon as possible."

Tom looked down at the attorney's business card. "And the paper is willing to pay for my entire defense?"

"Yes. And they will probably post bail as well, though I can't disclose how high they will go. Now, we will have to spend some more time together, of course. I'll want you to go over every minute of the past few days. If we can make a case to the judge that you were driven by the greater good, as they say, there's a chance we'll do just fine. I can't tell you how to plea, but if I were in your shoes, I'd probably say I was guilty of taking the file. You did what you did out of concern for national security and the wellbeing of all citizens, that sort of thing. You alerted the general public and the authorities to a major covert activity. You're a whistle blower who risked his life to expose an illegal program. If you had to do it over again, you would. It was that critical. Period."

Tom nodded slowly.

"There's a chance we could go for a plea bargain, but I have to get some more info out of you. Okay?"

"Fine."

The attorney stood and started to walk to the door. "By the way, in that story, you said a man by the name of Broderick tried to kill you, and was deeply involved in this thing. Are you sure that was his name?"

"Yes. That's what they called him anyway."

"CIA?"

"That's right. Why?"

"I checked. They claim there's no such agent with the CIA."

"Great," Tom said sarcastically. "Of course there's not."

"Don't worry, we'll find him. It's probably a cover name, or whatever the hell they call them. If we have to, we'll subpoena every senior person at the agency that we can. Get everyone on the stand, all the way up to the director. That should be fun, the case will probably be dropped just like that," the attorney continued, then turned and knocked three times on the door behind him. A few seconds passed then a guard opened it.

"Mr. Lassiter, I'll be in touch with you tomorrow. In the meantime, I wouldn't say a word to the suits sitting behind that mirror over there, other than you're protecting sources and can't talk. They just love it when reporters say that. Now get some rest. And don't worry," he said as he winked, a gray caterpillar of an eyebrow dropping briefly.

"Thanks, I appreciate your help." Tom took a deep breath.

CHAPTER THIRTY-ONE

Amidst a sea of reporters poised on the steps of the courthouse, mostly local hacks, and a few decent folks from the *Post*, the Volvo pulled to a stop near a red-painted curb. Tom was riding in back and wearing dark sunglasses. He was still surprised that attorney-Jack was able to get him out on bail.

His stomach grew nervous. He was worried about a phone call he received last night at home. His mom had answered and a man asked to speak to Tom Lassiter, and he wouldn't give his name. Tom got on the line and the man said, "Mr. Lassiter, you better not talk. Do what's best for yourself, just keep quiet and serve your time. If you don't, you'll be killed, and your family will be killed. Understand?" The line then went dead. After the call, Tom couldn't sleep all night and, when morning finally arrived, he contacted the FBI and told them about the threat. They already knew about it; they had tapped the phone line and recorded the entire conversation. "Don't worry," the agent had said. "We'll protect you." The words were not comforting in the least to Tom.

Tom was the last to step out of the Volvo. He waited for everyone else to get out. He then noticed Victoria approaching from across the street, dressed in a navy-colored skirt and jacket and carrying a briefcase. Yesterday she told him she would be there, though he suggested to her that she should probably stay away for her own good.

Reporters from television and newspapers jockeyed for position and quickly circled Tom as he walked toward the courthouse.

"Give us some room, please," Tom said firmly as he ushered his daughters and his parents toward the court entrance steps, cameras clicking noisily. Microphones and cameras were thrust at them from all directions. "Mr. Lassiter, Mr. Lassiter, just a word if we may—"

"You'll just have to read about it in the *Post*," he interrupted with a slight grin.

Someone in the crowd yelled, "Did you steal a file from the Pentagon, Mr. Lassiter?"

"No comment," Tom immediately answered. He had always cringed when he was told that, when conducting interviews. Now he could see that it was rather fun saying it. He looked down at his girls. "Up the steps, kids. Hurry now."

They reached the entrance door to the courthouse, but one more question blared out before the door could close.

"Mr. Lassiter, is it your fault that Iran fired missiles at the United States and Israel, as the Los Angeles Times reported?"

"Leave it to the L.A. Times," Tom said under his breath, standing in the doorway. He shook his head then swung around, reached up to the lens of the camera next to an obnoxious talking head, and shoved it away. He then turned, looked into the reporter's eyes and, barely moving his jaw said, "No, damn it, it's not my fault. I kept a much worse tragedy from occurring. It wasn't my fault. Now excuse us, please." He opened the courthouse door all the way, ushering in his family. "Go on in girls, Mom, Dad." They walked in.

Tom glanced out to the street once more just before going inside. Victoria was making her way up the steps and was being bombarded with questions. He was sure she could handle them though.

Inside the courthouse, Tom's attorney, the venerable and ostentatious B. Jack Slayter, approached from the other side of the huge hall, his double-breasted suit open and flapping in the air. Sixty-dollar haircut. He was carrying a briefcase made of some sort of reptile.

"Good morning, Tom." He extended a hand.

"I hope it will be."

They shook hands firmly and he gave Tom a solid it'll-be-all-right pat on the back.

"I don't think you have anything to worry about, Tom."

"I'm glad one of us feels that way."

"Well, shall we go in? It's time."

Tom nodded and thought, *guess the tar and feathers are ready.*

They made their way through large double doors and entered the courtroom. Tom noticed a bailiff walking in from a side-door entrance, then people streamed in through the rear. Nervous chatter filled the room. Tom and attorney-Jack sat at a wood table, about twelve feet long. Tom took a deep breath and looked about. There was dark wood paneling everywhere, and a couple flags flanked the front corners of the room. The court reporter appeared half asleep. Tom glanced over his shoulder to make sure his family was seated and okay. They seemed nervous but okay.

"Just stay calm," Jack whispered. "You want to look confident. You did nothing wrong."

Tom crossed his legs and undid a button on his jacket. Mr. Casual.

Twenty minutes passed.

"I wonder what the delay is?" Jack said, twisting is neck left and right.

Tom shook his head slightly. He just wanted to go home.

Finally, a door creaked open to the left of the judge's bench. Gray hair could just barely be seen poking in, then a waving hand and arm, cloaked in black fabric. "Judge Stephens?" Tom whispered to Jack.

"Yeah, I think so." Jack rose from his chair and leaned forward, trying to get a view. The bailiff finally saw the waving arm and walked toward the door. He disappeared into the paneling, a side room, with the judge.

When the bailiff returned he cleared his voice and said, "All rise."

Honorable Judge Carl Stephens entered, looking a bit disheveled. Assuming the bench, he moved his eyes to the defendant table with an expression that seemed to say that Tom needed a good swat on his reporter's-butt.

Tom's head lowered and the party began.

But seconds later, before another word was spoken, Tom noticed someone handing the bailiff a note, which he then took to the judge. The judge reached for his bifocals and seemed to read it at least two times. Tom turned to Jack and he just hunched his shoulders.

"Will the attorneys please approach the bench," His Honor said, folding the note and tucking it in a pocket."

Attorney-Jack got up, walked around the table, and made his way forward.

Tom thought, Lord, what now? The army at the prosecution table also stood and rigidly moved toward the judge (we're talking robots in cheap suits).

A minute later Tom saw the legal eagles nod their heads before the Great One at least six or seven times. To think I almost chose that path, kissing butts and sitting in cold courtrooms half the time, Tom pondered.

Finally, Judge Stephens looked up and said, "Mr. Lassiter, would you please join us in my chamber?"

"Yes sir." Tom got up and followed the bailiff.

His Honor continued, speaking to everyone seated in the courtroom, "Ladies and gentlemen, there will be a thirty minute recess."

Tom entered a paneled room filled with books on every wall, and what appeared to be antique furniture scattered about without a hint of design finesse. There was a desk next to a dirty window, and a couch and two blue wing-back chairs with ball and claw legs. The place smelled musty and Tom had to place a hand over his nose to keep from sneezing.

"Please, everyone sit down," the judge said, twirling his bifocals and pointing to the couch. He meandered around two file cabinets and sat in a high-back leather chair, then brushed a hand down over his face.

There was a knock at the door. "Come in," his Honor said.

The door opened and the bailiff peeked his head in. "Agent Delaney is here, sir. FBI."

"Very well. Show him in."

Tom thought, *What did I do now? More FBI?*

The door opened all the way and a large man walked in. He had a thick mustache and carried a shiny briefcase that looked bullet proof. He approached Tom first. "Mr. Lassiter, pleased to meet you." He extended his chubby hand and chubby fingers, one of which was smothering a gold and diamond football-related ring, or a school class ring.

"Please have a seat, Mr. Delaney," the judge said, reclining somewhat in his chair. He reached for a glass of water and took a sip. "Okay, let's get right to the point. What's the meaning of this interruption?"

"Yes sir, uh, if I may, I'd like to first inform Mr. Lassiter of an incident which just occurred."

"Incident?"

"Yes your Honor."

"Go on, please."

Agent Delaney turned to Tom. "Mr. Lassiter, I'm sorry to have to tell you that your house burned down about an hour ago and—"

Tom's heart seemed to crawl to his throat. "You have to be kidding me. We just left—"

"I know, sir. I'm very sorry."

"My god." Tom tilted his chair forward, shaking his head. "Arson?"

"Yes sir. No doubt about it. There was gasoline everywhere, and they even left the cans."

Tom suddenly appeared frantic, lifting his arms, palms open. "When is this going to stop? This is crazy."

At least, he told himself, his family was here at the courthouse with him, safe and sound.

Attorney-Jack turned to him. "I'm very sorry, Tom."

"Is there anything left?" Tom asked.

"No sir. It doesn't appear so," agent Delaney answered.

The judge coughed slightly and all eyes moved to him. "I'm very sorry, Mr. Lassiter. You certainly don't need any more problems right now." He shifted his attention to agent Delaney. "This news could have waited until the end of day, don't you think?"

"Yes, your Honor. But I have more, well, news, if you will."

"And what would that be?"

"Do you have a DVD player?"

"This better be good, agent Delaney."

"Yes your honor."

"There's a TV and DVD player behind those doors over there." He pointed to his right. "Go ahead. And make it quick."

Tom thought, great, another video. That's all he needed. He twisted sideways and watched Delaney snap open his briefcase. He pulled out an unlabeled DVD and walked to the cabinet the judge had pointed to. He opened the doors and inserted the DVD into the player, then hit the power button on the TV. He pressed Play on a remote control.

The video came on. It was one of the field reporters from CNN. Tom couldn't recall his name. He was just another Ken doll with stiff hair and perfect teeth, smart and articulate. The CNN logo and a digital clock graphic were shown at the bottom of the screen.

Tom glanced at his watch, then back at the TV. The video was of a broadcast made about an hour ago. Delaney turned the volume up and a little green bar shot from left to right at the bottom of the picture, then disappeared. Everyone listened and watched. The reporter said, "We now go to Washington for a breaking story."

The video changed. It was a picture of a group of microphones—ABC, NBC, CBS, CNN, and others. They were all clamped to a podium. Cameras were clicking away as a bald man in a black suit walked up to the podium. Tom recognized him immediately, even on the small TV screen. It was Senator Livingston of Maryland. Tom's mind raced, wondering what the hell this whole mess had to do with him.

"Thank you. Thank you all for coming here on such short notice," the Senator said, then forced a slight smile at the crowd. He looked nervous. People were moving by in front and behind him. Two more Senators approached—Schroll of Massachusetts and Porter of Florida. They appeared to be out of breath. They took their places on either side of Livingston, who seemed relieved to have some support. He continued, "Senator Schroll, Senator Porter, and I requested this

318

press conference to announce that we are calling for immediate hearings in regard to the recent crisis with Iran."

Tom stood and moved closer to the TV.

"We believe that illegal activities have taken place within the Central Intelligence Agency and the Pentagon. As you know, arrests have been made. We believe the American public has a right to know precisely how and why this crisis occurred. Therefore, we are calling on the President and the Attorney General to immediately create a bipartisan committee to review all activities associated with the crisis and—"

The reporters yelled out questions, interrupting the Senator. Livingston tried to continue but there was too much chaos, everyone talking at the same time, dozens of camera flashes going off. Senator Porter whispered something in his ear, then he continued, "If you'll calm down a bit, we'll take a few questions." He pointed to a lady directly in front. "Please, you, go ahead."

The video suddenly cut off. Then it turned back on just as quickly. Tom assumed that the recording had been edited down.

As the video resumed, a reporter asked, "What do you think about Mr. Lassiter of *The Washington Post* being prosecuted?"

"Well, I think it's a travesty of justice. He exposed a very dangerous and illegal program. We shouldn't shoot the news bearer. He's a critical witness to this entire mess."

With these words, Tom immediately felt a wave of relief wash over him. A Senator, on international TV, was taking his side.

As another question emanated from somewhere in the crowd, Agent Delaney leaned toward the TV and hit the off button. He then ejected the DVD and walked back over to a chair.

"Well, that was interesting," His Honor commented.

Tom sat down.

"It looks like you have friends in high places, Mr. Lassiter."

Tom nodded. "Yeah, I'm real connected."

The judge smiled at this.

Delaney cleared his throat. "Your Honor, if I may continue."

"Go ahead."

Delaney turned to Tom. "Mr. Lassiter, I've been asked by the Director of the FBI to communicate to you that all charges against you will be dropped and—"

Tom tilted forward again. "You're serious?"

"Yes sir. But there's a catch. You have to agree to serve as a witness in the forthcoming hearings you just heard Senator Livingston announce. No pleading the fifth."

Judge Stephens folded his hands upon his desk. "Sounds like a nice offer, Mr. Lassiter."

Tom said nothing. He was in shock. He wanted to scream for joy, but something was holding him back.

Agent Delaney continued, "We are talking full impunity, Mr. Lassiter. And we're willing to protect you and your family. We believe you're in tremendous danger."

Tom rolled his eyes. "You guys don't miss a beat do you. What do you mean, protect?"

"The Witness Protection Program, a new life, and a new identity. It's all approved. I have the papers right here."

Once again Tom was speechless for several seconds, then he asked, "You want me to just change my entire life? Lose my position at the *Post*? Just drop everything and move to some small town?"

"We don't see any other way, sir," Delaney continued. "We're reasonably certain that some sort of fringe group within the CIA will stop at nothing to keep you from testifying."

Gee, another excellent observation, Tom thought. His head began to throb as he thought about his house, which was now a pile of ashes.

"This morning's fire was simply a warning. They knew you and your family weren't there. We just don't see any other way, sir. And we need your testimony to sort through this."

Tom paused for a moment then continued, "You'll relocate and protect my entire family?"

"Of course."

"And what about James Clemens? He knows almost as much as I do."

"Yes, we're aware of that. He's accepted our offer and will also testify. And he'll disappear just like you. He has already been moved to a military hospital, and is under twenty-four hour protection."

"You guys move fast," Tom said, raising his eyebrows slightly.

"Yes sir, we do."

"I suggest you accept their offer," the judge put in. "You don't appear to have much of a choice."

Tom swallowed some air.

Agent Delaney removed papers from his briefcase. "Everything's been drawn up. All we need is your signature." He handed over a couple pages, then a pen.

Tom knew that the judge was right. He really didn't have any other options. He didn't even have a house to go home to. And he knew his family couldn't take any more of this craziness. They were sitting outside that door right now, not even knowing their house had burned down. He couldn't expose them to anymore danger. He read through the document, which basically said that he agreed not to contact any friends, relatives, or former colleagues, and he agreed to change his name. There were also several paragraphs on what was expected of him during the hearings. He raised his eyes to Agent Delaney and asked, "What about some money?"

"Sir?"

"You're taking away my livelihood. Everyone will know my face, if they don't already. I can't very well continue being a reporter."

"We're prepared to buy you a house, wherever you want, and give you enough money to get started in a business."

"How much?"

"It varies, Mr. Lassiter. I can't—"

"Look, you want me to sign my life away and just trust that the financial well-being of my family will be fine? I need to know some numbers. You must have some pre-approved range. Right?"

"Yes sir."

"Well, what the hell is it?" Tom asked.

Agent Delaney pulled another pen out and grabbed a business card from his shirt pocket. He scribbled a couple figures down and handed the card over. Tom took a look and quickly passed it back. "The high number will do. And I want at least five hundred thousand set aside for the house, not two-fifty. Is that doable?"

Delaney nodded.

"I need it in writing."

"That's fine, I'll have it—"

"No, I need it now."

Delaney hesitated, shaking his head a couple of times. "Fine, give me the agreement." He reached forward and Tom handed it to him. He scribbled some more.

Tom was sure that Agent Delaney and his FBI colleagues just loved the CIA. It was widely known at the *Post* that the two agencies were always competing and fighting for resources and more power. The FBI would do anything to nail the CIA and Tom knew it. Maybe he should have asked for more?

Tom continued, "If you wouldn't mind signing that, I'd appreciate it."

Delaney signed his name and handed the document back to Tom. Tom let attorney-Jack take a look at it, then read it once more and signed and dated the bottom. He was a free man! Well, almost.

Agent Delaney turned to the judge. "Can I use that copy machine over there." He motioned to a small copier, next to some file cabinets.

"Yes. Go ahead."

Delaney took the original and went over and made two copies. He came back, gave Tom the original, and sat down.

"Now, I need to know where you want to go, so plans can be made," he continued. "Where do you want to live?" He removed another card and handed it to Tom. "Write down what state you want to live in. Even the town, if you know."

"I can't think about it for a couple days?"

"Mr. Lassiter, you and your family will be moved directly from this courthouse to wherever you choose. Once the hearings begin, you'll be flown in and will stay under our protection. After what's happened, you can't risk delay. You need to get out of this area."

Tom placed the card on his right leg and pondered where he'd like to spend the rest of his life. He wrote down the first thing that came to mind. He handed the card back to Delaney, who read it to himself and said, "You'll be consulted on the house, of course."

Tom nodded. "Gee, that's nice of you."

"Very well, gentlemen," the judge said, then stood. "This was indeed interesting." He looked at the clock behind his desk and turned toward the door to the courtroom. "I better get in there." He moved his eyes to Agent Delaney. "If you'd like to have Mr. Lassiter's family brought in here, that would be fine. Arrangements can be made to take them out through the back."

"Thank you, Your Honor. But we have a helicopter on the roof right now," Delaney said as he rose from his chair.

The judge seemed surprised at this, as did Tom. The judge continued, "I guess you were pretty confident about Mr. Lassiter accepting the FBI's offer."

"Yes sir."

Tom also stood. His throat felt dry and his head was pounding even harder. He wondered whether he had done the right thing. His thoughts suddenly turned to Victoria and a chill shuddered up his spine. He turned to Agent Delaney and said, "There's a woman out there. I really need to talk to her. Can you bring her in here with my family and—"

"Victoria Brookshire?" Delaney interrupted, shaking his head.

"Yes, how do you know—"

"We know all about her. You better sit back down for a minute, Mr. Lassiter. We need to talk."

CHAPTER THIRTY-TWO

Vermont in the springtime is pure heaven—the bluest sky on earth, green maples everywhere, rolling hills, and the scent of boiling syrup floating through tiny villages. There are also glistening and pristine lakes, and even an occasional moose and deer running around. It almost makes you forget about the winters from hell.

Tom was sitting on the back deck, staring at Sugarbush Mountain. The only sound was from the breeze shuffling through the leaves and an occasional biker coasting down the road, brakes squeaking and that ticking noise emanating from the chain and gears. His daughter Emily was out in the garden helping her grandmother pick strawberries. Grandpa had gone fishing. His other daughter, Hayley, was working after school down at the bakery on route 100. Life could be worse.

The only bad thing was the isolation. It wasn't fair that he couldn't see Victoria. He had wanted to pick up the phone a thousand times to try and get a hold of her. Was she still with the CIA? Was she trying to find him? He missed her more than he could say. He had half a mind to just tear up the damn FBI relocation contract and drop out of the Witness Protection Program. The only thing stopping him was his family. He couldn't put them at risk.

The hearings were supposed to start in a week. He was nervous but wanted to get them over with. Agent Delaney, his only liaison with the FBI at this point, had said that he couldn't leave the house until after the hearings were over. So he was stuck here, staring at the mountains. The beautiful green mountains.

Wednesday morning. The girls were playing with the kids down the street at the Nettles' farm. The house was quiet, except for the TV. Tom had ordered a satellite dish a few days ago, and he hadn't turned the channel away from CNN since the system was installed. The media was all over the pending hearings, interviewing Senators and bombarding the White House with questions. Tom missed the action. But he didn't miss Washington D.C.

He took a sip of Green Mountain coffee. God he loved the stuff, though the buzz it gave him made his temples throb. He stared at his desk. It looked as messy as his old one in his office back at the *Post*. Maybe worse. On the left side was a stack of articles he had clipped from the *Post*. The staff had done an excellent job interviewing people and filling in the holes of what happened. How could they get along so well without him?

The doorbell rang, then he heard a few taps of the brass knocker. He wasn't supposed to answer the door but he left his desk and walked slowly through the hall, the wide-planked wood floor creaking beneath his feet. He hoped the security system wouldn't go off, which it tended to do whenever someone banged the knocker too hard. Then he remembered that his mom had turned it off. He approached the door.

Now there was knocking, the sound of knuckles on wood.

His pulse picked up a bit. Three people had come to the door the entire time they had been in Vermont (a Girl Scout, a farmer looking for a cow, and the telephone, cable, and power company man—all the same person). He leaned forward just as the door jiggled in its frame. Someone was pounding even harder. He looked through the peephole. It was at least forty years old and there was a crack through the middle of it, probably from the wonderful winters. He raised his right index finger and tried to wipe some of the muck off the lens. It helped a little. He could see that there was a human being out there anyway.

There was more knocking.

He decided to just talk through the door. "Yes, what do you want?"

There was a long pause, then. "Tom, is that you?"

He immediately recognized the voice. His hands flew to the deadbolt and he pulled and swung the door open.

"Victoria!"

She didn't say anything. Tears streamed down her cheeks. She rushed forward and threw her arms around him.

"Tom," she whispered. "I was so scared I wouldn't be able to find you. They wouldn't tell me where you were moved to. I was so scared I'd never see you again."

"I know, I know. I'm sorry." He pulled away from her a bit and looked at her. She was wearing jeans, boots, and a light blue sweater, very little makeup. And absolutely gorgeous as ever.

She wiped the tears from her face.

Tom said, "I was going to contact you after the hearings, I swear."

She again lunged forward and put her head to his chest. He rocked her back and forth several times.

"Here, come in, Victoria." They moved inside and he closed the door. "How did you find me?"

"I remembered that you said how much you liked living up here as a kid. I didn't have any other ideas, so I just decided to come up to Vermont and check. I remembered that you mentioned the Sugarbush ski resort area."

"But the house. How did you find—"

"Don't you remember? That day at the museum, in London, I told you about a house for sale here the last time I went skiing. You went on so much about Vermont and this area, I took a guess that you might end up here, and decided to come up and see what I could find out. A real estate agent told me three homes had closed escrow recently. Two were purchased by investors, for ski rentals. The agent described who purchased this house, and I just knew it was you and your family. I guess the CIA training paid off finally," she added, then smiled broadly.

"You're amazing." Tom leaned forward and kissed her.

"You were really planning on contacting me after the hearings?" she asked.

"Yes, of course. I actually wanted to contact you right away. But the FBI said if I did, they'd drop all support. And they said that I'd be jeopardizing everything, you know, the hearings and even your career with the CIA."

"There's no career, Tom. I resigned."

"Seriously?"

"Yes."

"Thank god." He gently wiped her cheeks with the back of his fingers. "Will you forgive me, Victoria? I just didn't have any choice. They wouldn't let me contact you. I'm the first witness they'll call. I just wanted to get the hearings over, and not screw up the investigation. I really didn't have any choice. I probably should have—"

"I know, dear. I know. It's okay." She hugged him tightly again.

They said nothing for what seemed like two or three minutes. They just held each other. Finally, she looked up at him. "Have you heard anything about James?" she asked. "Is he okay?"

"Yes, he's fine. The FBI won't let us talk until things die down. I don't even know where he is, but Agent Delaney with the FBI said he's doing fine."

"I'm glad he's all right."

Tom nodded. "Me too. He's a great friend. I can't wait to see him again."

Suddenly Victoria began to cry as she said, "Tom, I was so worried that I'd never see you again."

"I've thought about you all the time too. It's been killing me."

She reached up and raked his hair back with her fingers. "I just want to be with you. I don't care where."

"Victoria, I'll never let you out of my sight again. I promise."

They walked from the front entry area and toward the living room, which resembled a rustic lounge of a mountain resort. Layers of horizontal logs rose from the floor and formed each wall, then transitioned to a traditional A-frame two-story open ceiling where a large fan was slowly turning and casting a flickering shimmer of light upon the room. On the far side of the room there were eight French doors, two of which were wide open and leading to a cedar deck with a view of the Sugarbush ski slopes.

"This is beautiful, Tom," Victoria said as she ran her eyes over the living room, then toward the deck area. "And look at that view. Wow."

"Let's go outside. It's so nice out today, I opened everything up."

They walked through the open French doors, his right arm draped around her waist, her hand softly touching his back. They sat side-by-side in a cushy outdoor loveseat, which was placed next to a portable fire pit. Tom held her close and kissed her forehead, which was already feeling warm from the bright sun resting atop Sugarbush Mountain to the west.

The end

Thank you for reading *The First Witness*.

About the author

Todd Easterling is a Southern California novelist, originally discovered by the venerable Jay Garon-Brooke Agency in New York, of John Grisham fame. Todd was previously in the satellite and cable television industry, and has worked with companies such as HBO, Disney, Time Warner, and various media and wireless technology start-ups in strategic marketing, public relations, and corporate development in both vice president and consulting capacities.

He is currently in the final editing stage of his next book, tentatively titled *The Miracle Man*, which is along the romance-adventure story line of *The Horse Whisperer* by Nicholas Evans and which includes current topics such as cloning and genetic engineering. Todd is also working on a genetics thriller (title not announced), which has been referred to as the next step in continuing the brilliant Michael Crichton's legacy of *West World* and *Jurassic Park* (books and motion pictures). Over a period of many years, Todd has conducted research and obtained technical advice from the esteemed Dr. Ian Wilmut (first to clone an animal, Dolly the sheep) and Dr. Raul Cano, whose techniques formed the foundation of *Jurassic Park* (extraction of DNA from ancient tree amber).

Todd resides in the San Diego area with his family and Russian Wolfhound, Bentley. He has three girls, including twins (9 years old) and a 14 year old and is an avid advocate of international adoption. Todd encourages reader emails, press inquiries, and rights/translation inquiries via Twitter (@toddeasterling), Facebook, or LinkedIn, where his profile is in the top 5 percent most visited of 200 million member profiles for 2012. For more information on Todd's forthcoming suspense and thrillers, please visit www.ToddEasterling.com.

A final note from the author

Featured in the climax of this novel is, for many readers unfamiliar with military aircraft and technology, an aircraft which has a high powered laser built into the nose. Believe it or not, this is a real aircraft. The Air Force purchased a Boeing 747-400F and built a megawatt-class chemical oxygen iodine laser into it. The plane, which has been referred to as "747-ABL" (Airborne Laser) and more recently as YAL-1, was first tested in 2007. In 2010 a high-energy laser blast was used to intercept test targets, including two missiles. Due to budget pressures, funding was purportedly cut and the Airborne Laser, according to the Pentagon, made its last flight on February 14, 2012. The U.S. Secretary of Defense stated: "So, right now, the ABL would have to orbit inside the borders of Iran in order to be able to try and use its lasers to shoot down a missile in the boost phase. And if you were to operationalize this you would be looking at ten to twenty 747s, at a billion and a half dollars apiece, and $100 million a year to operate."

In February of 2013, the United States Department of Defense surprised many when it communicated that the Airborne Laser program is still alive, and that it expects to have two laser weapons ready by 2014 for both the U.S. Air Force and the U.S. Navy. The program is called HELLADS (High Energy Liquid Laser Area Defense System). This second generation of aircraft lasers are expected to be lower power and light enough to mount on planes much smaller than a 747.

In the end, hopefully these technologies will never have to be utilized to defend a country from a missile attack, and the citizens of all nations can learn to accept each other and peace will prevail.

Made in the USA
Lexington, KY
30 August 2013